DESTINY of FIRE

By the Same Author

The World Is Not Enough
The Cornerstone

DESTINY OF FIRE

ZOÉ OLDENBOURG

Translated by Peter Green

CARROLL & GRAF PUBLISHERS, INC.
NEW YORK

First Carroll & Graf edition 1999

Carroll & Graf Publishers, Inc.
19 West 21st Street
New York, NY 10010-6805

Library of Congress Cataloging-in-Publication Data is available.
ISBN: 0-7867-0577-9

Manufactured in the United States of America

Contents

A Historical Note

THE heroes of this novel are the Cathars, or Albigensians, a heretical sect which flourished in the Midi during the twelfth and thirteenth centuries. The Church preached a Holy War against them, and after a long struggle their religion was stamped out. This war is generally known as the Albigensian Crusade.

It may be of some help to the reader if I sketch out the historical facts: it is a dramatic story, and one of the cruelest episodes in the annals of Christianity. Besides, a perusal of the novel itself may not make it quite clear that it is, in fact, the Albigensians with which we are concerned. They almost invariably appear under the title either of "heretics" or of that which they used themselves, i.e., "Christians." (The implicit claim has been challenged not only by their enemies, but also by many of their latter-day admirers.) But despite their bold heterodoxies of doctrine, it is only fair to describe them in this way. The creed they professed may have denied God's Creation of the world and the truth of Christ's Incarnation; it may have rejected every Sacrament save that of baptism by the laying on of hands; it may have admitted the notion of metempsychosis, and so on. Yet it has been established that this creed was centered on Christ, with the Gospels as its sole Scriptural authority and the "Our Father" as its only prayer. We know that the Cathars' preaching rested above all on the example of their personal lives, and that this example was such that we may legitimately attribute to it the genesis of the Franciscan movement; St. Dominic, too, consciously and deliberately took it as a model of guidance. Even their worst enemies found nothing to condemn in the Cathars apart from their doctrines; and that is well-nigh miraculous when we think of the savagery with which they were persecuted.

Nothing of them survives. It was strictly forbidden to record a single deed or word of theirs which might present them in a favorable light; these Christians sans Cross have remained a mystery to posterity because no one ever succeeded in finding fault with their conduct. We know, too, that their doctrine itself was frequently misrepresented or misunderstood. The only authentic Cathar document which we possess today is a Book of Rites, entirely made up of a cento of New Testament quotations, together with a commentary which even a Catholic would accept in almost every detail.

If the Cathars have remained—in the eye of history at any rate— the heretical sect par excellence, that is because they were, on the eve of the war which obliterated them, halfway to becoming something much more than a mere heresy or a mere sect. They were crystallizing into a new Church, quite separate from the Roman tradition, and indeed independent of all traditional orthodoxies. It is not possible to appreciate this novel unless one bears in mind that these candidates for martyrdom felt themselves to be members of a strong, living Church.

Throughout the whole of the twelfth century Catharism spread to various centers throughout the length and breadth of Europe. From Bulgaria, its country of origin, it passed to Italy (where it became so powerful that the Cathars established seminaries in every large city, Rome included), to Languedoc and Flanders, not to mention the Balkans—it remained the major religion in Bosnia for two whole centuries. In Languedoc, by the end of the twelfth century, the Cathars had their own bishops, convents, and seminaries, and had organized themselves into parishes and dioceses. For many of the local inhabitants this creed was already that held by their fathers and grandfathers before them. Yet in this so-called "Albigensian" Crusade, the heretical Albigensians themselves hardly appear in any role except that of martyrs.

The Albigensian Crusade (1209–1229) brought the province of Languedoc under the authority of the French King, and restored to the jurisdiction of the Catholic Church a district which was threatening to break away from Rome altogether. Throughout this long and cruel war, King and Pope worked hand in glove to crush a country which asserted its right to political and spiritual independence. The war was not so much waged against heretics as against a people who, with their princes, had been guilty of the sin of tolerance—and against those Catholics who were fighting to protect their own fellow citizens.

When Pope Innocent III preached his Holy War against the Count of Toulouse and his vassals, this land of Langue d'Oc—a wealthy and civilized province, whose ancient culture ensured that it was open to every intellectual or spiritual current—split off almost openly from the Church of Rome, yet without ceasing to be a Catholic community. Raymond VI, Count of Toulouse, who belonged to one of the noblest families in Southern Europe (he was not only a cousin of the King of France, but also brother-in-law to the English monarch John Lackland and the King of Aragon), remained a Catholic all his life; and indeed most of the nobles who took up arms against the Crusaders were Catholics themselves. And yet, according to contemporary witnesses, the Church of Rome was so discredited throughout the area that the clergy were obliged to wear hats to conceal their tonsures: the very word "chaplain" had become a term of abuse, and the churches were empty. St. Bernard, who was already famous both as preacher and as reformer throughout Western Christendom, went to Albi in 1145 (over sixty years before the Crusade) and preached in the cathedral to a congregation of *thirty*.

Generally it may be said that the population of this province was hostile to a clergy that had become corrupt and venal. Religious indifference was greater here than anywhere else. A more serious matter for Rome was the fact that Catharism already had deep roots in the Languedoc countryside, was openly tolerated in the cities of the area, and ranked high in the esteem of the local nobility: in certain parts it had entirely ousted Catholicism. And for the Cathars their Church was the One True Church, while Rome stood for Babylon or the Beast of the Apocalypse. But it was useless for the Pope to appeal to the Catholics of Languedoc to fight against this heresy, so he preached a Holy War, and set Christians to invade a Christian country. It was not a war between Catholics and heretics so much as one between Northern Frenchmen (who were irreproachable, indeed fanatical Catholics) and the Frenchmen of the Midi, who at this period were not yet known as Frenchmen at all.

The army which in 1209 captured the town of Béziers (and, in a few hours, slaughtered the *entire* population, more than twenty thousand in number) was a powerful expeditionary force, composed entirely of volunteers—fanatics, adventurers, or ambitious men—and responsible to no one but its religious leaders. The commander-in-chief of this army was Arnaud Amaury, who, besides being Abbot of Cîteaux, was also a Papal Legate. Such an unheard-of atrocity had its effect: the country was not so much beaten by force of arms as paralyzed by sheer panic. But then, little by little, resistance began to stiffen.

Thanks to his military skill and the reinforcements which he received each summer, the leader of the Crusaders, Simon de Montfort, managed within a few years to capture and occupy most of the Languedoc strongholds. King Peter II of Aragon came to the succor of his brother-in-law the Count of Toulouse, but was defeated and killed at Muret. After six years of fighting, Simon de Montfort was solemnly invested by the Pope with the title of Count of Toulouse, and became (with the King of France's approval) the sole legitimate ruler of Languedoc. He was the "courageous Catholic gentleman" who had carried the cause of Christ to ultimate triumph in this area. The campaign (like any campaign where a numerically weak foreign invader is opposed to an exasperated and terrified local population) was quite exceptionally brutal. The ministers of the heretical Church, or Cathars,* were burned alive by the hundred, while ordinary poor folk—Catholic or heretic, it made no odds—perished in their tens of thousands.

* The term "Cathar," strictly used, denotes only the initiated, the "Perfects" or "Christians," as they described themselves: that is, the priests, monks, and nuns of the creed—though without the Catholic associations which these terms imply. The name derives from the Greek adjective *katharos*, meaning "pure." There is an admirably concise account of Cathar beliefs and practice in Sir Steven Runciman's *The Medieval Manichee* (Cambridge, 1947), pp. 147–62.—Trs.

The town of Toulouse rose against the usurper's regime and re-called their exiled Count: Simon de Montfort was killed in 1218, and the Crusade was defeated. Yet for seven more years the Cru-saders continued to hold out, losing town after town despite the support of the King and the Pope. However, when they had been, to all appearances, finally crushed, King Louis VIII of France invaded Languedoc in person, at the head of a vast army. This time his intention was to conquer the country and add it to his own dominions; but he still had the Crusaders' Cross as his emblem. In 1229 a peace treaty was signed. Through force of arms and, above all, through the power of the Church, which recognized as legitimate sovereigns only those who furthered Catholic interests, Languedoc was now brought under the sway of the French King. Against this French occupation, and against the Church which they detested more violently than ever, the men of Languedoc fought on for years and decades, disarmed though they were. The Inquisition instituted a police-state reign of terror which for sheer effectiveness has never been surpassed; and thus, slowly, the living strength of the conquered country was crushed and undermined.

Historically, the Cathars had to be forgotten; and their absolute pacifism paralyzed them when it came to any direct action. They went on preaching, succored the poor, baptized the dying, and went stoically to the stake when captured. Though the Church to which these priests belonged was by now well established, there cannot have been more than two or three thousand of them. The Crusaders burned nearly a hundred and fifty at Minerve, four hundred at Lavaur, eighty at Cassès—and these were only the larger holocausts. The Inquisition, too, burned many, in small scattered groups; at Montségur, one of their last strongholds, two hundred went to the stake. Ordinary converts who refused to renounce their faith were likewise burned; most converts, however, were less recalcitrant, and condemned only to life imprisonment. A hundred years after the Crusade there were no heretics—no Cathar heretics, at least—left in the whole of Languedoc.

Perhaps, by studying the way this Church of faggot-martyrs met its death, we can understand something about the nature of its life.

Preface

THIS book is a product of the imagination. None of the characters portrayed in it actually existed, with the single exception of Bernard de Simorre, who was the Catharist Bishop of Carcassonne at the beginning of the thirteenth century. The author has endeavored, by basing her picture on such scanty evidence as has been preserved, to convey the spirit of the Catharist religion as it really was: though it must be made clear that the Cathars were, first and foremost, great preachers—of whose discourses and sermons not one single word survives.

The present work is neither a chronicle nor colorfully embellished history. The action takes place marginally to history proper, which serves as a backcloth for it; major historical events—with the exception of the Count's entry into Toulouse—are deliberately kept out of the limelight, as being inessential for the story. The struggle in which these fictional characters are involved takes place beyond strict historical time.

This novel describes the resistance of the Cathars to the persecution of which they were the object both during and after the Albigensian Crusade. It does not treat this resistance as a whole, but concentrates on certain aspects of it: in particular it tells the stories of Ricord and Arsen, Aicart and Renaud, Gentian and Bérenger, and of nameless combatants, members of a Church which today is nonexistent, yet which in their eyes was the only true one. It is not my business to discuss the value of this creed, nor its possible chances of survival and similar problems. We only need to realize that there were people who believed in it with their entire heart and soul, and that their priests (with perhaps four or five exceptions, if we search the records closely) all preferred martyrdom to abjuration.

This novel, then, is a martyrology—hence its unilateral character. In a subsequent volume I intend to retrace the hopes and fears of other, different combatants—those who asked nothing except the chance to live. For the would-be faggot-martyr the route is mapped out in advance; he can recognize only one definition of Good and Evil. If we wish to understand the lives of such people, we have first to accept the universe in which they lived. In that inextricable tangle of conflicting loyalties and contradictory interests which make up the Albigensian War, these faggot-martyrs stand out as the men who had no choice. They were not the champions of a lost cause; they were not fighting for a "cause" at all, but for something which, as they saw it, could never be defeated.

They were the victorious ones. The second panel in my diptych will show the history of the vanquished.

Z. OLDENBOURG

PART ONE

CHAPTER I
Raymond de Ribeyre

THE Lords of Montgeil, in the Sault district, were such staunch believers that they never went to church. Only their eldest child had even been baptized.

Occasionally a traveller, on his way from Limoux to Foix, would make a detour through the Blau Valley, and ask the local peasants who owned that little castle, perched in so high and dominating a position above the river. The Lords of Montgeil, he would be told; a decent, easygoing family. If he could face the steep, difficult path which led up to the house, he could always be sure of a hospitable welcome, be he rich or poor.

Montgeil was not, strictly speaking, a castle at all, but simply a well-sited and fortified country house. Since the present owner had other things to worry about besides the maintenance of his walls, the place had become somewhat dilapidated.

Ricord de Montgeil, despite his forty-five and more years, was the most formidable hunter in the district. He ranged the countryside both on foot and on horseback, either alone or with his three servants; he went bareheaded, winter and summer alike, and always wore the same leather jerkin. It was fifteen years old, copper-studded, with the texture of oiled parchment. Those who met him greeted him as respectfully—no more and no less—as they would have done had he been lord of three full castles. He never quarrelled with anyone, and actually helped the peasants to poach on his preserves. He never handed over thieves or marauders to justice, and only exercised his right to forced labor when the situation urgently demanded it—during a drought, or when a debtor had failed to repay what he owed.

Ricord had five children living, four sons and one daughter.

While the boys were off roaming the countryside the girl remained at home, helping her mother with household duties: the only other females at Montgeil, besides the family, were two elderly servants.

Gentian and her mother lived at the top of the tower. Apart from this tower their home consisted merely of two flanking out-houses, built from rough stone. On the north, east, and west sides the tower was protected by a palisade. The hillside opposite was covered with dark pines. The sun's first rays never rose above it till the dawn-flush had faded from the sky and the entire household had long been up and about. When Gentian woke—and she was an early riser—her mother had already finished her prayers, and was lighting the fire in the living room.

"When you're married," she used to say, "I shall leave this house."

But Gentian had no desire to get married. Many of the smaller landowners down in the valley had already asked for her hand on their sons' behalf: she was now seventeen years old, a dark-haired, dark-complexioned girl, tall and lovely, with eyes the color of a wintry sky.

Mother and daughter resembled each other. Though she was now forty, Arsen de Cadéjac remained one of the most beautiful women in the whole of the valley. She was much given to piety, and spent more time tending the sick or visiting the poor than look-ing after her own household. She never took her daughter on these expeditions, for fear of possible unpleasant incidents. Gentian did not complain, but privately she fretted under this restraint. It is not always easy to be the daughter of religious-minded parents. Here was a young girl who knew how to read, who went to hear a ser-mon preached once a month with her family, who worked hard—and who spent the whole day thinking. The thoughts of a seven-teen-year-old girl, as we know, sprout and spread rather more rapidly than the rankest of weeds.

Ricord often left the house an hour before dawn, not returning till late that night, or even the following morning. When the men brought home their bloodstained booty, Arsen and Gentian would settle themselves by the hearth, together with the maidservants, and set about plucking the birds, cutting up the meat for pies, and preparing quarters or hams for curing. Ricord's hunting expeditions fed not only his own household but half the village as well. As she faced each fresh carcass Arsen felt the urge to ask its forgiveness. She went about her work in silence, lips compressed, yearning for the day when she would no longer have to perform such a task.

Ricord's four sons each possessed a horse. These creatures were at once their owners' pride and despair: in order to keep them fed and stabled the boys were obliged to spend much of their time going around the countryside in search of money. But where could a free-born, impecunious youth lay his hands on the stuff? What one of them won at hazard another would promptly lose the same way. Their harness and saddles were pawned, redeemed, sold, bought back again, while the four horses fed in a series of seigneurial stables all around Foix. The brothers certainly had no lack of friends. Since they were all inseparable, they were referred to collectively as "the four Aymon boys."

They took after their father in appearance, being, like him, tall, dark, and lean. When they smiled, they revealed teeth as strong and white as those of a young colt. They wore the same gray jerkins, winter and summer, girded their slim waists with leather straps in lieu of belts, and felt themselves equal to the richest young sprig in the district.

Imbert, the youngest, would sometimes put Gentian on his crupper and take her along to visit some neighboring family. Her public appearance unaccompanied by her mother gave no offense, since all the seigneurs in the valley were interrelated in some degree. The young people would settle themselves on the rush-strewn floor, beside the fire, and the girls would sing songs, chorus and solo. Gentian's voice was the most full-toned and fervent of them all.

William, the Seigneur de Frémiac's second son, said to her one day: "Your eyes are so beautiful that I can neither eat nor sleep because of them. If my father asked my Lord Ricord for your hand, would you marry me?"

Gentian hesitated for a moment. William's own eyes were so darkly miserable that she felt sorry for him.

"Oh, I know, I know," he went on. "You don't want to belong to any man. All you're interested in is saving your own soul. The fact that you're destroying mine means nothing to you."

"William," she told him, "I do not think I love you enough to forsake my maidenly chastity on your account."

That same evening Gentian said to her mother: "William de Frémiac has asked for my hand. What answer should I give him?"

"Is it my business to tell you?" Arsen asked. She was standing beside her bed, combing out her long hair prior to plaiting it up again for the night. "I have no wish to hurry you. Still, you are of marriageable age."

Her big dark eyes glowed, as a fire of coals will glow at its inmost heart. "Remember this," she said. "So long as you are here, I shall never leave this house. I shall never desert you till you have a house of your own, and a husband to protect you."

Gentian lay on her pallet bed, furs piled over her, unable to sleep. Her mother was sitting on the chest reading, a small oil lamp above her, the big book open on her knees. The girl saw her lips moving gently; from time to time she closed her eyes, as though repeating by heart the words she had just read. Then her great glowing eyes would fix themselves once more on the page before her. All that was visible in the circle of lamplight were those two white pages, the white sleeve of her shift, one long hand, and her head, bent in profile. It was very cold; yet, whatever the weather, Arsen always went barefoot at night, and wore nothing but her shift.

It was so misty a morning that the palisade was invisible from the doorway. Mountain, valley, and forest had all vanished; nothing remained but this milk-white mist, through which there struggled faint hints of the ascendant sun. From behind the portcullis, just visible between the shadows of the two outbuildings, there rang out the sound of a hunting horn.

The two travellers, who had come on foot, with no luggage apart from sticks and knapsacks, now strode across the courtyard, a pair of dark, silent, elongated silhouettes; and as they passed, everyone —servants first, then family—bent the knee to them. They were conducted to the ground-floor chamber in the tower, where a fire of big logs was blazing away on a hearth the size of a peasant's shack. Here too the fog had penetrated; but the flames licking up the chimney gave it a yellowish, luminous quality.

The women hurried in with clean towels and basins of warm water, while their menfolk hurriedly removed the cold leg of mutton that had been laid out for the morning meal, and hid it away in the storeroom. Ricord went in search of two bottles of the best wine from his own vineyard, while Arsen took down a brace of smoked salmon, and put a batch of fine wheaten griddlecakes to warm in front of the fire.

After the two men had washed themselves, they went into a corner near the window and said their prayers; the others discreetly left them alone while they did so.

Ricord's house was among those in which they were never obliged to prepare their own meals: they never would be served there with a cake or a dish of soup that contained a mere niggardly drop of milk or butter.

After the meal the mist slowly lifted, leaving the valley clear, though the mountains were still swathed in white vapor, and far below the river looked like a long streak of smoke. A mile or less away folk from nearby villages could already be seen trudging toward Ricord's tower, following the track that wound its slow way up the hillside. Good news travels fast.

The elder of the two men, Raymond de Ribeyre, had been a deacon for some years. He was about fifty, by no means an old man yet. His face looked pale against his black robe, and his hair, blond still rather than gray, was so curly that one might well have supposed the effect to have been achieved by artificial means. His features were so fine-drawn that they seemed the handiwork of some divine spirit rather than mere vulgar nature. It was known that his mother, an extremely pious woman, had restricted his diet from birth to almond milk, honey, and herbal soups: all his life no unclean matter had soiled his lips. Because of this his flesh, though firm and healthy enough, had the transparency of alabaster. His eyes were lavender-blue, big, and clear as a child's.

Arsen had heard him preach on many occasions, but this was the first time he had deigned to ask hospitality of her. When she began to tell him how overjoyed she was, he replied: "My sister, a time is coming when to receive us will be neither an honor nor a joy, but a sorrowful and perilous undertaking."

"When will this time be upon us?" she asked.

"It is here already, though we cannot tell the day or the hour thereof. Antichrist is girding himself mightily against Christ's Church, and comes among us to seal the faithful with his sign. In these days there shall be heard a great outcry in Rama, and great lamentation; for Rachel shall weep and mourn for her children, and will not be comforted. My sister, Rachel is the Church, and her children the faithful. And Antichrist will steal away their souls, for many and great will be their temptations, and I see not any end thereof."

"The harvest is full," Arsen said, "but the reapers are few. Tell us what we must do to prepare ourselves in the day of these great temptations."

"Let those who are in Judaea flee into the mountains; let not him who is in the field turn back to take up his coat."

Arsen stared miserably at the ground. She said: "But what words have you for those servants who wish to stay, their lamps lit, and await the Master's coming?"

The man made no reply to this. He moved across to the fireplace, settled himself in the straw, and sat staring at the flames as they licked up around the damp logs. His face was a still mask; his eyes did not so much as blink, yet they were brimming over with such agony of spirit that Gentian, who was standing beside the fire, put her hands over her face, and wept.

Out of the respect they felt for him no one present dared invite so revered a guest to take a chair. His companion rose from his bench and joined de Ribeyre at the fireside, taking care not to brush

against Gentian as he passed her. When he saw that she was weeping he asked her, quietly, the reason for her tears.

"Look there," she told him, glancing at de Ribeyre's face. "Look;
have you ever seen such agony as this? If *he* is thus afflicted, who
can refrain from weeping?"

"Take care," the man said, frowning. "These are frivolous tears.
You know neither the cause nor the object of his grief. You are like
a child, who cries when he hears others crying."

Gentian said, bitterly: "I would not wish to behave like a child."

"To wish is not enough," the man said. But then he looked at
that lovely face, a young girl's face, trembling now and tear-
stained, and reflected that her soul might perhaps be numbered
among the elect. Despite everything, a shade of warmth crept into
his impassive voice as he added: "It is written: Knock, and it shall
be opened unto you. You are never forbidden to knock."

Normally he avoided speaking to women; but this one, with her
countrified clothes and direct gaze, seemed more or less exempt
from the faults of her sex:

"You cannot knock in the void," Gentian said. "You have to
find the right door."

"I am sure you will find it."

She kept her eyes on the fire, not daring, out of modesty, to turn
her head toward him as he spoke. "Ah, my lord," she breathed,
"if that could only be true!"

The man in black decided to cut this discussion short; he moved
away from the chimney breast and stood in the doorway that
opened onto the courtyard, leaning against the jamb. There he remained, arms folded, watching the slow progress of the mist over
the crests of the nearest fir trees. He was not in the habit of talking
while his companion was occupied with prayer or meditation; now
he waited, as a valet will silently wait for his master to rouse himself from sleep.

Aicart de la Cadière was still a young man. He was nearly thirty,
and because of his extreme thinness looked younger still. He was
tall and slim, and rather more vigorous than one might have sup-

posed at first sight. His features displayed that stern yet noble
beauty often to be found in well-born gentlemen of Catalan der-
ivation: he was, in fact, a Catalan on his mother's side. His large,
dark, dreamy eyes made it difficult for him to discuss anything with
a person of the opposite sex. But since he was, so to speak, the
revered Raymond's shadow, his guardian, his very right hand,
Aicart had little time to concern himself with the souls of the faithful; his main function was a secretarial one.

The courtyard was already crowded with visitors. We'll never
get them all into this room, Aicart thought. He went out and gave
orders for a fire to be lit: the sermon would be delivered in the
open air.

So Raymond de Ribeyre preached out in the courtyard. The air
was icy cold; men and women alike were wrapped up in their
cloaks. Some stood, others sat on bundles of kindling. The young
folk kept feeding the fire with fresh wood to prevent its going
out. Raymond stood there, straight and rigid as a statue, perched
on the trunk of a big felled oak. He talked and talked; his voice,
despite a slightly monotonous quality, was fine and resonant. His
pale face, gilded by the fire, resembled a flame flickering above
some tall black candle.

He was preaching on the thirty-seventh verse of the seventh
chapter of the Gospel according to St. John: *In the last day, that
great day of the feast, Jesus stood and cried, saying: "If any man
thirst, let him come unto Me, and drink. He that believeth on Me,
as the Scripture hath said, out of his belly shall flow rivers of living
water." But this spake He of the Spirit, which they that believe on
Him should receive.* Raymond de Ribeyre spoke of the thirst that
was slaked yet never quenched, and of the living water more pure
than crystal, brighter than any diamond, fresher than morning dew
—water of which one could never drink enough, for thirst was
turned into eternally reviving joy, and the spring which is in the
heart never ceases to flow. For such a thirst there is no final appease-
ment; a soul united to the Spirit is like a plant, ever in need of the
sun, striving upward toward it, swelling and burgeoning, till it
brings forth its fruit in due season; it is like the fire that consumes

where it is nourished, and makes its fuel kindred to the sun, and cannot live except by waxing great and seeking fresh nurture where the desire so takes it. . . .

Night was falling; the burning faggots began to cast long black shadows against the stonework of the tower, and illuminated the faces of those nearest the fire with a dull, reddish light. The listeners huddled more closely against each other, partly to get nearer the speaker, partly to keep warm.

When the sermon was over, another good hour passed while the faithful filed by the two men to receive a blessing. They could not set out for home that night; they settled down in the outbuildings, in the tower rooms, and around the fire in the courtyard, sharing out the provisions they had brought with them. For the most part they remained silent; when they did speak it was in a whisper. Raymond's voice still seemed to float in the atmosphere, carrying with it a peace that no one dared to disturb.

Since it was long after sunset, the two visitors would accept only a little bread dipped in water. Ricord and his family wanted to copy their example as a token of respect; but Raymond gently admonished them, saying that it was quite enough for him and his companion to be obliged to fast, without the additional distress of causing their hosts unnecessary inconvenience. He was a courteous and affable man; he next apologized for the indiscreet zeal which had led him to keep his flock out in the open air for hours on end, at the risk of their catching bad colds or coughs.

Aicart, who hardly ever dared to raise his voice publicly in his master's presence, nevertheless managed to observe at this point that the spirit must be served before the body.

"Not always," Raymond said, with that faint smile which resembled a fugitive ray of sunlight. "Not always, my friend. Far from it. When a child is crying with hunger, would you feed it on sermons? Many of the faithful are still children in the Spirit. Anyone who forgets that is lacking in charity."

Aicart's only response was a smile, which carved two long vertical lines down his lean cheeks; it conveyed simultaneously contrition and trust, and spoke eloquently of the friendship which bound the two men together.

"My lord," Gentian said abruptly, flushed but sure of herself, "all the time you were speaking I did not feel the cold. It was as though there were a great warmth spreading from my heart. Doubtless I am ignorant in the Spirit, but I believe I could live my whole life through on sermons."

"Well, *I* was cold," the deacon said, with just a touch of mischievousness in his voice. "My blood is old; yours is young."

"Please excuse my daughter," Arsen said, with some embarrassment. "I have never managed to teach her good manners."

"It is written: Fathers, do not grieve your children. Your daughter has spoken as her heart directed."

Gentian, with the assistance of the two old servants, was now ladling out pea soup into the bowls. She had sworn not to eat anything herself that evening; despite being extremely hungry she felt as light as a feather. Raymond's radiant features and blue, sun-bright eyes shone continually before her, and her mind dwelt on that living water which gleams like diamonds.

Arsen was saying to the deacon: "Very soon now, if the Church deems us worthy, we shall be able to take the habit and begin our probationary period of service. Personally, I am waiting till my daughter is settled in life; my husband will leave the house to our eldest son as soon as we have discharged our debt to the Church."

After his brother's death Ricord had not always managed to keep up payment on the five-hundred-sou legacy which the dead man had bequeathed for the use of the righteous. There was still eighty sous outstanding, and in the mountain districts money is hard to come by.

"Have you at least found your daughter a husband who is of good family and a true believer?" Raymond asked her.

His hostess sighed. "There is no lack of such husbands," she said, "but my daughter has refused them all."

Raymond's companion asked if it was not a pity to drive the girl into accepting an inferior condition of life. "The question of money need not come into it," he added. "My aunt, Dame Adalays, would gladly waive the dowry and take her in for a probationary period at the establishment she maintains in Foix—always supposing the girl herself so willed it, and if my brother Raymond approves."

"I am the least of men after the flesh," said Raymond de Ribeyre, without looking up. "Who am I to approve or disapprove?" His disciple interpreted this as a rebuke.

"Ah, my lord," Arsen said, "I know too well how eagerly she would desire such a thing. But as it is written, one should think long and well before taking the field with five thousand men against an army of ten thousand. It is better to send ambassadors to treat with the foe rather than expose oneself to the shame of defeat. So my own sainted mother did for me. Many young girls mistake their natural pride for a longing toward God."

"Go on, Aicart my friend," Raymond said then, "speak." His voice was a little weary, yet vibrant with tenderness; he reproached himself for imposing his will too strongly upon the younger man. But to judge from Aicart's burning passion to save souls, his Aunt Adalays's house would have needed to be the size of Foix itself to accommodate them all. I'm getting old, the deacon thought. Who knows? Perhaps he understands young people better than I do.

Aicart spoke of the dangers inherent in a bond that risked at once the destruction of soul and body alike, and might bring new souls especially to perdition. "A soul that is still young turns to God with greater ardor, and learns the lessons of the Spirit with greater docility. It is cruel to force a young girl into marriage against her own desire."

"Ah, my lord," Arsen said slowly, "the desires of young girls are like apple blossom. It is not seemly to desire God according to this fashion."

Gentian sat there in the shadows behind the bench and listened to every word. Why, she wondered, must I wait for old age before I can know true joy? What use will the Divine Spirit be to me when I am an ugly, decrepit, worn-out creature? She was weeping

now, for the unearthly beauty of Raymond's face and words had
pierced her to the heart. "What would I not give," she whispered,
"to have knowledge of the Spirit revealed to me!"

That evening she knelt at her mother's feet in their high bedchamber and besought her for a long while, sobbing and crying.
Her mother wept too, but silently.

"Mother," she said, "am I so unworthy of the Good Life?"

Arsen sat motionless on her chest, under the little oil lamp. Her
clasped hands rested on her knees; her great eyes were wide open
and brimming with tears, like those of a stag at bay.

"I wanted you to be happy," she whispered. "I wanted you to
have fine children and a husband who loved you. Doubtless that is
a sinful desire, but it is so strong that my heart cannot struggle
against it. My beloved child, when I think of the life you crave, I
am afraid for you. I feel I know you too well. If you ever lived to
regret having set yourself on this road, truly it would be better for
you then that you had never been born."

"I am no coward," Gentian said. "Fear will never make me renounce my desires."

"Gentian, suppose you cannot stand the ordeal of training and
initiation? Suppose they send you back home? Would you not harbor bitterness, either against yourself or, worse, against God and
His Church?"

"If they send me home I shall kill myself."

Alarmed, Arsen said: "How could I agree to expose you to such
suffering?"

"The suffering you speak of has come already, Mother. It is here,
among us. Who knows whether the lightning may not strike our
house tomorrow? And if it does, I shall have died without drinking
from the Spring of Life! I am not afraid of death, but I cannot bear
the thought of living my life out in ignorance, like the beasts of the
fields. And how am I better than the beasts if I have no part in the
Spirit?"

"Go, then," her mother said, in a broken voice. "I would cut
the heart out of my own breast rather than see you weep any longer.

Go, my wild, headstrong little dove. Leave us if you must. My heart tells me that your life does not lie there; but a mother's heart is blinded by pity, and I no longer understand your ways. Tomorrow I will speak to your father and the holy men. I am sure Master Aicart will plead your cause well."

Ricord, as was usual with him, said little. He was not by nature of a taciturn disposition; but instinctive modesty forbade him to speak out in the presence of these men, when they were clad in the Holy Spirit and he was a miserable sinner. He believed that a man should not discuss matters of which he has little understanding, and left to his wife the task of interpreting his thoughts. He felt sad; he had not supposed that the moment of parting would come so soon, and in such a fashion.

Ricord and his neighbors accompanied the two travellers as far as Chalabre. Ricord lent the deacon his only horse, and himself walked ahead leading it by the reins. This honor rightfully belonged to him, as head of the house in which the holy men had been received. Raymond's companion rode on a horse which belonged to the Seigneur de Frémiac.

Even those travellers who had horses at their disposal went on foot, the better to show their respect for these servants of God. The procession made its way through the valley, and all along the narrow track by the river peasants stood waiting to cast fresh straw under the horses' hoofs. Some even spread out their woollen cloaks: it was not every day that Raymond the deacon visited this part of the country. His reputation was such that even the Catholics themselves regarded him as something of a saint.

When they dismounted outside the walls of Chalabre, the two men were once more obliged to bestow individual blessings on all the faithful. Aicart in his heart of hearts felt this to be a great waste of time, since each man insisted on kneeling and prostrating himself three times, according to the Rule. Raymond de Ribeyre was not worried about wasting time; he was always behindhand. Sometimes, at a gathering of high solemnity, he would allow himself to be delayed for hours on end; the faithful clung to him like flies to a honeypot, and he was by nature patient almost to a fault.

"I shall never forget this day, sir," Ricord said. "Pray God that I be found worthy to serve the Church!"

The wind was whipping his hair about his head, and he put one hand up to restrain it. He had one of those serious faces, unsmiling for the most part except for his eyes; but the joy which now shone from those eyes was simple and frank and made him look ten years younger. He had already quite forgotten about his daughter and his domestic worries; now he was just a man who had been lucky enough to accompany the deacon and lend him a horse.

"May God make a good Christian of you," de Ribeyre said. "Satan is making ready a hard ordeal for us. Guard yourself against falling into temptation—you know to which temptation I am referring."

"Sir, may my hand wither before I—"

"Do not speak in this way," the deacon said, with a melancholy smile. "One day you will regret it."

The two men in black were welcomed to Chalabre by the Town Council and leading citizens, and conducted to the church. This edifice had long since ceased to be used in the normal fashion. All crosses had been removed, and the paintings of saints on the walls had been carefully whitewashed over. Raymond could preach here without any risk of profaning his cloth.

Between them they had a busy day of it. There were two gravely ill persons in the town who were demanding to be baptized; many of the faithful had been perturbed by rumors of war, and were eager to hear the deacon's counsel on such matters. Raymond told them the same as he had told Ricord: namely, to be on their guard and not to succumb to temptation. And despite the entreaties of the Chalabre councillors, when night came Raymond de Ribeyre and his companion left the town.

"Friends and brothers," Raymond said, "do not suppose that this decision is dictated by any scorn for you or lack of friendliness on our part: our Lord Himself has made it known to me that I must not remain here. I beseech you, for the love of God, do not escort us for more than half a league on our way. Tonight we need neither guides nor a bodyguard."

"My lord, if rumors have reached you of some supposed traitor, some brigand who has sold his services to the Catholics, rest assured that such creatures could not harm you while you remain in our district."

"My friends, I have never gone in fear of traitors or brigands; any more than I was afraid when I spoke last Sunday in Carcassonne, to a congregation that numbered clerks and priests among its members. I would never budge ten steps off my chosen path through fear of our Church's enemies. God forbid you should think I scorn you! I know well that your district is one of those in which the Faith of Christ has been worthily honored since the time of our forefathers."

It was a chilly night. Flames crackled over the dead branches and twigs, making the star-clustered sky seem a deeper black by contrast. Of that vast nocturnal landscape which lay spread out at the two men's feet, all they could now see were a few pine trees, lit by the glow of their campfire.

Aicart could make a fire in all weathers, and from any sort of kindling. His master loved to sleep out under the stars; houses stifled him. He could never have enough fresh air, and open spaces were never wide enough for him: it was vital for him to be able to pray beneath the naked heavens, in some high place for choice, far from all human habitation. "Do I impose too severe a penance on you, my friend?" he would ask Aicart. (He never called him "brother" or "comrade"; always "my friend.") Penance? No; rather, a favored privilege. From his youth onward Aicart had come to know the fearful joy to be had from these lonely nocturnal vigils: the body crucified by hunger and exhaustion and the struggle to stay awake; the soul bewildered by great black abysses, voids of the mind where voiceless, formless spirits dwelt.

I make the fire, Aicart thought. If my thirst becomes overpowering I drink a little water from the flask—and thereby commit a

breach of the Rule, which I have to purge with such lengthy pre-
liminary prayers that sometimes I forget my thirst in the process.
For years now Raymond had been in the habit of letting no drink
or food sully his lips from sunset to sunrise. Hunger is the body's
best friend; when one lives with it continually there is little in this
world of which one goes in fear.

Sharers in the Bread of Heaven, Raymond whispered silently,
partakers of the Water of the Spirit, bound by the Mystic Robe and
the Celestial Fire; shades among the living, adults among the children in the Spirit—Ah, this life of eternal watchfulness, burned
by Pentecostal fires, the single sacrifice made once and forever.
From the day of our ordination we cannot close our eyes, even in
sleep. Our very night is light. Of that warm, secret, animal self
which every man carries within him, and which distinguishes him
from all other creatures, no particle remains to us. We are public
men, exposed day and night to human and Divine scrutiny alike.

Raymond stood erect to pray, arms uplifted, his back resting
against the trunk of a pine tree. He could remain in this position
for hours: delicate and sensitive physically though he was, he no
longer felt the most cruel cold when engaged in prayer. Strike him,
he would not so much as feel the blow; burn him with a red-hot
coal, still he would not flinch. His face, harshly lit now by the fire,
had divested itself so completely of its fleshly attributes that it
seemed a mask in molten metal, wrought and shaped by the flames
—mouth half open, eyes unnaturally enlarged, each muscle quivering yet motionless, taut to breaking point. How could this fragile
reed sustain such pressure, not once but night after night?

On this occasion his prayers were both more sorrowful and more
concentrated than ordinarily. Tears streamed down from his eyes,
and his forehead was so heavily bedewed with sweat that his very
eyebrows were wet with it. Aicart had never attained the experience
of this kind of prayer. He stood there rooted to the ground, scarcely
breathing, his mind a blank, stiffening his body in order to keep
himself upright, as though some mighty wind were bowing his
shoulders.

The fire was dying down; time to replenish it. First with twigs and dead leaves, then small broken branches. All the time Raymond stood still in prayer, his lips drawn back now in a strange smile, calm as the smile of a dead man. His eyes shone with light.

Aicart thought: I would die for you, master. Ah, master, I cannot bear to see you suffer! Speak to me—tell me what grief this is that has gained possession of you— No one knew better than Aicart what depths of joy Raymond's eyes could, on occasion, conceal; yet Aicart loved him even more strongly for his grief than for his joy. He, Aicart, was the sole witness of this agony; it remained as it were a secret between his master and himself.

Recently this mood had become more marked. Was it possible that rumors of war could so rack such a man as Raymond? Aicart stared at the fire, blazing up cheerfully once more, sending out little yellow or bluish flames to lick through the fresh fuel. Look at it, he thought, dancing, soaring skyward; it has found nurture, it is growing, transforming itself into an oriflamme of light. A symbol of life, he told himself: fire fed on eternal fuel, destroying at once itself and what it devours. It is both friend and enemy: a seeming friend to those who never come to close grips with it. Look; I put my hand near, and its warmth is good; I thrust my hand into it, and instantly am transfixed with agony. *Thou shalt not deny thy Faith through fear of death by fire, by water, or by any other means whatsoever.* During the testing period of our novitiate we dwelt on such an ordeal in our thoughts, with that peculiar joy which the young experience in the face of danger. We tested ourselves secretly, laying one arm against a flaming faggot. Pain beyond measure, sharp delight of pride and the five senses. Childish vanity.

Before you receive baptism you still have a choice. Once granted that solace, you become a man without power over his own life, a body surrendered to the Rule just as this log is given over to the consuming flames. The body can inure itself to anything, with the possible exception of death by burning; but once you have reached this extreme point, it is a little late to turn back.

Who knows? Anything might happen. Aicart reflected that the news of the Crusade now being mounted in the North had led certain Catholics to put on outrageously arrogant airs; they were beginning to hold their heads high once more, and threaten you with the stake for the slightest intemperate word. A fine sort of argument, and just what you would expect from a parcel of heathens.

Raymond lay sleeping like a corpse, stiff and pale: it was impossible to tell whether he was breathing or not. At times Aicart became convinced that the spirit actually left his frail husk of a body, only returning when its owner needed to use it once more. If it was true that certain fortunate souls achieved occasional reincarnation in the flesh—not to expiate sins, but through love of their fallen brothers on earth—then without doubt Raymond's soul must be numbered among them. During the eight years they had spent together, Aicart had failed to discover the slightest imperfection in his master—except, in the last resort, his excessive patience with sinners. Did not Jesus Himself decry the Pharisees as hypocrites? he had asked. "Ah," Raymond would say, "and am *I* then Jesus?"

This was why Aicart used to stay awake by his master's side till his strength failed him, sometimes holding his hand over the brazier to prevent himself from falling asleep. His own case apart, he was of the opinion that Peter, James, and John had shown up rather badly (before their baptism by fire, that is) in allowing themselves to doze off on the Mount of Olives.

Aicart lay stretched out on the cold ground, arms folded behind his head, and stared at the sleeping deacon's profile, lit now by the reddish glow of the dying fire. Long curly ringlets of hair, straggling over forehead and cheek, gave his ageless face a young, almost a graceful air. A three days' beard shadowed his chin and upper lip, reminding one in an unexpected fashion that the revered Raymond de Ribeyre was a man like other men, who needed to use a razor. It was nipping cold and the air was pure and fresh; in the sky the stars had begun to fade. Aicart shut his eyes, suddenly overwhelmed by sleep. There was nothing to worry about. You could rely on Raymond to wake you at the right time for morning prayer: he knew what time it was even when asleep, like the birds and beasts.

When the sun rose Aicart perceived a score or so of men and women from Chalabre at the bottom of the hillside. They were sitting in little groups among the young pine trees, a couple of hundred yards from the spot where the two men had passed the night. They must have followed them at a safe distance and tracked them down by means of the fire; indeed, they must have spent the whole night there, watching and praying, not daring to light a fire for themselves, lest they betray their presence.

"Will you not go and speak to them, brother? It seems to me that they deserve it."

"They have no need of my words," Raymond said, slowly. "Come, let us begone. If we take this path through the wood, they will not be able to tell which way we have gone."

"These people have shown great faith by their action. Can you leave like this, without saying a single word to them?"

The deacon's face was impassive, almost hard. "This generation seeks for a sign," he said. "As God is my witness, I have no wish to be that sign. I said what I had to say yesterday: I was not preaching to the town walls. And indeed, if their faith is as great as you maintain, they have no further need of me."

"Ordinarily," Aicart observed, "you show greater patience to those who deserve it less."

"Aicart, my friend, are you not really saying to yourself: 'I am the companion of a true light of the Church, a man whom God has so glorified that all he needs now is to be carried up alive to Heaven in a chariot, like the false prophet Elijah'? It is in such a way that the servants of the Beast do honor to their leaders. Do not read bitterness or mockery into these words; truly I love you more than I have ever loved any living creature. But for the love of God, do not glorify in your heart that which does not deserve to be glorified, else one day you will pay dearly for it."

Aicart said nothing, but strode on ahead, using the tip of his staff to hold back such low-growing branches as might scratch his friend's face. He did not feel hurt; Raymond's rebuke was well merited. Three months earlier, during a General Assembly of the

Brothers of Christ's Church, the question had been raised of creating a new diocese to serve the Foix district. The project had been abandoned, partly because of the threat of war, but also because the Bishops of Toulouse and Carcassonne, Monseigneur Gaucelm and Monseigneur Bernard—both of them extremely old men— might have been grieved by such a decision. The faithful round about Foix had, indeed, no fault to find with either of them; they wanted a Bishop of their own simply for the sake of convenience and local prestige: it was in their part of the country, they asserted, that the true Faith had been longest established and honored. To cut a long story short, at a certain point in the proceedings some of the brothers (by no means the least among them, either) had thought of Raymond de Ribeyre for this new position. He was a native of Foix and, despite his comparative youth, renowned for the Christian virtues he displayed.

On that occasion Raymond had said to his companion: "You want to see me a Bishop, do you? Why not Pope as well? You are not yet free of the desires of the flesh." But at the age of thirty who was? When one lived according to the Rule, natural concupiscence was transmuted into ambition, or a passion for controversy.

"A leaven for the Pharisees and Sadducees, eh, my friend?" Raymond said. "The Catholic priests who lead an impure life are not the worst, by a long way."

"Ah, master, it is through my love of the Church that I would have wished to see you made Bishop; what other man could serve the Church better than you? Do *our* bishops live in palaces or wear cloth of gold or have an armed militia to collect their tithes?"

Remembering this, he said now: "My brother, why did you refuse to speak to these folk from Chalabre, when you had just spent a night at Montgeil in a married man's house—a man who was an ex-soldier and the father of a family to boot?"

"His wife is one of God's elect," Raymond said. "I can see a path of glory awaiting her. But were the faithful miserable sinners, their hospitality would always be too great an honor for us. The time is coming, my friend, when we shall have to say to them: To that place where we go you may not follow. And this parting will be so dolorous that at times I wish I had never been born."

"Ah, my brother," Aicart exclaimed, utterly dumfounded, "is your suffering then so intense? What have we to fear? Persecutions? There have always been persecutions. Is not the faith of our flock growing daily? Do not the princes and barons of our country honor the Church? We have heard enough and more than enough of war—at Carcassonne, Limoux, Termes, and Lavaur! Yet even war is preferable to pestilence. If they dare to launch this Crusade against the Christians, will not the Great Whore be unmasked once and for all? Will not the day come when her raiment will finally be torn from her, as it is written in the Scriptures?"

"Do not try to comfort me," Raymond said, with melancholy tenderness. "I am not a child. Aicart, my friend, I do not want my weakness to cause you any shame. Only the sons of the Great Whore can believe in their own unfailing strength; they are so deluded by the lying lures of the flesh that they take themselves to be God's creatures.

"So the Great Whore will be unmasked, will she? The worse for us, if we look to profit by public catastrophe, and act the part of vultures, that grow fat by devouring the bodies of the dead! And you: are you seeking to gather in souls through hatred of our enemies rather than by the love of Christ? In very truth, such souls will be damned more surely than if they were under the yoke of Babylon!"

"Brother," Aicart said, "these are hard and bitter words. It is right that we should hate evil."

"Aicart, we are not allowed to kill so much as a rat, yet you talk of hating men! The man who says: 'I hate evil' deceives himself utterly. He does not see Evil, only individual men whom he thinks of as evildoers. Whosoever shall say to his brother, 'Raca,' * shall be in danger of the council: but whosoever shall say, 'Thou fool,'

* A contemptuous epithet, signifying "worthless," in use among the Jews at the time of Christ. See Matthew 5:22, from which this passage is borrowed.—Trs.

shall be in danger of hellfire, since we have embraced our Lord's ordinances, and therefore must answer to the utmost letter of His every law. Such a judgment is just; but hatred must always lack justice."

"Your words are hard to understand," Aicart said, eyes on the ground. "Pray God enlighten me with the grace of His Holy Spirit, for my understanding is sadly imperfect, and I cannot assent to what you have just told me."

CHAPTER II

The Chosen

GENTIAN was not passionately addicted either to prayer or to reading. She enjoyed singing: she was always the first up into the granary or down in the cellars; she was an enthusiastic poker of fires. When she went out with her mother, she picked whole basketfuls of berries or mushrooms; it never occurred to her that she had got enough. In springtime, she used to go out into the woods and come back with great armfuls of flowers and greenery to decorate the house. At the moment she wanted to pluck the joy of eternal life, because nothing so wonderful had hitherto offered itself to her desires.

As she waited for her day of departure she had occasional pensive moods, when she would let book or needle fall; at such moments her cheeks began to burn, and her eyes became as clear as a rock spring. She looked so lovely that the two old servants had their breath quite taken away, and said there was no doubt now that the good Lord had chosen her to bring honor on her house. William de Frémiac, who loved her, no longer dared speak to her of marriage.

"I could not have asked for a better match, William," Ricord told him. "But what can a father and mother do when the soul that is their child has heard the voice of God calling her? One day you too will hear that Call."

Ricord had heard the Call himself, fifteen years ago, and was in no danger of forgetting it.

The four brothers returned home at the beginning of Lent, and accompanied their parents and sister to Foix. The farewells were cheerful ones, as was only fitting when a young girl was to have the chance of pursuing the Good Life. Dame Adalays, the Superior of the community, received her joyfully. "Be happy, dear child, that you have been granted the desire to follow true wisdom," she said. "Think no more of your own faults; they are nothing. Think rather of God's love, which is all-embracing. One day, perhaps, the Church will deem you worthy of the full Christian life."

Gentian kissed her father and brothers; but when she came to her mother she wept.

"Very soon I shall forsake this world," Arsen told her. "When you see me again I shall be wearing the black habit."

"So may it be for me also, Mother. Pray God I soon win through to this high honor."

"I have to say 'Thy will be done,' not 'My daughter's will be done.' I can neither increase nor diminish the love which God has for your soul. My love is all I possess; and that is little enough."

"How much it meant to me, though, Mother! What a loss I shall suffer in never seeing your sweet face again. If God promises to recompense us a hundredfold for such things, the joy He gives us must be great beyond all reckoning."

"Great, indeed," Arsen said, "but not of the sort which we suppose. At the hour when that joy comes to you, like a thief in the night, will you be sure of recognizing it?"

Ricord's four sons had to stay on in Foix for a few weeks longer; they escorted their parents on the homeward journey, a full two leagues' ride. Each one of the four vigorously asserted his claim to the honor of carrying their mother on *his* horse. Despite their perpetual absence the four boys—Sicart, Olivier, Renaud, and Imbert —were devoted sons; they took as much pride in their mother as other young men did in the lady they served. For penniless youths the delights of love constitute a luxury further beyond their reach even than a knight's armor. Ricord's four sons were decent and godly young men, who could at least boast of a mother whose name was a by-word for piety throughout the countryside. They themselves were pious after their fashion. They had frequent brawls with comrades who were Catholic (or passed as such); they had a cordial hatred of all tonsured monks, and sprang off their horses whenever they saw a Christian approaching in the distance.

Arsen was not worried on behalf of these robust, easygoing sons of hers: poverty is no vice when it is willingly accepted. She knew that the friendship which existed between them all protected them both from debauchery and from the temptation to enrich themselves at their neighbors' expense. Sicart was now in his twenty-third year, and was thinking of taking a wife, against the day when his mother would quit the house.

As she watched all four of them remount and gallop away down the little track that skirted the mountainside, turning around in the saddle and waving enthusiastically as they went, Arsen felt a deep stab of pain pass through her heart. She was thinking of what Deacon Raymond had told her, and what was being talked of in the town. It was virtually certain that this time, at last, Antichrist was about to launch an all-out attack against the Church of God; down in the plain the summer that followed would be a summer of war. Béziers and Carcassonne were a long way off, folk said, and any enemy who got up here would have to be a clever devil indeed: though it might be nearer the mark to say that anyone who comforted himself with such an argument would have to be very frivolous and very stupid. A horse could do the journey in two days, a pigeon in one—and Satan's notions in less than an hour.

Antichrist will send his servants by their thousands and ten thousands, Arsen thought, all armed with weapons of death and marked with the sign of the cross. It is not only death in the flesh that they bring for our bodies, but the devils that go by the names of hatred, cruelty, and fear; and many are the souls of the faithful that will succumb to them. My sons are tall and strong and skilled in the use of bow and javelin—and have neither helmet nor armor for their protection. Ah, God protect their tender hearts against anger, and their breasts against the spears of the enemy!

"Woman," Ricord said, "is it these rumors of war that make you so sorrowful? Would a war really matter to us? Our children are free and owe allegiance to no man."

"No, God be praised, they do not," Arsen exclaimed, shaking

her dark head. "But we have taught them the profession of arms, seeing the servitude of our condition in this human life; and such a profession in itself forms a very great temptation. I know, too, that this will not be a war like other wars; many indeed will perish in it."

Husband and wife were sitting together on a heap of stones in the shade of a vast olive tree. Their horse stood cropping the grass on the lush hillside; above and behind this wide slope, with its vineyards and black plowed fields, the mountains stretched away, increasingly blue as they approached the horizon. The sky above them was unclouded, and showed vivid blue through the tree's gray, latticed leafage. Arsen said a grace and then undid her bundle, which contained some bread and a few dried figs for the journey.

"How many more meals will we have together like this?" Ricord asked. "Our daughter is in good hands now; we ought not to linger together any longer."

He felt melancholy; the figs which he took from his wife's open hand seemed better to him than honey-steeped ginger. At forty Arsen herself had the beauty of ripe fruit: her face was smooth and firm, her eyes the color of hazel or dark honey, her eyebrows like two tiny ermines' tails. She was so beautiful that even after five years of chastity Ricord was still sometimes troubled by thoughts of carnal love. When we are parted, he thought, when our hands can no longer touch, when we are obliged to greet each other from a distance, as though we were strangers—who knows whether even then the memory of our long loving friendship will keep us from sleep at night?

She said: "Ricord, I feel that I have reached the summit of a high mountain which I have been climbing, step by step, ever since childhood. There are still a few flowers and some grasses growing here; and when I look at them my heart beats as it never did for the great apple trees of my childhood. From where I stand I can see tall snow-clad mountains, glittering bright as the sun; when I look down, valleys and villages and forests lie before my eyes. And everything seems so tiny that I could cover it all with the shadow of my hand. Giddiness assails me—I could never make my way down again. Yet if I climb still farther I shall be burned by the sun, frozen by the snow—and my heart is wrung with fear at the thought of it. To free myself wholly will mean abandoning everything; and my soul is distressed to its depths, for I am as much a part of you as the root is of the ground which nourishes it."

"I am not hurrying you," Ricord said gently. "Stay at home for as long as you need to prepare yourself for your new life. As far as I am concerned, it will certainly take a year, if not more, to pay off my debt and settle the matter of the inheritance. For the present you will be able to lead as solitary an existence up in the tower as a prisoner in his cell. In this way, though we shall still be under the same roof, we shall gradually get out of the habit of seeing each other."

"Why am I not a man?" Arsen said. "Then I could have been assigned to you as travelling companion. Yet I have no real regrets: if I had been a man I would never have known you as I know you now, or loved you as I do."

The ways to salvation are strange. In his youth Ricord's reputation had been so bad that Arsen's parents had wept with distress on the day of their daughter's marriage. He was of a quarrelsome, impatient, and haughty temper, always ready to draw his knife or fling a gauntlet in someone's face. He was smitten with so sudden a passion for Arsen that no one, except Arsen herself, believed it could possibly last. It turned out a better match than many, though it was by no means perfect: the love that united husband and wife was so fierce that it produced real suffering. Though neither was ever jealous or unfaithful, a dozen times every day they tormented themselves and each other, to the point where they actually longed to die. In six years they produced five children, all of them strong and good-looking. Then, when he was about thirty, Ricord received a visitation from God, in a particularly cruel fashion.

He was travelling to Carcassonne with several of his friends and relatives, to render homage for his land, as in duty bound, to the local Viscount. On this particular day an execution was due to take place in the main square of the town, and a large crowd had assembled there. The Montgeil party, being on horseback, were in a more advantageous position than the rest to view this spectacle; and out of curiosity they halted by the doorway of a large house some twenty paces from the scaffold.

The condemned man was a dangerous brigand, convicted of murder, rape, and gross sacrilege; so his death was to be a hard one. He was led into the square, his hands and feet shackled, while the crowd pelted him with stones and filth as he passed. At the foot of the scaffold a priest awaited him, bearing a cross. The executioner and his assistants were busy checking that the wheel turned freely, laying out their pincers, and preparing the lead, which was heating up in a caldron set on a tripod. The man paid no attention to the priest; he was watching the executioners, thoughtfully, mouth gaping open, like some scared child about to be birched. Before he mounted the steps of the scaffold his shackles were knocked off. He made a great sign of the cross, and then went to meet his executioners with humble docility, head bent, like an ox going to the slaughter.

Ricord wanted desperately to turn his head away, but he could not take his eyes off the man's face. The brigand was a big, powerful man, and well inured to physical pain: this was by no means the first time he had been on the torturer's block. His nostrils had been torn out, while his right cheek and both shoulders bore the marks of the branding iron. At first he merely clenched his teeth and groaned. But when molten lead was poured into the wounds that had been made on his arms and thighs by the pincers, his self-control vanished: he threw back his head and howled like a wild animal. The sheer volume of sound was terrifying; it seemed impossible that any living creature could keep it up for more than ten seconds without dropping dead.

When he was bound to the wheel he continued his outcry. At each revolution Ricord saw that gray-haired, bloodstained face borne past him, hanging upside down, with its O of a mouth and its huge, terrified, beseeching eyes: *Stop it,* they cried silently, *what are you doing to me? And why, why?* On either side of the wheel his arms and legs hung, thin flaccid bags of black, bleeding flesh, their bones reduced to meal.

The man's mouth, bloodless-blue, still shrieked in agony, and his lost, defeated eyes seemed continually to beg for help. Something was happening inside Ricord, he knew not what. Why had the features of this tortured victim suddenly become haloed with reddish light, and begun to move toward him? Every muscle and nerve in his body was stretched so taut that he seemed to feel them all vibrating, like ropes near breaking point. Then a voice as resonant as any trumpet cried out: *"Ah, brother, brother, forgive us!"* He did not realize at once that the voice had been his own.

One of his cousins gripped his arm and told him he was out of his senses.

At this point Ricord was utterly overwhelmed by what people later described as his "madness": he pushed forward into the crowd, still mounted, and in imminent danger of trampling down women and children. He held his arms high above his head and shouted: "Stop it! Get out of here, all of you! It is your own brother, your own father you are treating like this! How could you inflict such horrors on any living creature?"

He uttered these words in a thunderous voice that rose high above the roll of the drums, the howls of the tortured man, and the clash of bells in the church steeple. For a few seconds everyone was quite still. The wheel ceased to turn, the executioners dropped their staves. For one split second Ricord had a vision: a devouring fire seemed to lick about the heart and bowels of every single soul in the square. The fire of pity that burned him had, however briefly, descended on them as well.

He wheeled his horse about and rode out of the town without looking at anyone; and so intense was the fire that glowed from his eyes that the soldiers at the outer gate did not dare either to stop him or to ask his name.

For a long while he galloped on, never slackening speed, convinced that this headlong flight of his was due to anger. He followed a random course along the stony tracks that led toward Les Corbières; his mouth and throat were parched, as though he had drunk nothing for two days. Then, as he was passing through a black, rocky, pine-clad gorge, he felt his horse sway under him, and just managed to jump clear in the nick of time, into the thorn-bushes that lay thick about the ravine. The horse collapsed beside him, and only just missed crushing him as it fell. Twice it tried to stagger up, and then its head fell back finally, on a pillow of dead twigs and brushwood.

As he gazed at the beautiful creature that he had killed by his lunatic behavior, Ricord found himself, at last, able to shed tears. He wept for a long while, his face buried in the horse's long, fine-muscled neck.

For two days Ricord wandered through the mountains. On the third day he saw a fortified village, perched high up on one side of a rocky spur, and made his way up there to beg some bread. When he returned home, after a three weeks' absence, his children failed to recognize him, so thin had he become, so feverish and deep-shadowed his eyes.

Arsen said: "Your cousins told me what happened, of course. They think you're out of your mind; but that's only because they're singularly stupid themselves. What you heard that day was the voice of God."

"I do not know if it was God's voice or not, my beloved; but certainly there is no longer any rest or peace of mind for me. Thirty years long my heart slumbered in ignorance, and its awakening was so hard a thing that death itself would have been preferable. One thing I must tell you which will please you little: neither for you nor for any other have I felt such love as rose burning in my heart for that tortured fellow creature—my brother indeed—and for all like him. Wild beasts may devour one another, but man is worse still; the evil in him is without name or bounds. Since I have learned what changes a man's face can suffer, your own features have seemed less lovely to me. If I can still bear to face life, it is only because I have a feeling my own death will be similar, if not more agonizing still. So great is the weight of evil in this world that any man who aspires to find good there is a traitor to his brothers and to God.''

"These are hard words," Arsen said. "Why do you love me less than some brigand, a murderer of innocent people? And why, being innocent yourself, do you expect to die a felon's death?"

"Before God's face there are neither innocent nor guilty: only lost souls. Of my own soul I reckon little, it is nothing but a burden to me now; what does it matter that this soul should be saved when others are being lost? Would *you* care to eat at the King's table if you knew your children were starving to death?''

"Place your trust in God, Ricord. Remember Christ's words: *Holy Father, those that Thou gavest me I have kept, and none of them is lost, but the son of perdition.* Who knows whether the man you saw may not have been such a one?''

"If he had been, Arsen," Ricord said, "the fire would never have burned in my heart as it did. And for what do you suppose the Good Thief was crucified? Why, for theft and murder. But *he* saw Jesus nailed up beside him, on a cross like his own; whereas this fellow human being I watched the other day had no one beside him except a priest who was hand in glove with the executioners.''

"Ricord," the girl said, "are you suggesting that every thief might have Christ crucified beside him in the moment of his death? Christ only appeared once on earth.''

"He came to light a fire on this earth; and the flames of that fire burn today in my belly, so that my thirst will never be slaked. I am an ignorant man; and even though I were to let myself be flayed alive by inches, I could not in this way learn anything that might lessen the distress of so much as a single one among my brothers. And till I have learned *that,* I cannot face my own life.''

From that day forward Ricord renounced the profession of arms, and no longer showed himself in town or castle, lest he succumb to the temptations of anger; for rage burned in his heart against all those who had the power to harm others. When spring came, he sought counsel of that venerable figure Bishop William, who administered the See of Carcassonne for the heretical Church. He remained ten days in the Bishop's house, fasting and praying, before he was admitted to Monseigneur William's presence. The Bishop's advice was that he should continue to abide by the secular laws of the land till his children came of age: this would give proof of his capacity for faithfulness in small things, as it is written in the Gospels.

This seemed a stern ordeal to Ricord. "Is not a man who suffers evil in silence," he asked the Bishop, "more culpable than the very criminal, who acts out of ignorance?"

The Bishop said: "When the woman put a handful of leaven into three measures of meal, did she then set her bread to bake at once? No one would have cared to eat her loaves if she did. What are ten or twenty years in the sight of God?"

"If I abide by Satan's laws," Ricord said, "am I not myself a servant of Satan?"

"My son, we all serve him with every breath of air that we take, since our body is his handiwork. Resign yourself. You still have money in plenty to spend on whoredoms: and the names of your strumpets are Anger, Impatience, Ignorance, and Presumption. Only when misery and a hunger for the good things of the Spirit have eaten into your very marrow—only then will you know a true desire to turn back to our Heavenly Father."

Ricord did not yet possess a hunger for the good things of the Spirit. It was a different hunger that devoured him, a consuming pity for the wretched creatures whom his newly opened eyes now perceived at every turn. On his way back home from Carcassonne he gave away his horse to a lame beggar, his cloak to an old half-naked woman, and his shoes to a young boy whose feet were covered with open sores. He knew such things were of little or no avail; he felt like a man who sees his friend devoured alive by swarms of wasps and mosquitoes, and who manages to kill one or two individual insects. The others still remain, crawling in their thousands over the victim's tortured body. Out of sheer impotent rage Ricord lay down on the stony track, and wept. He thought of little children tortured by brigands, of violated women, of old men left by their sons to die of hunger, of peasants hanged for poach-ing, of the cripples and lepers. Wretchedness in the body makes the soul ugly as well, driving it so far from God that it is in peril of never finding Him again.

When Ricord returned home his wife did not inquire where and how he had lost his second horse, though she wept with him at the news of the Bishop's decision. "My beloved," she said, "since this is how it must be, let us promise one another to surrender ourselves to God's service on the very day Gentian is married; and from henceforth let us live as brother and sister, and renounce all worldly possessions except what is needful to prevent our children from starving."

Ricord said, bitterly: "What good does it do for our life to appear virtuous in the eyes of the world? Let us drink and be happy; there is not one of the children starving to death on a dunghill at this very moment who would be one penny the better or worse for such a gesture. Why should I not raid the abbeys and churches? There is enough gold and precious stones and fine stuff and corn and wine stored away in them to feed every poor person in this district for the next half century. Why should I not kill with my own hands all these lying grandees who offer the poor salvation in return for money, and deface that image of God in which they are all made?"

"Listen, Ricord: in this world, at least, the powers of evil have mastery. Jesus Christ did not bid us kill and plunder; He told us of a Samaritan, who saw a wounded man as he passed by, and took pity on him."

"The Samaritan saw one victim only; I can see thousands. I feel as though my eyes had the power to pierce through walls, and see things twenty leagues off. I feel that all those I have failed to help are dead by my doing; it is just as though I were to stand by and watch our own children being butchered without raising a finger to protect them."

"Ah, beloved," Arsen said, "I see you love me no longer—" and she burst into a storm of sobbing.

So deep was Ricord's distress that he did, in fact, imagine his love had died, and that the only emotion he felt for this beautiful

young woman (now condemned by him to so austere an existence)
was pity and nothing more. But time passed: six months, then a
year, and Ricord resumed his occupation of the marriage bed. He
was young still, and had not yet succeeded in casting out the
demons of desire from his blood.

One dark summer night he went in search of her, in the granary
where she now slept, picking his way to her pallet through heaps
of dried lavender, carded wool, and freshly dyed linen: the scent
of herbs was as strong as spiced wine. Arsen received him so joyfully that it seemed the night was lit up for them with the brilliance
of a dozen suns.

"May our sin be laid to his charge through whom the angels
fell!" she whispered. "My love, let us drain desire till we are
weary; for truly this love of ours is as strong as the tides or the
winds of the South. Who can struggle against it? Let us surrender
to it gladly, without repining."

"Arsen, I wish this night could last forever," Ricord said. "Tomorrow we will find ourselves as we were yesterday; and henceforth there will be two spirits, two desires in our hearts, ceaselessly
striving for mastery. Can one long for two good things that are
clean contrary each to the other? My heart longs for them both with
equal intensity."

"A day will come when you no longer desire me," she said.

"May that day never come. When it does I shall be dead, even
though I still live and breathe."

"No, Ricord; I pray it may come. Then nothing will be able to
separate us."

For ten years they continued to live together as man and wife.
All that time they were wearing themselves out with toil, working
harder than any peasant, for their duties were onerous and they
were trying in addition to maintain a Christian way of life. The
land was theirs, yet they only took as much rye and sheep's-wool
and olives as they needed for survival, and very often gave that
away too, for there were always folk ready to beg it of them. From
stark necessity no less than charitable Christian motives Ricord

would sometimes go between the shafts of the cart to help a sick peasant, gather in olives at harvesttime, or lend a hand in person at the oil press.

The boys were growing up now, as wild as young wolves, and their father spent half his time teaching them to draw a bow or handle a spear; they took turns riding the one horse left in the stables. Ricord was by no means happy at the thought of teaching them the use of arms; but it was the one skill he possessed, and a day would come when his sons might well need to fight for their lives. The year that the youngest of the four boys turned fifteen, Ricord sold his crop of olives and that season's vintage for hard cash, borrowed fifty sous from his brother, and bought four horses. After that the boys regarded their father as though he were Jesus Christ in person. They were not ungrateful children; in fact, so little used were they to receiving gifts from their parents that each rare present was worth a king's bounty in their eyes.

But with Gentian it was different. She was the youngest of the five, and the only girl, so that her parents could not stop themselves from treating her as though every favor was no more than her due. Arsen failed to nurse the four children she bore after her husband's conversion: she was working so hard that they all came into the world small and sickly, and she herself lacked the milk to give them. Her natural tenderness for these tiny beings, so quickly lost to her, was transferred to Gentian. And the thought never left her mind that the girl's wedding day would also mark her own separation from Ricord: because of this the child became yet more precious to her. When Gentian was twelve, Arsen took her up to sleep in the granary at the top of the tower. Henceforward Ricord's place in the bed was filled by his daughter, and he himself went there no more.

From that day on his passion for hunting grew until it became an obsession. It was in vain that he told himself all this game went to feed those who could procure neither bread nor meat for themselves: the truth was, he hunted for his own pleasure. "Purification comes by degrees," his spiritual adviser told him. "It is best not to kill at all; but killing animals is better than killing men, and hunting better than the practice of carnal intercourse. In this way one substitutes a lesser sin for a greater one." The saintly old man had no notion of the anguish or exultation a man can experience when he views his quarry, looses a shaft at it, or slits its palpitating throat. In fact Ricord sometimes took pity on the creatures he stalked, and would come back home carrying a wounded fawn, or a bear cub whose mother he had just dispatched. His heart was forever torn with pity, yet he could not separate from this emotion his taste for blood. At times he was driven almost to distraction, so contradictory were the elements of his life—prayer, renunciation, and those savage pleasures which alone allowed him to fulfill his true nature.

Arsen had overtaken him on the road to the Good Life; she read much, and meditated on Holy Writ while she was spinning or cleaning vegetables. They often discussed the subject together. "Why," Ricord would ask, "did I not follow the Master on that day when he appeared to me, embodied in the most outcast of His sons? Our Bishop is like those of the Romish Babylon: he hearkens to the voice of worldly wisdom. I am more than forty years old, yet the bonds which tie me to the world and the flesh are stronger than ever they were."

"Would you trust your own judgment rather than that of a man born in the Spirit and chosen by the Church? He sent you back home because you had not yet quenched your thirst for sin. On the day he has assigned to you you will enter the Church, and your obedience will not pass unnoticed."

"I do not know if that day will ever come, Arsen. It may be that I will die before then; it may be that other tests await me first. A voice has spoken to me, saying: You have slain defenseless animals, and one day you will be led to kill men likewise."

"God forbid!" Arsen cried. "God keep you from such a sin! Do not even utter the thought: it is a temptation in itself. You are getting older now, and the day is not far off when we shall have no further obligations in this world. You are a free man; no one can force you to fight."

Arsen often meditated on the parable of the pearl of great price. Without knowing how, she had herself found this pearl, one winter evening when, after having sat up with a sick woman, she was climbing the path back to her home. The woman's groans still echoed in her ears; she was tired and cold, her thoughts dwelling on the fire at that moment burning in the great chimney.

Completely exhausted, she sat down on a big boulder and thought: I can go no farther, even though I die of cold. The icy wind stung her cheeks and wrenched at her cloak. Tears started from her eyes. And then it seemed to her that she was no longer conscious of her body. Someone was there, close by her; someone so vast that by leaning on his hand she could have crossed the sheer gulf that divided her from the far side of the valley. She could see nothing before her but the gray mist and the tops of a few pine trees; yet she felt herself to be in the presence of such beauty that neither her children's faces nor sunlight on mountain snows could give any notion of it. She realized that no unhappiness could touch this beauty; that evil was away and somewhere different, in another world.

Then she rose and walked effortlessly to the door of her house; and her joy was so great that she was incapable of thought. As she crossed the courtyard her two dogs came bounding up to lick her hands and face; she smiled at them. She could not keep this intense joy to herself. In the main hall she found three beggars, two neighboring landowners, and Gentian. All of them stared at her as though she were a ghost, so pale was her face and so burning bright her eyes; but she did not even notice their attention. She served them with supper and joined in their conversation; but the words she spoke seemed to issue from another's mouth. That night, in her bedchamber, she found herself unable to explain the incident to her daughter; for a long while she sat in front of her oil lamp, staring at the gray stones of the wall. The features of the Beloved One were outlined there—yet without form or color, for in sober truth all was gray stone and nothing more. But she saw Him, and knew that she would never forget Him as long as she lived.

Henceforth her love for her husband and children both increased in intensity and took on a sorrowful quality, as though she had discovered them to be made of elements as ephemeral as flower petals. The beauty which she had glimpsed through her heart's awareness had the solidity of a block of marble, and was as vast as the sky: all earthly things faded into insignificance by comparison. *For as soon as the wind goeth over it, it is gone, and the place thereof shall know it no more.* Now she waited for the day when her great withdrawal should be made, yet did not see in it either joy or renunciation. She simply knew that to this end she must come, as the tree must bear its fruit. Who can ever tell whether such labor gives the tree joy or sorrow? The fruit must needs come, and only its Creator can say why.

Yet the pain of leaving those one loves is great, and instills a fear like the fear of death. Many times Arsen shivered in her heart when she thought of it.

The house seemed empty without Gentian. Ricord and his wife sat down to table, together with their farm hands (who had long since graduated to the position of fellow laborers) and one or two guests, travellers passing through the district. The old serving-woman brought in bread, wine, and bean soup; Ricord cut the bread with his great knife, putting a slice aside for the absent Gentian. Till now he had never realized how much he loved the child; he continually found his eyes straying to the door, as though he expected to see her come in, hair flying wild, cheeks reddened by the wind.

Isarn de Cadéjac, who was a relative as well as a neighbor, said to him: "Don't be so downhearted: we all know the strength of a young girl's desire. She'll be back home again in six months, and you can marry her off next spring."

"Ah," said Ricord, shaking his thin dark head, "may God will it so!" The words burst from his lips like a cry of pain. He had not intended to utter them; he was well aware of the impiety they contained.

The talk around the table was largely of the Crusade being

organized in the North. They had known for a long while about
the overweening insolence and insatiable pride of the Papal emissaries; they were used to such behavior. But this new Pope, who
had occupied the See of Rome for ten years now, was a visible in-
carnation of the Spirit of Evil, and disposed of most formidable
powers: by his lies he had seduced princes and barons alike, and was
now preparing to hurl them against the Church of God. He had
preached so indefatigably, and written such innumerable letters,
that King Philip of France had permitted his barons and vassals to
raise the Cross against their own peers; he had not shown himself
willing to put a stop to such villainy, for all that he was cousin-
german to the Count of Toulouse.

"My friends," Ricord observed, "this most redoubtable Pope
raises levies which he never pays, and then promises them property
which is not his to give. Surely Catholic folly knows no bounds
when this Pope *still* exacts obedience from his subjects after declaring murder a work of charity? Such a pronouncement is posi-
tively driving souls to perdition!"

Isarn de Cadéjac said: "Some Catholics are rather like workmen
who have a bad master. If the workman cares for his craft, he will
pray God for his present master to be replaced by a better, and go
on with his work. Catholics are no more witless than any other
folk; they simply stick to the Faith in which they were brought
up."

"All the same," Ricord said, "you need to be a little weak in the
head to go off and commit murders out of love for your Faith."

"These Northerners," put in Pierre de Frémiac, "are credulous
folk, easily led, and full of every sort of superstition. They are so
devoted to warfare that the man who has killed most pagans in
the Holy Land is reckoned the best Christian among them."

"Why, they are pagans themselves," Arsen said. "What else
could you expect from them? They are led on by worldly desires,
such as pride and the appetite for booty. Plenty of men who are
neither Catholics nor Northerners behave in the same fashion. It
is a disaster for all of them no less than for us."

"You are worried because we have grown-up sons," Ricord

told her. "Do you really think these Northerners so powerful? They are only coming for a forty days' campaign. What large town could anyone take in that time? Carcassonne and Béziers both have supplies for six months and excellent garrisons."

"Oh, the towns will hold out," Isarn said. "It's in the country-side that the shoe will pinch. If they really march down with an army of ten thousand men, as they say, the damage will be fearful. The districts beyond the mountains will sustain such losses in cattle, vines, and crops that they'll be impoverished for three years, at least."

"Wars are like hail or pestilence," Arsen said. "We endure them, and they pass. My only fear is lest they lead too many souls into temptation."

That evening Ricord and Arsen had a long discussion about the decision they must make.

"Suppose the child changed her mind, or was found wanting in strength? Is she to come back here and be entrusted to the care of her eldest brother? Sicart is a good boy, but much too young to give her guidance—especially after such an ordeal."

"My love," Ricord said, "I would pay dearly in order to keep you by me still; but do as your heart bids you. Supposing the girl *does* have to come back to us: I am ready and willing not to leave home myself yet, but to wait till she is confirmed in her vocation."

"Ah, Ricord, you know very well that these fears of mine are only excuses! My flesh is weak, and shrinks from the act of sacri-fice. I am afraid to leave you, just as the traveller putting out to sea fears to abandon his native soil. Unless you renounce the world at the same time as I do, I shall never bring myself to it. I could not take one step toward God without you."

Finally they both agreed to wait till their daughter's period of probation was over. Neither of them could entirely believe that Gentian had left the secular world forever.

In the convent, meanwhile, under the supervision of the good ladies of Foix, Gentian was learning to read the Scriptures accord-ing to the Rule, and to interpret them in accordance with the traditions of her Church. Above all, she was learning how to toughen soul and body alike, so that one day she might be fit to endure the ordeals of the Christian life. During the day she was obliged to sweep out rooms, scrub and polish the flagged floors, and scour dirty pots; her nights were given over to meditation and prayer. If she fell asleep, she was sent back to her dormitory: this was so cruel a humiliation that the girl no longer found sleep a pleasure. If she let it be seen that she was hungry, she was given bread—and being thus condemned to make public admission of her weakness, she developed a deep repugnance for bread.

After two months of this regime Dame Adalays sent for her and said: "We have been watching you for some time now. You are proud, stubborn, and obstinate. It would be much better if you went home to your parents."

Gentian had been warned by her companions that the same thing was said to every girl during her initial period of probation. She said: "My lady, I would rather spend the rest of my life scrubbing out latrines and sweeping the courtyard."

"Do you then hate your parents so much?" Dame Adalays inquired. "Would you have me believe that they are perverse and impious persons?"

"Do not mock me, my lady, I beseech you. Show me some pity. My longing for the true Way is such that even my parents, for all their goodness and kindness, seem only shadows to me now. Pray God help me to conquer my own natural vices!"

The old lady agreed to keep her on, without any promises as to the future, but only (she said) because Gentian had entered the convent with Monseigneur Raymond de Ribeyre's approval. In point of fact she judged the girl to be capable of turning out an excellent Christian.

Toward the end of May Raymond de Ribeyre once more passed through Foix and went to preach at the convent. Gentian was astonished to see the change that had been wrought in him during these few months. He did not actually look older; but his features had sharpened and his eyes grown larger, while his countenance seemed more transparent in texture than ever.

He spoke for a long while to these young girls of the immense
and irreplaceable treasure which virginity of heart and body offers
—that virginity which, he told them, was the fountainhead of all
power and virtue. This was easy to believe when one looked at
Raymond himself: his strength was not as the strength of other
men, great prophets and well-tried Christians though they might
be. From his untouched body there radiated that kind of tran-
quillity which can be observed in the eyes of very young children.

"That man or woman," he declared, "whose chastity has never
failed either in deed or thought, is already half triumphant over
Satan, and has rendered powerless the work of death to which end
our body was created. Beloved daughters, there are many sorts of
glory promised to the elect, to each according to the gifts he has
received and brought to fruition. Yet none is more wonderful and
enviable than that promised to the one hundred and forty and four
thousand; for they alone will have the power to sing the New Song
before the Lamb. And as it is told in the Revelation of St. John
the Divine, none but they may learn that song.*

"How often, O my beloved daughters, should we meditate on
the pricelessness of this gift! Once we have lost it we are deprived
for all eternity of wisdom unparalleled, that wisdom which comes
from knowledge of the New Song. And when in time to come we
assume the gifts of prophecy and of tongues, the power to preach
and the faith that can move mountains, with all this we still should
not be capable of learning the New Song, nor of following the
Lamb whithersoever He goes.

"When Satan formed our body from the clay of this earth, he
did not complete his work. The soul submits to the laws of the
Evil One as a prisoner, not a willing accomplice. Though carnal
desires urge it on constantly toward sin, yet the soul remains free,

---

* Revelation 14:3: "And they sung as it were a new song before the
throne, and before the four beasts, and the elders: and no man could
learn that song but the hundred and forty and four thousand, which were
redeemed from the earth. These are they which were not defiled with
women; for they are virgins. These are they which follow the Lamb
whithersoever He goeth. . . ."—Trs.

so long as the body has not sealed a pact with its creator by accomplishing that work of death which reduces it to the level of the beasts. But do not suppose, beloved daughters, that purity of body is in itself a good work; it is no more than the visible expression of true inward cleanliness. It is necessary, but not all-sufficient; our thoughts, too, are of the flesh. Their power is such that one glance can make us guilty of adultery, and we are more defiled by the thoughts in our hearts than by any carnal contact, as the Scriptures teach us. Bear yourselves like apprentices learning a difficult craft. They do not know whether they will become master craftsmen; they only know it is quite certain they will *not* unless they do their work as it should be done."

When she heard Raymond's words, Gentian examined her conscience in all good faith, yet failed to discover any impure thoughts lurking in her heart. God grant, she thought, that I am able to preserve this precious freedom my whole life through—even though it means disfiguring myself, or shaving my head— No, I shall not leave this house until I have been baptized in the Spirit.

Raymond de Ribeyre smiled at her in recognition, and asked if she was not missing her parents very much.

"My lord," she said, "I attach no value to the affections of the flesh."

"That is to be expected in one of your age," he replied gently, and she thought she detected a faint shadow of reproach in his voice.

"My brother," Aicart asked his companion, "do you think this young girl will one day become a good Christian?"

"She is only a child," Raymond said. "After all, have not we ourselves had the Call since childhood?"

Since childhood. Aicart had gone to school at the heretics' seminary in Carcassonne—like his brothers and most of his playmates. At the age of fifteen he had announced to his parents that he wanted to give his life to the service of God. His mother, with true feminine frivolity, looked forward to seeing him a Bishop in next to no time—or at the very least, a deacon. He had all but renounced such ambitions, having very early ceased to be numbered among those one hundred and forty and four thousand of whom his master had just spoken in his sermon; but God's grace had proved stronger in the end.

The group of young postulants, in their gray robes and white veils, made a pleasant spectacle; yet Gentian stood out among them all by reason of her height and boyish slimness. Aicart followed her with a thoughtful eye, reflecting that Nature herself on occasion fashioned creatures who gave some notion of what the angels would be like, had they visible bodies: frail, yet hardy and proud, and innocent of any sexual characteristics. Perhaps this virgin was destined to shine among her sisters like a diamond among the pearls in a king's crown.

"You know," Raymond said as they left the convent, "there is one advantage women have over us, my friend: God has spared them the temptation to make a profession of killing. How often, at the seminary here in this town, have I not seen young men eager to quit God's service, inspired by false notions of honor!"

"The war will never come to their part of the country," Aicart said. "What would the French do here? The terrain is difficult for invaders, and the soil barren. We all know these fellows are more eager for loot than indulgences."

Raymond said: "Please God it may be possible to buy them off with gold! Their army is already preparing to march; and if the Count of Toulouse thinks he can stop them with promises alone, he is making a great mistake. It is useless offering a soldier all your possessions; he will always believe he can get a little more by using force."

All the talk in the town was of this Crusaders' army. It was known to be extremely large, and much encumbered with noncombatant pilgrims; there was little likelihood of its maintaining a prolonged siege in midsummer. If the Viscount did not halt their advance earlier, they would dig themselves in outside Béziers, and the district around the town would suffer in consequence. In the Carcassès area every town and fortified position was already so chock-a-block with cattle and refugees that it was almost impossible to force one's way through on horseback. It looked as though people were taking all the threats of the official clergy at their face value.

In Foix itself they found a Cistercian friar—a young man, very full of righteous wrath—haranguing the crowd in the square out-side the church, and predicting all manner of retributions for the impious. Raymond and Aicart, together with several other brothers from Foix, pressed forward into the square to hear his sermon: the fellow had a great reputation as a preacher, and had already made several most regrettable conversions in Carcassonne.

"I stand among you," he cried, "as the prophet Elijah stood among the idolaters and the priests of Baal: alone, indeed, but strong in the sustaining hand of Almighty God!" (He was not, in fact, alone; the Cistercians in the town were a rich and highly re-spected foundation. Nevertheless, it took courage to speak as he was doing.) "To punish Pharaoh's disbelief, the Lord God in olden time sent down the ten plagues upon Egypt, and the enemies of the One True God saw their land plunged into desolation. To punish Jezebel's abominable deeds, the Lord God sent drought into Israel, and it was in vain that the priests of Baal offered up their sacrifices! Look, my brothers, at the priests of Baal who are with us in this very place, whose souls are blacker than the robes they wear! They may affect an arrogant air as they listen to me, yet they are trembling in their hearts: will their false prayers have the power to avert from our land the storm which is ready to burst upon it—the floods in spate, the trumpets proclaiming God's judg-ment? At this very moment the holy army of Christ's warriors, protected by the Cross of our Saviour, bearing bright swords and drunk with divine anger, is marching down the Rhone Valley to-ward us. For ten long leagues that army's banners fly, and the whole river is covered with its ships!

"Unhappy people, you who have blindly put your trust in these false apostles, these purveyors of Hell itself—behold them, and see! Is it to their feeble hands, so lavish with illusory blessings, that you will look for help? It is in vain that that impious Jezebel" (he meant the Count of Foix's sister, though he dared not name her openly) "promises them her support, and her fortune to share among them. They are well skilled in the acquisition of gold and silver, it is true; but over the last six months—nay, the last year—they have been beseeching their Master, Satan, that is, to cast confusion on all Christian hearts, and sow discord in the army of the Crusaders—and with what results? Why, the army of Christ has assembled, and made itself ready for battle with prayers; and now it is on the march, like a great pillar of fire, or the tidal wave of the Flood itself, ready to pour out upon this God-denying land the wine of its divine fury!

"Ah, that righteous and terrible drunkenness, that wine of divine fury! Every street and square will be drowned in a sea of blood, a torrent turning the rivers scarlet! You say to yourselves: The scourge will not touch us, we are in a safe place. Madmen! How many of you have relatives and friends in the threatened districts? You fools, once the heavenly fires are kindled they must needs spread; the lies and false oaths of your counts and barons will not protect you!

"Let the priests of Baal tell you whether they have the power to ward off this scourge from you! See, I raise my hands heavenward —without fear, O Lord, humbly, surely, setting my trust in Thee! The heavenly fires are already lit, they are approaching now, ready to consume these false prophets! Look at them"—the preacher pointed toward the group of men in black, who stood listening to him with impassive disdain—"look at them, unbelievers that you are! Their bodies are vowed to Satan, and the fire that will consume those bodies is already flickering over their heads. I can see it! I can see it curling about their bodies, burning into their very vitals! Not one of them shall escape! I call down the flames upon them, I consign them to burn for all eternity, through the power of the Holy Spirit that clothed my unworthy body at the time of my ordination. Yes—in truth and verity was I clad in the Holy Spirit, anointed and consecrated, by the will of Holy Church—the One True Church, the Church of the Apostles, Confessors, and Martyrs, the Bride of Christ and Mystical Body of Jesus!

"Impostors and seducers, generation of vipers, who has taught you to flee from the wrath of Heaven? Here you stand before me, dumb and trembling, with not a word to say for yourselves—soft, fearful, meeker than doves, saying: Why should men war against such as us? But it is not so long since your blasphemies, sacrilegious acts, and violent words brought fire and blood upon this country-side, and scandalized even your own heretical flock! Did you not incite the populace to break God's holy Crucifixes to pieces, and to befoul Church altars with their own excrement?"

William de Ventenac, one of the deacons from the Ariège district, advanced on the monk at this point, observing that it was difficult to speak when you were not permitted to get a word in edgeways.

"For the rest," he went on, "it would be a simple matter to refute the numerous falsehoods and heretical statements with which your speech was stuffed from beginning to end. The God whom you invoked is not the True God, the Father of all good Spirits, but an evil deity, athirst for blood and murder; it is a vile blasphemy to say that our Saviour Jesus Christ ever adored such a God!"

"You deck yourselves out with the most holy Name of our Lord Jesus Christ as though it were some stolen garment," the monk cried, "merely to seduce the people! You may pay lip service to Him, but your true master is Mani. You will not find one single passage in Holy Writ which tells you that our Lord ever regarded the God of the Old Testament as a devil!"

"Your own words condemn you," William said. "They show beyond doubt that you do not serve the God of charity. The folk who hear us are our witnesses: is it fitting to credit our Heavenly Father with such vile sentiments as anger, and to speak of His drunkenness? You compare yourself to the prophet Elijah. Was Elijah, who with his own hands cut the throats of four hundred and fifty priests of Baal, any better than a common butcher? Will a God who does not wish for the death of a single one of His creatures look kindly on the torrents of blood you tell us of? What are those heavenly fires you promise us, your adversaries, but an ordinary bonfire of logs and faggots, kindled by sinners who rejoice in the sufferings of their fellow men?"

"It is easy to deceive the people by such arguments," the monk retorted contemptuously. "You have appointed yourselves masters both of Providence and of God's will. You mock and blaspheme the Divine Mysteries; the secrets of the Divine Love have become such commonplaces in your hands that you proclaim them at every crossroads. But when it comes to your own mysteries, you keep *them* to yourselves; your flock hear not a word about them. You will find some difficulty in explaining how one soul can occupy several bodies, and just where one can find these 'heavenly spirits' of yours, that you cause to descend upon the elect of your Church by the laying on of hands; and just what our Saviour's 'seeming body' consisted of—not to mention how God is supposed to have had two sons, and Satan two wives!"

"Listen to me, Pierre-Bernard," said Aicart, going up to the Cistercian, "it is not our present concern to embark on a discussion of such high matters. As I see it, you were telling us about this army, which you call Christ's army, and which is coming to turn this land of yours into a waste of fire and blood. Us you refer to as priests of Baal, and reproach for not having been able to halt the advance of this scourge by our prayers. But why do you not tell all these good folk now listening to us that it was you who brought this selfsame army into being—by your own prayers, by the intrigues of your bishops and the letters written by your Pope, by the preaching of your monks and their lying promises of pardons? It seems to me, therefore, that it is not we so much as you whom the people should accuse."

"When a surgeon amputates a gangrenous limb, it is not the surgeon whom you should blame, but the gangrene."

"If you must talk of gangrene," Aicart said, "why do you search so far afield?" (With all the good will in the world he could no longer control his bitterness.) "Do you dare to speak of *us* as gangrenous limbs, when your bishops spend all their time hunting, and sell their livings to the highest bidder? When abbots force poor folk to work for them without pay, and then take their land? When your priests have concubines, souse themselves in wine, and preach no more than one sermon a year?"

"How long, O Lord, how long?" cried the white-robed Cistercian, pressing his hands to his forehead. "How long must we endure the insults of the ungodly? Come, pluck off my habit, stone me as others like you once stoned our Blessed St. Stephen! I am ready to be sacrificed. O Lord, look down upon your beloved Spouse, now lying on the ground, while the impious spit upon Her, strike and revile Her! See how Her robes are torn to shreds, how She bleeds from countless wounds, like the traveller attacked by robbers on the road between Jerusalem and Jericho! O Lord, behold, here are those who have attacked and insulted Her, still holding their heads high, still laughing at Her sufferings, still loading Her with the vilest of names, still daring to reproach Her for miseries of which they themselves are the sole cause! O Lord, have pity on Your Church in this land, for the Pharisees mock and humiliate Her as Christ was mocked and humiliated on the Cross!

"False prophets that you are, who else is it but you has weakened the Faith in this country? Who else is it has robbed the poor of the consolation of the Blessed Sacrament, or by infamous calumnies brought our bishops and priests into disrepute, deluding simple souls with false and diabolically inspired wisdom? You have told them, *Ye shall be like Gods, having knowledge of good and evil*; you have unburdened upon them, for their confusion, such mysteries as they cannot comprehend; you brand us as idolaters because in all humility we venerate those relics and holy images which speak to us of God—while you cause your flock to fall into worse idolatry by making them worship *you*! Be well assured, we have no fear of you; for the immaculate Body of our Lord, offered and sacrificed every day for the sins of the world, is that Good Samaritan that preserves our Church from your attacks, and will bring Her triumphant through the centuries!"

"Then what need have you to summon the armies of the North to your assistance?" Aicart cried. "These Crusaders of whom you speak: are they, too, Good Samaritans? Is our blood, for which you seem so athirst, the oil and wine you need to pour into your wounds? Is it we you blame for the disorders of your Church? God knows *we* have never imposed our Faith by force of arms, or corrupted men's souls with money and honors; if many of the faithful have come to believe us, it is only because your own Church furnished a living argument against itself, and proved us to be in the right! You know very well, Pierre-Bernard, that till recently you did not dare to show yourself in the streets of Carcassonne without a hat, or wearing your habit. Has your Church suddenly acquired holiness and purity since you took your vows among the Cistercian friars?"

"Indeed and indeed," cried the monk, crossing his arms, "let Him who did not judge the woman taken in adultery judge between us now! Let him who is without sin cast the first stone. *We* do not claim to be free from sin; yet you are proud enough to declare yourselves sinless. In this way you delude the credulous— and we know very well how to take this so-called 'purity' of yours. It ill becomes you to reproach our priests for their luxurious living, Aicart; it is common knowledge that you and your fellows are secretly addicted to the crime of Sodom; *that* explains the mystery of your apparent chasteness. You call our Church 'the Mother of fornications,' yet you yourselves attract converts by allowing them to live in the most shameful and vicious state of debauchery; this is what lies behind your professed contempt for the marriage sacrament!"

Aicart recoiled a step at this. "Only the spirit of prostitution that inspires every son of the Great Whore could ever have produced such words!" he cried. "You should be grateful to us, Pierre-Bernard; it is only out of respect for us that these good people here are not now casting stones in your face—"

"Come away," Raymond said, taking him by the hand. "Let us leave this unhappy man. Why should you lose your temper over such commonplace insults?"

"Ah, my brother," Aicart said, his lips still trembling and the fire of wrath still bright in his eyes, "it is not the insults alone. I knew this man in my youth; our parents were near neighbors. How could *he* have believed all the infamous slanders that are spread concerning us? The Great Whore must needs utterly corrupt all she touches, and the man who serves her can henceforth live only by lies. Her acolytes hate the very name and works of Jesus Christ; it is only as a screen for their true purpose that they still bother to invoke Him."

"They say much the same of us," Raymond remarked. "Think no more about them; it will only lead you into temptation. God has granted me the grace to see that their souls—ignorant and defaced by the mark of the Beast though they be—sometimes possess fine qualities and would be capable, in a different bodily existence, of finding the road to salvation. Suppose you had a convert who was a prostitute's son: would you advise him to spit in his mother's face, or kick her out of the house? Let us pray rather that the spirit of Jehovah may not descend upon us in our turn, and make us like the salt that has lost its savor."

Aicart thought of the "wine of God's wrath" and the seven cups that the angels poured out. Dear God, he prayed silently, the time is not yet ripe, the harvest is barely begun. May Christ's Church emerge from this ordeal stronger than ever!

At the beginning of June, Sicart went to see his parents. This visit was rather different from the others. The young man was dressed up in new clothes, had had his hair cut short, and appeared somewhat agitated. He ate little; he also tended to laugh very loud and gave elusive answers when questioned. In the evening he asked to be left alone with his mother.

"I've done something which would annoy Father very much," he told her. "Please speak to him on my behalf—and when I say *my* behalf, of course, that includes my brothers too. You know how we swore never to be separated from one another—"

"And *you* know very well," his mother interposed, "that swearing is forbidden."

The young man made a gesture of impatience. "That isn't the

point at issue, Mother. Listen: we are leaving next week for Carcassonne. The Baron de Saissac has taken us into his retinue. We are of age, after all."

He seemed angry, but Arsen realized that underneath he was ashamed of himself and more than a little scared. These boys would have jumped over a cliff rather than cause their father any real displeasure.

"Have you thought this over carefully, Sicart?" she asked. "There is a war in the offing. The Baron de Saissac is one of those responsible for the Carcassonne garrison, and his retinue will be among the first to man the defenses."

The young man looked at her in some astonishment.

"But of course, Mother," he said. "That is why we did it. We are not interested in the money."

Arsen went very pale. "You know very well," she said, "that he who takes the sword shall perish by the sword. No one has attacked you. Why should you go out of your way to commit such a sin?"

"The Viscount needs men," Sicart said. "And we hold our lands from him."

"But you know very well," Arsen persisted, "that your grandfather long ago freed himself from all military obligations, when the land was parcelled out. The Viscount possesses certain rights over this land itself, but none at all over our persons. Nor does anyone else."

"All the more honor to be gained by fighting, then. Mother, you can't *really* want the French to come here laying down the law for us, telling us what we should or shouldn't believe? Look, they are already on the march. Some of them come from places a hundred leagues and more away. We are sitting here on our own land: should we not await their coming spear in hand? Ought we to make them think we are greater cowards than they?"

"Are you so concerned with what Frenchmen think of you?" his mother asked disdainfully. "Just because they do evil, do you have to copy them so as not to be outdone?"

"But it is *they* who are attacking *us*," the young man asserted, in some embarrassment. Arsen glanced at him tenderly.

"You are young, Sicart," she said. "If your heart tells you that your duty lies there, then follow the promptings of your heart. But be well assured of this: if you do such a thing out of mere vainglory, you set yourself lower than these Crusaders themselves, who have taken up arms out of mere ignorance."

Sicart looked at the floor and thought for a moment.

"No, Mother. I could never be lower than such creatures. I have good friends who think as I do. We have attacked nobody; men who are defending themselves are always in the right of it. Besides, it is men of our own country and Faith who are in peril."

Arsen sighed. "I will speak of this matter with your father," she said. "He is a man; he will agree with you."

Sicart had omitted to mention one reason for his departure, however. He had fallen in love with a married lady, whose husband came from the Carcassès district and was a most redoubtable warrior. Sicart wanted to win this gentleman's respect. Besides, the lady herself still adhered to the old religion; she even attended Mass. Sicart wanted to show her that those who followed the heretical Faith were no less courageous than anyone else.

Ricord was sorry to see him go, but did not reproach him or hold him back. "A pity your brothers didn't come with you," he said. "Still, this will be a short war, God willing, and there won't be so many lances for you to break."

PART TWO

The war was not, indeed, lengthy; yet it was such that it caused more terror, destruction, and loss than a hundred ordinary wars could have done in ten years. Here was evidence enough to show what the devil of violence could do once its leash was slipped. It was not really a war at all. You do not fight against a tempest or a plague of locusts or a pack of mad dogs; you escape if you can, and hit back when and how you get the chance to. These murderers of women and children found every door open to them, all knees bent in homage—so long, at least, as the shock caused by the shedding of innocent blood was still fresh. A time would come when people were no longer capable of feeling shocked by anything.

When the Great Terror swept over Béziers the sky turned black and the sun shone red as blood. From Montpellier to Toulouse, from Perpignan to Foix, a huge wave of panic and stupefaction surged across the countryside and then slowly ebbed, leaving untold ruin and destruction behind it. Yet the war was not over; it was only just beginning. The enemy army was no longer there; but it left in its stead a fear stronger than hatred —and a new Viscount, charged with the task of holding the area in the name of the Pope at Rome.

Who would dare to march against this Great Beast? His food was human flesh, and he slaked his thirst with blood. Where he set his foot the earth rotted away, and his breath poisoned the air for a hundred leagues around. Yet a day would come when men would see that their enemy was human, and could be slain.

CHAPTER III

First Temptations and Ordeals

T HE days passed miserably for Arsen, who was now alone in the house with one old serving-woman too old for further work. The men were busy with the wine harvest, while Ricord was away in town with his cousins and brothers-in-law. Of her sons she had little news, though she knew them to be alive; they had retreated into the Corbières district with their liege lord's forces.

On several occasions she had given hospitality to refugee families from the North, who were fleeing over the mountains to Catalonia. She asked them if the war could ever reach Montgeil.

"Who can tell with people of this sort? They'll come back with another army in the spring."

"And what could an army do in these mountain gorges?"

The men would say nothing to this, while the women and girls would shake their heads. "What could they do, eh? You ask that after the things they've done already? They stormed a town in one day and left not a single creature alive in it; clearly the Devil is in league with them."

"What news from our noble Raymond?"

"He is at present in retreat, at Laurac; he sends a message to you to remain steadfast, and to pray. With God's aid he hopes to visit your area this winter."

If only I could see his blessed face, and hear his voice, Arsen thought. If only my soul could be fortified by the power of the Spirit in him! But in these days, when the servants of God are hunted down by Antichrist as thought they were dogs, will he still be able to continue his preaching? She felt the urge to go to Laurac herself; she had an aunt there who had taken the veil in a Cathar convent, and it was this same convent which she had selected for her own period of probation.

She had good news of Gentian: the girl was making light of such things as fasts, physical labors, and nocturnal vigils. Perhaps I was wrong, Arsen reflected; perhaps after all she has a true vocation. But there was anguish in her heart, and that night, sensing a severe ordeal ahead of her, she read and reread the Psalms as a preparation for facing it. And indeed, such an ordeal did come upon her—but from the quarter in which she least expected it.

Ricord came home one cold, sunny October day when the sky was as bright as the blade of a new-forged sword. He was (as he had been for some months now) calm and taciturn, and so dispirited that his wife thought he must be going into a decline. He no longer went out hunting, nor, indeed, did he work; he divided his time between seeing his friends in town and sitting up in the granary reading the Scriptures. On this occasion he was even calmer than usual, though his wide, staring eyes seemed fixed constantly on some astonishing or horrific object. At first Arsen wondered if he had had a call from God; but very soon she saw that it was not God in him. She mounted to her chamber as usual that night, and soon afterward in he came—stiffly resolute, head held high as though he were marching into battle. She snuffed her little oil lamp and shut the big book that was spread out across her knees.

For a moment they stared at one another. Then with an abrupt gesture Ricord fell on his knees before her, knocking his forehead against the cedarwood cover of the sacred volume she held.

"My love," he said, "my joy, my life, I have come to tell you that our paths are no longer fated to take the same course, either in this world or in the next. Go where your desires lead you, without further thought of me. May the sins that I have made you commit never be laid to your charge. We are no longer husband and wife. But tell me one thing—say you will still love me as a brother, whatever I may do!"

Arsen did not move; but her hands tightened a little upon the book.

"And what," she asked, "could you do to make me stop loving you?"

"Arsen, I am turning soldier again. I have a strong arm, a quick wrist, and a well-trained eye. If my body is still of some use, let it serve to destroy the evildoers; for whatever may pass, my soul is lost now to God."

Arsen set down the Gospels on her coffer and stood up.

"These are blasphemous words, Ricord. Your soul is *not* lost! I am your wife, and I will not let you destroy yourself; if you do, it will be over my dead body. I will not let you go and befoul your hands and your heart with work that any mercenary brigand could do better than you—for a mere ten sous a week!"

Ricord said, grimly: "No one will do this work better than I. Besides, my love, when our sons went off to fight you raised no objections, did you?"

"It wasn't the same thing, Ricord. They are young, and their souls are ignorant. Yours is not. Christ prayed for those who knew not what they did; He did not pray for Judas."

At that Ricord too stood up, and took his wife by the shoulders.

"Who are you to call me Judas?" he asked. "Who told you my judgment was any whit inferior to yours? For fifteen years now I have been trying to comprehend the ways of God. Now, after all I have seen and heard, I realize it is good for a man made of flesh and blood to feel hatred: not to hate evil is to love it. If I saw a soldier raping you, I would feel sheer delight as I smashed his skull in. I cannot help it if this is my own personal kind of madness; I cannot help loving every violated woman, every child whose throat has been cut, every old man pitched out of a window under trampling horses' hoofs—all with the same intensity of love I feel for you. I would take greater delight in killing men who had harmed little children than ever you could in the perusal of Holy Writ."

"Ricord, can this be you speaking? Do you suppose that by using the Devil's weapons you can make yourself stronger than the Devil? All he will do is avail himself of your services to do yet more evil. The Enemy always orders his deceptions in such a way that any blood which is spilled flows, invariably, from innocent veins. You will see that Popes and Bishops and Kings are never exposed personally to attack, since the Devil looks after his own; and he will find ways of guiding your hand in such a fashion that you will be led to slaughter men who might have been touched by saving grace."

"The grace of God will never alight on those who wear the Cross. If they have witnessed the things that have been done in its name, and not turned their swords against their own leaders, or gone into the desert to weep tears of repentance for the rest of their natural lives—if instead they still wear that infamous sign on their breasts, and are actually proud to do so—why, then they are men no longer, and have nothing to lose any more!"

"Who are you to fathom God's ways? Has He not warned us in prophecies? Men will persecute you in My name, He told us; the day will come when any man who slays you will believe he is serving God. Again He said: Blessed are they who are persecuted for righteousness' sake—"

"Woman, your unfulfilled love is driving you to dishonest argument. Did I say anything about those who are persecuted for righteousness' sake? These are blessed indeed; but poor old women going to Mass, or little children, or men whose only thought, day and night, is of earning their bread—all those outside the Fold who have never even dreamed of justice or righteousness—are we to let *them* be treated worse than cattle in the slaughterhouse? What can I say to those who only want one thing—protection against murderers? This is what I shall say: 'If I could kill all these accursed devils with my own hands, I would do it: not a single one of them that crosses my path will escape me.' "

"Ricord, remember the prisoner on the wheel at Carcassonne. You took pity on him; and yet this was a man who had killed innocent people."

"Woman, will you have done with your false arguments? Had I ever seen this man sitting at his ease in a coat of mail, with armed companions all about him, and bearing a bishop's blessing? *He* never supposed that his actions would get him into Paradise. But when you are dealing with men whose hearts have been so degraded that they actually mistake evil for good, any harm you may do them is good in itself."

"Who made you a judge?" Arsen cried. "Who made you a judge? Man's ignorance is boundless. You yourself are liable to mistake evil for good; what then can you expect of these Northerners, who have never had occasion to hear the voice of the Spirit? When Jesus said that His kingdom was not of this world, He was condemning all worldly things except love. He forbade even His angels to pull up the tares, and angels can see more clearly than we mortals can!"

"The fated hour is come," Ricord said. "Soon even the most ignorant will see this clearly. Arsen, you care for the sick and wounded; you must know well that protection of the body is also protection of the soul. When you have to deal with such men as these, who are worse than scorpions or serpents, you fight them with whatever weapons come to hand. When I find them, I might perhaps try not to kill them; I shall cut off their hands and put out their eyes instead, to stop them from doing further evil."

"Go!" Arsen cried, bursting into tears. "I have no wish to see any more of you! I hope your soul is reborn in the body of a man blind or deaf, or as some monk's bastard, or as an executioner! I loved your soul with all my heart, and now you want to make it hideous in my sight. God judges the souls of the slain, but Cain's soul is judged by his brother's blood. The sins of those fellow men slain at your hands will be passed on to you; the evil that is in them will adhere to your soul, and you will become one with them."

"I have already made the sacrifice of my soul, Arsen. Remember in your heart the man you once loved. If I become the kind of person you needs must hate, so much the worse for me. But even that is not so bad as seeing what is happening, yet standing by inactive, with folded arms."

"Go, then, do what you will, if your soul is so weak that the mere sight of blood engenders a craving for blood in it! Go and bay with the hounds. Begone from my sight! The Devil has finally caught you in his snare. I have nothing further to say to you."

"Give me one last kiss, Arsen. It may well be that I shall die fighting; I may never see your face again."

She put both arms about her husband's neck and touched his dry, lined cheek with her lips.

"Forgive my hard words. Even God has not the right to condemn; and how should I then condemn you? May God reunite us one day, despite your deeds. Tomorrow I shall leave this house, and no longer be your wife. It will be hard indeed for me to walk alone on the road we should have travelled together!"

Ricord kneeled once more before her, and then took his leave.

The following day Arsen left home, alone and on foot, taking with her some bread and olives for the journey, together with the only objects of value she possessed: a silver necklace left her by her mother, an amethyst brooch, and a pair of bracelets inlaid with enamelwork. A poor enough dowry, and one of which she felt a little ashamed; hitherto she had never lived on charity.

Thirty leagues; that meant several days' journeying. Days of wind and rain, over rocky paths where pebbles slid underfoot. Ever since war had come to the countryside, Arsen had feared the possibility of unpleasant wayside incidents; much unhappiness had sapped her courage. So she went by forest paths and hunters' tracks: she knew the district well. In order to counteract her fatigue, she began to recite in her head every passage of Holy Writ that she had learned by heart.

In addition, she prayed. Let my own thoughts die, let me forget all other words, for they are as nothing. O Lord, who alone art living, true and good, have pity on us, mere vessels of lying delusion that we are! If we have not Thy truth, we are nothing. Deliver us from the temptation to seek Thee elsewhere than in Thy person. When the whole universe cries out that Thou hast lied, and that evil is too great for love to conquer; when the very angels come down from Heaven to tell me that Thou art in error—then grant, Lord, that I do not betray Thee, not by so much as one quickened heartbeat! Beloved Lord, I do not pray for my sake, but that Thy purity may never be defiled through me. O Lord, Thy Holy Law is mightier than all the wretchedness of every man who has lived or shall live till the end of time; as a spider's web against the sun, so is our world confronted by the truth of Thy love.

She tried not to think of Ricord, but her heart still ached for him. Ricord, she thought, you are a weak soul, one of little faith, a house built upon sand. And the rain descended, and the floods came, and the winds blew, and beat upon that house—ah, such floods and winds as have never yet been seen, in this or any other country; and who then would cast the first stone at you? Once you aspired to the condition of a disciple, Ricord. But now you have become mere matter once more, a prey to the hazards of the flesh, which knows none but its own law. Let my affliction be as the exhaustion of my limbs or the agony in my loins. It is of the flesh, as all afflictions are of the flesh. Only in God is there no affliction.

It took her six days on foot to reach Laurac, and when she got there she was welcomed as a long-expected sister. But for all their great courtesy, these pious ladies could not wholly conceal the confusion into which this war had thrown them.

"You thought you were coming into a haven of peace, my child," Dame Agnes de Roquevidal, the Superior of the community, told her, "but in fact you have entered a house of tribulation."

"It matters little to me, my lady," Arsen said. "In the Lord all things are joyful. Will you one day accept me among your sisterhood?"

"The Church will decide," Dame Agnes said, and went on to tell Arsen what great pleasure it gave her that so lovely a woman, still in her prime, should manifest this great desire for the Good Life, and had not waited for old age before turning to it, as so many others had done.

"These are hard times," she said, "and we shall have need of women who can stand every kind of fatigue and danger. For some while now," she added, "we have been hearing of your exemplary life. We know that both you and your husband have borne public witness in your conduct to all the most estimable virtues. For a woman such as you I do not think a long probationary period will be required. I can say this to you, since I know you are wholly devoid of sinful pride."

Arsen burst into tears. "No, my lady," she sobbed, "I certainly have no reason to be proud of myself today, whether or not I once did." And she told Dame Agnes of her parting from her husband, and the temptation to which he had succumbed.

"You are not alone in this, my child. Some have been still more sorely tested; there is one among our number whose brother went over to serve the forces of Antichrist. Bear in mind that we should blame no one, since Jesus has said that He came not to judge men. And do not forget that by torturing ourselves with the sins of our near ones, we are already prejudging them."

Arsen knelt down and kissed the hem of the old lady's habit. Then she withdrew to her aunt's cell to begin her preparation for Holy Baptism. For over six weeks she dwelt in silence and solitude, without receiving any news from the outside world, living on a diet of rye bread and water mixed with a little wine.

Her aunt, Dame Serrone, lived by the rule of silent prayer, and never spoke to anyone except to say Yes or No. She had been living in the Laurac convent for more than twenty years now, and was deeply respected by the community. She was a tall, thin old lady, black-haired still, but so dry and withered that it seemed unlikely the worms would find any sustenance on her skeletal body when she was dead. The skin was stretched tightly over each bone, unwrinkled, without the least trace of fat beneath it.

Arsen never dared to say a word to her, and tried to make the old lady forget her very presence. But she was aware of the presence of that Spirit which dwelt in her, exactly as one is aware of the heat of a fire. For hours on end Arsen would remain on her knees, reciting the "Our Father" in a low voice, while her black-clad companion, kneeling three paces away from her, was repeating the same prayer silently. Arsen learned more from her than she would ever have done from countless lengthy sermons and disquisitions. The expression in her aunt's gray eyes was no longer that of a human person; another Being looked out through them.

They were so full of stern compassion and unconscious majesty that Dame Serrone, it was plain, had long since almost entirely forgotten her own existence.

O Lord, Arsen thought, when the day comes for the Holy Spirit to enter this miserable body of mine, shall I not die, as Ananias and Sapphira did, who received the Spirit when they were unworthy of it? Just as they wanted to keep some portion of their property for themselves, so I nurse earthly affections in my heart. My aunt was already a widow when she surrendered herself to God.

Arsen no longer bothered to count the days. She only knew that the sky was lighter every day when she awoke, and that sometimes Dame Serrone would linger at the window of her cell, gazing out at the clouds, white or rose-pink or gray, that hung high above the town ramparts. The sky itself was already a spring sky.

"Dear Aunt," she said, "can you read portents or signs in the clouds?"

"No," the old lady replied.

"Tell me, Aunt: will this coming year be a hard one for us?"

"Yes."

"Will we soon drive the enemy from our soil?"

"No."

Ah, God, Arsen thought, how can I prevent my thoughts from dwelling on worldly things—on my children, who may be going into battle, or on Ricord? O Lord, if this spring is to bring us so many ills, then may it never come!

On the day of the spring equinox Raymond de Ribeyre came to preach in Dame Agnes's house. Such a crowd attended to hear him that he was forced to deliver his sermon out of doors, despite the bad weather. There was a great gale blowing: shutters banged to and fro, tiles were wrenched from the rooftops. Raymond spent two hours outside the main door of the house doing nothing but bestow blessings on the faithful. He spoke of the ordeals inflicted on the Church by the powers of evil, proving, by citations from Holy Writ, that these times had been foretold, and that people should not allow themselves to be distressed by them. Aicart stood at his side, very pale, eyes lowered, biting his lip like a man in great pain.

That evening Dame Agnes presented her new postulant to the preacher: he appeared delighted to see her again. Arsen stared at him, deeply moved but also somewhat surprised. He had discarded his black habit; the brown doublet and woollen bonnet he now wore gave him a strange appearance. It was like seeing a piece of fine gold plate set out on the kitchen table. Arsen told him this; she had been long enough acquainted with him to allow herself such familiar remarks.

"I suppose I shall have to smear grease all over my face, then," he said. He was smiling, but his eyes remained sad. "We have to take care not to succumb to the temptation of martyrdom. It is not our black habit of which the faithful stand in need. Dressed as you see, we have passed safely through towns and by castles where there is a price on our heads."

Arsen said: "I can't believe that no one recognized you."

He smiled again, a smile of real happiness this time.

"Those who did recognize us said nothing. It is very important that I should bear witness to this: it may lead the faithful to a spirit of greater forbearance. In Carcassonne and Limoux we met certain clerics and monks, and they too affected not to have seen us."

Then he sighed and turned away, his eyes brimming over with tears. This was so unexpected that Arsen dared to ask him the cause of his unhappiness. He shook his head.

"What is the use in hiding it?" he said. "I had gone to Carcassonne about the necessary affairs of my ministry—but also to be present at the last moments of my sister according to the flesh. I was unable to get into her presence; I found out afterward that she had died without receiving baptism. Because of me—because they knew she was my sister, that is—they kept a close guard around her deathbed, and none of our brothers in Christ was able to go near her."

"I understand how you feel," Arsen said, "but I thought you were free of all carnal affections?"

"We are not perfect, and those whom it has been given to us to know most closely we also cherish most dearly. She was a woman of great piety, who was fervently awaiting the day when death would at last make her worthy to enter into the Communion of the Spirit. My sister, the sorrow I feel for her I also feel for every other woman who will come to the same pass; and they will be many."

For a few moments he knelt in prayer; then he announced to Arsen that the Church deemed her worthy to receive Holy Baptism, and that she must begin her fast that very night, since the ceremony would take place in three days' time.

For three days Arsen fasted and kept vigil, alone in a turret cell, with no company except the light of the sun. She failed to feel any joyful sensations during this period, and decided that God was testing her by withdrawing His presence from her. At the same time she felt so utterly emptied of all earthly thoughts that it seemed to her she had never loved husband or children, never felt compassion for the misfortunes of others. She was alone in the world; she remained where she was the whole night through, like one of the Foolish Virgins, beating against a closed door. And behind that door there rang out the joyful songs of the Marriage Feast.

Lord, Lord, she prayed, open unto me!

I know you not. I have never known you. Your lamp is out, and the bolts are drawn, and you shall have no part in the mystery of My joy.

Lord, it matters little to me that I cannot behold Thy joy; but if Thou hast no need of me, what need have I of myself? Behold me laid in my coffin with six feet of earth above me: that great Light of Thy being will yet never lose its brightness. All that is not of Thy essence is dust and nothingness. Let me vanish forever, let my body and soul be as though they had never existed, O Lord! If they are not of Thee they are less than nothing. Since the only true sorrow in the world is Thy absence, may all of me that is not Thine be destroyed! Here I stand, O Lord, alone in the night; I no longer ask that Thou shouldst open the door to me. All that belongs to

Thee has been always near Thee, since the beginning of time.

On the day that two black-clad women came to fetch her into the great hall of the convent, Arsen remained wrapped in silence, and as melancholy as though she were being led away to her death. But when she saw the hall itself, all ablaze with wax tapers, and the white linen cloth spread on the table, and the faithful all gathered to receive her into the Church, she understood the meaning of that passage in the Acts of the Apostles that speaks of Pentecostal tongues of fire. She heard Raymond de Ribeyre addressing her, and made the required responses; yet it was not her own voice that replied. She felt as though she were caught up in a vortex of flame, and her heart burned so fiercely that she almost felt herself shrink away from its heat, as if from a torch: this happened in the instant that Raymond placed the copy of the Gospels upon her head.

When she exchanged the kiss of peace with Dame Agnes, then with Dame Serrone and the rest, she still found some difficulty in moving in this invisible robe of flaming scarlet which had descended about her. Strange, to become like a kindled lamp, to hold within oneself an incorruptible flame, to be transformed from a creature of flesh and blood into a temple that housed God Himself. A flawed and fragile temple, but what matter? There was none other for Him on this earth.

Arsen remained at her prayers till evening came, kneeling before one of the windows in the great hall, gazing out at the roofs of the town, and the ramparts, and the great vine-clad slopes that rose behind them, checkered with black fields and crowned with thick forest. Her mind was empty and unthinking; but in the familiar outline of that countryside, in the sloping thatched roofs and the stone walls, her eyes could read the immense, unappeasable anguish of a world ceaselessly breaking up and rotting away, consumed by that most terrible of all evils, absence of God. In a dimension that spanned all space and time she seemed to see countless thousands of souls, in deathly torment through this absence, like children beaten to death and drowned in mud. Yet she did not even feel a twinge of unhappiness. In this instant it became clear to her that the flame had already been kindled on earth, and the time of fulfillment was at hand. The hour had come when every soul would be filled with the knowledge of God, as the waters cover the sea.

"My sister," Dame Agnes told her that evening, "we all bless God for the great favor which He has deigned to bestow on you; and we would dearly love to keep you with us for a long period. But the times have changed, and you are to be summoned elsewhere. Our house will always be available to you as a place of refuge if danger threatens—always supposing that God wills this town to be spared the ravages of war."

"Where am I to be sent, Mother?"

"Master Raymond will tell you. Your travelling companion is to be Sister Fabrisse, who was formerly the Seigneur de Brézilhac's widow. May God grant you both a true understanding of one another, and may nothing separate you except the death of the body."

Arsen said nothing; she inclined her head and withdrew. She hardly knew Fabrisse de Brézilhac, who was a woman of about her own age—tall and slender as a taper, with fair hair and a peculiarly lovely voice. They met that evening in the refectory, prostrated themselves before each other in turn, and then kissed three times, on either cheek. Fabrisse seemed as joyful as any woman who had found her own long-lost sister; she was a person of great natural courtesy.

"We shall have to get thicker soles put on our shoes," she said. "I gather we are going to be condemned to the Wandering Jew's life for a year or so."

Arsen replied that there was nothing she enjoyed more than such an existence, and the two of them fell to discussing it as though it were some pleasure trip. So strong are the habits engendered by this world that, even on so supremely solemn a day in her life, Arsen found herself exchanging casual pleasantries with her companion, and was not even astonished. What was there now she could either say or do that was not countless leagues below this other Universe in which, all undeserving, she now had her part? She felt oddly empty, a husk stripped of its fruit. What remained was not *she;* this strange self lacked all familiarity.

"My sisters," Raymond de Ribeyre said, "I will presume, if I may, to repeat to you words which our Saviour said: I am sending you forth as lambs among wolves. Yet it is not I who send you; I have my orders from our beloved lord and Bishop, Monseigneur Bernard, who takes the distressed condition of the faithful in this district very much to heart. The perils of our times have forced us to abandon that habit which was the outward and visible sign of our vocation; so you, who in your worldly stations were ladies of noble birth, now go forth dressed as common laborers' wives. Do not, my sisters, regard this as a reason for vexation, but as an instance of God's grace, a sign sent to illumine our ignorance. It is not through the vain ostentation of our apparel that we shall win fresh brothers in Christ, but by the power of the Holy Spirit which is in us. Let us in all things be even as those to whom God has summoned us. You will spin and weave in their workrooms, and dig the soil shoulder to shoulder with peasant women. You will nurse their children and bear their burdens. You will seek out the lowest in the land, and serve them: you will nurse the prostitutes and give food to the lepers. Such things you will do as far as possible in secret, to avoid drawing attention to yourselves. Do not forget that in these times your lives are precious: where you are to go there will be no other persons fit to bestow the Holy Spirit on the dying."

Arsen said: "Is that a woman's task? Can the Bishop ask us to do such a thing?"

"It is a task for every Christian, my sister. As the Apostle said, there shall be neither man nor woman, Jew nor Greek, but all shall be one in Christ. Truly these words show us that from the day when you have received the Spirit you are no longer women, just as I am no longer a man. Though the semblance of sex and a respect for traditional custom give men a privileged position in the divine ministry, such is not an article of faith laid down by Christ: the salvation of souls comes before anything else. As it is said, the gnat can pass where the fly cannot. You are skilled in the care of the sick, and so can more easily gain access to the bedsides of women in danger of death. The gift of the Spirit that has been granted you is full and complete: God bestows nothing by half measures. Go then, and may the Lord keep you from the blasphemy of doubting your own powers!"

"Where then are we to go, Monseigneur?" Fabrisse asked him.

"Make your way first of all to Castres. Here you will find lodging in the house of one William the Tanner, and friends to tell you where you must go next."

The two women set out together, knapsack on shoulder and stick in hand, clad in plain gray dresses which barely reached their ankles, and with white shawls over their heads. Fabrisse sang hymns as she went, putting them to various popular airs. On the evening of the first day they had to take refuge for the night in an abandoned farm. Fabrisse collapsed on the damp, straw-covered ground, and began to sob.

"Take heart, sister," Arsen said. "This journeying on foot has wearied you."

"Ah, no," Fabrisse said. "I am not weeping for weariness, but at the thought that I shall never again see my other sisters in God, nor the house where I used to live. I had to tear myself away; I was too attached to it. You and I have a hard road to climb to Calvary: the flesh is weak, and weaker in us than among those who do not know God, for they at least possess the illusions of their hearts. Make no mistake about it: cold, fear, and hunger are worse temptations than pride or luxury."

Arsen thought herself already well acquainted with fatigue and hunger, and was astonished by her companion's words. Very soon she learned how true they were, however. It is a hard thing indeed to be hungry and frightened when you know that there is no meal awaiting you at home, nor, indeed, so much as four walls where you can be sure of shelter. There is no respite, no dallying: friends receive you joyfully, but never shelter you for two days in succession, and even the poor folk are sometimes distrustful of you. Two women who never separated were liable to create suspicion, and in some places they had to live apart and only meet secretly, at night.

From Castres the two women were sent to Carcassonne: this town was solidly held by the French, and none of the brothers in the area could safely stay there, except for a day or two at a time, and in hiding. Conditions, too, were wretched in the extreme, especially in the suburbs, which had been half destroyed during the siege the previous summer. Many folk, for want of pastors and from fear of the enemy, had relapsed into their ancient errors; many more died impenitent, while the misfortunes of war led poor people into a life of sin. Arsen was well acquainted with the poverty that prevailed in the countryside; but that in the towns was far worse. Women would sell themselves to soldiers for a crust of bread, while men would turn thief or informer.

From April till June fresh contingents of Crusaders passed through the town from the North; the flow of troops never ceased. The banners of every land fluttered in Carcassonne: the place was thick with blazoned shields and fine armor, with thoroughbred horses in their bright-colored trappings, with plumed casques and pennants and lances. Arsen's heart was wrung with pity for these young men, thus lured with the bait of worldly magnificence into such acts of crime. She saw strapping young squires sauntering past her in the street, some of whom bore a close resemblance to her sons. They would push their way into houses in search of women, or overturn shopkeepers' stalls and throw stones through windows simply for the fun of it, like children. One of them tried to embrace her one day. "Would you wish your mother to be treated in such a way?" she asked him; and as there were tears in her eyes, and her expression was somewhat forbidding, he let her go. She added: "I feel great pity for your soul." He asked if she had any children, and did they get enough to eat? Ah, misery, she thought: can ignorant souls be so corrupted? In their part of the country these poor people have never heard of salvation; they are as innocent as beasts of the field. Who is to bring them to God?

"It may be," Fabrisse was wont to observe, "that those who kill them are not doing them such a bad turn after all; when a man has sunk so low, death at least prevents him from further self-destruction."

Arsen shook her head. "No," she said. "You do not make dirty linen white by befouling it yet further. Evil is not killed by evil."

She made the assertion, and yet at times the temptation to doubt it assailed her. There was too much evil, too much misery, too much terror abroad: then let those who have brought this war upon us reap what they have sown! We have done nothing to them. They are here to pillage and burn, to kill men and destroy their souls through fear. No, we have done nothing to them: our men have never invaded their lands, to rape their women and mock their Faith, or burned their bishops and priests like so many heaps of filth. We asked nothing of them; their Pope was doing us enough harm already without their assistance.

"Fabrisse," she said.

"Yes, my sister?"

The two women were spending this particular night in a hayloft above a stable. They had been hidden there by the head groom, a kindly soul; people were beginning to know them about the district.

"Fabrisse, I didn't wake you up, did I?"

"I can't sleep. I keep on imagining I hear footsteps down below."

"Ah, no—those are only the horses! Listen, Fabrisse; a thought has just occurred to me. Raymond told us, did he not, that we should be in all respects like those to whom God has called us? But the similarity is going beyond our outward garments; we are beginning to think as they do, too. At least, *I* am, very frequently. Do you believe God demands that of us, besides everything else?"

Fabrisse had her face pressed to a crack between two boards, through which she was watching the deserted street. The moonlight, falling between two shadowy lengths of wall, lit up a butcher's shop-sign. Behind the gabled rooftops, with their black and silver tiles, a reddish glow lit up the night sky: there was a banquet going on in the Bishop's Palace.

"Arsen, my sister," she said, "how can we tell? How are we to know what God desires of us at this moment? Our thoughts are like our bodies; they are no purer than blood or sweat. Prayer and Holy Writ always excepted, no utterance is ever truly good. Why should we trouble our heads with such things?"

"Why indeed?" Arsen said. "We are, after all, nothing." She thought of those women who had received the final Sacrament at her hands and had died at peace with God. O my dear sisters, she thought, I am the weakest and least worthy of you all; yet since God has made of me the vessel in which He conveys the Water of Life to your lips, He will protect me from all gross defilement.

"Fabrisse," she said, "I am very much afraid we shall have to leave here tomorrow."

"How shall we go? The street is very probably watched."

"Out by the back courtyard: it gives onto the ramparts. The groom here is running a terrible risk in sheltering us."

"Not so grave a risk as we run," Fabrisse said bitterly. "But you are right, all the same; we cannot compromise him."

They left at dawn, and spent ten days scrubbing floors and washing dishes in the house of a certain pious believer, who had taken to making great friends of the Crusaders as a cover for his other activities. All the time they were waiting for a message from Laurac, which never came. The master of the house brought his family and friends to see them; these visitors would closet themselves in the bedchamber with Arsen and Fabrisse, to pay them their humble respects and listen to their counsel. The men would talk of the war, and swear that the Count of Toulouse and the King of Aragon would soon come with their armies and drive out the French invader.

It was here that Arsen had her first news of Ricord since that winter: someone informed her that a certain "Lord of Montgeil" was raiding isolated detachments of Crusaders, at the head of a band of Spanish mercenaries. Of all those who had encountered him, it was said, not one survived to tell the tale. Arsen concealed her distress as best she could; she did not dare admit that this man was her husband—the more so since Ricord's conduct evoked such universal approval.

"Fabrisse," she said at last, "the days are slipping by, while countless souls are lost daily through sin and the sword—and we sit here at our ease! It's time to move on. If the town becomes too dangerous we'll turn north and follow the armies. There are so many vagabonds on the roads that no one will pay any attention to us."

"Do you want to get us raped?" Fabrisse asked. "We are not even allowed to carry knives for self-defense. Would you risk seeing Holy Writ trampled underfoot by drunken riffraff?"

Fabrisse gave the impression of being very timorous but in point of fact was a good deal tougher than most. Now, laughing, she began to smear her overpale face with a mixture of red clay and ashes. The result obstinately refused to look like sunburn.

"Anyway," she remarked, "the responsibility is out of our hands now. It is up to God to take care of us."

All through that summer they travelled about the ravaged countryside, weary and sick at heart, frequently more concerned with saving their own lives than aiding their neighbor. The vast misery of war unfolded before them: hanged men dangling from the branches of olive trees, women driven crazy, abandoned children, eviscerated cattle, burned fields; the vines all uprooted, castles and towns deserted and smoke-blackened. Nor would this year see the end of it: from countries far afield an endless supply of troops poured in, some even from Germany or Flanders, their language so rough and outlandish that no one could understand a word of what they said. They enrolled Navarrese and Brabantine mercenaries and marauders, as though there were not enough of these villains roving the countryside already. A plague of locusts could not have done more damage, and would certainly have occasioned less transgression.

Never had there been seen so many blind or maimed wretches, hands and feet lopped off, screaming, cursing, begging to be put out of their agony: their condition defied treatment or comfort. Babies were abandoned by the roadside in such numbers that they could not all be rescued; and some of them were eaten alive by vultures.

The enemy camp lay spread out all around Minerve. The whole of the surrounding countryside was covered with white or colored tents, horses and siege engines, countless campfires: from a distance it looked like some gigantic fair. Traitors that you were, men of Narbonne, you shamefully threw in your lot with those other, human vultures, who bore the scarlet cross on their breasts; to revenge yourselves on your rivals in Minerve you sold your souls to the Devil! After the siege was over a huge bonfire was lit outside the city; it could be seen from miles away, and attracted attention by reason of the acrid, bitter smell its smoke gave off. May that smoke, the spectators prayed, burn the executioners' eyes and hearts to all eternity!

Such shrieks and screams and yells of agony had never before been heard: more than a hundred unhappy martyrs were being burned alive simultaneously. On this day Arsen and Fabrisse had taken up a position at the bottom of the hill, mingling with the crowd of peasants and fugitives: all of them, their fear of the soldiers forgotten, were weeping openly. Ah, blessed saints, you who have been as fathers and mothers to us, how fearful is your martyrdom! How cruelly these accursed devils have bereft us of you! Fabrisse and Arsen wept with them. Our Father, they prayed, Thy kingdom come, Thy will be done on earth, let not Thy just servants suffer longer at the hands of these devils! Raymond de Ribeyre had gone to the stake that day, and many other Christians with him. Aicart, his companion, had left him to undertake a mission in the countryside beyond Laurac, and thus did not share his martyrdom.

Four days after this massacre Aicart assembled a crowd of the faithful in a woodland clearing near Ventajou. He was older and leaner; his eyes showed black in that emaciated face, like two dark gaping holes in a stone wall.

"Brethren," he cried, "no pity for these devils! God has granted us one favor in our troubled times: He has revealed the visible sign by which we may know a soul accursed. This scarlet cross they wear on their breast is that same red mark with which the Devil seals his own. Brethren, a soul which has been utterly lost and degraded by its sins may sometimes incur the fearful penalty of being reborn in an animal's body: so we must, so far as we are able, respect all living creatures. But be well assured, no soul that God has created can ever be found in a Crusader's body. The hour has struck when the Beast must at last reveal his unmistakable mark. These so-called men are really creatures of the Devil in human guise!

"Even though you may be perplexed by their noble mien or handsome features, remember that such things are a snare and a delusion: the Devil is skilled in deceiving just men. God has not forbidden us to crush serpents—and how much worse than serpents these beings are! They are not only gross in their substance; they represent the very Spirit of Evil incarnate!"

Arsen rose and asked leave to speak.

"Master Aicart," she said, "it is not I who utter these words, but the Spirit which moves in me as it does in you. If I interpret the Spirit ill, I pray your indulgence, my sisters and brethren, for the infirmities of the flesh in me. Do not forget that the Devil, who is well versed in deceit, can also deceive simple or ignorant souls by causing them to carry this outward and visible sign—which is, after all, not a supernatural sign, but merely two strips of crimson cloth. And though what you say, my brother Aicart, may be true, yet the blood which flows from these accursed men's bodies has the same color as the blood of just men; and the cries of anguish which these men utter are indistinguishable from those of the just. By telling folk that killing is a good work you put their souls in great peril. Men are ready enough to kill without any prompting from us."

"My reverend sister speaks like a woman," Aicart said. "I shall never kill anyone with my own hands; the Rule forbids me. But let anyone skilled in the handling of arms reflect: for every single Crusader he spares, he may render himself responsible for the deaths—horrible deaths—of ten of his own brethren!"

"Take care," Arsen said. "It is fleshly sorrow that inspires you to utter such harsh words; you are mourning the death of your companion and our beloved friend Raymond de Ribeyre. Jesus said: My Kingdom is not of this world. You are seeking to act as though it *were* of this world, as though we could establish it in this world by main force!"

"My sister, when Jesus wept over Jerusalem, He wished to make us understand that it is permissible to weep for an earthly city if just men inhabit it. As God is my witness, the tears I shed over our profaned and martyred cities are not occasioned by sorrows of the flesh. As God is my witness, the agony I feel at the loss of my friend is not the sole cause of my misery—nor of this harshness which you find so shocking. We have given a promise not to fear death by fire; and we should not fear it for our friends' sakes any more than for our own. But to those of the faithful who ask our guidance we should say: To resist evil by violence is a lesser sin than to acquiesce in evil through cowardice. For souls who have not yet received the gift of divine light there is no middle course between the two."

Arsen bowed her head. "God save you, my brother Aicart," she said. "In the Father's house are many mansions; and there is none can see truth whole and clear, except the Son of God in Heaven."

That night Aicart broke bread, and blessed it, and many of the faithful shed tears over it as they ate.

"Be of good cheer," Aicart told them. "Our Bishop, Monseigneur Bernard—whom God has preserved from the hands of brigands—will soon send you new pastors. Remember what has been said of the Church: The gates of Hell shall not prevail against her. A hundred and fifty Christians have been burned; but a thousand more will come to replace them. And as for the Mother of whoredoms and adulteries, intoxicated with the blood of the martyrs—so terrible a fate is being prepared for her at this very moment that your hearts would shrink in terror at the mere thought of it! Did not Jesus say: Let not your hearts be troubled? Did He not also say: I have overcome the world? If He has overcome the world, then it is written for all eternity that the Church must triumph in the end; and the time is now nigh."

Before leaving the district and setting out on the road to Toulouse, Aicart bade farewell to Arsen and her companion. "I cannot tell you," he said, "how my heart bleeds, nor how troubled I am in the flesh: our brothers' martyrdom has robbed this world of such a brilliant light that we seem now plunged into dim shadow. But though my affliction may have torn from me such utterance as shocked you, I do not believe I have sinned gravely against the Spirit. For even in this world there are some causes that are more just than others; and for souls that have not attained to purification there are degrees of sin." Then he added: "My sister Arsen, I passed through Foix this spring, and saw your daughter. I found her increasing in wisdom and in the gifts of the Spirit, and well-nigh ready to receive Holy Baptism. She begged me to ask your blessing for this day when it comes."

Arsen pressed both hands to her heart, breathless.

"Then you will see her again? Ah, if only I could go with you! Tell her that I give her my blessing—for hunger and cold, for terror and tears, for every bitterness that a life without hope can offer; for according to the laws of the flesh we cannot look to any hope. She was born of my flesh, and it is that flesh which I love in her: against the compassion of my own heart I am powerless. I cannot wish her the kind of life I lead myself. May God grant us to meet again one day, in the place where there will be neither mothers nor children, neither husbands nor wives, neither friends nor enemies, but one Christ in all of us."

That night, in an old abandoned woodcutters' hut, Arsen lay in Fabrisse's arms and wept, for Aicart's words had opened up old wounds which she had believed to be healed.

"What lunatic creatures we are," Fabrisse said. "Truly, we ought to be locked up! We fear this life for our children as though it were the greatest misfortune imaginable—yet we would choose no other life for ourselves. Have you forgotten that the wisdom of

God seems madness to mankind—and not only in a metaphorical sense?"

"Ah, if that be madness," Arsen said, "let us continue mad to the end! In the midst of this nightmare of blood, fire, and mortal agony let us sing joyfully: for if it is true indeed that God has overcome the world, who else but us is there to tell it? Let the women weeping over fresh graves forget their tears, and follow us. When love is madness, it knows no bounds; and there are enough children by every roadside for all the mothers who have lost their own. As for those who were once my husband and my children, I am dead to them; I could wish I had never known them."

All that winter the two women remained in the town of Limoux, where a burgher gave them a house in which to care for orphans and the disabled. They kept themselves hidden, and, to avoid discovery, themselves performed every menial chore ordinarily undertaken by the most humble servant. But despite everything they were denounced, and just managed to escape from the town in time, disguised in men's cloaks. O God, Arsen thought, if even charity is barred to us, whither shall we turn?

"In the days before we received the Spirit," Fabrisse said, "we could deceive the whole world: we went to Mass, ate our meat, and succored the poor without let or hindrance. In God's eyes, then, it is clear, truth and faith are more important than all else. We have not abandoned the suffering; their trust in us is more important than a crust of bread. They know that it is on account of our Faith that we are thus hunted."

"Are *we* going to retreat to some safe hiding place—inside the walls of a castle, or high among the mountains—while these poor God-fearing souls are exposed daily to the whims of the invader? I shall never leave this district. Even if we live in the woods we shall find people to succor still, and gather the faithful together to hear the Holy Scriptures read."

"Yes," Fabrisse said, "but we must keep on the move the whole time. It's a good thing winter is over now."

CHAPTER IV

The Scarlet Crosses

THE fifteen men lay concealed behind a group of gigantic boulders, high above the road and overlooking it. Their skins were burned black from exposure to the sun, and grimed with dust for good measure; at the moment they were lounging at ease, greasing the strings of their bows and arbalests. Despite their appearance they wore good French coats of mail, and were armed with fine brand-new weapons. Some had colored scarves tied around their necks or waists; others sported earrings and embroidered shirt sleeves. Their leader was worse dressed than any of them: he wore a tattered leather jerkin, clumsily patched shoes, and a piece of gray cloth knotted around his head in lieu of a hat. Curling iron-gray hair fell over his forehead, and his thin hard face looked as though it had been carved out of seasoned oak. His eyes were exceedingly dark and lively, with deep brownish circles beneath them.

Now he lay flat on his belly on a shelf of rock, watching the road below. About a hundred and fifty yards off there was a sharp bend; the road itself was fairly narrow, and beneath it the hillside dropped steeply away, dotted with large stones and an occasional pine tree. Presently two horsemen rode into sight; they wore long white surcoats, and their helmets glinted in the sun. The man signalled to his companions with one hand, and then dropped back into his former position, like a pointer scenting its quarry. The little cavalcade continued toward them; there were about a dozen men on horseback, and many more on foot, most of them with the scarlet cross sewn upon their breast.

"Comrades," Ricord whispered, "there are fifteen of us, and they are at least forty. Aim for the foot soldiers first, and be sure that every one of your shots strikes home. I will do my best to stampede the horses. Once we have discharged our volley, let us charge down on them. Not a single man must escape."

Arrows and bolts hissed through the air; the valley was filled with shrieks and the shrill whinnying of horses. Ricord's men left their place of ambush and began to heave large blocks of stone down onto the track. Three of the horsemen tumbled over the edge and rolled toward the stream at the bottom; the horses of the remainder went milling around in their tracks, trampling the wounded. Ricord's band consisted of old soldiers who knew their job backwards. Confronted by these howling, club-swinging raiders, any man might well have supposed himself to be dealing with devils straight from Hell. Out of the forty ambushed, only half a dozen managed to escape, by rolling down the hillside and hiding behind handy rocks. All the rest were finished off, either with knife or club; they had been taken by surprise and scarcely had a chance to defend themselves. More than one head was so violently smashed in that the features were no longer distinguishable; many corpses had been trampled over with such brutality that their armor was unfit for further use.

Four of the horses were captured alive, and led away off the track. The victors proceeded to bind up their wounds and wipe off the blood that had spurted over their faces and hands.

Ricord said: "If we follow the course of the stream we'll get the ones that escaped. First I'm going to take my share of the booty. You can strip them afterward."

Quickly, with the point of his knife, he ripped through the stitches in the scarlet, blood-spattered crosses. Then he tore them off the white and gray surcoats these Crusaders wore above their chain mail. In this way he collected twenty-seven crosses, which he stuffed inside his jerkin, against his chest. This done, Ricord's men stripped the corpses, sorted out all arms and armor which remained in good condition, and piled it on the backs of the horses.

It was a long time since they had had such good hunting; most often the detachments numbered no more than ten or a dozen men. On this occasion Ricord had killed eight of them with his own hands.

"A good haul, my friends," he said. "But we must not forget the fugitives. Let us grant them the martyrs' crown as well, lest they become jealous of their comrades. At least three of them were wounded; they cannot have got far."

One of the soldiers lugged a corpse forward by the feet, preparatory to rolling it down the hillside. "A good fellow, this," he remarked. "I wouldn't have minded having him in my own company; he fought well."

"A wolf will defend itself bravely, too," Ricord said. The dead man was very young, hardly over twenty. Ricord recalled that not so long ago he had felt a twinge of pity for the animals he slaughtered.

Eight days later they pounced on a small armed detachment that was escorting an abbot on his white mule, together with four monks. The soldiers were killed first of all; next the abbot had crosses slashed into his face and tonsured head, and was lashed by the heels behind his own mule. Trembling, the monks prayed as they awaited their own turn. Ricord, who disliked seeing anyone —even monks—tormented for the mere pleasure of it, told his men to hang these poor wretches as quickly as might be. The four victims seemed much relieved at the realization that they were not to be tortured, but begged a respite of execution in order to make their last prayers.

"What is the point?" Ricord asked them. "Your false prayers will not save you. If your God were the true God, you would be martyrs for your Faith, and would have no need of prayers."

Three of the monks were duly hanged; but the fourth still knelt there, apparently oblivious to his surroundings. His features were fine, his expression gentle: this man, Ricord thought, could not be among the damned.

"Brother," he said to him, "are you blind? Can you not see that your Faith leads men to murder and other grave sins?"

"So does yours, obviously," said the monk, "since I have just seen you kill numbers of your earthly brethren. Leave me to my prayers, if you please."

Ricord admired the dignity this man displayed in the face of death; he sensed very clearly that such courage was not diabolical in origin.

"Let my Faith be," he said. "You are unworthy to speak of it— as indeed am I. Look: I could spare your life and take you to certain men who would be able to guide you toward the true Light."

"Leave me to my prayers," the monk repeated. "I have not much time left."

Why did I ever speak to him? Ricord asked himself. Am I to see him hanged there, too, beside his comrades? He knew that it was dishonorable to use a man's fear of death to procure his conversion. But is it not better, he thought, that this poor wretch should die now rather than linger on in his own execrable faith? After seeing what he has seen, he will never allow himself to be converted.

The monk was still praying, his face turned heavenward, neck outstretched. Ricord went up to him and drew a dagger quickly across his throat, reflecting that this way he would not suffer too much. The blood spouted out, drenching the coarse white woollen habit; the man's face remained peaceful, lips a little parted, with hardly any trace of astonishment in his expression.

Never afterward was Ricord to regret this gesture; more often he was to remember it as an act of mercy. Yet the agony that gnawed at his heart became more powerful still from this day on. We have been told, he reflected, that it profiteth a man nothing to win the whole world if he lose his own soul. God knows I have never tried to win anything for myself, not so much as the price of a button. All I wanted was to protect the weak and defend the innocent; and on that basis the loss of my soul is perfectly justifiable. Then why should I be so afflicted when I think of it, as though I were losing a close personal friend?

The life he had been leading for nearly two years now was not an unhappy one, but at times it bore hardly on a man who had hoped one day to earn the appellation of "Christian." What he had to do was not something that could be learned in the pages of Holy Writ. The companions he had chosen were men who, except in wartime, would richly deserve to hang from the nearest gallows. He had got them by promising them all the booty, down to the last farthing. They were professional mercenaries, who killed because they enjoyed it: such were the sort of whom he now stood in need. He knew very well that he was not fighting for honor's sake, but simply to exterminate as many of the enemy as he could. He was the hunter still, though his quarry had changed from animals to men: there is no such thing as honorable warfare when dealing with wild beasts.

A score of times he came within an ace of death, for occasionally he was bound to attack seasoned troops; yet he would never wear so much as a cuirass, let alone a coat of mail. Because of this lunacy his men worshipped him, and firmly believed he bore a charmed life. Let it never be said, he often told himself, that I have plundered to my profit; I am neither a brigand nor a looter. Let it never be said that I tried to protect my body: I wear the same hunting jerkin as I would to go after wolves. If murder is the Devil's handiwork, then the Devil will look after his own. And in the event, it seemed, the Devil did so; in some fifty surprise attacks he was wounded only six times, never severely.

He made his band both fear and respect him. But simply as a result of having to live with them, he felt his heart becoming hardened, and taking on the horny insensitivity of a horse's hoof. They were evil men, and he knew it; he told himself they were essential for the work he must do. Then, little by little, he came to realize that their indifference to death—their own no less than another's—was a powerfully insidious habit, one which deformed the soul just as the exercise of some exacting physical trade can deform the body. He felt himself becoming like them—and worse than them, indeed; for they were as innocent as animals. They loved wine and fine clothes better than all else; when they were drunk they were equally liable to gouge out a prisoner's eyes or burst into tears at the thought of their mothers. Ricord recalled something Arsen had said: *He prayed for those who knew not what they did; He did not pray for Judas.*

At times a mood of black, intolerable despair would descend on him, which could be relieved only by the sheer joy of killing. He knew that the only reason these men admired and followed him with such devotion was that they reckoned him to be the fiercest of them all. Even in this accursed brotherhood honor came before money; and their honor consisted in the degree of cruelty they could attain.

After the defeat of the Count of Toulouse, their work became harder, since the Crusaders held the greater part of the country-side and were beginning to get their adversaries' measure. The Grand Army had withdrawn, and the troops who remained were brave and canny fighters, well versed in guerrilla warfare. In every town and throughout the country districts a notice had been posted, signed by the Bishop and Simon de Montfort, the new Viscount, which offered a reward of five marks to anyone who captured a guerrilla commander, dead or alive.

"It will be a hard winter," Ricord told his men, "and we shall have to go into hiding in the woods. What will you live off? These clerics will travel little during the winter months, and will be heavily escorted when they do. You cannot rely on getting much plunder from that source. So I advise you to quit my service and find other masters, who will pay you a living wage."

"We could get good wages anywhere," they replied. "We could go to Foix or Toulouse, to Gascony or Aragon—or even join the Crusaders in Carcassonne. But in your service we can boast of having done good work. The Count of Foix would put a man such as you over a company of two hundred Aragonese mercenaries."

Ricord reflected that one day things might indeed come to that. Yet he still found the thought of profiting by his sins a repugnant one, and could not bear to relapse into the worldly temptations he had known as a youth. At times he sought refuge in those castles which were not yet occupied by the Crusaders, and was well received there: he had a reputation as a gallant fighter. The wife and daughter of the castellan would wait upon him at table in person; everyone urged him to talk of his exploits, but on this subject he preferred to remain silent.

"Plenty of men would dearly love to do what you are doing," they said, "if it were not for their wives and children. Those who took their families and left the area acted wisely—though they did leave their serfs and vassals at the mercy of the invader. You have greater freedom, since you are not yourself a local man."

"I cannot blame you for your submission," Ricord told them. "With enemies such as these a dagger in the back troubles no consciences. But next spring, when the King of Aragon and the Count of Toulouse have mustered their troops and joined forces, we shall be able to make a concerted effort and drive every Frenchman out of the country."

When he spoke thus with men of his own rank and class, Ricord gradually became aware that he was beginning to forget why he had decided to fight in the first place. He was turning into a regular professional soldier, whose greatest concern was to kill as many foemen as possible; he found himself wanting to boast of the dozens upon dozens of scarlet crosses he possessed, and which constituted his sole booty. Was he fighting to defend the poor and helpless, or in the hope of collecting another hundred crosses? One cannot think of two things at once, he told himself, and his mind had to be on the business of killing.

On a certain day in November the woodcutter who was sheltering him came around with the news that two "holy ladies" were hiding in a wood outside Minerve, some three miles away. Ricord, who had encountered no Crusaders for some while now, was in the grip of a deep, nameless melancholy at the time; but he went off with some townspeople to the place where these women were gathering the faithful for prayer. He seldom had the chance to pray nowadays, and hoped to cleanse his soul by virtue of their presence. After the massacres at Minerve and Lavaur, those of the brotherhood who survived were forced to go into hiding, and their places of refuge were revealed only to reliable people.

He found the women in a clearing, beside a large wood fire. As the faithful passed in front of them—each prostrating himself as he did so—they bestowed their blessing on them in turns. They stood very straight and slim in their long brown cloaks, and did not have the appearance of age. Ricord awaited his turn, eyes on the ground. Then the sound of a well-known voice made him raise his head. The taller of the two women was just then readjusting her hood, which had slipped back, revealing her face. How like Arsen she is, Ricord thought. Perhaps this is her aunt. Then, as he drew nearer, he saw who it really was.

She had not really aged; but her sunburned, fleshless features seemed made now from some wholly different substance: so, doubtless, would the face of St. John the Evangelist have appeared, or any other happy soul whose life span had been extended by God's will to a thousand years. But alas, it was not even a thousand years that separated these lips from those other, softer lips, that had once given and received kisses: it was all eternity. She was dead to him forever, consumed by the Spirit, no longer mother or wife, but God's vessel.

These eyes will see me yet not recognize me, he thought.

He went up to her and prostrated himself in his turn: there was nothing he could say apart from the prescribed words of veneration: "Pray God make me a good Christian, and bring me to a good end."

Arsen raised her thin hand, so brown and scored, and her lips trembled.

"May God make you a good Christian," she said, "and may He bring you to a good end."

There were about fifty men and women gathered about the fire afterward, while the two women stood up on a huge boulder, reciting verses from the Gospels in turn.

"I am the true vine, and My Father is the husbandman."

"Every branch in Me that beareth not fruit He taketh away; and every branch that beareth fruit, He purgeth it, that it may bring forth more fruit."

"Now ye are clean through the word which I have spoken unto you."

"Abide in Me, and I in you."

"As the branch cannot bear fruit of itself, except it abide in the vine; no more can ye, except ye abide in Me."

"I am the vine, ye are the branches. . . ."

". . . If a man abide not in Me, he is cast forth as a branch, and is withered; and men gather them, and cast them into the fire, and they are burned—" As Arsen uttered these final words, she felt her voice fail: she burst out sobbing, and raised both hands above her head.

"Ah, my friends," she cried, "my sisters and brethren, as God is my witness, it is not I who weep now, but He who is in me! For all those who have not remained in Him, for all whom these cruel times have sundered from Him, for all those who are withered branches, who have been cast into the fire to burn! This fire can no more be extinguished, nor the burned branch ever again bear fruit! My brothers, my friends, God's sorrow over these lost souls is keener than that of a mother who sees her own child tortured! He is Infinite Joy—yet for our world His features are the features of affliction. To Him a thousand suns are as nothing if their price is one lost soul!

"Even when you see the enemy spread foulness and blood over the face of the earth, stand fast in Christ Jesus. There is no justice here below except the Devil's justice, no truth but the Devil's truth, no wisdom but the Devil's wisdom. Verily I say unto you, God is not of this world, and never has been, nor ever will be. My sisters and brethren, God is a frenzy such as no human mind can conceive; God is insensate Love—limitless, all-consuming, unreasoning Love! To hearts such as ours, compact of stone and mud, He seems so wild a frenzy that we prefer to die rather than endure Him!"

She stared straight in front of her as she spoke, across the flames; all the time she held her clasped hands above her head, as though she were suspended from some dark invisible cord.

"Sisters and brethren, I know these are hard sayings; but what right would I have to speak otherwise to you, if such indeed is the Truth? If you seek some other thing, and not God's Divine Frenzy,

go to those who promise you salvation for a little money, unleavened bread, and servile obedience. Verily their madness is
greater still, but it is madness as this world knows it. If you would
judge by the laws of this world, go to them, for your hearts are
with them already."

Tears streamed down from her eyes as she spoke, flooding her
cheeks and running into her mouth. Most of the women who stood
listening to her were in tears themselves; so were several of the
men. It would have been better for me, Ricord thought, had I seen
her dead and laid in earth. I could have spoken to her then, I
could have mourned at her grave. But what can I say to such a
woman as this?

Fabrisse was singing hymns now, her strong voice made a little
harsh by the cold, yet true and lovely still: men and women re-
sponded to her in chorus. The night was long, and before it was
out the fire had consumed a whole load of faggots, and more.
Slowly the sky grew pale, and the tall black shadows of pine trees
began to stand out against it. The two women warmed their hands
at the fire: they were exhausted, shivering with cold, and as if just
aroused from sleep. A group of peasant women clustered around
them as they waited for the time to recite morning prayers.

Once again Ricord had a long period of waiting, for everyone
wanted to bring his problems to the "holy ladies"—a case of illness, a particularly cruel bereavement, some burden on the conscience. But about noon they asked to be left alone to pray in peace.

What is there for me to say to her? Ricord wondered. He did
not actually feel any urge to speak to Arsen at all; but the recollection of their children, and the twenty-five years of married life they
had shared, somehow compelled him to wait on. At last he came
before the two women. After kneeling to receive a blessing, he
asked a favor: might he talk with them after they had concluded
their prayers?

"Ah, my dearest friend," Arsen said, "how I have prayed for
the blessed chance of seeing you again! When I recognized you last
night, my heart leapt like a wounded deer; I had been so afraid
that we were doomed never to meet! This lady is Fabrisse, the com-

panion whom God has bestowed upon me; her family comes from the Laurac district, and she was married to William de Brézilhac. God send everyone so worthy a comrade on his travels!"

Fabrisse gave her characteristic laugh, dry yet affectionate, and observed that Dame Arsen was the first highlander she had ever struck who was easy to live with.

"People from your part of the world," she said, "generally regard us as worldly, frivolous folk; quite right, too."

Ricord reflected that this woman *was* somewhat worldly, indeed, and that she was a graceful, still attractive creature. Intense pity stirred in him at the thought. Here are women, he told himself, worthy of the very highest marks of respect, before whom kings should bow down in homage; yet they are hunted down like mad dogs, and if they are caught they will die something worse than a dog's death.

Aloud he said: "Arsen, we parted in sadness, and I count it a great honor that you should rejoice at this meeting of ours. Every human being seeks to do good in his own fashion, and according to the enlightenment he has received from God. Last night you wept over my soul. But if it be true that the love of God is madness, do not judge those who are themselves mad!

"As God is my witness, this is not the kind of life I desired for you; nor, indeed, is it the life for which you were preparing yourself. Do you want me to see you dragged through the streets with a rope around your neck? Do you want me to watch your writhing agony in the flames, with faggots piled high about you? If you still have any regard for me, leave this area and go up into the mountains, where our Christian community has found a refuge; there at least they have their own homes.

"My own life has become hard enough. There is a price on my head; I cannot get more soldiers, and I have not a penny to my name. I had sworn to continue the struggle as long as there remained any strength in my body. But in order to convey you and your companion to safety I would be prepared to leave this district. You will be less suspect and better protected if you have a man with you; and you will not be lying if you say I am your husband."

"No," Arsen said. "We thank you for so generous an offer, but we will be of more use here."

Ricord said, gently: "I too am more useful here than I ever could be serving under a regular command. Listen, Arsen: I have been through Foix and Toulouse, from Perpignan as far as Barcelona; and I have seen many men ready and willing to fight. Apart from the Count of Foix, anyone capable of using a sword is either afraid of being excommunicated or waiting till things settle themselves. Our sons are spending their time in guardroom or castle courtyard, kicking their heels, playing dice, and listening to the latest news. Things have come to such a pass in this country that unless a man wants to go over to the enemy there is no one he can enlist under; he has to fight on his own. That is why I am regarded as a sort of bandit. But I have done nothing worthy of reproach; on that score my conscience is clear."

Arsen was sitting on a fallen tree trunk, head bent, hands clasped around her knees. Fabrisse, who still remained on her feet, threw some twigs and dead leaves onto the dying fire. The morning sun shone cheerfully; the pine trees cast long, blue, striated shadows across the gray, trampled-down grass in the clearing.

"Why do you not speak to me?" Ricord said. "Must you always judge me so harshly?"

Arsen looked up at him: a long, pensive stare. She seemed not to have heard what he said.

At last she said, in a voice that contained something like tenderness: "Your hair has turned gray."

"What has that got to do with what I have been telling you?"

"Nothing. Once upon a time I loved to comb out those curls of yours, and now I may not so much as run my hand over them. How eagerly we looked forward to the coming of these gray hairs! Yet what have they brought us? Tribulation, bitterness, misery."

"You at least have found peace," Ricord said.

She smiled; her gaze wandered slowly over the deserted clearing, with its muddy path and pile of blackened ashes.

"When we are alone," she said, "we keep the fire going all night for fear of wolves, and take turns staying awake. Yet when we hear a rustle in the undergrowth, we say to ourselves, Pray God it be a wolf, not a man. Is it not said that the peace of God passeth all understanding? The Spirit brings us whithersoever it will, but our soul stands naked and alone in the face of affliction and evil. For pity is like some fiery potion that sears our inward parts; and there is no remedy for the burn it inflicts."

"Who knows that better than I? It has deprived me of my reason. Do you desire that I should remain in the woods with you both, and follow you as your escort?"

"No, Ricord. Your heart is set on another road. Suppose that, in order to save the lives of many innocent people, I had been forced to prostitute myself to some common hangman: you would not have approved my act. Yet you are committing a sin a hundred times more serious, which destroys you far more irrevocably! The laws of this world are so cruel that it may even be better to do evil, if your soul is blind enough to see some good in it. And indeed, scarce one man in a hundred thousand is not blind; and among the hundred thousand ways of prostituting oneself to the Devil, yours, perhaps, is not the worst."

"Go to," Ricord said, rising to his feet, "I know very well it is not the worst. I do not hold your harsh words against you. Nothing remains of the love that once existed between us; our hair has turned gray, our children have forgotten us. I can scarcely recall the ecstasy that your body once gave me: for years now I have not so much as touched a woman—I have always stayed faithful to you. The bond that we imagined to be so solid was only a bond of the flesh. Two years apart, and our separate ordeals during that period have sufficed to make us strangers to one another.

"Arsen, do you see this bag I carry at my belt? It contains enough red cloth to sew you a great mantle—if the seamstress were willing to piece all the crosses together, strip by strip. Each one of them was got at the price of a man's life. Of your compassion remember those men, too: I did not kill them gladly. But if I encounter others, and can kill them, I shall do it with greater joy than hitherto, since now I have seen you once more. When I think of the harm they might do you, I shall feel increased in my strength."

He knelt before her, and she stretched out one hand over his head.

"May God make a good Christian of you," she repeated, "and bring you to a good end."

Then he knelt in front of Fabrisse, who pronounced the same formula over him. He departed in a thoughtful, melancholy state, almost wondering whether he had not dreamed the whole thing.

The path which so many feet had trodden the previous night was now deserted. It wound its way between moss-grown rocks and thorny thickets; small streams flowed across it, great boulders blocked it, and finally it vanished once more in the depths of the great pine forest. It was a good league's journey back to the town. Ricord reflected that, all things considered, it would be easy enough to penetrate the women's retreat. A casual patrol riding through, an official search, an informer: any of these would be enough. There was in the town a certain elderly cleric, highly unpopular despite having been born and bred thereabouts; it was well known that he prayed privately for the Crusaders' victory. This man might very well denounce them if he had occasion, Ricord thought. Equally, he might not. Suppose he wanted to do so: fear would not prevent him; he would leave the district under military escort, and find a place at Carcassonne or Narbonne. Must he be punished in anticipation of a crime that he might not even intend to commit?

Arsen, he thought, oh, Arsen: once I called you my dove, my beloved. Now my heart is so parched that the one great love of my life seems mere childish folly. If she had come to me today in the likeness of her twenty-year-old self, I should have looked at her just as I now look at this great stone, with its patches of black moss. I am old; anger and pity have consumed my inward parts. All I feel for her is pity, since I seduced her mind and set her upon this hard road: women are frailer than we, and she has burned herself away in the fires of Love like a fly in a candle flame. For her soul I can do nothing; it inhabits a different world. But may I die a shameful death if I do not protect her noble body, worn and ravaged though it be, from all outrage! If blood must be spilled, let it not be hers.

When he reached the woodcutter's hut he took the woodcutter aside and said: "Since you give shelter to a man such as myself, you must needs love your country. Come, then, give me one of your axes, take the other yourself, and let us go into the city, to the great square where the fountain is. We shall see whether the men in these parts have courage—or whether they should be wearing skirts, like the women."

"The men in these parts," observed the woodcutter, "have never loved looters—or traitors."

Ricord stood on the great wooden well-cover, brandishing his ax in the air like a flag, and shouted: "All those here who dearly love Frenchmen and clerics, speak up, tell me your names: I have something to say to you! And let all who do *not* love such creatures hearken to my words! I am Ricord de Montgeil. The man who captures me will gain much wealth—though I do not think he will enjoy it for long! He who follows me will get little reward, and be a hunted man—but again, not for long. They will tell you I am a bandit. Believe you me, I have never taken a penny for myself, nor have I attacked any save my country's enemies. Know that I am related to one of those good ladies who live in the forest, and am of their Faith, as my father and grandfather were before me. Know too that I have always cared more for the poor than the rich, and for the weak rather than the strong!

"Our foe possesses horses and siege engines, spears and bucklers, swords and crossbows. He has chain mail, helmets, greaves, and gauntlets of steel. He holds the walls of our castles in fee, with granaries full of our corn and cellars laden with wine from our vineyards. He enjoys our women, from country and town alike. His men are so well fed and armored that it is small wonder if they fight well. The real men are those who have nothing but stout thews and a strong right arm; when *they* fight, it is not for the sport of it. Brothers, we are a hundred to their ten, a thousand for their every hundred: *we are stronger than they*. Let the man who lacks an ax bring a sickle; if you have not a sickle, then bring a knife; if you have not a knife, then cut yourself a cudgel, or fill your knapsack with stones!

"They are safe enough in their castles; but let us make them realize that once outside them they are always open to attack; let us get them so scared that they needs must draw their swords before passing any wayside rock or thicket! Then they may go back whence they came, taking with them their abbots and bishops and all the rest of their bloodthirsty crew—for just as they pretend to drink our Saviour's blood, so in truth do they drain that of our brethren!

"You, yes, *you*, who are staring at me now—you who are younger men than I am, you boys who have not a score of hairs in your beard yet—you live in good houses, all of you, where fires are lit daily—yet you let women old enough to be your mothers live out in the depths of the forest in log cabins—women of such sanctity that one tear of theirs is worth all the blood in your bodies! Are you worse than the very beasts of the field? Or is the life which is good enough for these women not good enough for you?

"The summer's labors are over and done: the harvest is gathered, the vintage is trodden, the olives are all picked. Do not stay at home, idling your time away! The hunt is up! If you love your country, do not stand by and watch it devoured alive! God and Christ Jesus are on our side, the God who forbids us to kill women and little children, or to wrong the poor: those who follow me will waste neither their time nor their labor."

That day Ricord gained thirty followers, and set them to collect axes, bows, broadswords, forge hammers, even pitchforks and scythes. It was decided that the group should leave town and camp out in the woods, near the Toulouse road. From this position they would be able to harry scouts, stragglers, and military dispatch-riders.

These townsfolk were hopeless soldiers; one Spanish mercenary was worth ten of them. But they were willing enough, and angry into the bargain: that very night the elderly cleric and all his family were slaughtered in their own house.

CHAPTER V
The Church Militant

THE following year Arsen and Fabrisse, with an escort from the Bishop to guide them, went south to Mirepoix. They badly needed this respite: the horrors which daily met their eyes on all sides, coupled with increasingly bad news, had both exhausted and deeply depressed them. It seemed that the Devil was indeed triumphant on earth, and that he was strong enough to rob all lost souls of their chance to win salvation. He had caused more than four hundred Christians to be burned in Lavaur, and more than a hundred on one pyre in Cassès; while the slaughters and burnings in Carcassonne and other towns were relatively infrequent, and by comparison not worth mentioning. The mountains were no longer a safe place of refuge. The town of Foix was badly overcrowded, and crammed with men-at-arms. The celibate orders (both of men and of women) had been forced to abandon their houses and seek refuge in friendly châteaux, or turn caves into hermitages.

Bishop Bernard had summoned all Christians whom his emissaries could reach throughout the Carcassès area to meet him in the Château de Mirepoix. Only about three hundred persons attended this gathering, over and above the knights and men-at-arms who belonged to the district, and a considerable number of the faithful—though the latter were warned not to stay in the locality for too long: it was vital not to attract the attention of such enemy detachments as might be patrolling the countryside thereabouts.

Long indeed was the list of casualties that the Bishop and his elder son read out to the surviving brothers, in order to make them aware of how the Church of Carcassès now stood in this, the fourth year of the war.

"There were more than a thousand of us," the Bishop said, "and our Church was justly spoken of as the most powerful in the land —though I do not say this to glorify ourselves at the expense of our brothers in Toulouse or Albi. At present, even with our new recruits, we barely number four hundred. But, sisters and brethren, let us take care not to ordain overhastily such of our flock as have not yet had their faith sufficiently tested. In these troubled times a postulant's fervor, admirable though it may be, is no guarantee of authentic faith.

"Let us also guard against ordaining those who, being ill instructed in the Faith and knowledge of God, might forget what true teaching they have acquired, and thus fall into heresy. Such people, though believing themselves to be serving God, would in fact be serving the Devil, and would sully the purity of our Church's doctrines with the imaginative fancies of their own hearts. Let no one among you say: 'The Holy Spirit that was conferred on me speaks now through my lips'; for the Spirit speaketh indeed, yet we know not how or when, since it is written that this Wind bloweth where it listeth.

" 'By this shall all men know that ye are My disciples, if ye have love one to another.' Did our Lord mean that love according to the flesh which today makes our tears to flow for those brothers and sisters who are gone from us? Far from it: the love He spoke of was that which binds all souls and spirits in God. So strong a bond is this that no man who endures it thinks his own thoughts any longer, but all as one think the Words our Saviour spoke, and lose themselves therein, and are consumed by them, as straw in the fire!

"He prayed not for the world, but for those who are beyond this world. Dear sisters and brethren, do not believe, as some simple souls believe, that He prayed only for those elect who have received the Holy Spirit. Every soul, from the most pure to the most erring, is outside this world to all eternity, and destined one day to return to the bosom of our Father. Let none of you so scorn a soul still wrapped in ignorance as to reveal to that soul anything but the pure doctrine of Jesus! Let no one among you say: 'This knowledge is too high for the poor in spirit; they must be brought by roundabout ways to their salvation.' There is one Way, and one only.

"This was ever the most pernicious of temptations; it was this caused Rome's downfall, and by this that the Devil lured our forefathers into idolatrous ways. There are those among you who say to their flock: 'Your souls shall be saved since the cause in which you fight is just.' By such words they put these poor folk's souls in great danger. For our cause is, indeed, both good and just; yet the Apostle has said: 'And though I bestow all my goods to feed the poor, and though I give my body to be burned, and have not charity, it profiteth me nothing.' Let no one among you entice his ignorant brother with a promise of salvation in return for some work in the flesh, worthy though that may be; for so do those against whom our struggle is!

"By this shall the world know that you are His disciples: let His Word shine forth in you, let it be your standard and your sword, your buckler and your raiment, your food, your labor, and your repose. Above all, keep His Word. Have no other desire or care than to enter into it, to be clothed and fed with it, till, God willing, the Word be manifest in you; for you will not win souls by a persuasive tongue, nor yet by good works. But if you become as windows, through which your brethren may perceive God's light, then you will have helped the Father to find His lost children once more."

The following day, in the castle armory, by the light of every taper and flambeau that could be collected from ten leagues around, the Bishop ordained thirty postulants, all of them men and women of mature years. The young ones he advised to return, for the time being, to the world. Among these latter was Gentian de Montgeil.

For over three years now Gentian had been preparing for the day when she would be received among God's Elect. She was neither idle nor frivolous, yet people always told her she lacked maturity. She was now in her twenty-second year; after three years of vigil and fasting she had become a lean, pallid creature, who almost seemed a young man in disguise. Her eager, quick expres-

sion had got her nicknamed "the Falcon"; her spiritual advisers
thought of her as a gifted child, but one who had not yet succeeded in ridding herself of all her devils. On the day when the
community was due to leave Foix, Gentian, together with three of
her companions, asked whether they might, as a favor, go to Mirepoix and participate in the meeting convened by the Bishop of
Carcassonne. She had frequently been told that she could not be
confirmed in the Spirit except by warrant of the Bishop.

When she thought of the misfortunes with which the country
was oppressed, Gentian shed no tears, as her friends did; she was
astonished at her own hardness of heart. Ever since the news of
the massacre at Minerve a vision had haunted her. She seemed to
see her mother's face, its skin all bloody and blistered, burned to a
crisp, eyes bursting, mouth wide open and screaming; yet this
vision caused her neither fear nor unhappiness, but merely a kind
of exaltation. She used its brutal details to temper her own heart
and senses; with grim and astounded delight she thought: If I
could stand that, I could stand anything. This is the cup which we
must drink, and the baptism wherewith we are baptized. As He
once demanded it of the Holy Apostles, so He now asks it of us;
and blessed are those who reply: We can endure all. Ah, my sweet
and gentle mother, let not my heart be troubled on your account;
if you ever suffer such a martyrdom it will be for God's sake! As
for myself, I shall go singing to the pyre.

The day when she heard the Bishop's request that young postulants of both sexes should return to the world, Gentian wept, for
the first time in three years. And on that same day she found out
that her mother was among those present at the meeting, with the
rest of the ladies who had come from the Carcassès district. The
postulants were given quarters in the barns and outhouses of the
château, and only saw the elect from a distance during the cere-
monies; besides, Gentian lacked curiosity, and was no gossip.

It was Aicart—recently promoted to the office of deacon—who,
having learned how sharp was the young girl's disappointment,
judged it advisable to tell her of her mother's presence.

"My lord," Gentian said, "you were the very first person who encouraged me to pursue the Way of Truth; it was you who long ago persuaded my mother and the noble Raymond to let me follow my vocation. You have not the right to abandon me now—you must intervene with the Bishop on my behalf! He does not know us; he judges us simply by our age. But God can call a soul to His service at any age, even in the cradle, or in the mother's womb, as it is written in the Psalms! You know me; it is your duty to speak up for me."

She had fallen on her knees now, head upturned, eyes desperately seeking his face. Aicart turned away lest he be stirred by pity for her.

"My daughter," he said, "who am I to set myself up against the decisions of my lord the Bishop? I am the youngest and least worthy among the deacons. And in truth I do not know you; it is the leaders of your own spiritual community who must speak for you."

"Master Aicart, without you I might never have renounced the world—yet you claim not to know me! Take care that you do not become that one through whom offenses come, the one for whom it were better that a millstone were hanged about his neck, and he cast into the sea! Without you I might still be in the world, perhaps married by now, and long since resigned to my lot. To make me renounce my desire now is more cruel than tearing off my breasts with white-hot pincers could be!"

At these immodest words Aicart felt his heart quicken, and the blood mounted so fiercely to his head that for a moment he was dizzied; he was not yet thirty-five years old, while the girl was both young and reasonably attractive. Since he had long supposed himself free of such temptations, he felt some alarm; his first instinct was to cry out: "Hence, you have a devil!" Then he controlled himself; he had no right to offend a pure and innocent soul. In a low voice he said: "It is not a truly charitable desire that can make you speak thus."

"I did not mean to hurt you," Gentian cried impulsively, and with naïve amazement. "I thought nothing could ever hurt you. I am not saying these things reproachfully; I am begging you to take pity on me."

"I have already told you that your most revered mother is here. It is to her that you should speak."

"You know very well that I have renounced all affections of the flesh. What can my mother do? She has never wanted to believe in my vocation. You are a deacon; you have greater authority. Think: if you reject my plea you risk damning my soul. Where am I to go? My brothers are soldiers, my father is fighting among the Albigensians, while my mother has given herself to God and cannot take me with her."

Aicart remained silent. Gentian thought: That's better, I've touched him; he's hesitating. She tried to guess what this man's own thoughts might be. There he stood before her, stiff and straight, arms crossed on his chest, eyes lowered, lips set in a stern line. She was amazed that she had never before noticed how extraordinarily handsome he was. Even with its present expression—stern, tense, withdrawn—his face made her think of one of the three young men in the fiery furnace, suffering Nebuchadnezzar's upbraidings. Does he think me so utterly unworthy of salvation? she wondered.

Finally she said: "Why do you stand there saying nothing? Why don't you answer my question?"

He shuddered; he had to make a great effort to keep his eyes on the ground.

"Say no more to me," he muttered. "I can do nothing for you."

"No!" she cried. "I can see that you feel pity for me. Did not our Lord say, Knock? It was you who reminded me of that, long ago; I have never forgotten it. Did He not say that we must not fear to ask and ask again, when it is the Bread of Heaven that we seek? I will be like that widow who exhausted the patience of the unjust judge. You have the right, and the power, and the necessary authority; you can gain me admittance into the Church. Ask my sisters whether I have incurred any reprimand during the whole of my three years as a novice!"

"I told you to say no more to me."

"Yet you are still listening. So you believe that I am not wrong. Monseigneur, there are many mansions—and many ways. Is youth in itself a fault? Is it culpable to desire passionately that which every soul should desire? God alone knows men's souls; you cannot judge them. He has brought me to you; do not reject me."

"Very well," Aicart said, in a brisk, impersonal voice. "I will mention your case to my lord Bishop. Now go, and pester me no longer."

In point of fact Aicart had been guilty, not exactly of a lie, but at any rate of an equivocation that sounded as though it were a promise. He begged an audience of Monseigneur Bernard that same day, and spoke to him about the girl from Montgeil as frankly as he could. He said he believed her to be sincere, but also hotheaded, full of pride, and little suited for the life of the Spirit. He made no attempt to conceal the carnal desire which attracted him to this young girl, and asked the Bishop to impose on him a penance and a period of retreat, since he did not feel worthy to continue in his ministry after so shameful a lapse.

The Bishop advised him to practice more frequent bloodletting, and not to waste time over futile thoughts. He also said he would find a noble and honorable family where the girl could be placed, either as maidservant or companion. Aicart felt he had acted for the best, after all.

For eight days now Arsen and Fabrisse had been enjoying a Paradisal existence: it seemed to them the life of the elect before God's throne must be cast in the same mold as this one, a sequence of communal prayer, conversation with friends, meditation, and the reading of Holy Writ. After the years of loneliness and fear, this intimate communion of brotherly love and trust was sweet indeed. Sweet too, for weary bodies, was it to rest in a house where one's only obligations were the hours of prayer and communal meals. Like pilgrims at the end of their journey, those who had led a hard life in forests and trudging long miles from place to place now relaxed into childish unconcern. What did tomorrow matter? What concern of theirs, even, were the misfortunes and miseries in the world outside? They would be back among them soon enough: but for now, God have compassion on all weary hearts!

Among those few dozen Christian women attending this gathering, Fabrisse found five or six of her old friends, and learned about the deaths of many others. Dame Agnes and Dame Serrone had both been burned at the stake in Lavaur. Arsen wept; yet she felt no real affliction. Her heart had bled too long, for too many friends; at present it was numb and wanted nothing but a little warmth. Fabrisse was coughing and spitting blood; Arsen herself had such sharp pains in every joint that she was unable to sleep. They had both passed through plenty of houses—a day here, two days there—but most often they had slept in the forest; always well forward, deep in occupied territory. They found that this mode of existence was, in fact, less risky than relying on the protection afforded by castle or château; it was still impossible to carry a forest or mountain by storm.

"Fabrisse, my sister," Arsen said one day, "before the war we had no idea what true joy was. Could we have guessed two months ago that we were to be reunited with our brethren in the Church, as in the old days? It is as though God had welcomed us into His Paradise."

"In some ways misfortune can be a blessing," Fabrisse said. "Perhaps, when the war is over, we shall come to regret its absence."

"So long as it *is* over, I would be prepared to miss it for the rest of my life! Sometimes I begin to think that you and I will never see the end of it."

Fabrisse sighed, and passed one hand across her sweating forehead.

"This illness of mine isn't dangerous," she said. "It's caused by cold weather. Summer isn't far away now."

The sisters from the Carcassès district were lodged in the weaving room, now transformed into a large dormitory for the occasion. The castellan's wife, a pious lady who herself had a sister in retreat at the Foix convent, looked after her guests as attentively as she could. She was continually having special dainties sent in to them: platefuls of choice fish, honey cakes, vintage wines. Sometimes she asked leave to bring her daughters and maidservants to see them: the visitors would stay kneeling in the doorway, eyes riveted on these saintly women as they read the Gospels or said their prayers.

Arsen thought: A month of this sort of life would tempt us into spiritual pride. Still, the laborer is worthy of his hire; and where shall we be tomorrow? She and Fabrisse, together with about a dozen of the younger women, were due to go back into the Carcassès area: the Church in those parts had been so sorely tried that the faithful were in danger of relapsing into Romish idolatry for lack of pastors. Those with previous knowledge of conditions there were better equipped to reorganize such believers as remained.

"For the present," the Bishop had told them, "the harmlessness of the dove is not enough; you must also possess the wisdom of the serpent, as our Lord prescribed. In order that you may the better elude the Devil's vigilance, you will travel in groups, two brothers and two sisters together. In each district you come to you will be known, not by a false name, but by some title or occupation in conformity with mundane requirements. Let yourselves pass as travelling hawkers, laborers, landless gentlefolk or out-of-work craftsmen, whichever seems most convincing and appropriate. This will not involve you in actual lies; you will not be obliged to make such claims yourselves. Those of the Faith who give you shelter will do so on your behalf. If and when you deem it necessary, you will be at liberty to separate from your brother or sister, and present to the world the appearance of two married couples. In such a case, however, each person concerned should maintain close contact with his real travelling companion, and always reside in the same place, whether it be town, castle, or village. None of you should take upon himself the least decision—about changing his district, for example, or holding a public meeting, or offering consolation to a dying person—without his companion's advice and consent. Our Lord sent out His disciples two by two, saying:

'Wheresoever two or three are gathered together in My name, there
am I in the midst of them'; but of a solitary man or woman He
never said the like. Two of you together represent the Church; but
one man alone, though he may be endowed with every gift of the
Spirit, resembles a hammerless anvil or a bow without arrows; one
man alone is hard put to it to conquer his individual will.

"Do not allow either the perils or the needs of your ministry
to lead you into any infringement of the Rule of the Church. In
times of stress we impose stricter discipline. Let none of you, in
seeking to deceive the vigilance of the Enemy, expose himself to
the risk of also seeking to deceive God. Let no one touch any
impure food, even with his finger tips; and if, for appearance's
sake, you are obliged to wear a knife at your belt, remove the blade,
and retain only the hilt and sheath. The Rule is the beginning of
obedience; he who sins against obedience destroys his own soul
and hinders the working of the Spirit in him, while he who consciously commits a single breach of the Rule has already destroyed
that Rule in his heart."

In a calm and somewhat melancholy mood the travellers prepared for their departure. The women patched their clothes, the
men repaired their shoes. The garments brought as gifts by the
faithful were distributed to the elderly, while offerings of money
were shared out equally among them all.

The summer is here, Arsen thought: God be thanked, we shall
no longer be cold. The summer is here; and how many swarming
crows with their scarlet crosses will it bring down on us?

The evening before they were due to leave, the lady of the
château came and told Arsen that her daughter was there, and
wanted to see her.

"So God has granted me this joy after all," Arsen said. "I
never hoped to receive it. How great is His bounty to me! I thought
my child was in the mountains; and she was here, only two steps
away from me!"

She dropped the cloak she had picked up and ran to the door.
Gentian was there; she had not even the time to kneel in greeting.

Her mother clasped the girl in her arms, and covered her cheeks and forehead with kisses.

"My little dove," Arsen said, "how tall and beautiful you have become! My heart is so full of happiness it can hardly bear it— that lovely hair of yours! And those bright eyes! Did *you* expect to find your old mother here?"

Gentian was weeping; she did not know whether it was for joy or sorrow. She thought she had hardened her heart; yet at the mere sound of that once dearly beloved voice, she felt herself become a child again. She slipped out of her mother's embrace and sank on her knees.

"It's true," Arsen said, smiling, "that I can bestow a blessing on you now. Tell me, though—have you found your true joy? Are you soon to enter the Church?"

The girl stiffened, and her expression became hard with disappointment as she said: "Mother, they are sending me back into the world."

"Not for long, my dove! When this war is over—"

"Mother," Gentian exclaimed, "don't you understand anything? Take a fish out of water for a quarter of an hour, and it dies. Mother, they want me to take a place in the Seigneur de Chazès's family—they have a château near Castelbon. To wait on his wife and daughters—I, who have never waited on a living soul!"

"The war has reduced many girls of noble family to living in strangers' houses," Arsen said. "Your uncles have left the district and have a house here no longer; I would be glad, myself, to know you were somewhere safe. You know the kind of risks a young girl runs in wartime."

"Mother, it is an affection of the flesh that makes you speak thus. In the old days virgins were known to bear witness to the Faith; they held their own with princes and converted the infidels."

"Then we must presume that in those times men were less perverse. I do not know how God protected these virgins you speak of, but I know only too well what life is like today in a country where the soldier reigns supreme. Be thankful that you have found some generous people who are willing to take you into their family: you would make me ashamed if you dared to complain of your lot."

"Then I shall shame you still further," Gentian said, "because I *am* complaining. My heart has burned with the desire to enter the Church for so long now that it is wholly consumed, and nothing can give it life again save the Sacrament that God has promised to those who truly desire it. Perhaps my heart is at fault, but who has the right to judge that? Mother, for three years now I have lived on my hope, and now I have come to the end. Are we to believe that baptism was instituted only for those, like yourself, who have always been good and pure? A stubborn and hardhearted person can be refashioned into a wholly new being. I do not lie when I tell you that I am nothing but an empty house now, ready to receive seven devils, all worse than the old one!"

Mother and daughter sat on bales of straw beside the door, while servant-women and visitors went to and fro, brushing them with their skirts as they passed. Gentian was talking in that loud, resonant voice of hers, which made the women stop and listen to what she was saying. She appeared not to notice them; her cheeks were flushed, and she tugged with nervous impatience at the long locks of hair spread out on her shoulders. Arsen sat erect and stiff, clasping her interlaced fingers ever more tightly in her lap; she was in tears.

"Have I come here just to see you cry?" Gentian demanded. "Are these tears your only reply to my questions? Do you remain unchanged, has the Spirit not made a different woman of you? Can you do nothing but weep and wish me in safety, like any other mother? You are leaving tomorrow. Will you be content at the thought of abandoning me to strangers? Do you suppose that all you need to do for any young girl is to lock her up in a strongbox like a gold coin?"

"What do you want of me?" her mother asked, in a broken voice. "Am I God? What can I do to help you? I am no longer even your mother; I have no part in you. According to the laws that have been laid down in our country since the war, you are an orphan now. Your father and I have both gone beyond the law. You are free; you need obey no one."

"Mother, I do not wish to cause you pain; but I see that henceforth I shall be forced to manage my life alone."

It was said of Aicart de la Cadière that his promotion to the rank of deacon had come as an inheritance; as Raymond de Ribeyre's companion for ten years he had been raised to the diaconate simply because his superiors wanted to honor the dead man's memory. At least, this was the opinion of those who did not care for him. In fact he was regarded as a man with only mediocre qualifications for the life of the Spirit; but his pugnacious energy made him a natural choice in those hard times. His place had been sought by men who were both older and more learned than he was: men who expressed their regret at the Bishop's thus resigning himself to the use of any fuel for the fire.

For these reasons Aicart and his companion left the château in a highly un-Christian frame of mind. A few days' respite, they felt, had been enough to renew all the bad old spirit of discord and intrigue; those brothers who lived a sheltered existence, well out of all danger, paid more attention to theological disputation and questions of precedence than to the struggle against Satan.

Renaud, Aicart's companion, was a man of about fifty: a tall, burly ex-blacksmith, as strong as a bull. He was one of those rough-spoken, quick-witted preachers who were openly accused of sympathy with the heresy held by the Poor Brethren of Lyons *;

* That is, the heretical sect of the Vaudois, formed independently of the Cathars at Lyons about 1170, and showing distinct characteristics, with a bias toward evangelicism. See C. Schmidt, *Histoire et Doctrine de la Secte des Cathares ou Albigeois* (1849), p. 68; and for a more modern treatment of the subject in English, Sir Steven Runciman's *The Medieval Manichee* (1947), pp. 124–25. These two books are essential reading for anyone wishing to make a further study of the Catharist heresy; in many respects they complement each other. Another most valuable study is J. Guiraud's *Histoire de l'Inquisition au Moyen Age* (Paris, 1935–8); and Mme Oldenbourg has now herself produced a scholarly, well-documented, and exhaustive study of the Albigensian Crusade and its climax, the massacre at Montségur, entitled *Le Bûcher de Montségur* (Paris, 1959).—Trs.

and indeed, the common people hearkened more readily to him as a result. He declared that in wartime old prejudices must be put aside, and that they should go forward hand in hand with the Lyons community. "For," he would say, "though their spirits may be in error, their hearts are not. Satan can recognize his true enemies better than we can; does not Rome press as hardly on them as she does on us?"

The two men, escorted by three armed attendants drawn from among the faithful, were approaching Carcassonne, where they had to make a halt in great secret. It was a clear night, and the road was deserted. It was dangerous to move by day, since Aicart was well known in the district. The three men-at-arms talked in a low voice, fearing they might disturb the meditations of their reverend companions. Aicart was looking up and watching the stars, in order not to let the hour of prayer pass wholly unobserved. There was such anguish in his heart that he could have wished never to need to look down at the earth again.

For more than two years now his heart had bled, and would not be staunched. For more than two years every step his new companion took throbbed through his head as though he had been struck by a mallet. Aicart had to struggle hard to stop himself from hating this worthy, estimable man, whose only fault was to be so different from the friend he had lost. The ox, Aicart thought, lets itself die of pure apathy when it loses its yoke companion; and the ox is a mere beast of burden. To us such weakness is forbidden —yet would that I had passed through the fire when he did! From my earliest youth he was the light of my life; the nights when I did not sleep at his side and the meals I have eaten apart from him I can number on the fingers of both hands. Today his spirit shines out among God's angelic host; yet such is the Devil's power that he can turn even the best and purest things to poison. By that very friendship, that great friendship which I bore him, my friend has pierced me to the heart, and those who have taken him from me have made him my worst enemy, since on his account I endure such suffering.

O Lord God, Aicart prayed, who hast such compassion for all souls that through fear of losing them Thou lettest this world continue to exist—O Lord, the blood of the just cries out to Thee from our wounded hearts; to save ten drops of the Water of Truth Thou wilt permit a whole mountain of evil to exist! O Lord, Thy pity is cruel; Thou givest unequal measure. Through the power of evil the flesh dominates the spirit—dost Thou know, O Lord, the strength of the flesh? The man whose bowels are torn out with pincers is but flesh and blood, though he may be the purest of the pure—

"Brother," Renaud observed, "it is the hour for prayer. Forgive me if I have disturbed your meditations."

"Thank you, brother. Please excuse my negligence."

The two men stopped; the soldiers left them by themselves and squatted down on their heels a score of paces away. They were utterly exhausted and stared at the two religious brethren with a certain grudging admiration: the latter, even after a ten hours' march, were capable of setting off again as though they had slept all night. They had limbs and hearts of steel. And if ever they got themselves caught, the soldiers thought, their number was up for certain. In order to get into Carcassonne they had to be at the outer gate before dawn, so that the guards (who had been fixed in advance) would not yet have been changed.

Beside the road, on the edge of a black, plowed field, the two men knelt and repeated the Lord's Prayer, text and gloss, prostrating themselves slowly after each verse; they were as solemn and impassive as though they had been in a candlelit room crowded with the faithful.

The soldiers lay stretched out in the grass and chatted in low voices to keep themselves from falling asleep.

"Are you sure of the sentry, anyhow?"

"Of course I am. He's my brother-in-law, I tell you. His daughter's been carrying on with one of those Northerners since last autumn, from Picardy he is. My brother-in-law says: 'It's an ill wind that blows no one any good.' "

"I haven't got any daughters, thank God. Think of all the bas-
tards this war has left us with; we can't drown them all, that's
certain."

"I'll tell you something, William: this Picard, now—if my
brother-in-law tells the fellow to go and sleep in his own bed,
there's no more cash, see? He pays for what he gets—"

"The girl must be a rare beauty, then. Still, if I were your
brother-in-law, I'd spend quite a few nights sharpening up my
knife against the day when our lot recaptures the town."

"Hey, you two," the third man said, "can't you find a more
decent subject while these holy brothers are praying?"

"Ah, well, I suppose it's a sin; but life's always pretty dirty in
wartime."

All three of them were thinking that the holy brethren's prayers
had gone on far too long: in order to arrive on time they would
have to prepare themselves for a six-mile forced march. They knew
what scorn and contempt any guide would incur who was clumsy
enough to let these men be arrested—men whose inability to tell
a lie rendered them especially vulnerable. Their guide was the
guardian of a priceless treasure. The enemy could only kill men's
bodies, but the death of one of God's ministers robbed souls of
salvation.

In Carcassonne, Aicart and Renaud were able to confer the baptism of the Spirit on some twenty seriously ill persons. Some of
these, fearing they might never again have the chance to purify
themselves and die a good death, deliberately hastened their end
by refusing attention and nourishment—a practice which shocked
some of the faithful. Aicart declared that, though he did not encourage such practices, every soul was free to choose its own way
once it had achieved unity with its heavenly essence—the death
of the body being a lesser evil than mortal sin.

After eight days of comings and goings by night in the outlying
parts of the town, scrambling through windows and over barn
roofs, preaching in kitchens by the light of a single candle, the
two men left Carcassonne. It was not common sense to stay there
any longer, and they were eager to get to their own "parish" in

the Minerve area: a rich Carcassonne merchant had, at Aicart's suggestion, placed at their disposal an estate he had there, on which he also ran a sawmill.

The preachers left town accompanied by the merchant's son, who was to sign them on as "sawyers"; they knew nothing of this trade, but were fairly well aware that in their case it would involve little manual labor.

That summer the harvest was rich. Though there was great fear of the enemy, nevertheless men who have grown accustomed to danger become skilled deceivers. It was possible to gather the faithful in their hundreds for a public sermon almost within bowshot of some enemy-occupied castle: in the woods perhaps, or some abandoned hamlet. Those who before the war had gone to Mass no longer cared to be reminded of the fact, while many clerics and priests came to hear the sermons, saying: "We do not hold your Faith, but we cannot endure to serve bishops such as these: they have abandoned our country to foreign domination."

PART THREE

The great sun that had arisen beyond the Pyrenees was extinguished almost before it appeared, devoured by the black dragon, and the land was plunged into darkness. Night had descended upon men's hearts: they wandered about like lost souls in broad daylight, no longer knowing which road to take.

Since the noble King of Aragon is no more there to protect us, and the other kings have abandoned us to the Church and her Crusaders, from whence will our salvation come? Foreign lords are like wolves in the sheepfold: the land entrusted to their authority is not their own, and all they think of is plundering it for their own enrichment. Accursed be the Church that violates not only God's law but man's, and robs men of the rightful possessions they inherited from their fathers! The very pagans do not act thus.

Behold the judgment of God: the Devil shall strike down all those who in true sincerity of purpose rise up against him. It has been made plain that the King of Aragon and those who fell in battle with him were just men: Satan knows how to pick his victims. All honor to those whom Death has taken; and God's mercy on those who live still!

CHAPTER VI

The Passion of Ricord

AUTUMN colored the hillsides golden and rusty red, and brought chill mists to the valleys. Scarcely one field in four was tilled; the others remained yellowish gray, like an old man's beard. On the slopes lay rows of torn-up vines, roots in the air, black and twisted, like an army of devils petrified in mid-flight. Even the most frugal of troops now found it impossible to live off the land; it was becoming increasingly difficult to raid enemy convoys, since the Crusaders too had acquired some knowledge of the terrain.

Ricord had about two hundred men in his band at the moment, but could not rely on the local burghers to keep them victualled. Your average burgher was only too glad to let you defend him, but kept his corn in the granary and his cash under lock and key. Ricord thought: It is not seemly behavior to withhold bread from poor peasants who may get none till Christmas. But the soldier too is a human being, and one who leads a hard life: battles and ambushes and man hunts in summer, in winter cold and starvation; while if he lets himself be taken alive he is liable to be roasted alive, or to suffer mutilation. Every laborer, even though his hands are not clean, is worthy of his hire.

For fifteen years now I, Ricord de Montgeil, have lived by the labor of my own two hands. My children's bread, the wool my wife spun and wove, the game I shot—all these I have given to the poor. Often when I came home from a day's hunting without any food for my own household I would explain that the poor folk down the valley stood in greater need of it. And now, after fifteen years of this life, I have turned looter, and send my men out to get their food where they can find it. Alone, a man can think about his soul's salvation; but God has set in my heart an unassuageable anger. Alone I am nothing: with my men I can inflict hurt upon our country's enemies.

Already I have lost too many of these followers of mine, by cruel deaths at crossroads or in city squares: yet their mutilated corpses, dangling from trees, have not scared those of us who survive. The soldier deserves his pay; to dice endlessly with Death is a hard trade.

During Christmas Ricord made his men camp in a certain wood close to a grotto where two saintly hermits lived. Despite their widespread reputation, these holy men had hitherto enjoyed God's protection: the grotto was difficult of access, and the approaches to it were guarded by reliable sentries. Among Ricord's men there were some staunch believers; and anyone, be he a mere brute beast, needs to cleanse his soul during the great Christmas fast.

The faithful had to await their turn for several days, and then clamber up the face of the rock in little groups; there was a great number of them hoping to see the holy men. Meanwhile they remained scattered about the valley, where they lit fires of brushwood, and grilled their fish or mulled their wine. The sick went up first, and the dying were hauled up on mattresses to which ropes had been attached.

What with the stench of unwashed bodies and foul linen, the air in the grotto was extremely unpleasant to breathe. The hermits' actual cell had been made from a hollow cleft in the rock, and here they kept tapers burning day and night; the gifts of the faithful never failed. They were old, black-robed men, with long, white hair; it was said that they had not left their cell for the past ten years. The elder of the two was vowed to silent prayer; only the younger spoke to the faithful.

He sat on a high stone seat, from which he never shifted, his hands clasped on his knees. His long, fine, close-shaven face looked as though it were modelled in brown wax. When he spoke, he did not look at the devotee kneeling before him, but kept his eyes fixed on a great square cross carved in the rock wall.

"My son," he said, "God has not sent us here to pass judgment on worldly matters. Of such things we know nothing. You speak of what is far from our understanding. In God's eyes a war destroys as many souls as a great famine; the death of a king differs in no respect from that of the lowliest beggar. You speak of the enemies of our country; but God has no country, and only one Enemy. In truth, the affairs which preoccupy you do not of themselves possess either truth or substance; they resemble those castles of mud and pebbles which little children construct."

Ricord said: "I am very nearly an old man now. I know only too well the nature of those evils which destroy men's souls. Death and anger are not mere child's play."

"You are wrong, my son. All things human are child's play, and less than child's play: its shadow merely. For there is no truth in the body and all that pertains to it—our thoughts, our passions, our individual wills. Only one thing in man is true: his agony of soul. Like a caged beast, the soul struggles and writhes in its longing to be united with that celestial Spirit which it has lost. In this alone men are not children; for each immortal soul is by itself greater than the whole world, which is mortal.

"As children are greater than the mud castles they build, so men's souls are greater than their lives. The children engage in mock battles; they kick over their playmates' castles, and run wailing for their mothers; but an immortal soul can no more be destroyed than a block of marble can be dissolved in water."

"If there is no true substance in evil, then," Ricord asked, "why should it cause us such affliction? Do you call the torturing of innocent people till they die *child's play*?"

"My son, all is shadow and child's play, save the cry of a soul cut off from God. The hands of the executioner are not in themselves evil, nor are his pincers and red-hot irons. There is no evil in the heart of an executioner, for he is made of perishable matter, whose law is to obey the Devil who molded it. But the agonized cry of an outraged soul is like that of a child to its father: both appeal and accusation. Could you be so blind as to doubt our Father's compassion?"

"No," Ricord said, hesitantly. "But if I have of my own free will caused the deaths of other men, what fate will God hold in store for me then?"

"The executioner's fate: eternity of darkness. The murderer and the voluptuary inflict their own punishment on themselves: they bring their soul by violence down to the level of their body, and plunge it into a black pit where it loses all power of distinguishing good and evil."

"I can see evil still," Ricord said.

"Evil is everywhere; the whole world can see it. But to see the good is another matter. In every man there is a tiny window, as it were, designed for this purpose, but obscured with vapor, and dust, and every sort of impurity. It is so hard to see through this window clearly that we often mistake one thing for another, and are covered with confusion. But you have done worse: you have put up a great wooden shutter in front of this poor window, and have scarcely one slender crack left for a little daylight to pass through. In these times there are many, many souls such as yours."

Ricord returned to his men in a thoughtful and scarcely reassured mood. The old man's words had brought him little comfort, and he no longer found any satisfaction in prayer. A strange bitterness took possession of him. If the very people he was defending regarded him as butcher and brigand, what was left for him? The war was not nearly over. He could no longer find refuge in the châteaux, for they were either occupied or had surrendered. More than one landowner in the district secretly approved of him, yet did not hesitate to treat him as a common bandit. He was much less concerned with ending the war than with seeing that he was not taken alive.

At present the Crusaders no longer maintained regular fighting armies in the area; instead, they were hunting down the guerrilla bands that had gone to ground in the forests. Could one, Ricord asked himself, forbid troops to plunder when they got no pay, and were hungry? Nowadays the Crusaders had no difficulty in getting the villagers to give them information. "They came through here a couple of days back," they would say, "on their way up the valley.

You'll find their camp on the other side of the mountain yonder."
Truly, O Lord, our mud castles and pebble fortresses are very dear
to us; and so is our hatred, dear Lord, for henceforth it is our sole
possession. Better to bang that wooden shutter fast, and not let a
single ray of sunshine filter through it. My heart is old and tired;
all it desires now is the blood of those who have butchered my
country. Such blood is good to look upon; it has not the same color
as the blood of innocents.

Near Moissac Ricord's band was broken up: more than fifty of
them were killed, another score or so had their hands and feet
lopped off and were hanged from the nearest trees. The Crusaders
lost only a dozen men, and they were small fry; the rest had good
coats of mail.

"Where shall we make for now?" the survivors asked Ricord.
"They're bound to find us again soon with all these wounded."

"Brethren," Ricord said, "better a swift death for some than the
rack for us all. Take those who cannot march, and finish them off
—and may God have mercy on us; it is for Him that we are fighting."

Scarcely one in three of Ricord's men still concerned himself
about God; the rest thought above all about not being taken. Yet
even so they felt proud to be told that they were soldiers of God.
What remained of the band now retreated toward the district
around Minerve, hoping to join up with some stronger and better-
armed detachment.

"O Lord God," Arsen cried, "Thou hast summoned me, and
I am here. Wilt Thou now make me regret my obedience? To follow Thee I have abandoned my child, left her alone in the world,
delivered her into the Tempter's hands. If I have not even been
able to save the souls of those I loved, how then could I be
worthy to serve Thee?"

She wept so copiously throughout this prayer that finally her
companion rebuked her, saying that she was allowing true prayer
to degenerate into mere self-indulgence.

"What can we do, my sister?" Arsen replied. "We are living in a wretched and pitiable age. Human instinct is not dead in us, only held down."

"Ah, that I know well; there is a great price to pay if we will attain to joy in God. I too had my time of tears, during my first years in the convent. The devil of barren tribulation has a hard life: he wears the appearance of neighborly love."

"Oh, barren love," Arsen said, "unprofitable love! *That* is the thorn in the flesh of which the Apostle speaks. It is only just that I should pay the price for my life in the flesh; I have not yet forgotten its joys."

The two women were at present living in the lumber yard attached to the big sawmill: they were employed in various tasks, such as repairing clothes and doing the washing. When they went around the area on circuit they always had two or three men with them as an escort.

The Bishop had not been wrong to trust Aicart's abilities; the sawmill developed into a prosperous and more or less peaceful community. It even boasted a Catholic chaplain (a clerical convert, in fact), and every Sunday, for appearance's sake, a large body of the faithful would attend Mass in the nearby town. There were rather too many visitors at the yards, and, indeed, too many inexperienced workmen; but no man could be signed on unless he had the password.

One fine day the Bishop paid a visit to the sawmill in person, disguised as a candle-seller; and indeed, so many candles were lit in the big timber shed on this occasion that it shone brighter than any church on Christmas Eve. Three new ministers were ordained, and several others reconfirmed in their ordination. There was much need of this latter ceremony: the hazards of war exposed Christians to many temptations and infringements of the Rule.

From a member of the Toulouse brotherhood Arsen had heard news of her daughter, and her heart had found no peace since. It was not good news. Gentian had gone to Toulouse with one of her companions, the daughter of a noble and wealthy widow. Among the nobility of the town the young girl had acquired, not exactly a bad, but certainly a dubious, reputation. They said she received visitations of the Holy Ghost; she fell into trances, and made what some took to be prophetic utterances. On the day of the battle of Muret she first fainted, and then foretold the death of the King of Aragon and of many other knights whose names she had not so much as heard before. For eight days she remained in bed, unable to eat, and bleeding from the mouth and nose: she said she was dying because of all the blood that had been shed in the battle. She also on occasion made public pronouncements, in the presence of her hostess's friends. Since the town was, for the moment, under the Bishop's control, and the girl's utterances contained frequent pointed references to the Bishop himself, her situation was a dangerous one—all the more so since the noble lady in whose house she was, not being of a timorous nature, openly boasted that she was sheltering one of God's elect.

Arsen had always considered large cities to be places of perdition, and Toulouse worse than any other. She was far more concerned for her daughter's soul than for her body: by now she had witnessed so many horrors that physical fear seemed to her the merest childishness. The day when she learned that her second son, Olivier, had been killed at Narbonne, she had not the strength to weep. She gave thanks to God for having accorded her child a quick and honorable death: a pure heart did not lose its chance of salvation by such a demise. Blessed are those, Arsen thought, who have not been led by their ignorance into the ways of evil, and who will be reborn in a happier life! My son will never know what miseries have been spared him.

One day a soldier arrived at the sawmill, desperately ill, his right arm rotted away with gangrene. For two days and nights he had been hunted through the forest, and now he had come here to die as a Christian. He brought with him a letter from Ricord, for his wife.

"Noble lady and deeply revered companion," Ricord wrote, "I do not know if you have heard that our son Olivier is dead; he was on the wall at Narbonne, and a crossbow bolt lodged in his left eye. We shall never see him more; ten years of calling his name would not bring him back to us. This bereavement strikes me so cruelly that it has well-nigh robbed me of my reason. Beloved sister, I put my honor, my life, my very soul in peril without consideration either for myself or for you; but I still hoped that the evil would spare our children, that they would live to see the end of our tribulations, and return home once more.

"It is not my old, worn-out body that Satan has been pleased to destroy, but that of my young and handsome son. I have good tidings of the other three; but when one hears good tidings of a soldier one must needs fear the worst. If they have won a high reputation it is by risking their persons constantly. Yet I rejoice at the news nevertheless, for if they must live in this world, it is well that they should live according to an honorable code.

"My dear, dear friend, do not feel either fear or regret on my behalf. One day my courage failed me, and Satan sent me comfort of a bitter sort: how could I withdraw from the fight when I still had my son to revenge? May God grant that we see one another again when this accursed war is over. The joy of that will be such as to make us forget all our afflictions, and the whole land will be covered with beacon-fires as thick as blossom on an apple tree in spring. Never will our country have known such happiness, and it will be by our tears and blood that we shall have won it. The measure is so full now that God's justice cannot long be delayed.

"Of your great and generous bounty, pray for your faithful companion and servant."

Before he died, the soldier was able to see Arsen and talk to her about her husband. This man worshipped Ricord like a saint: never, he said, was any commander more just to his men, more wholly devoted to God's cause, more relentless in pursuit of the enemy, more selfless, sober, chaste, or more inured to all danger. "For such a man," he told her, "one would really go through fire and water; he never wronged a living soul." Arsen was amazed at this in her heart of hearts, for the soldier had just been telling her how Ricord clubbed foemen to death when they fell off their horses, and had monks hanged, or cut their throats. But then she told herself that this man was right. Such was the blinding power of the flesh that one did not *see* the enemy as one killed him; what one struck seemed no more than a kind of wooden puppet. Ricord, Ricord, Arsen thought, Heaven grant that it was thus with you, and that in your heart you never wronged anyone!

Aicart de la Cadière was enjoying (without any mental reservations or ulterior motives) the pleasure of solitary travel—or, at least, with no more than a simple member of his flock for company. That special companionship imposed by God could be either a comfort or a stern ordeal, according to His unpredictable will.

For some while now the deacon had resigned himself to treating his new companion as a cross he must bear without complaint. He could not find fault with Renaud in any way: the man was tireless, invariably good-tempered, humble, virtuous, a staunch laborer in God's cause. The two men had never exchanged a cross word or so much as an unkind glance; each would have given his life for the other. Yet they did not feel any mutual friendship. Sometimes a mole on the chin, or an overloud voice, or an indelicate way of blowing one's nose can be quite enough to produce such an antipathy. The Devil, failing in his efforts to corrupt the elect with major temptations, afflicts them with such small vexations which, by daily repetition, finally become unbearable. When Renaud was out of sight, Aicart was quite ready to praise his worthy qualities.

He was now on his way to Toulouse, where he had to meet several of the brethren, and renew his contacts with such of the faithful from the Carcassonne diocese as had been forced by the war to seek refuge in the city itself. These folk, he had heard, were allowing themselves to slip into various regrettable errors of conduct. They defied the authority of their local ministers, refused to pay their debts, and had relapsed into certain superstitious practices: for example, they venerated as "relics" the ashes and bones of those martyrs who had died at the stake.

Furnished with a letter from the Bishop, which he carried sewn into his belt, Aicart was travelling disguised as a cloth merchant; the lay member who acted as his guide was a clothier from Toulouse. These deceits practiced at one remove no longer pricked his conscience; they were merely irksome in so far as they exposed him to infringements of the Rule. At this moment he was reduced to saying his prayers silently, while he waited with a group of fellow travellers for the ferryboat that would convey them across the Garonne. Among them were some women, with whom he must avoid all physical contact—yet without excessive discourtesy; and one or two drunken men who were singing a lewd song.

The river was in full spring flood; its yellowish, fast-flowing waters had risen high enough to submerge the bushes along the banks, and even the young willows. The ferry made slow progress, struggling against the current. Aicart, sitting on a pile of canvas covers in the bow, concluded his prayer in a state of mind which he knew all too well, and for which he condemned himself bitterly. He felt that someone was watching him; and though he was not exactly frightened, he was, so to speak, held captive by those staring eyes, in the sense that he had no way of being certain that they were friendly. Several times already his face had betrayed him, but always in towns, where it was easier to shake off pursuit.

But no, the man watching him now was no traitor. I ought to have seen it sooner, Aicart thought: how well he knew that expression, full of affection and reverence, which he so often encountered on chance-met, unfamiliar faces during his journeyings! It was in vain that he told himself that his individual personality had nothing to do with such a reaction; the pleasure he derived from it was not wholly devoid of pride. The man who had now recognized him was a lean, tense person, dressed in a poor-quality leather cuirass. His short black beard was sprinkled with white hairs; there were deep-etched wrinkles at the corners of his eyes, and the eyes themselves glowed with a flame of inner joy. Yet on his sorrowful features this joy shone like the lurid glow that hangs above a burning house.

Aicart smiled, to make him understand that his, Aicart's, period of prayer was now over. The man drifted across to him, as though inadvertently, and said in a low voice, keeping his eyes fixed on the swollen river: "There are five of us here, my lord, who would rather be cut into little pieces than allow one single hair of your head to be harmed."

Aicart said, half smiling: "My hairs are not worth that much; and I do not know whether you and I intend taking the same road."

"If you will do us the honor of accepting us as your escort, your road shall be ours."

Aicart distrusted such willing volunteers, who were inclined to sin through sheer excess of zeal. These, besides, looked suspiciously like soldiers of fortune, wandering freebooters, so he advised them to think rather of their own safety. But as their leader was the famed Ricord de Montgeil, who had hunted down Crusaders in the Carcassès district with such notable success, the deacon agreed to let them accompany him for a league or two, so that they should not fancy he disdained their company.

He recalled now that this Ricord had formerly been a man of austere ways, and one well instructed in the Faith; so he lavished on the old soldier all those special sorts of solace which he knew were liable to move him most. Aicart was aware that the war had aroused a frightful bloodthirstiness in many of these wolves who had become lambs for love of their Faith; such men must be handled with care, for their souls were devoured by a spiritual thirst that could never be appeased. The road back was closed to men like Ricord; they resembled windfall apples, fruit that had dropped from the bough.

"When you pray to God, my brother," he told Ricord, "what is the first thing you ask of Him? Why, that He will bring you to a good end. This means that life is never good of itself; only death can be either good or bad. This body of ours is a filthiness, utterly offensive in God's sight; yet we bear it with us to our dying day, as the leper bears his sores. That is why death alone is good— that death which delivers us forever from the bondage of the flesh. No man should be so cowardly as not to hope for such a death.

"For merits in this life, whether good actions or pious thoughts, are as nothing. Against God's shining purity the life of the saint shows well-nigh as sin-besmirched as that of the criminal. The difference is so small, my friend, that even the eye of the angels has never discerned it. It is only in the final moment of dissolution that we become free to choose between lies and truth."

"Our life is by no means too long a preparation for this choice," Ricord said, "and many men, because of the war, are so plagued with earthly tasks that they scarcely have time to pray."

"My friend, no living person has ever so much as glimpsed the splendor of that harvest of reclaimed souls which will one day arise from the earth, like a great field of wheat in which every separate ear is a star. When that day comes the laborers and the sowers and the harvesters shall share in its joy. But what of those who protect the field against the ravages of hare or boar? Will their recompense be the less? Will not the Lord say to them on that day: 'Come and sit on My right hand, all ye who saw Me naked and bleeding and exposed to the knives of murderers, and who raised your swords in My defense'? And they will say: 'Lord, when did we ever see Thee under the assassin's knife?' Verily these too shall share in God's peace, even as they shared the labor."

"My lord," Ricord said, "such promises are not in Holy Writ. It is your generosity in the flesh that makes you speak thus."

"No, my friend. These promises are written in letters of blood, on this same martyred soil that we tread underfoot today. When the Pharisees said to our Lord: 'Master, rebuke Thy disciples,' He replied: 'I tell you that, if these should hold their peace, the stones would immediately cry out.' There are times when not the stones only but the very wells and trees and city walls cry out and testify in the voices of those many thousand souls who died cruel deaths there! Truly, the man who has not stopped his ears to that cry—even though death find him in a state of sin—is making ready for a better life, and is very near his final deliverance."

"Ah," Ricord said, "would to Heaven every man might have the joy of hearing such comfortable words! I have lost one of my sons in this war. Blessed indeed are they who do not know the pangs of fleshly affection."

Ricord and his company bade the deacon farewell, and knelt to receive his benediction. Aicart recommended them not to put themselves in unnecessary danger, and gave Ricord an ancient fragment of Greek copper, with three notches cut in its rim.

He said: "If ever one of you finds himself in imminent peril of death, let him, if he can, send this piece of metal to any minister of God who may be in the neighborhood."

Ricord hid the copper fragment in the tiny leather pouch that hung from the sheath of his dagger, and watched the deacon and his companion dwindle into specks along the Toulouse road. He thought: Happy the father who begot such a son. May God preserve him, as He did the three young men flung into the fiery furnace. What would our lives become without shining lights of God? Then his heart sank as he thought of the deacon's face: would it not betray him more surely than ever the black habit would have done? He was filled with burning compassion for this frail creature, blown by the wind of the Spirit, like a feather on the breeze, from town to town, from one peril to the next. Ah, he thought, if only we could build a rampart with our bodies to protect all such men—if only we could cheat the executioners, and die in their stead! What agonies would one not accept as the price of such an honor?

When, O Lord, have we seen Thee under the assassin's knife? When was it? Lord, it was *Thy* throat I slit, not the monk's; *Thy* skull I split the other day, not the skull of that young, freckle-faced boy. Murderers, murderers of murderers, till the end of the world —where should we seek Thee, Lord? How can we recognize Thy face? O Lord, when we protect Thee against the murderers, it is Thee whom we kill. I know it, Lord, I have always known it, yet I cannot stop: every man must drink his cup to the bitter dregs.

CHAPTER VII

Aicart

FOR months now Gentian had been living in a dream, where all was scarlet and black and gold; a dream in which the faces of the dead mingled with those of the living, and the sun was liable to rise in the middle of the night. She was not at all happy: the tumult in her blood kept her ears ringing continuously with battle cries, with shouts of triumph or agony, while her eyes were flooded with so brilliant a light that at times she could not see her actual surroundings. She reached the point of wondering whether she had not died long since and been reincarnated in some alien body, so strange was the life she was now forced to lead.

The room she occupied was small and round. Its stained-glass window was fitted with heavy bars, and looked out over a narrow street. One could see little through it apart from the house opposite, with its pink wall and little square windows; and the gray flagstones down in the street, divided by a noisome water conduit; and a couple of tall stone posts fitted with heavy iron rings, which were used for tethering horses. From dawn till midnight a continual stream of people on horseback or on foot surged past the house. The shouts of hawkers, water carriers, and tumblers mingled with oaths, bursts of laughter, and the neighing of horses; sometimes people came to blows, and stones would rattle against the window bars. The church bells were rung six times every day.

In spring and summer it was advisable to keep one's windows shut because of the filthy stench in the street outside; the air in the rooms was hot and sluggish, and Gentian found the smell of perfumes, burnt amber, and Eastern spices quite overpowering.

The room was hung with crimson tapestry, which showed a pattern of birds and foliage; the coffers were covered with painted leather. Gentian had two young maidservants allotted to her service, but hardly ever spoke to them except to ask to be left alone. In point of fact she was never left by herself for very long. The rich luxury of the house in which she was living did not bedazzle her; but occasionally the patterns of the tapestry or the carving on the lectern would set her dreaming.

Because of the horrible dreams she had had in it she did not like this room of hers. But in the main hall, where she often sat with her hostess, the Lady de Miraval, she felt herself keyed to so intense a pitch of awareness that it terrified her. Her body vibrated silently, like a cord stretched to breaking point—taut, so taut, so charged with latent power that she felt as though she could push the walls over with a single tap of her elbow. Sometimes, among the Lady de Miraval's many guests, she would see a face that caught her attention: this frightened her, because she did not enjoy the vision that was likely to follow. Once she was imprudent enough to exclaim: "My God, the poor woman! Fancy losing both her son and her lover on the same day!" This double disaster did, in fact, overtake the unfortunate lady in question—but not till a month later, when both the young men involved fell fighting, side by side, near Foix.

"Can you see my son?" they would ask her now, or "Can you see my brother?" To all such poor, foolish creatures she returned the same answer: No. In three out of four cases she in fact saw nothing; and when she did it was more often than not bad news. "Ladies," she would say, "for pity's sake do not torment me like this! It was not for the sake of such visions that God laid His hand on me. He is testing me severely enough already; do not add to my burden the fear of causing you grief." The ladies—and indeed the men too—bowed to her wishes, and passed on their inquiries through the Lady de Miraval or her daughter.

The Lady de Miraval was a still beautiful woman, intent on adorning her soul with virtues in the same way that she decked out her person with jewelry. In consequence she had a notable reputation and standing among the high-born ladies of Toulouse.

Despite wartime conditions her town house was still lit with a mass
of wax candles, and twice a week she gave lavish banquets, with
music and dancing: her stables were not large enough to hold all
the guests' horses. In her house people spoke their minds freely.
Those suspected of indiscreet gossip outside were more than likely
to end up with a dagger between their ribs at some lonely street
corner: the Lady de Miraval's serving-men lacked neither courage
nor devotion to their mistress. The noble lady herself was highly
respected by those in authority, and knew that she stood beyond the
arm of episcopal justice. When she went to church priests and
clergy greeted her with deference, even though they knew her to
be so shameless a heretic that she openly mocked the Mass and the
Church's most solemn doctrines.

Her daughter came back from her convent with a companion,
whose family had been scattered by the war. Alfaïs de Miraval was
always glad to give hospitality to impoverished daughters of the
nobility; but she hardly expected to discover a phoenix among her
doves, as she always referred to them. She developed an inordinate
passion for Gentian de Montgeil, giving her the guest of honor's
seat at her table, loading her with gifts, and watching the least
change of expression on her face with a view to anticipating her
desires. How, she wondered, had this strange clairvoyant power
first come to descend upon the girl? In the beginning she had kept
silent most of the time, as though too scared to speak, coming to
life only when she sang. Her voice was so lovely that the Lady de
Miraval decided to teach her music, so that she might accompany
herself on the cittern. Gentian very quickly learned to play this
instrument, and became particularly adept at improvising songs—
though they more often treated of war than of love.

After the battle of Muret, which made so many widows and
orphans in Toulouse, and left the town wide open to attack, Gentian de Montgeil found herself promoted to the rank of prophetess;
and that was no less than her due, for she had been in such agony
of mind on the day the battle was fought that she all but died of it.

When the possession came upon her she would speak of angels
falling from the heavens like arrows of fire, and of the mighty

clamor that all the souls who had died ill sent up to Heaven, and of the victory that God promised to the Count of Toulouse—in the foreseeable future, she said, but after many misfortunes. When those who had not met Gentian said she was nothing but a hysterical child, Alfaïs de Miraval was wont to reply that she, Alfaïs, knew the difference between an emerald and a green glass bead. And in point of fact this young girl was possessed of so powerful and striking a voice that simply to hear her speak dispelled all doubts about her. What she said pleased a good many people for reasons which had little to do with spiritual grace. Monseigneur Foulques, the Bishop of Toulouse, Count Simon de Montfort, and the Archbishop of Narbonne were condemned by her to such torments that her listeners thought: May God heed her words! Her times of inspired utterance apart, she was a modest, simple, somewhat melancholy girl; neither the gifts she possessed nor the attention which they drew upon her made her in the least vain.

One day the Lady de Miraval had a somewhat stormy discussion with several ministers of her Church. Since the latter were compelled to live in hiding, and were in any case hostile to worldly pleasures, they came to see her only at night. On these occasions she would assemble her whole household, together with numerous friends and acquaintances; in this house one could always be certain of hearing a sermon through without any untoward interruptions. On the day in question, the Lady de Miraval's spiritual adviser, that venerable figure Jacques d'Ambialet, happened to observe that it was unfitting for a girl who had not received the Spirit to preach in public and make prophecies.

"The Spirit," retorted Lady Alfaïs, "bloweth where it listeth; this child has undergone a lengthy period of preparation, and I judge her worthy of admission to the Church."

"The Church judges otherwise, my lady. Please make the girl realize that she has no authority to say she has been sent by God."

"Then it is your business to confer such authority on her!"

D'Ambialet, who was a mild person by nature and had great respect for Lady Alfaïs, explained the girl's position. She was answerable to the bishopric of Carcassonne, and could not be bap-

tized by a Toulouse minister. The old man, overflowing with
charitable condescension though he was, had a soft spot for Gentian de Montgeil himself: he was delighted to learn of Deacon
Aicart de la Cadière's presence in Toulouse on a special mission.
So it came about that, at Jacques d'Ambialet's request, Aicart was
led into another meeting with the person he had hoped never to
see again in this world.

"Yes," he told the old man, "I do know her—in so far as we *can*
know a woman, in other words hardly at all. But her mother, who
is a true Christian both in word and in deed, has never believed in
her sense of vocation."

Jacques d'Ambialet observed that a girl's mother, whether Christian or no, was not always the best judge.

"This girl," he said, "has declared to me that you encouraged
her in her vocation when she was living with her family."

"That is true," Aicart said, lowering his eyes. "At that time the
noble Raymond was still among us, and I was a different person.
At the moment, even if we did not have formal instructions from
our Bishop on the subject, I would do nothing to encourage a pre-
mature sense of vocation."

"But nevertheless," the old man asked him, "have we the right
to abandon a soul in mid-career? Who knows whether this particular soul may not be going out of her wits from sheer despair, because, though intensely aware of her heavenly Spirit's presence, she
yet must perforce suffer in isolation? I have known several similar
cases. Does the disposal of God's divine grace rest in our hands?
Are we to judge who is worthy of it? None of us has ever been
worthy; and yet we have received it."

Aicart told himself that this old fellow (however venerable)
was well past adapting himself to contemporary conditions; he
was still living in an age when the security of the convents allowed
even the most mediocre of vocations to develop and blossom. He
said: "We can never meditate sufficiently on the parable of the
sower: every soul is new ground, and the one we are discussing
seems to me to be stony soil, where the seed grows fast, yet withers

at the first touch of sun. Are we to copy our enemies in Rome, and regard our baptism as a miraculous panacea that can create something out of nothing?"

"Look at yourself," the old man said. "Were *you* a fountain of pure light on the day of your ordination? For forty years I have struggled in vain to be worthy of the ministry entrusted to me; yet I shall never dare to claim that in me the Word found fertile soil."

"Very well," Aicart said. "We shall look into the matter together, and see if a new period of probation may suitably be granted to this girl. I advise you to summon her for interrogation in private. One should never allow this sort of person to suppose that they are regarded as anything out of the ordinary."

Jacques d'Ambialet was lodging with a merchant who dealt in ladies' shoes, purses, belts, and other similar objects made from highly worked leather. Gentian went thither accompanied by the Lady de Miraval's son and daughter, and slipped through into the back part of the shop while her companions lingered out front, examining belts, gloves, and dancing pumps, and haggling with the proprietor.

D'Ambialet sat bent over a small table, pen in hand, reckoning up columns of figures on a long paper scroll. The table itself was covered with various documents and little piles of coin. He was a good accountant, and had the most recent quotations for every European and Eastern currency at his fingertips; so there was no difficulty in justifying his presence in the shop. Aicart was also there; he stood examining a heap of purses in embossed leather, which lay piled up on the big chest.

When Gentian saw this small, fleshless old man, with his white and curling locks, acting out the role of a bookkeeper, and the deacon beside him, disguised as some wealthy client, a strange feeling of pity took possession of her. It was as though the doctrine which teaches that the soul must pass through various successive lives as part of its self-redemption had here found a visible embodiment. She was not certain she recognized this handsome man in his doublet of rich cloth: it was he, yet not he. Despite the somewhat stiff nobility of his gestures, he looked so exactly like a man of the world that she felt a shade embarrassed at kneeling before him to ask a blessing. He stretched out his hand, with that imperturbable gravity which comes from repeating the same gesture and formula hundreds of times. "May God make a good Christian of you," he said, "and bring you to a good end." She rose, curtsied, and then knelt before Jacques d'Ambialet.

"My child," the old man said, "you must not be shocked by these outward appearances which we are compelled to assume on account of the secular authorities. God is present at all times and in all places, and more especially wherever two or three Christians are gathered together in His name. Now, Master Aicart the deacon, whom you know well, is ready to question you on your Faith, and offer you such advice as may be appropriate."

I was not wrong, Aicart thought. This woman is a snare of the Devil. She certainly looked lovelier than on previous occasions, since she was now dressed in the costume proper to a daughter of the nobility. Her tall slender body was draped in a green robe that fell in heavy folds about her, and her long black hair was barely restrained by the blue veil that covered it. Yet one had only to glance at her to realize that she cared nothing for her beauty, nor for the raiment with which she had been provided: her gray eyes were fixed in burning concentration, as though she were some wild beast poised ready to spring. Aicart felt his blood congeal in his veins, so terrifying did her expression seem to him: indeed, it was no longer a young girl he saw, but Satanic temptation incarnate.

Gentian faced the two men, head held high, hands folded in her lap. She forced herself to pray; she besought God to inspire her with words of humility and wisdom. But without knowing why she felt both tense and obstinate, a prey to some incomprehensible fury which she could barely control. Why should the spirit that possessed her on *this* day be one of pride and rebelliousness? Like the virgin St. Catherine before the Emperor, or St. Barbara facing her own father—was it her place to teach her masters a lesson? She held her peace.

Aicart said: "I am most happy to see that worldly temptations have not diminished in you that most legitimate, indeed, most praiseworthy desire, which should be the sole aim of all living souls. But God has fixed no limits on the delays our patience must endure, since even the longest life is less than the winking of an eye in His sight. You are an impatient soul, and a violent one; what would you say if He were to impose a penance on you—that you should remain knocking at the gate for the term of your natural life?"

"I would make very sure of a quick death," the girl exclaimed, passionately. "You cannot withhold baptism from the dying."

"You are wrong. The Rule forbids us to confer the Holy Spirit on a disloyal person, who has not honored his commitments to the Church. One who deliberately rejects his imposed penance and does violence to God's will is not one who honors his commitments. Your reply is not that of a Christian."

Gentian rose to her feet. "But you were even younger than I am when you received the Spirit!" she cried. "I am twenty-two years old. Were you any less impatient then than I am now?"

This shaft hit its mark squarely. But Aicart had no wish to discuss his own position. This girl possessed a knack of forcing him to face unpleasant thoughts long buried: the memory of his youth, tormented by the demon of carnal desires, now all but blotted out those fifteen stainless years which had followed it. This woman, he reflected, is my superior; she has her virginity still, and I have not. If it were not for the presence of that saintly old man, I would tell this arrogant girl just how powerful the devil of the flesh can be, how burdensome and humiliating the weight of eternal chastity. I would tell her how hard I find it to keep my eyes on this silver chandelier while I am addressing her, as though it held some heavenly sign or vision for me. I would tell her how hard it is to feel a hypocrite and a liar, yet not have the right to speak one's belief aloud. Must I then fall back into the torments of adolescence when I am on the very brink of maturity? My head is so over-whelmed by the tumult in my blood that I no longer know what she is saying, let alone what I should properly reply.

She was, in fact, discussing her feelings of disgust for the worldly life: the lewd, immodest glances she had to endure, the necessity of coming in contact with impure foods, even at times of attending services conducted by Romish priests. "I have been purified and cleansed," she continued, "and stripped of my old garments—yet you refuse to replace them with new! Why do you persist in leaving me in so unnatural a condition? I swear to you that there is no deceit in the spirit that visits me; I get more suffer-ing than joy from it."

Aicart said: "I do not know this spirit of which you speak."

"It is a spirit of vision and deep compassion," Gentian replied. "It contains neither impurity nor any taint of sinful pleasure. I did not ask to receive it, and it has never distracted me from prayer. Nevertheless I feel I cannot now pray with my former steadfastness of purpose. I am like some half-severed vine-shoot, in danger of withering up. While I remain outside the Church my life is a shame and a misery to me!"

Jacques d'Ambialet sighed. "Calm yourself, my child," he said. "Do not despair. The Church seeks nothing but your spiritual good; it ill becomes you to blame her."

Gentian cried out that there was only one unique Good, and, turning on the deacon, accused him of harshness and lack of zeal.

"Must my fate yet again depend on you, whose heart is so hardened against me? Once upon a time I lost my temper with you, and because of that you still harbor resentment—which shows your liability to human weaknesses. What right have you to decide the fate of any soul, as though you were God? *And why do you always avoid looking at me?*"

"I am not answerable to you," Aicart said, as calmly as he could. "It seems to me that we have heard words aplenty from you, not one of which suggests to us for a single moment that you are animated by the spirit of charity. I have no advice to offer you but this: take a husband, and live according to worldly ordinances. In twenty or thirty years you *may* begin to understand what God demands of your soul."

Gentian swayed as though she had been struck: she flushed, then turned deathly pale.

"I had not looked for such cruel words," she said, abruptly. Then she sat down—or rather collapsed—on the settle. Her limbs no longer supported her, and the room whirled green and black before her eyes. I am dying, she thought. So much the better.

Jacques d'Ambialet reflected that, while the deacon was far too young to talk to women, the advice he had given was by no means bad. Forty years' ministry had taught the old man that women who were liable to fainting spells often lacked a proper sense of vocation.

"I'd better go and get some water for her from the proprietor's wife," he told Aicart. "Next time try to hide the cutting edge of your truths under a few flowers of rhetoric. Quite apart from any question of charity, we must not risk being exposed to scandal."

Now Aicart was alone with her. The beautiful, waxen-pale girl lay sprawled on her back among the cushions that covered the settle: he could not turn his eyes away from her. He had seen so many extraordinary women; one could, he reflected, expect *anything* from them. Yet could so lovely and young a creature die so suddenly? Since he could not touch her directly, he took a copper pestle that lay on the table, and laid it gently, first against the girl's forehead, and then on her cheeks and lips. The touch of cold metal brought her around, and she opened her eyes. Aicart did not have the time to turn his own away.

For an instant they stared at one another in lost amazement, as solemnly as a pair of lovers. Then Gentian sat up and adjusted her veil.

"Tell me, Master Deacon," she now said, in a quite different voice, "tell me why you are so harsh with me."

He did not know what to answer, but merely continued to stare at her. There are moments when to resist temptation becomes as hard as to stop breathing. It made no difference; she had understood.

This, he thought, is something men kill for. He strode swiftly to the far end of the room, recollecting that Jacques d'Ambialet and the merchant's wife were likely to come in at any moment.

Gentian found herself wondering by what miracle it had come about that she was now alone with this man, who had looked at her with the eyes of desire. In what life had they lived that moment? She would have given anything for another glimpse of his ardent, unhappy face, for the chance to understand— But now he stood three paces' distance from her, head averted, twisting the copper pestle round and round in his hands.

The merchant's wife came in with a glass and a jug of fresh water.

"It's the heat," she said. "Come now, drink. . . . This young lady has a delicate heart," she explained to Aicart. "The Spirit has tried her sorely. Has she had some horrible vision?"

"To be quite honest, I don't know," Jacques d'Ambialet said, irritably. "But for the love of God stop this endless talk about her visions. It's just that sort of gossip which gets people sent to the stake."

When they were alone once more, the two men looked at one another with rather more rancor than they would have wished. Because of the vaguely ridiculous situation in which they had just found themselves, they felt a certain mutual annoyance. The incident was not serious, but decidedly disagreeable, Jacques d'Ambialet had seen quite a few women roll over in a faint at his feet, too, in the days when his hair was less white and fewer wrinkles seamed his face. Nowadays his attitude to such Mary Magdalenes was one of indulgence, tempered with a certain involuntary disdain. As soon as they came across a man within the age of temptation they both spoke to him and looked at him in quite a different way—so much so, indeed, that they became quite unrecognizable.

Now he calmly sat down at his desk again and said: "I feel I perhaps would have done better to spare you that irksome task; the fact is, you were in a better position than I to decide the case."

"God grant we have no worse troubles than this to face," Aicart remarked dryly. He stood there, arms folded across his chest, staring at the cushioned settle where, a few moments before— How did it happen? he wondered. She isn't blind or half-witted; clearly I have nothing more to lose in her eyes.

He asked himself how he could contrive to see this woman again before the day was out, and speak to her alone. It was impossible to act otherwise; throw a stone into the air, and it must needs fall. Scorn the flesh, and the flesh will have its revenge: when it raises its voice, there is no way but to hold one's peace. There is nothing I can say to you, for all your virginal eloquence; our status debars us from overwordiness. It is only with my body that I long to speak to you, and to make you understand the reason for my harshness. . . . Yet how can I see her again? There is no question of clever trickery in our world: the gates are guarded, not by go-betweens or accomplices or lackeys, but by our own comrades, whose vigilance equals that of any prison warder, and is infinitely more perspicacious. And even supposing one had lost all shame, all self-respect, by what means could one accomplish the seduction of a daughter of the nobility here, in the heart of the city?

Despite himself, Aicart cast a hate-filled glance at the little old man, so imperturbably occupied with his accounts. At this particular moment he could have wished him six feet underground. He knew only too well what that silence conveyed: that he, Aicart, was still a mere belated novice, struggling in the arena of human emotions. Have you not learned, the silence asked, how to avoid such accidents? The truth is, Aicart thought, that we can understand one another fully without uttering a word; we all have the same thoughts, we are like plates cast in the same mold. There are days when this is very wearisome. For years now we have unlearned all but those words which directly concern our ministry; it is as difficult for us to do evil as to walk upon the waters.

He bowed humbly before the old man and said: "Forgive me,

most reverend brother, if I have in any way offended you, whether by word or deed."

"Forgive me," Jacques said, rising, "if any word or glance has escaped me which can have wounded your feelings."

They kissed one another thrice on either cheek, according to the Rule; and then Aicart knelt down to say his prayers. He was due to leave for a part of the town where street fighting was actually in progress: here about thirty of the faithful from the Carcassès district, who led a communal existence together, were expecting him to go and bless bread in their house. He carried messages for some of them, and money for others. At nightfall he had to see a certain sick person whom he could not safely visit in broad daylight; and after that there was a sermon to preach, in a seminary which during the day underwent transformation into a potter's workshop.

He who leads such a life, Aicart reflected, has no individual will. He is less than a man, a tool merely. We do not own two bodies; we go where we must go, say the words we have to say, neither more nor less. That is the rule. And even though it is hard to bless bread with impure hands, we do not let our distress appear. In wartime one cannot refuse a mission through mere scruples of conscience.

Gentian returned to the Lady de Miraval's house dejected and distraught. She felt as though she had received a heavy blow on the head, or were drunk. Can one, she asked herself, endure such an outrage without flinching? Neither desire nor pain, only a vast amazement. Can it be true that I am now a mere nothing, a soulless body, fit only for such a life as the beasts of the field live? Why should I care? I am so cowardly that I cannot even hate the cruel man who treated me so ill. If I could still see his face as I saw it once today, perhaps I would then understand whether I hate him or not. Beyond question when he looked at me there was the desire of love in his eyes. How can it be that I am more inclined to obey a man I know to be sinful than one I believed just and virtuous?

Jacques d'Ambialet acquainted the Lady de Miraval with the decision regarding her protégée: his brother Aicart, deacon of the Minerve district, who knew both the young woman and her family very well, was of the opinion that she did not possess those qualities necessary for admission to the ranks of the elect, and was a victim of that overexalted state of mind characteristic of her age and sex.

"Well, well," the Lady de Miraval said. "A curious lack of insight on the part of so respectable a person."

"I cannot be the judge of that, my lady; nor, I fear, can I act against his recommendations. We have incurred enough criticism already for meddling in the affairs of the faithful from other dioceses. This girl is a visionary. She ought to be married off as soon as possible; there's far too much talk about her in the neighborhood. She is drawing suspicion on herself without the least profit to her immortal soul."

"*Suspicion?* But I am quite competent to hide and protect her. Our Catholic clergy is not yet entirely in the pay of the French! Would anyone destroy a virgin's life for such mean motives?"

"No one has violent designs on her, my lady. But since both her parents have placed themselves outside the law, it is your business to take care of her. If I were in your position I would not take upon myself the responsibility of exposing a young girl to any useless danger."

"Is there a worse danger than marriage?" the Lady de Miraval cried, indignantly. "Since when have you been counselling your flock to kill the soul that the body may be saved?"

Because of her wealth the Lady de Miraval could and did speak bluntly to everyone, whatever his station. Though she constantly postponed the day of her entry into the Church, she was a skilled theologian, more than ready to advise the elect on matters of doctrine. Her friends used to say that she would have readily taken the habit if the episcopate had been open to women: she considered the reservation of this privilege to men an injustice. "You obviously need female bishops to take care of women," she often said.

"Are men capable of understanding our thoughts?" But despite
such mildly heretical aberrations, Lady Alfaïs was wholly devoted
to the Church; she spent half her time organizing collections, or
supervising needlework schools and convent workrooms; she daily
received a score or so of beggars below-stairs in her own house.
Could a woman so ardently devoted to the cause of freedom agree
to abandon her little dove to some man's embrace?

"My child," she told Gentian, "I love you with so pure an affection that I will never willingly see you defiled in this way. No man,
be he deacon or bishop, has the right to violate our will."

"My lady, I have received such a blow that I feel I shall never
recover from it. The times in which we live are so hard that the
breaking of my vocation matters little: but I have no wish to become a cause of scandal. I have been told that I do not possess
charity; the truth is that I am thinking only of myself. I have become a burden to my own nature. I might as well follow the common highway; that at least should break my pride."

"Be patient: when the war is over you will return to your convent."

"My lady, the old days will never come back. This war will go
on till the end of the world. At least I shall have the consolation
of telling myself that the sons I bear will avenge our dead. Many
women have endured this shame: you yourself, for example, or my
mother, who is the most saintly of women. Is it for me to put myself forward as the lily of the valley or the incorruptible flame?"

The old days will never come back. In what glorious raiment
will God's Church emerge from this blood-bath? We have committed the sin of pride; we have come to believe ourselves established in security and prosperity. We have forgotten that persecution is the Christian's lot, and that it will be so forever till the end
of the world.

His mission now concluded, Aicart was on his way out of Toulouse, escorted by two men-at-arms, and leading a mule laden with
clothes and food for the brothers in the Carcassès area. How great

a temptation it is, he reflected, to flee this vagabond life and withdraw to some mountain hermitage, where the enemy's forces have
not yet penetrated. If only our adversaries were content merely to
destroy our bodies! It is the soul that is degraded by this life of lies
and compromises. *They* flaunt their tonsures and monastic robes
everywhere—a practice which sometimes earns them a devil's
martyrdom; and so they know very well that by abjuring our own
habit we profane our ministry, and that the impure objects with
which we unavoidably come into contact render the Spirit inopera-
tive.

We are only human. If the Spirit, through some unheard-of
miracle, consents to dwell in the dunghill of our body, it burns
there like some flickering candle flame, always threatened with
extinction. Yet we, through rashness or sheer lunacy, carry our
lamps unshielded in the midst of a hurricane. To bear witness to
the Truth we bear a false habit, a false name, and false excuses.
Take care, Aicart told himself, lest your deacon's rank and your
power to confer the Holy Spirit do not become false in their turn,
and you yourself become the prince of liars.

Can God still make use of a soul that is guilty of the sin of
lewdness? While my beloved brother was yet at my side no such
thing befell me. What evil thought could have withstood his gaze?
Those eyes destroyed evil as fire consumes scraps of straw. My dear,
dear companion, three summers and four winters I have lived
without you; and this is the fourth spring now. My soul grows
weary, my body withers: God should never allow such separa-
tions. The heart wears away when it is condemned to fight alone,
to beat against the void. May God have pity upon the hearts who
love things divine with an earthly love.

I have broken the Rule: I have not been able to love my admirable companion, my partner in work and toil, who shares my
couch and my daily bread. And Satan in his cunning offered me
another sort of love. To the imprisoned soul that spurned its
fleshly envelope he made known, by trickery, a new companion:
an Eve of such bodily charms that Adam's soul was caught by them
like a limed bird. God-a-mercy, a *woman*! For Thee, O Lord, they

are our equals, souls destined for salvation; but to us mortal sinners they mean plague and death.

And what use is it to starve oneself, to eat nothing but a slice of dry bread at sunrise; to have one's body bled white, or very nearly, and be so exhausted that one can see nothing but green and red circles where the road and the trees should be? What does it avail to recite the Lord's Prayer if each word echoes like a hammerblow in one's head, because one is too enfeebled to pray properly? Besides, one falls into a state of mental lewdness, when thoughts no longer remain obedient to the will: given the least chance I would manufacture some excuse to return to Toulouse and find this creature once more, given the least chance I would go and beg her forgiveness for having offended her. The flesh is more prolific of trickery than even the most accomplished *jongleur*. And why just *one* woman, when they are all of equal worth? Satan knows what he is about when he tempts us with one fixed object— just as the weight of a hammer concentrates on the tip of a single nail. This is the stupidest of all afflictions, which leads us to believe that our thirst can be slaked by one wine only, drunk from a single cup, this and none other, this and none other—for if I had not seen her, I should never have known this thirst. . . .

Renaud panted painfully at each stroke of the ax, and never managed to keep up with his comrade: one cannot turn woodcutter without practice. Renaud was fifty years old, and fasted more than was reasonable. The two companions imposed three hours of such work on themselves every day, as a kind of discipline.

"Let's stop now," Aicart said.

"I would very much like to. But when one is tempted by anger it is better to go on working."

"Why should you be angry? I have already told you I shall not go without your approval."

Renaud dropped his ax and wiped his forehead.

"*I* have already told *you* that I shall not keep you by force."

"And *I* have already told *you* that if it were not absolutely necessary, I should not dream of leaving the district at this juncture."

"The only necessity lies in your imagination. There are only the two of us here: there should be ten at least. Yet you abandon your duty for a scruple of conscience!"

"I shall be back in two months' time, at the very latest."

"Who knows where *I* shall be when those two months are up? You must be well aware that temptations to which one has not yielded are like the dishes of rich meat one sees in dreams. If the Spirit in us could not avoid being defiled by our thoughts, it would not remain there a single day, even with the purest of men."

"I will tell you something frankly, my brother: if men such as ourselves do not yield to this sort of temptation, it is very often through pride, or fear of dishonor. We are like dogs on the leash. The Rule can be infringed by evil thoughts, too."

Renaud, who was leaning against a tree, now knitted his heavy brows in an attempt to reflect on this. He did not understand. He was a peaceful man, firm and sure in his belief, and as little bothered by his own thoughts as by the flight of a mosquito. For all his natural generosity he occasionally told himself that God, with the intermediary assistance of the Bishop, had wanted to try his patience by imposing such a companion on him—an impatient, intolerant, authoritarian creature, with a weakness for private attachments. These things apart, Renaud loved him in Christ, and held him to be a good Christian.

"Thoughts," he said, "do not depend on our personal will. The mistake is to believe oneself something when one is nothing."

"Do you really believe," Aicart said, not without humility, "that it is as easy as that to truly understand one's nothingness? My brother, ought we to be like those Romish priests who say: 'What matter if our hearts are impure? A doctor can be greedy and lustful, but so long as his remedies are good he remains a good doctor'? The grace of God is not transmitted by mere physical contact, like leprosy: when we deceive men we are deceiving God also. It is said that a corrupt tree cannot bring forth good fruit."

"You are not a corrupt tree."

"My brother, that is something which I alone can know, after

God. If I do not obtain a renewal of my vows from the Bishop, I am like the salt that has lost its savor."

"Take care lest you fall into the sin of doubt and false humility," Renaud said.

"I am not yet so far abandoned by God as to know doubt and false humility. I have told you already, I want your blessing on my departure, since it has been revealed to me that I must put off this journey no longer."

With a somewhat bad grace Renaud at last gave his consent. Four of the brethren had already left the district during the winter; two women had been captured and burned at Albi, and another had died of an illness. The sawmill was not so safe a refuge as it had been. Renaud did not want his companion to incur any suspicion of having fled the area through fear of danger.

Once he was on his way, disguised as a beggar, with his copy of the Gospels hidden under his rags next to his chest, Aicart no longer found that the journey was difficult or that time dragged for him. He felt that he was on the right road now. It was as though he were going to a second death, a new baptism, a new destruction of his soul through the Spirit. It had taken him two full months to resign himself to this, so great is the lure of sin and self-complacency.

My beloved friend, he thought, have I truly betrayed you?

The meanest man is strong enough to light a fire and burn ten, twenty, a hundred of the just in it. My only friend was destroyed by creatures unworthy to kiss the earth where his feet had trodden. He used to say that the world has no power over us. He was wrong. The world has had power enough to separate us: in this world body is stronger than soul. For his soul is now in perfect joy and happiness: but when he was alive I only had to see him tighten his lips, or blink, to know whether he was happy, or upset, or tired—

What would he have said at this moment? How can I tell? I was a different man when he was there.

He never knew ordinary temptations, except by hearsay.

It is possible to fear the thought of being purified. I am going toward my new baptism as though to a Calvary, for it seems to me that I shall not survive it. This love of self that one must stamp out takes diverse forms, and is tenacious of life: some men only manage to rid themselves of it together with their very skin and flesh.

That tall, smooth, fresh thing—a naked body, a virgin's body! For me it is as though I had never known any woman; my youthful sins were the merest child's play. To hunger for *that*, totally, from the roots of her hair to the very pit of her belly; to know that this hunger will never be satisfied, never, at any place or time, in any circumstance whatsoever! It is this word, this eternal, limitless *never*, that sears our hearts. And in the end we come to love the hunger itself.

We destroy ourselves by violence: two or three weeks hence this passion will be quite dead.

Despite the serious drain on his strength caused by the humiliating position in which he had found himself during the past two months, Aicart had no doubts whatsoever about the efficacy of his chosen cure. A man determined to ask for a second laying on of hands comes to resemble a twice-baked loaf, which can neither become harder nor yet turn moldy. Aicart had known several of these twice-risen Lazaruses; in their various ways they were all like men who had endured torture—either embittered, or possessed of an inhuman detachment from the world.

You will forget even the friend whom you never wished to forget, he told himself. For God he was a saint among the elect, but for you the occasion of a fall from grace. *I have never known you, Raymond.* You are nothing but ashes now; you were never anything but corruption and nothingness, mere flesh consumed by God. All that is not God is vanity; and *he* was not God. All fleshly affections lead to the death of the soul. O Lord, hast Thou not humiliated me to prove that there is none other Love on earth than Thine?

Aicart knew of a hut in the woods near Carcassonne where two brethren of the Faith had their abode, and he made up his mind to spend the night there. It was not good to remain solitary for too long. In the company of these two men prayer would be easier, and thoughts less vagrant. There are days, he thought, when one needs the company of one's brothers more than bread or water.

He was surprised to see that the track was far less carefully camouflaged than usual. When he reached the hut he understood why. At first the stench of decaying flesh made him start back; then he went up to the doorway. A man lay there on the ground, so thickly covered with ants and black flies that he looked like a mere heap of swarming insects. The earth in front of the hut was heavily trampled, and there were blackened bloodstains on the door jamb.

For once in his life, though he was not superstitious, Aicart felt panic-stricken. He had come to hold converse with friends, only to find himself confronted with a mass of stinking carrion. Was this, then, life? The one true and certain fact, rather—Death. Which of the two brothers was it? It would be a clever man who could tell now. Even without the grievous loss which the death of a Christian represented, there had still been a most foul sin committed here. Murder. What man had dared to do it—and why?

This was some footpad's crime, Aicart thought. The authorities do not leave the bodies of heretics to rot; they would have burned the body and the hut too. There are some folk who believe us to be rich. May God forgive them. Perhaps these two brethren were making a collection at the time—who knows? Perhaps they had been tortured in an effort to make them reveal where their treasure was hidden. Poor mad fools! Everyone knows that we are the last men on earth whom anyone would entrust with a treasure: indeed, we never know where our money is hidden. People are so stupid.

Mastering his repugnance, Aicart went into the hut. A cloud of flies buzzed around him and settled on his sweating face. He wanted to find out if the man who had gone had taken his Book with him. On hands and knees he searched among the debris on the floor, holding his breath as long as he could. The Book was there, hidden under an upturned soup bowl, and swarming with ants. He would have come back to look for it if he could, Aicart thought. What's to be done? Maybe he was wounded, or broke a leg— *Which of them is it?* Ah, it must be Raoul, the younger one, who got away. The old man had crippled feet. Aicart gave one last glance at what, in all probability, had been the body of a tall old man with melancholy eyes, and then strode out of the hut. In his hands he bore the Sacred Book, still befouled with dried blood and soup stains.

A voice inside him said: Don't go searching for Raoul. If he has not come back it can only be because he is dead. So. Another two comrades the less. Another two—and because of a stupid incident, the idiocy of some foreign soldier. Ah, but a wounded man can live for several days, he answered himself, to be devoured alive by hunger—and the vultures. Raoul is a tough, healthy fellow, forty years old at the outside.

He was about to commence his search (after a rapid recital of the Lord's Prayer) when he heard a clear young voice calling to him from a nearby thicket: "I shouldn't waste your time, friend; you'd only come back with nothing in the bag." And a fifteen-year-old boy came running out to meet him.

"It's a miserable business," the boy said. "Were you wanting them for a dying man, by any chance?"

"No. Not for a dying man."

"Worse luck for us," the boy said. "Both our pastors are dead now. It must have been the Basques who did it; they fear neither God nor Devil. I found Master Raoul lying behind the Ravens' Rock, with his head stove in and his hands and feet all burned. And the man I'd been sent to fetch him to needed him sorely."

There is nothing for it, Aicart told himself resignedly. I shall have to stay till tomorrow. I cannot get out of it now. Aloud he said: "If you were seeking consolation for a dying man, I am the person you need."

"Truly?" the boy asked, peering up at the thin, fine-boned face that remained half hidden in its unbleached linen hood. The man's expression reassured him; he gave a wide, trusting grin and knelt for Aicart's blessing.

"Well now," Aicart said, "who is it? A relative of yours?"

The boy's face became serious again.

"It won't be easy, Monseigneur," he said.

"He is being watched, then?"

The boy blushed and drew from his belt an old piece of Greek copper, marked with three notches. "He told me to show you that," he said, and put it in Aicart's hand.

Aicart bit his lip. He had not expected to see this token come home to him again.

"I know," he said. "The man is a soldier, isn't he?"

"Yes, Monseigneur—" The boy appeared to hesitate.

"Very well. Where is he? Far from here? Is he wounded or ill?"

"He is in prison, Monseigneur. In the Great Tower at Carcassonne."

There was silence for a moment. Aicart, somewhat taken aback, stood there thoughtfully twisting the scrap of copper round and round in his hand.

"How will I get to him?" he asked at last, in a low voice.

"I am the jailer's son, Monseigneur. My father will be able to let you through. Please do not refuse, Monseigneur; he is a very brave man. His name is Master Ricord; he's the one who's killed so many Crusaders."

Ah, God, Aicart thought, that it should be he of all people! How did he come to let himself be taken alive? Aloud he asked: "When is he to be executed?"

"In two days' time."

"So soon?" Aicart said, slowly. "Do you know by—by what method?"

The boy frowned. "They have done quite a lot to him already. Because he is of noble birth they will cut off his head. But first his arms and legs. It's very painful, you know."

"I know. It's a long business. How will you get me inside?"

"My father will lend you some clothes—he'll pass you off as a relative. Monseigneur Raoul got through three times that way. One time he even dressed up as a priest!"

Aicart reflected that Raoul was still more or less unknown in Carcassonne—in those quarters, at any rate, where it was vital he should not be recognized. Ah, well, he thought, they too have lost many of their number by death or dispersal, and anyway the town has become one large hostelry. I am not a giant or a hunchback; all I need to do is to conceal my face. So he drew his hood well forward over his face and followed the boy. As an extra precaution he wrapped a piece of dirty rag around the hand that held his staff. Your hands will betray you quicker than your face, he thought. Fifteen years' toil cannot change those long, slim fingers, or make them pass for those of some manual laborer.

They made their way across the town, skirting through back streets and outlying quarters.

"Wait till you see the square in front of the Bishop's Palace," the boy was saying. "It's all decked out with flags and suchlike for the departure of a pilgrimage—any day now. They sing special Masses before they go—you never saw such a display. Flags waving, horses all caparisoned in silk, every knight wearing his colored surcoat to church. And this new Bishop they've sent us, they say he's after heretics like a mad wolf. Of course, he's from the North; this isn't his own part of the country. He's been the ruin of plenty of folk. Consuls even. You know the saying, 'Flay a sheep once and you can't shear it twice'? It's wrong, quite wrong. The French are so powerful that they can find a way to flay us twice and have us thank them into the bargain! They've given the merchants and bankers their houses back, with what little was left in them, and now they're forcibly billeting Crusaders on them all; worse than rats in a windmill, that is. There's Master Peter Jaufré, and Master Isarn de la Cadière, too—though he goes to church like any Catholic! The Bishop forces him to lodge Crusaders because of his youngest son, the one who turned heretic."

Aicart had known for some time now that his father lived more or less by favor of the Bishop and the troops he was forced to lodge in his house; yet despite this he was a true believer, and, being old, ran a considerable risk of dying without the Consolamentum. All this because he stubbornly persisted in clinging to his home.

"Ah, the life they make us lead," the boy went on. "All the soldiers that come through—why, if you started counting their banners, it'd take you till tomorrow. They don't stay long—long enough to grab, but not to pay. As for the girls, if there are ten of them in the town who are still as they were, we ought to count ourselves lucky. These devils marry all the rich heiresses straight off, and the girls' fathers daren't refuse them. There are weddings every day from Easter to Whitsun. My father says he doesn't want to lose his job; he's waiting till the other lot are behind bars instead of the ones in there now. Then we'll have a good laugh, he says."

"There will be nothing to laugh about. Your father follows an ill trade."

"I know that. Still, he goes to hear a preacher whenever he can."

Aicart was watching some Crusader horsemen ride past, flaunting robes of embroidered silk. I was born in this town, he thought, and now it has become a den of thieves. How long must we endure this shame?

He was obliged to spend the night at the jailer's home. The jailer had recognized Raymond de Ribeyre's former companion instantly; he waited impatiently for the moment when they were alone together and he could kneel before Aicart.

"We don't have an easy time of it either, Master Deacon," he said. "It's not like being in one of the Bishop's prisons here, but they keep an eye on me just the same. If I got myself caught, they'd think I was making a good fat profit out of it."

"And aren't you?" Aicart asked. "Do you *really* never take money?"

"Well, when folk can afford it, I don't say no. But for this brave fellow who's to die a martyr's death the day after tomorrow I wouldn't take one solitary sou, not if you was to go down on your knees and beg me to. They say he's killed more than three hundred Crusaders in four years."

"You're a strange man, aren't you?" Aicart said gently. "You say that—yet you work hand in glove with his executioners."

"That's life for you, Monseigneur. You have to give the Devil his due, though; I've helped quite a few men to die in peace."

"That's true. But take care that the Devil's portion does not come too large."

In this house Aicart would accept nothing but water, in which he would soak two biscuits he had brought with him in his knapsack. He hated the thought of seeking lodging in a prison; but where, he reflected, does war not force us to go? It was enough to make anyone believe in signs and portents: his journey could hardly have had a worse beginning. And to crown it all, the man he had to ordain on the morrow was the father of that person whom he must keep forever from his thoughts. Usually he forbade himself all feelings of personal pity for the dying and their kin. But how could he keep pity out in such a case? The girl was bound to hear of her father's death in the end; and such a trial would, surely, prove more than she could stand. Poor child, he thought, grasping your visions as a baby will clutch at a sword! Suppose your spirit ever played so cruel a turn on you as to show you your father's body, dismembered alive by the executioner's ax? Men can hazard their lives in this ruthless game, and lose; but justice demands that women should be kept out of it. Will this child ever recover from the outrage done to this very flesh of her flesh?

Such uneasy misgivings disturbed his prayers and kept sleep from him. He had distressing dreams in which the girl reproached him tearfully for the death of her father. He swore to her that he had nothing to do with it, and tried to comfort her as best he could by stroking her shoulders and cheeks. Even in his dream this physical contact both frightened him and filled him with a kind of terrible joy. This feeling of joy, through its sheer violent intensity, always woke him up. O Lord, do other men know what it is to have a hand that tingles and grows thin with the desperate need to touch, if only for one single instant, a woman's cheek?

It is night, Aicart told himself. Somewhere very near here a man is waiting to receive from your hands the hope of salvation.

Because of that your hands are not truly a man's hands: every gesture, every contact has been foreseen and foremeasured, even unto death, and not one jot shall be added to the sum thereof.

The following morning Aicart was obliged to change his clothes for a burgher's dress and a red woollen cloak, and was taken into the prison while the warders were having their breakfast. "This gentleman would like to offer you a flagon of Spanish wine," the jailer told them. "He is the Sieur de Montgeil's nephew, and wants to keep his identity secret. He has come to bid his uncle farewell." The men scarcely glanced at the visitor; the day before an execution they were in the habit of turning a blind eye to such matters, since they reckoned that any man who was to be chopped to bits in forty-eight hours was entitled to enjoy his last day on earth.

The cell was small and gloomy: its only window was a narrow slit just below the ceiling, and such daylight as penetrated this was reflected from the face of the outer wall. The occupant lay slumped on the floor in his chains, trying to sleep. He had at last discovered a position in which he could stretch out almost to his full length, despite the gyves around his wrists and ankles with which he was fettered to the wall. When he heard the door open he started up with a groan and tried to kneel. Through the half-light Aicart made out a puffy face, its beard all clotted with blood, and two naked arms, swollen, inflamed, covered with long, dark weals.

"My brother," he said, "may God protect you on this day."

The eyes of the condemned man seemed to be making a fearful effort to focus on Aicart. Unable to maintain his kneeling position any longer, he fell back against the wall with a dry rattle of chains, and propped his head in a niche which God knows how many previous occupants had gradually hollowed from the stone.

"How—how can it be *you*, Master Deacon?" he croaked; and there was a querulous note in his voice, despite everything.

"God has indeed willed that I should be in the right place at the right moment. The man you were expecting is dead."

"If I had known it would be you," Ricord said, "I should never have dared to send for you."

Aicart said: "The risk is very much the same for all of us. Myself or another."

"That is true, Monseigneur. But we think less of it when it concerns a man we have never seen."

Ricord spat out a little blood and wiped his mouth with one fettered hand. Then he went on: "I was afraid I might be in no condition to talk. The inflammation has gone down now, and I'm a bit better. They broke all my teeth. Monseigneur—will I make a good end? They have tortured me so much already that I am good for very little more. My head is on fire."

"My brother, it is the same for every man at the moment of death. If they have weakened your body, so much the better; you will suffer less tomorrow. A spent man can die suddenly, with only one arm severed."

"May God hear your words. Ah, Monseigneur, the body is a paltry thing, I know; but it is not pleasant to think of its being carved up thus, like an ox—and even an ox is slaughtered first. The whole town will be there to watch me, and hear my cries. If only my children might never know—"

"They will be proud of you, my brother. Every man who is not a traitor to his country will say that you are a martyr."

"Some deaths are uglier than others. I am still lucky in one way: at least they are going to behead me. They could not condemn me as a traitor. I have never taken an oath either to the French or to any leader who has served them. I know them: they wanted to have me alive."

"Do not think any more about them."

"Yes, Monseigneur: I wish to think of them for one moment longer. Here, then, is my confession. How much I have hated them, you and the whole countryside know: of all those I could catch I spared not a single one. I have not borne myself like a soldier, who fights only so long as the enemy can resist him. For me these creatures seemed unworthy of a soldier's steel. I slaughtered their wounded and cut the throats of their monks, for these unarmed men are worse than the fighters, and it is right that their cloth should not protect them: these are they who brought this war upon us. I have led dozens of my own soldiers to their deaths; we have finished off several of our own wounded whom we could not carry with us. And in order to keep our fighting men well fed, we were obliged to take poor people's bread.

"But I have never regretted any part of what I did. To destroy our country's enemies there is a need of men such as myself, who shrink from nothing. And another thing I will tell you: I was wounded, and taken alive, and shown around their camp like some animal at a country fair, and dragged right through the town with shackles on my legs—and beaten, and branded with red-hot irons, and stretched on the rack—God, if you knew what *that* was like!— and *then* they tried to make me say whether I had any 'accomplices.' What accomplices? The whole country is on my side, barring the clergy. And then they tortured me again for the sheer pleasure of it, even after sentence had been passed. And they condemned me to a brigand's death, because here it is they who make the laws; so that I shall not even die by the laws of my own country, but at the whim of some foreign soldier.

"And here is my true confession, the truth, the whole truth: I feel no hatred toward them for what they have done to me. I pardon them freely, and would be glad to be able to forgive them as well the ill they have done our country. Because that ill they have done me is no more than my just deserts; whatever they do to me I am still in their debt, and God grant this is the only ill thing they have ever done! And in truth I no longer have the strength to hate them; pain has driven the hatred out of my body, and one ill cancels the other. And if you will of your bounty pray our Saviour Jesus Christ on my behalf, I have good hope that He will show me compassion, despite the little regret I have for my faults."

"My brother," Aicart said, "you must now renounce such thoughts, and all others like them; for the moment is at hand when your soul, God willing, will find its Holy Spirit which it lost on the day of its fall into the flesh.

"Indeed, this ordination is not that which tradition demands, since I alone am here to confront you, and I am a man little worthy

of the title of 'Christian.' But the Church is present here on earth
in its every member, be they already crowned with glory or still
endowed with their fleshly semblance. God gives me the authority
to address you in their name. It is not a man who stands before you
here, but God's whole Church; and the words you are about to utter
will not be spoken to a man, but to the Church. It is the Church
that, through my voice, will expound and recall to you the meaning
of the Lord's most sacred Prayer, so that you may be fittingly prepared to receive baptism of the Spirit."

Once again Ricord tried to struggle to his knees, but fell back,
with a sad smile. Solemnly, taking great care not to get a single
word wrong, he repeated after the deacon the Commentaries on the
Lord's Prayer. He felt awed, as though the whole Church were
actually gathered together there to decide whether he understood
the Prayer as he should. Shackled, half naked, a mass of open
weals, reduced to so wretched a physical state that he felt unworthy
even to lift up his eyes—ah, God, it was in this utterly humiliated
condition that he now had to present himself before the Church
for admission to the ranks of the elect!

Aicart spread out a scrap of clean cloth on the ground before
him, and placed the Book in his hands.

"Ricord," he asked, "are you willing to receive the spiritual
baptism of Jesus Christ?"

"Yes; I am willing. Pray God give me the strength!"

Since his time was limited, Aicart followed the rite for the dying.
When he placed the Gospels on Ricord's head to confer the Holy
Spirit upon him, he felt a great calm descend upon his own soul, as
though he, too, had just received baptism. For God's grace does not
descend upon every dying person, but only on those who receive it
in true humility: then only does its presence become sensible, and
we know ourselves in the presence of a new being. Thank You,
Lord, Aicart thought: I have not lied to this man. He is truly purified and clothed in the Spirit: there are now two of us here
gathered together in Thy name.

He bowed to the man who was henceforth his equal and comrade, then kissed him on either cheek. Ricord remained silent, not

wishing to profane the solemn moment of the sacrament. Gravely and thoughtfully he stared at the Book which the deacon had placed in his hands again. I had to come to this pass before being judged worthy, he reflected. God has rejected my life; He only wants me dead. For life is nothing: only death is real and true. My personal truth was embodied in this death. Lord Jesus, I do not ask to sit at Thy right hand, but in the outermost chamber of Thy Heaven, whence I may see the mere reflection of Thy glory. I deserve no more than that.

Why must he die so soon? Aicart wondered. He would have made a fine harvester in God's vineyard. Aloud he said: "Is there any message you wish to entrust to me, my brother? I will doubtless see your wife. Have you nothing to say to her?"

"No. What could I tell her that she does not already know? Go now, Monseigneur—God has granted us a longer time together than I had dared to hope: we must not put Him to the test. It would be a grievous misfortune for us all if you were caught."

Does he still need to be concerned on my behalf? Aicart asked himself. I have seen many dying men, but what lies ahead for him is something worse than death. "Farewell, my brother," he said. "Pray as long as your strength lasts, and do not take any nourishment. In your present condition the end may come sooner than you think."

Ricord shook his head. "No," he said. "I shall last a long time. Almost to the very last moment. I know that now, and I do not think I care. My sons are grown men, and will understand—but ah, if only I could have spared my daughter this horror! If you ever see her again, speak to her of me, let her know that I died well."

Aicart reflected that it would have been wiser to leave town as soon as he could; but his compassion for the man who was to die remained too strong. If I mingle with the crowd before the scaffold, he thought, perhaps Ricord will see me, and feel less isolated.

He could not stay any longer in the jailer's house. He resumed his mendicant's garb and made for the central part of the town, where he knew a house once listed as "safe." But he was out of luck: a knight from Champagne had been billeted there, together with his men, so that their unwilling hosts had to make do with the attics. The soldiers, now installed in the living room and kitchen, were decent enough fellows: they assumed Aicart was begging alms, and thrust a crust of whole-meal bread and a scrap of bacon into his hands.

Nevertheless one of them said: "You're a bit young for this game—or a bit old, eh? Wouldn't do you any harm to set you digging trenches."

"Ah, leave him be," another soldier broke in, "he must be getting over an illness, he's nothing but skin and bone."

Meanwhile the lady of the house had come downstairs. She took Aicart off to her own quarters so that he might wash his hands, and threw the bit of bacon to her dog.

"Ah me," she said, "all the sinfulness we see nowadays on account of this war! For God's sake, Master Aicart, do not stay in our house—my son-in-law is so scared that he'd beat me if he knew I'd taken you in."

"Please forgive me," Aicart said. "I will go now. May God protect you."

"Ah, Master Deacon, if it were just my responsibility I wouldn't mind—but *he's* been half out of his mind ever since he had these troops in the house. He'd lick the shoes of the Bishop's mule if he thought it'd get rid of them—not just the Bishop's mule either, that of his lowliest clerk! There's no doubt about it, either—soldiers may come and go, but it's the clergy who rule the town!"

Aicart had no alternative but to seek some other refuge. He wandered from street to street, unnoticed among the crowd of passers-by, beggars, hawkers' carts, and beasts of burden gathered at the drinking troughs, resigned to spending the night in some doorway. He had eaten nothing that day: the soldiers' bread was defiled by its contact with bacon, and it had not occurred to him to ask the old woman for another piece. As a result he felt exhausted and slightly giddy.

An ecclesiastical dignitary, robed in white and mounted on a mule, was with some difficulty forcing his way through the water-carriers and hawkers of vegetables that barred his path: Aicart had to throw himself backward to avoid the mule, which had taken fright at a dog and reared up right beside him. His hood slipped back as he did so, but he dared not adjust it too quickly for fear of attracting attention. A clerk in the abbot's train glanced at him, and knitted his brows in astonished recognition. Then he turned to rejoin his companions. Don't run, Aicart told himself. Walk on as though nothing had happened. Once I'm around that street corner he'll never find me again. But a huge timber dray blocked his passage.

The clerk ran after him and put one hand on his shoulder.

"Tell me," he said, "have I not seen you somewhere before?"

"I do not know."

The man hesitated, scrutinizing the false mendicant with close attention.

"Tell me: are you not Aicart de la Cadière?"

It would have been easy to say: "I don't know whom you're talking about," to shrug one's shoulders and turn away. Or to say: "No, my name's William Vidal, I come from Béziers—" But Aicart had known very well that one day he would have to answer this direct and brutal question, though hitherto he had avoided it as best he could. *I know not the man.* It is not ourselves merely that we deny, Aicart thought: it is our Saviour, our vocation, Rule and Spirit together. This man will believe me, because he knows we never lie. Or else he will say: These men are just like anyone else when their own skin's in danger.

"Yes," he replied, "that is my name. But it would have been better had you not asked it of me. If you are a man of charitable heart, you will let me go my way."

But the clerk had now grasped him firmly by the shoulder, and did not loosen his hold.

"I should be excommunicated if I did such a thing," he said. "Even if I wished to, I would not have the right to release you."

"Would you not be ashamed to betray a citizen of your own town?"

The clerk said, angrily: "You heretics have neither town nor any country—unless it be that of the Devil, whom you serve. It is you who have brought this war upon us. Come with me."

Aicart was well aware that the crowd would never side with a tonsured cleric if they saw him alone; but already two of the clerk's companions had joined him.

"This man is Aicart de la Cadière, the heretic," he announced. "He has told me so."

The two clerks stared at Aicart with a certain involuntary respect. A fine catch, they thought. These men who had come forth living from Hell stood in no need of the stake to become firebrands of Satan: their diabolical pride betrayed them the moment they opened their mouths.

"Follow us," the first clerk said. "No violence will be done you. You will be handed over to the compassionate mercy of the Church."

"I know the Church's mercy," Aicart said. "You have delivered our country to Rome and the French: take care that one day the people do not show you the same sort of mercy in their turn."

The passers-by, curious at first, now dispersed; they had no wish to witness the capture of a heretic.

"I shall not budge an inch," Aicart said. "If there is a warrant out for my arrest, I wish to surrender myself to the Bishop's bailiff."

"Do you think you're still living in the days of the previous Bishop and Viscount? You should count yourself fortunate to have fallen in with us. Others might not have treated you so kindly."

When they reached the Bishop's prison, Aicart lodged a protest at the clerk of the court's office against his illegal arrest—a purely formal gesture. His own position was something worse than illegal. He was a Consul's son masquerading as a beggar; he was also the heretical minister whom the whole town had seen, before the war, going about in his black habit. All these clerks had done was to lay hands on a public malefactor.

How long, he wondered, will they leave me alive? They have

no need of a lengthy interrogation. Usually the proceedings last two days, four at the most. *My God, four days at the most*—if by any chance both the Bishop and his deputy are away, that is. Generally two days are enough.

Aicart felt a vast wall slowly rising in front of him, as high as the heavens and as heavy as the earth. It was very close, right against his face: if he took one step forward he would run his nose into it.

Finished; this life of his was at an end now—though how he would die he could not yet bear to think, and in any case such agony was unimaginable. This life of his was at an end, far from his brethren, far from the Church, in a vain struggle, among men who would not so much as let him pray in peace. He so desperately needed to pray.

O Lord, he thought, it is not so much for my body that I fear; it is my soul which is ill prepared. I lack long experience of prayer: I was ordained too young. My fifteen years' ministry has been spent in work which was profitable enough to the Church Militant, but not for the glorification of God in my soul. I have so defiled that Spirit in me by evil thoughts that I am well-nigh fallen back into that animal condition from which my baptism raised me. I believed that with the coming of old age I would at last be able to fulfill that task to which I had been called.

I have been like the bad servant who sweeps in the middle of the room, but neglects the dark corners, and who, through excessive diligence over small tasks, allows his Master's treasure to be pillaged.

O Lord, it was not through any ill will toward Thee.

He perceived that his hands were trembling, and folded his arms across his chest, hugging them against the Book that was sewn in under his jerkin. It's true, he thought; they have not so much as searched me. Neither my Book nor my money has been taken. The room in which he stood was a kind of large square antechamber, the windows of which looked out onto a small garden. Two lay brothers and a clerk stood whispering together in low voices near the door. They avoided looking at him, just as when he passed they had avoided touching his garments. For them he was like a plague-carrier—and did not he regard them in the same way? These few days left to him would perforce be spent among men for whom he was beyond the pale of humanity.

He realized that he must not let them see his agitation, or they would mistake it for fear. Outside the window, beside a white-washed wall, a man in a white woollen habit was sprinkling the flowers with water from a ewer: the ewer had a long, slender spout. If this good old man accidentally crushed one of his flowers, Aicart thought, he would be quite desolate. Yet tomorrow, when he hears that a man's body is to be burned alive, he will glorify God.

One of the lay brothers now came up to the prisoner and asked him if he would like something to eat or drink. He replied that he would gratefully accept some bread and a jug of water, but nothing else. Daylight began to fade, and two oil lamps were lit, one before the crucifix, the other at the entrance to the chamber.

Aicart asked whether he could not obtain a cleaner garment, and one better suited to his station, if he was prepared to pay for it. At first his guards refused, declaring that they were forbidden by law to render a heretic any such service. However, they were well enough disposed toward him; and finally, after a whispered consultation, they had a kind of long-sleeved brown robe brought in, doubtless left behind by some previous prisoner who had no further need of it. They also told him that my lord Bishop had been informed of his presence, and was delegating the task of questioning him to the Bishop's deputy, immediately after Vespers.

Aicart said his prayers standing beside the window: he hated the idea of kneeling and prostrating himself in this profane place, under the eyes of his jailers. It was a mild night; here and there a church bell sounded, and in the distance he could hear voices chanting: measured, monotonous, quite unearthly in their serenity.

O flawless Peace, he prayed, Ocean of Light, our Father: Thou who hast engendered the pure souls only and not those that are evil—for as Thou art in Heaven, so are they, and come from on high to return on high again—

Hallowed be Thy name, may it shine in and through Thy servants;

Thy kingdom come: Thy kingdom which is Christ bringing light to every soul chosen for salvation, Thy kingdom which is Christ and Christ alone, one Vine with myriad branches, each one pruned and fruitful;

Thy will be done on earth: for Christ said, I am come to do the will of My Father, and He alone has done it, and that will shall never be fulfilled save in Him and by Him, through those souls in whom He reigns supreme, with undivided power.

Give us this day our supersubstantial bread *—not as unto the Jews, who ate manna and are dead, but that True Bread which is the Spirit and the Life, Thy true and real teachings that are the soul's only bread: that food of Christ which is to do the Father's will. Give us strength today to achieve this Bread, which is His very flesh and blood, this true and veritable bread which is His word: especially today, O Lord, for this is Thy servant's day of grace, the day when, even though my soul yields, my body will still bear witness to Thy will. . . .

"Come," the lay brother said, "follow me."

Aicart turned, and saw that two men-at-arms stood behind him, together with a third, who bore a torch.

"I would have liked to finish my prayer," he said.

One of the soldiers grasped him by the arm, but Aicart shrugged his shoulders and said that there was no need to drag him there by force. As he walked he resumed his interrupted prayer.

And forgive us our trespasses: O Lord, they are many, and Thou alone dost know and canst forgive them, even as we forgive them that trespass against us—those who persecute and do all manner of

* This Cathar variant on the normal version of the Lord's Prayer results from a different interpretation of the Greek word *epiousios,* which is almost impossible to render precisely, and contains a certain ambiguity of form. "Supersubstantial" is a quite feasible rendering. Cf. Runciman, *op. cit.,* p. 166, who explains it as "a literal translation of the so-called Nikolski gospel, the Slavonic gospel of the Bosnian heretics."—Trs.

evil against us—freely, and with a generous heart, for they are as ignorant of their debt to me as I, O Father, am of mine to Thee. My debt is infinite; but theirs will soon be paid.

My God, the effort it takes to keep my eyes lowered and my head bent! Here I stand, face to face with my iniquitous judge, the first and last I shall ever confront; here I stand, before the very Tribunal of Satan.

How many times in his youth had he imagined this moment, trying to picture it in advance, preparing his answers, conjuring up—to harden his will—every detail of the final agony! In those days he almost regretted that he had not lived in the days of the martyrs, and would doubtless have been amazed to learn that he would one day endure their fate in sober earnest. Even now he was not yet old enough to avoid a slight thrill of pride at the thought that the moment had come for him to pay for his vocation with his life.

There was a white wall in front of him, with a black crucifix on it, and a man in a white habit and black cloak ensconced in a high-backed chair, with two other men sitting on either side of him, on stools. On their left a scribe waited behind his desk, pen in hand.

The Bishop's deputy, who was the Prior of the Diocesan Chapter, was a man of about sixty: tall, with quick, lively eyes, an aquiline nose, and a mouth that was firm without being hard. Aicart knew him. He thought: This is a fellow townsman of mine, yet he serves a foreign Bishop. The odd thing was that Aicart hated these men more for their assault on his homeland than for their enmity to his Faith. The Prior was speaking now, in a tranquil, almost gentle voice. He said that since the crimes which the accused had committed were a matter of public notoriety, there was no need for prosecutor or witnesses; but nevertheless, if the said Aicart, son of Isarn de la Cadière, considered himself falsely accused, the Diocesan Tribunal would not refuse him the right to summon witnesses in his own defense.

"Do you desire an interpreter," the Prior asked, "or shall we conduct the proceedings in Latin?"

"I do not need an interpreter; and please be so good as to record the fact that I am calling no witnesses."

"Very well. Aicart de la Cadière, do you admit having professed, and publicly taught, doctrines contrary to the Catholic Faith?"

"I admit it."

"Do you further admit having embraced the doctrines of that heretical sect known as the Cathars, and having received from the hands of these said heretics ordination as a minister of their religion?"

"I admit it."

"Do you also admit that, both by word and by deed, you sought to injure Holy Church, and turn the souls of the faithful away from her?"

"If by those words you understand the Romish Church, yes, I certainly did so. But that Church is not Holy Church."

"Do you admit," the Prior asked, "that you are a forsworn apostate from that Faith which was given you at your baptism?"

"I have never forsworn the Faith I received at my baptism. The 'baptism' of which you speak is nothing but a superstitious and pagan custom, and is utterly useless as a means to our salvation."

"Do you believe that no man can attain to salvation except through that Faith which you profess?"

"I believe so most steadfastly."

"Do you believe that a man who wholeheartedly embraces the Faith of the Holy Roman Church can in no wise be saved?"

"Yes, I believe that to be so."

"Do you admit having professed, and publicly taught, the doctrine that the Holy Roman Church was the Beast of the Apocalypse, the Great Whore of Babylon, and the Throne of Satan, besides other yet more abominable blasphemies?"

"I admit that I both professed and publicly taught such doctrine: but I reject the term 'blasphemies.'"

"Do you admit having professed the doctrine that the world in which we live, the earth, the heavens, the stars, and all things visible were not created by God but were the work of the Devil?"

"I admit it."

"Do you admit having professed, and publicly taught, the doctrine that our Saviour Jesus Christ was never incarnate in the flesh, and was neither crucified nor rose again from the dead; that He never instituted the Sacrifice of the Mass, and that the bread and wine consecrated by the priest are not in veritable truth the Body and Blood of Christ?"

"I admit it. Why do you bother to ask me?"

"My son," the Prior said, with unexpected gentleness, "you believe yourself in the presence of wolves who are eager to devour you; but the truth is otherwise. In me you have an indulgent father, ready to close his eyes to your past faults; I do not see in you the man you have been, but the man you could still become. Just as a doctor seeks to diagnose the symptoms of a disease, so I am seeking to put my finger upon your errors that I may afterward refute them, and bring you to see the light of Truth. I am not here to be your judge, but to enlighten you. The Saviour said, I judge no man; and therefore we on earth have no right either to judge or to condemn. With charity and patience we admonish those who go astray, that we may lead them back to the way of truth. You are an educated man; but your knowledge, notwithstanding, is gravely inadequate, and a little learning can prove more pernicious than ignorance. If you were better acquainted with the writings of the early Fathers, you would not have fallen into those lamentable errors which have brought you here."

"Such writings do not exist," Aicart said. "Ours is the only Faith that has been true since the very beginning, and it is *you* who have been led into heresy by Pope Sylvester. He it was who instituted the reign of idolatry, and caused the ruin of many Christian souls."

One of the Prior's two assistants stiffened at this, as though in an attempt to control his anger, and said: "It seems to me we have heard enough, Most Reverend Father. What do you hope to get from this man?"

By his accent Aicart knew him to be a Frenchman, and for a moment his curiosity was aroused. He even felt himself seized by a vainglorious desire to embark upon a controversy with this foreigner. For years now he had spoken no Latin, and practicing the language again carried him back to the days when he could argue his Faith at the street corners, with any cleric on earth. But the Prior raised his hand and said: "We are not here to discuss our Faith, but yours. Divine Truth has no need of self-defense against error, and nothing you say can be detrimental to that Truth; for the words of the fool are like stones, which he casts into the air and which fall back on his own head."

"The blind man who was healed said to the Pharisees: 'Will ye also be His disciples?' So I likewise say to you: 'Why do you question me if your ears are shut in advance to my words?'"

"Could I not say the same of you?" the Prior asked, with a smile, switching abruptly from Latin to the Languedoc dialect. Then he rose, came forward to Aicart, and put a hand on his shoulder.

"My son, I tell you yet again: it is not judges before whom you stand here, but physicians. Consider: have you been browbeaten or maltreated or put in irons like a criminal? You know how severe the secular arm is upon those such as yourself. This the Church deplores: it is not your death that she desires. Christ wishes no man dead. If it were possible for us to shield you from the penalties of the law we would do so: there would be more joy among the angels in Heaven over the repentance of a man like you than for the salvation of ten men such as I am. I beseech you not to close your ears against my words through obstinacy, or from a desire to prove your courage. See, I have left my judge's seat, and speak with you now as one man to another: my heart bleeds for you, I swear that."

They paced to and fro in the room as they talked, their shadows sweeping slowly across the white walls. Aicart kept his arms folded and his eyes lowered: though he was not really listening to what his interrogator said, he was amazed by the man's genuinely kindly tones, which made his words fall pleasantly on the ear.

"If you are trying to comfort me," he said, "please understand that I have no need of such help. And I do not feel any hatred toward you."

"I want to save your soul. Why should you allow yourself to expiate one moment of blind stubbornness with an eternity of tor-

ment? Can you honestly say that your soul is fit to appear before
God's Judgment Seat in its present state? Even your own religion,
false and riddled with error though it be, admits that salvation
may be attained only through a perfect and stainless life."

"What do you want of me?" Aicart said. "I find your remarks
hard to understand. I make no claim to perfection, nor to a stainless life."

The Prior contemplated him with deep compassion. "Listen," he
said. "You are a young man still, and a handsome fellow. It is
impossible for you not to have thought about women at all. You
know as well as I do that God's perfect Love cannot dwell in a
heart to which impure thoughts still gain access. If we destroy you
today, we expose you to the risk of never knowing eternal bliss.
You need time to come to maturity, by way of fasting, abstinence
and solitude, meditation and prayer, the study of Holy Writ and
the ceaseless offering of your life to God."

"What do you want of me?" Aicart repeated. "I still cannot
grasp your meaning."

"My son, I do not ask a miracle of you. I know very well that
your false beliefs cannot be rooted out in a single day. But you
can, with one word, give your soul the chance of one day attain-
ing salvation; and you have no right to let that chance slip. There
will be no demands made of you. You will not be asked to name
your friends, or to reveal secrets of your Faith concerning which
you prefer to keep silent—unless you are yourself later driven to
do so by repentance. It will be enough that you declare your renunciation of your past errors—even though in your heart you have
not yet renounced them. I only ask you to take the first step; I will
trust you for the rest."

At this point Aicart felt his self-control momentarily slipping.
He wanted to vomit. Ah, should he not have foreseen that he must
needs be exposed to every affront—even this? He lowered his eyes
and turned his head aside, so as not to let the Prior see how con-
torted with disgust his face was.

"I did not think I had given you such an impression," he said.

"I did not imagine I had behaved in such a way as to give you the right to take me for a coward."

"My son, would I have spoken thus to a coward?"

"Though through my sins I may have had the misfortune to merit so flagrant an insult, at least I never expected to hear it from the mouth of a compatriot. Did you suppose you would obtain, *from me,* simply by talking, what you only wring out of a thief or bandit with the greatest difficulty, and after torture?"

"Ah, my son, what use to deceive yourself? Would you have flown into such a passion if my words had not moved you?"

Aicart gave the Prior a startled, indeed a somewhat disconcerted, glance. Was this man *really* incapable of understanding?

"Ah, well," he said, wearily, "after all, your opinion of me matters little to me now. You belong among beings lost and accursed, beasts with human faces, that lack all heart and understanding. I regret having lowered myself so far as to have spoken to you. Do not waste your time any more; I shall answer no further questions."

The Prior went back to his judgment seat, and the interrogation began again; but Aicart never opened his mouth. The clerk who noted down question and answer had to content himself each time with the phrase "Refused to reply." The Prior's two assistants, who were not so patient as he was, asked the prisoner insulting questions, such as "Do you admit professing the doctrine that adultery, incest, sodomy, and other such abominations are preferable to marriage in God's eyes?" or "Is it true that you permit members of your Faith to commit incest with their mothers, sisters, or daughters for a certain financial consideration?" Aicart was so sleepy that he could hardly stand up straight, and had to dig his nails into the palms of his hands to keep awake. It's a trick, he thought. They want to get me utterly exhausted, so that if they ask me: "Is So-and-So a member of your Church?" my face will give the truth away. He tried to concentrate his mind on words of prayer, but drowsiness jumbled them all up in his head.

"—Did your father know you were in Carcassonne?" a voice asked him.

He said nothing. Afterward he thought: I would have done better to say No. They are well aware that any testimony I give is the equivalent of formal proof. Oh, what does it matter? There are other people for whom I could not deny it.

At last his two warders came to take him back to his cell. God, he thought, I shall be able to sleep at last.

He had to walk down some steps, and then a door slammed behind him, and he was in a cold, black cell. There was some moldy straw on the ground, and a pale glimmer of light up near the ceiling hinted at a window. And then, as though by magic, two minutes after he had stretched out on the floor, drunk with sleep, Aicart suddenly felt so wide awake that he was sure he would be unable to sleep at all that night. His heart was beating too violently.

Why can I not forget this man, he asked himself: this man who called me his son, and spoke gently to me, and said, "My heart bleeds for you"? A toad's caress is harder to forget than a blow from a cudgel. Ugh, they even turn the desire to save our souls into something ugly. O Lord Jesus, if—which is impossible—obedience to Thy laws were to rob me of my salvation, I would still happily obey Thee.

O Lord, one can still obey for the wrong reasons. For us recantation is so deadly a disgrace that even supposing—though it is monstrous so much as to imagine it—I believed I could thereby attain salvation, my body would shrink from the dishonor.

O Lord, this man, damned as he was, said to me, "Perfect Love cannot dwell in a heart to which impure thoughts still gain access"; and I have not succeeded in avoiding such impure thoughts. Have I not longed for a woman with desire that overmastered my reason? But, O Lord, be Thou the Judge betwixt me and them. I tell myself: They accuse you of abominations, and your heart is consumed for a pure, chaste maiden—yet you have not dared to touch her save with a copper pestle. O Lord, they believed me capable of the vilest act a man can commit, though the merest shadow of sin put me in terror! But to tell the truth, if I saw that girl here before me now, I should say to her: I am a man. I am going to die.

One does not lie in the face of death. If I could sleep with you tonight my flesh would be no more humiliated than it is already; and at least I should know a joy of which men who do not live as we do can have not the faintest notion. . . .

O Lord, I have not haggled over the cost of my life. I am surrendering it at Thy first demand, even as I promised on the day of my ordination. But for good or ill, this *was* my life. Let me contemplate it now for the last time.

I loved a friend, and he was taken from me. O Lord, he was so much worthier than I that in that Heaven of Heavens where he now is I shall never see him again—not even from afar, not even through the Seven Spheres of Light. The love I bore him was more than any mortal creature's due. You, ignorant woman that you are, I did not love *you* truly; my feelings were lust merely—lust of the flesh, lust of the eyes. This was nothing, woman: no more than a warm breeze blowing over apple blossom, a simple, gentle, perishable emotion. It is not there that a man's true life lies. And may God spare you this life, in your virginal ignorance: may He spare you all debauchery of the heart and the unfathomable temptations of pride!

There came the sound of bells, and he heard, quite near yet high above him, the night watchman's drawn-out, melancholy cry. The prison was in the heart of the town, and its moat ran alongside the street. As a child, on stifling summer nights, Aicart had heard the same lonely, vigilant call. Our house is not far away, he thought. Oh, my father and my mother, what agonies I am laying up for you in your old age! It will profit you little to say: We disowned him long ago. These people will still suspect you of having been in touch with me.

Prime has been rung. Still two hours to wait before daylight. Before you pray, consider whether your brother has anything to reproach you with— God! Was *this* the way I was about to begin my prayers? Stubborn creature that you are, *submit to the Rule:* would you cherish your hatred above God's law? Were you going to pray just after you had treated your brother as a thing accursed, a beast with human face? Ah, I know what you will answer, in your craftiness and cowardice: This was not my brother, but an enemy. But it has been said: Love your enemies, bless them that curse you. You cannot argue yourself out of that.

If he neglect to hear the Church, let him be unto thee as an heathen man and a publican. . . . . Yes, but is it said that one should abuse heathens and publicans? You have happily violated the first Rule laid upon every Christian, by saying in your heart of hearts that to one about to die all things are permitted. *Heaven and earth shall pass away, but My word shall not pass away.* Reflect and consider: what is the miserable, petty rebellion of the flesh in one man who is to die—even as thousands die every day?

The publicans and prostitutes point to the way we should go. That old soldier, with more murders on his conscience than you have conversions to your credit, said of those who tortured him: *Whatever they do to me I am still in their debt.* But you have been ordained to a divine office: are not you forever in the debt of every man alive? Because you have become accustomed to seeing rich and poor kneeling before you, do you therefore allow yourself to raise your voice against people who are not of your religion and have no reason to respect you?

When dawn came Aicart had very nearly won back his peace of mind. So great is the power of the Rule that neither place nor time can prevent a man vowed to this discipline from forgetting his individual self. Through the years and the sorrows of life, through the temptations and the joys, two things remain constant: the bread of the soul, the impregnable bastions of faith.

Truly, Aicart thought, you are so small a thing that it matters little whether this is your last day on earth, or the day before the last. You and your petty temptations, petty rages, petty remorse— vanity of vanities!

The interrogation began again. There were no more questions to be asked, yet the Prior remained determined to convert this prisoner, and did his best to explain his various errors to him. Aicart, sorry now for his intransigence on the previous evening, apologized to his judges.

"I realize," he said, "that when you exhort me to accept what you believe to be the truth, you honestly suppose you are acting in my best interests. You have received this doctrine from your masters, and cannot yourselves be held wholly responsible for it."

This apology annoyed the two clerical assessors; but the Prior had heard similar sentiments before. He told himself that one should never despair of saving a sinner, and was only sorry that he had too little time at his disposal to achieve a conversion: an obdurate heretic never remained in the diocesan prison for very long. The present government and, indeed, the Bishop himself wished it thus: swift retribution was better calculated to strike terror into the faithful and to keep up the troops' morale. The soldiers, who had come all the way from their Northern provinces to defend their own Faith, were shocked at never seeing any heretics burned, and complained that episcopal justice was both corrupt and complaisant—an unfair accusation. The reason why so few heretics were caught lay in the difficulty of keeping order in a country given over to the anarchy of warfare.

The Prior, who was a man of sincere faith, found such impatience deplorable: it might be legitimate in itself, but it did very little for the cause of the Church. Granted that a case of plague must be isolated, need the patient's body also be destroyed? Surely to cure him would be an example that might result in the cure of further souls? And could so serious a malady be extirpated in two days, especially when the patient, taken by surprise, was holding out, with the energy of despair, against any attempt at treatment? This man is young, the Prior reflected, and therefore less deeply corrupt than some of his fellows. Truly, among these heretics it is not the heart which is corrupt, but the intellect: *here* the gangrene of error is to be found. The heart's conversion may be achieved in an instant; but that of the intellect needs many years—or a miracle.

"My son," he said, "I am praying for you. I spent the whole night in prayer, for your words wounded me grievously, and made me feel that I too was at fault. If I myself had been called upon by infidels to recant my Faith, I should have replied as you did— though perhaps less heatedly.

"Are you blind, my son? You are not an unintelligent man. You live in a country where the excellence of Holy Church is attested by splendid shrines and cathedrals, by the saintly lives of countless most venerable monks and nuns, by the lofty wisdom shown in the writings of innumerable learned scholars—to mention only matters of human piety. You have been shocked at the sight of certain unworthy ministers and evil shepherds. Do you suppose that I am not more shocked by these things than you? You are less exposed to temptations than they are. Do you count yourself so perfect that you can afford to cast the first stone at them?

"My son—and indeed you are young enough really to be my son—do not suppose that I am a hardhearted man. The sight of your strong and noble body, so full of life, wrings my very bowels with compassion; you have in it a splendid instrument destined to serve the glory of God, yet you want to see that instrument destroyed. Your faith is like that of the Pharisees: it exaggerates the demands imposed by Divine Law, merely to achieve self-glorification. It compels you to extend your compassion to the lowest of living creatures; yet you have no compassion for human weakness. What blind stupidity leads you to believe that the light in living eyes, the beauty of human features, the sun, the flowers, and every wonderful thing you can see in the world about you are the work of the Devil? What madness drives you to hate life so much that through your diabolical pride you come to desire its total renunciation? Your old parents are still living; you have brothers and sisters and friends—have you no pity for them? Have you thought of the sorrow you will cause them?"

"Are *you* in a position to tell me that?" Aicart asked, with melancholy disdain.

"I am not a judge," the Prior said. "I have accepted my duties in a spirit of obedience. The law that compels us to hand you over to secular justice causes us much suffering in our hearts. I am a servant of the Truth. All I have to give you is that Truth. I can only say: My son, I ask that you accept this trial, even though it seems less endurable than death itself, because I know, with utter certainty, that it is your one chance of salvation, either in this world or the

next. I pray, beseech, and implore you, cast away all pride, for
you should be beyond pride; all thought for your honor, since a
man who wishes to serve God can have no other honor than God's.
Try for one instant to say to yourself: *I am human and fallible.*
Perhaps I do not know what the Truth is; but I am ready to make
any sacrifice in order to know it better. I have tested this Truth,
and lived by it, and in every fiber of my soul I know it to be real.
I guarantee that once you have surmounted this first bitter ordeal
you will not be disappointed."

"I could say as much to you," Aicart observed, as calmly as he
could. "Recant your Faith, receive baptism at my hands, and mount
the scaffold with me. Then I will recognize in you a friend and a
brother. I am not telling you this in a spirit of mockery. But you
are asking me to do something which is utterly impossible for me.

"You can believe in the goodness of your Faith, since it has preserved enough of Christ's outward appearance to dupe credulous
souls: the Devil himself can create nothing that does not at least
possess the appearance of goodness, for otherwise he would not
be the Father of Lies. But the tree shall be known by its fruits.

"I could demonstrate the falseness of your creed from Scripture,
for in my younger days this was a matter which much occupied my
mind. But now I am more mature, and used to judging faith by
deeds rather than words—though I do not neglect words altogether. I have no need to make accusations against your Church:
your own bishops and Popes do that, with their attacks on 'rotten
fruit,' yet cannot see it is the tree that should be cut down. You are
a man not without kindness of heart; yet you confront me with a
proposition that says: Take it or leave it; accept my Truth, else you
die. To tempt souls thus is unworthy, for the flesh is weak, and
few men so detest life that they actively wish for death. I do not
want to die. I am myself a minister of my own Faith, and I believe
that Faith essential for salvation. But if I saw our bishops condemn men to death for their Faith I would say: God's Truth is not
in this Church. I would recant then, without a moment's hesitation."

"My son, can you not see the suffering which the imposition of this law on us causes me? In truth it is not the Church, but the harshness of the secular arm, that lays such a penalty upon all who disturb public order. We are mere torchbearers who go on in front to light the way: we can neither strike nor shield those footpads and wild beasts that our torches reveal. And we have not the right to put the torches out, either."

"I have not been a thief to my flock, nor yet a wolf. Those whom your brethren despoiled and degraded came to us of themselves; we did not constrain them. We imposed no tithes on them; we have not used their sweat and blood to build churches for ourselves. We have not threatened them with the stake in this world and all the tortures of Hell in the next. Freely they came to us, and laid down their goods and their lives for our sake. I am the least among the Church's servants, and the least worthy; but I can speak boldly, since it is not the man but the Christian whom you condemn in me. And charity forbids me to say who these footpads and wild beasts really are."

"It is easy," the Prior said, "for one whose hand is not on the helm to find fault with the steersman. What do you know of our labors and burdens, the ambushes laid for us at every step of the way? You have reaped in fields where we have toiled, and stolen some thousands or hundreds of thousands of souls from a Church that has brought whole peoples and kingdoms under Christ's dominion. And indeed you *are* thieves, and unworthy sons, thus to trample on the bosom of your Mother.

"And if the crime of parricide is punishable by death, with how many deaths should we not punish *your* crime? It is less cruel to murder one's mother than to drag her through the mire, spit upon her body, and dishonor her with vile calumnies. If a man who does such things deserves to be hated, how much more does he merit such hatred who, having done the deed, boasts of it vaingloriously?

"If I have felt pity for you, it was less for your body's sake than for that of your soul, which has sunk to such depths of vileness all unawares. For, painful though it is to me to say it, you deserve death more richly than any man alive."

"Others deserve it more, and have done so in the past—those

whom the soldiers you summoned burned, at Minerve and Lavaur and many other places; and those others who, God willing, will yet escape you! But those appointed to bear their palms before the throne of the Lamb, clad in white robes and washed in the blood of the Lamb, those same who have suffered great tribulation through you and yours—when on the Day of Judgment they wish to forgive you, and plead on your behalf, they will be unable to do so; for nothing will be left of your souls. They will have vanished for all eternity into the gulf of the void, and their master with them!"

After this Aicart had nothing to do but read through the verbatim report of his interrogation and append his signature to it. The Prior then pronounced sentence. He declared that the accused, Aicart, a citizen of Carcassonne, son of the noble Isarn de la Cadière and Marsilia de Cajar, was an apostate, a heretic, and a rebel; and that, this fact being admitted, agreed, and proved, the Church, seeing the said Aicart's stubborn obstinacy, hardness of heart, and perseverance in error, did hereby declare him cut off forever from the communion of the faithful, and abandoned him to the secular arm, recommending that his judges should not pronounce against the said Aicart any sentence involving mutilation of the limbs or other irreparable bodily harm.

When he heard the final words of this sentence, Aicart could not prevent himself from smiling.

"Is it God or men that you are trying to deceive?" he asked.

He was at once made to realize that he was no longer under the protection of the Church: one of the warders struck him. The Prior remarked that he would not tolerate such brutalities in his presence, and gave the order for the prisoner to be removed. The bailiff's escort had been waiting for a good half-hour at the prison gates and were becoming impatient: they were afraid that the heretic might play a dirty trick on them by recanting at the eleventh hour.

So Aicart returned to the prison where the jailer, two days before, had given him shelter. He felt utterly crushed; his head throbbed, and his body was drained of all its strength, as though after prolonged torture. Was this, then, the fear of death? A whole night left to live still, fifteen or sixteen hours—ah, even in this cell, with gyves on your wrists and your head shaven— This body, this wretched, blood-hot body of yours, quivering with life from the marrow in its bones to the very tips of its fingers, would be well content with this cell, this bed of straw, this jug of brackish water— Do they but know how rich a man is with such possessions?

He would not exchange them for a king's throne: all he wants is someone to tell him that it will go on like this forever, or for a year, or even for a month. Every kind of denial seems permissible to him, any vile act: what would the body care for mere words?

Yet with a word I can still stop this thing befalling me; and the word will be my death, for I shall never utter it. Not through the fear of being shamed before my fellows, nor for my own self-respect, but simply because the law imposed upon me is stronger than my own will. With all my heart and soul I wish I could say that word; but I shall not, ever. O Lord, I want to live; and Thou art Death!

O Lord, I have no knowledge of this other life that awaits me, and I have well-nigh forgotten that which is being taken from me. These few hours I still have left are more precious to me than the thirty-five years of my life put together, more precious than eternity itself.

How can Death be *good?* Death is the Enemy. It is obedience which is good: joyless, hopeless, endless obedience, stripped of all pride, the animal obedience rendered by our humiliated flesh. Yes, O Lord, I am but flesh, and the flesh desires to live! I have not even the strength to say: I have loved Thee unto death—I know nothing any more, I only know that I shall not deny Thee.

The great market place echoed loud and long with Ricord's last song to the glory of Arsen, a song that was a scream of agony and a cry for help and a prayer all in one. Lashed to the wooden horse that had been set up in the midst of the square, he cried out ceaselessly, in so powerful and heartrending a voice that the soldiers and knights who pressed around the scaffold to witness his agony felt their own hearts wrung with anguish, as though they were watching the death of a friend. They had largely forgotten that the man before them was a bandit and a cutthroat: it was a hard business to stand there and see his gray hair turn white before their eyes.

At first he had steeled himself against the torture, and suffered in silence; then he had fainted, till they revived him by throwing ice-cold water in his face. At that he had begun to cry out, calling on Arsen: *Arsen, can you see me? Arsen, Arsen, our children! our children!* He clung to this name to stop himself from howling like a wild beast; each shriek of agony was *Arsen! Arsen!* and nothing more, for he seemed to have forgotten all other words but this. Only at the very end did he mutter the one word, "Mercy."

When they turned that mutilated trunk over onto its belly to behead it, the man was already dead. His hair was white, his beard and face all dabbled red with blood; his eyes were staring, and his mouth yawned open, a black hole.

A few days later there was thrown into a pit of quicklime the body of the noble Lady Marsilia, mother of Aicart de la Cadière. The old woman, desperate to see her son for the last time, had slipped out of the house and joined the crowd around the scaffold. She returned home pale and in a sort of daze: then she began to rock herself to and fro, and to throw herself about, twisting and turning in all directions, like someone who was tied up and trying to wriggle free. All the time she kept uttering long, rattling sighs and groans, unlike any sound of which the human throat is capable: she neither saw nor heard anything that was going on around her.

At times she would come to her senses, press one hand against her forehead, and cry: "Ah, God, God, is such suffering possible? They made him suffer too much—they made him suffer too much!" Then she would begin writhing and struggling again. After three days of this she could stand it no more; she shut herself up in her room and cut her throat with a razor.

Old Isarn de la Cadière, summoned before the Diocesan Tribunal, swore he had always abominated his son's Faith and had had no contact with him since the beginning of the war. He also declared his devotion to the Catholic Faith, the Bishop, and the new Viscount. His goods were confiscated, professedly as a penalty for his past tolerance, and he was forced to leave the town, together with one of his daughters, who was a widow and kept house for him.

"May he be damned to eternity," old Isarn cried, "for causing his mother's death and bringing such tribulation upon me in my old age! Why could I not have seen him laid in the grave when he was yet an innocent child? I should have strangled him with my own hands the day he was born."

"Father, Father, what a wicked thing to say! He is one of God's martyrs!"

"Do *I* have to be a martyr, eh? Did I bring him up so that he might destroy me? Can God permit my child to endure such a death, yet leave me alive still?"

CHAPTER VIII

Gentian

MAY God pity the sad complaints sent up to Him by the women of any country at war—women rich or poor, married or widowed, old grandmothers and young maidens! No more love or happiness for them; now they are poor deposed creatures, useless burdens, flaws in the steel, keepers of empty houses, spinners without wool, laundresses with no shirts to wash! Brides of a moment, empty-armed mothers, women in love with no lovers to serenade them.

Their tender hearts are raw and red now, crushed ceaselessly between hammer and anvil, so beaten and bruised that in the end they no longer feel the blows. In the days of hatred and fear loving is a hard business. Better to be orphaned from birth, alone in the world, old, solitary, or deformed—better to have a heart as hard as any lump of granite.

You, girl with dry eyes, hardheaded girl: such joys await you in this world that you ought to give thanks and praise to your Creator. How should he be vanquished, when he is at all times and in all places the victor? He is our Lord and Master, he who was the most beautiful of all the angels: praise be to him, I dispute it no longer.

Through the red and blue glass of her window Gentian watched men bearing the fleur-de-lis banner march down the street. They wore no armor, their faces were open and smiling: their horses' harness was brand-new, studded with gold; they bore the scarlet cross on their white surcoats, and their standards were fringed with silk. Louis the Lionheart did not even have to fight. When he gave the order for the walls to be levelled, and disarmed his men of their swords and crossbows, the gates fell open before him. From

him we looked for justice, and he has thrown out our Count and
set the Beast in his stead; he has betrayed us, and the King of
France has not lifted a finger to defend us, but has let us be
crushed, and then sent his son to receive our homage. From him
we looked for justice, and he has not dealt justly with his vassal
and blood-brother, but has sent in his stead the wild Beast, the
butcher, the murderer of the most noble King of Aragon.

This is what the King has done to us, the King who owed us
justice: he has set our executioner as master over us, and sold the
sheep to the wolf. He has betrayed his race and lineage and the
whole nobility of every Christian country, not to mention his own
knightly honor: against our legitimate overlord he has upheld the
usurper.

O Louis, Prince of France, why can I not see *you* in my visions,
outstretched on the field of battle among corpses, gnawed by
wolves? Are my visions of disaster only for those dear to me? Ah,
Simon, Simon, if I could see your accursed face I would have no
difficulty in foreseeing the death that awaits you, and my heart
would rejoice thereat; for we shall see justice done ourselves, and
your death will not be a pleasant one!

Gentian was not at this moment alone in her room: but the
visitor who now spent long hours with her every afternoon was not
some easily dismissed servant. Bérenger d'Aspremont came of a
noble Toulouse family and was related to the Lady de Miraval; he
was, moreover, a knight, and exceedingly well favored. A man's
love is not like a necklace, which one can remove from one's neck
and place in a coffer; it is a golden chain to ensnare the feet. He
says he is dying for love of you, and that no lady was ever so
desired. "For one kiss from you," he says, "I would go to the
world's end." Which means: marry me first, and I shall go to the
wars thereafter. Bérenger wanted to go over into Aragon to join
the Count's troops there. He said it was love that held him back
in Toulouse.

"Will you love me the less, once you are married to me?" Gentian asked him.

"No: but if I needs must die, I shall have known the peak of happiness first."

As a result of her capricious and changeable moods, not to mention the advice given her by Jacques d'Ambialet and a suitor who was both persistent and lavish with his flowery compliments, Gentian found herself betrothed. After her father's death she had felt so miserable at not being a man herself that she had accepted Bérenger simply because of his knightly spurs and skill at swordplay. There were many other reasons as well, since in this world we do not always do what we want so much as what others expect of us: Gentian had little experience of worldly etiquette, and was only too ready to conform to it. After her previous setbacks she no longer dreamed of returning to her convent.

Bérenger d'Aspremont was thirty years old and had loved many women. The rules of love demanded that as a man grew older he should aim at increasingly lofty conquests. It was no Countess or Princess that Bérenger had chosen for his lady, but a poor girl all alone in the world, the daughter and sister of outlaws, a provincial who did not know so much as the language of love. But the first day he had set eyes on her, standing there tall and slim in her white dress against a background of scarlet tapestry, trembling in the wind of her own spirit like some tall poplar crackling in the flames—on that day Bérenger swore to have no other loves till he had won this woman. This was, of course, the sheerest lunacy: the girl had about as much taste for love as a horse has for meat.

Since he was no longer a youth, he was bold enough to declare his passion openly, and received a courteous rebuff: "Do not eat your heart out to no purpose," Gentian told him. "I am sworn to love of a different sort. You must seek a remedy for your ailment elsewhere."

He wore her favors, green and white, on his sleeve; he restricted himself as far as possible, at meals, to dishes which she had touched with her own hands; and in the evening he kept vigil outside her window, bareheaded, his cloak spread out on the ground as a token of submission. He was as adept as the next man at singing or declaiming verses, and the girl found his voice pleasant enough. But when she heard of her father's death she became so miserable that he no longer dared to speak to her of love.

By dint of seeing her at close quarters daily he came in the end to find her more desirable than any other woman in the world, with her deerlike manner, that dark complexion, and those sea-gray eyes, and her direct, ingenuous expression. Like some importunate visitor who, unable to obtain admission by way of the front door, afterward tries the back yard, so he now began to think of marriage, which would at least gain him the maiden's body. There are many men, he reflected, who find their way to their lady's heart in such a fashion.

The Lady de Miraval, who was his cousin, told him that this was known as putting the cart before the horse. "Why," she inquired, "do you want to marry a girl who has no money and is not in love with you?"

"Would it not redound greatly to my honor if I won such a woman?"

"Love may be honorable, cousin, but marriage is most often a contract. Would you dare demand of so pure a virgin the services you habitually expect from your concubines?"

"There are many men," said Bérenger, "who consider it great good fortune to be able to sleep with the woman they love."

"I do not call *that* love," the Lady Alfaïs said. "Still, this war has degraded so many noble and beautiful things that I cannot blame you. There is no room in the present age for either virtue or true courtesy."

Gentian said: "If I must live according to worldly laws, it will be with you rather than anyone else, since I feel that you love me loyally. My body I can yield up to you; as for my heart, which you desire so much, in truth I know nothing of it, though I do not think it is made for love."

There is no creature crueller or more brazen than a young woman. They are always driving men to do more than they either can or ought, simply because they love to hear of blood and danger.

Surely, they cry, you will not soil your lips with an oath of loyalty to the usurper? How can you remain kneeling at your lady's feet when our country is suffering so much? They all say such things: it is not their fathers or brothers they weep for but the shame that is upon their native land. And love in their eyes takes on the color of blood.

On that day, as Bérenger sat watching the lady of his heart, she stood up by the window, trembling, actually stamping her foot with rage, and said: "Still they come marching past, there is no end to it! How long shall we be left to endure this dishonor? You are a knight: how could you have brought yourself to surrender your sword to them?"

"Do not fear, my lady: I have kept the best one for myself."

"Why am I a woman? The worst possible insult one can bestow upon those of your sex is to treat them as women. Is the feminine condition one of natural cowardice? *We* are not even asked to swear oaths."

"My lady, if I had refused to swear that oath, I would have had no alternative but to go into exile the same day; and with the property remaining to me I could hardly have paid for the upkeep of a dozen soldiers. But they will pay dear for making us swear, you may be sure of that."

"Ah, that's what they all say!" the girl exclaimed bitterly. "*We submit only to gain time.* And what good has that done us so far? It was because the noble Aimery de Montréal served the Crusaders to begin with that the flower of our chivalry later suffered the affront of seeing him dangling from a gibbet! You will be treated as traitors, not as enemies."

"Does that matter?" Bérenger said. "To betray such masters is a real pleasure. And if I think of gibbets at all, my lady, it is not of those which they might one day make ready for us; it is of those which, God willing, we shall one day raise with our own hands for more than one traitor to this country! This war has made treachery a thing to boast of, and turned the hangman's trade into a fine profession. Since of your bounty you have deigned to choose me as your husband-to-be, have no fear that I will bring dishonor either on your favor or on the name which you will bear."

"Ah, I do not question your valor. How should I presume to do so? But we women are passionate to excess: if I were a man I should have opened this window, taken my bow, and put an arrow through one of these fellows' heads, just to avenge my brother, who himself died in exactly the same way."

"Do not worry: the day will come when such a death seems too good for them. *They* will go down before hammers and hatchets and kitchen knives. Another year or two, and Simon de Montfort will be hunted through the woods like a mad wolf, and then flayed and hanged."

"Ah, Bérenger, have you forgotten that their Master is the prince of this world? For them he does his miracles, and against him neither good reason nor faith in God will ever prevail on earth."

She was pacing to and fro between the chest and the bed as she spoke, her hands clasped under her chin, eyes hard and brilliant.

"My friend," she went on, "what breaks my heart more than anything else is the thought that we shall never, *never* be able to do anything worse to them than they have already done to us. Suppose we hang them, or torture them, or gouge their eyes out, or chop them into little pieces: they have done these things to just and innocent persons, while we would merely be punishing murderers. Even supposing we were powerful enough to invade their country, to burn down their homes and rape their daughters, still they have already served us in the same fashion, without any aggression on our part. They would be getting no more than their just deserts, while we have done nothing to merit such treatment."

Bérenger said: "All I want is to see them out of this country. When they're gone we shall be able to live in peace. I would gladly cry quits with them for the rest."

"Have they cut off *your* father's arms and legs, and stuck his head on a spear above the city gates? I should rejoice for my father's sake, since he is now in Paradise; but how are we to treat those who have done these things to him? Are they to get off scot-free to their Northern castles, and make a joke of the whole business with their wives? Can we let them do that?"

"My sweet," Bérenger said, rising and taking the girl by the shoulders, "you must not think any more about your father's death. It is cruel past bearing. What grim times that force women to harden their hearts thus! The sex is made for tenderness and all gentle courtesy. Ah, this is strange lovers' talk we are having!"

With her eager, thoughtful eyes Gentian searched Bérenger's features. She saw a proud, high-colored countenance, a mouth both strong and handsome; his thick hair was curly and brown, and so long that it fell over his forehead almost to the eyebrows. A sinewy man, as quick in his movements as a thoroughbred: thoughtful, courteous, and learned too. Is not my betrothed a fine man? Gentian reflected. Would not my father have been proud of such a son-in-law? Has not my mother always wanted to see me married? What does it matter now? Nothing can cause me fear or shame any more. Here I stand before my Enemy who is my friend, with his hands on my shoulders and his breath hot on my cheek.

What else have I to lose? The French have entered Toulouse, the country is sold and betrayed—and my father's long struggle is ended. "Ah, Bérenger," she said aloud, "why have you chosen me to be your lady? I am neither beautiful nor skilled in courtly manners. For three years I lived in a convent, exhausting my body with prayer and fasting and vigil. I am twenty-three, which is old for marriage. I am exceedingly ill instructed in those gentle, tender ways which you will look for in me."

"My lady, I need a wife such as you, one I can look up to. And if the chances of the flesh lead us to bring forth children, they will need a mother strong in the Spirit to guide them to their salvation."

All was ready for the wedding, and now even the Lady de Miraval was anxious to see it accomplished. Since Bishop Foulques had been master of the city, it had not been advisable for any girl who had visions to remain too long unmarried. And though Gentian's visions were less frequent now, they had become bloodier than ever: she saw the Bishop himself, together with his acolytes and servants, all bespattered with gore, moving across a corpse-strewn field like plunderers after a battle.

The engaged girl had not a penny to her name: the prospective bridegroom was obliged to provide her dowry before the wedding. To make over house and lands to the daughter of a man who had suffered public execution as a rebel against Church and Sovereign was a somewhat perilous honor. But to the Chancellery clerks and the Consuls alike Ricord de Montgeil was a hero, and this marriage served to enhance rather than diminish Bérenger's reputation.

The bride was making ready in her chamber, with the aid of the daughters of the house: she was in a state of deep distress and agitation. Dame Alfaïs, who was supervising her preparations, smilingly reassured her.

"If you go into a shop owned by a Mohammedan or a Jew," she said, "simply to buy some scent or any other similar feminine trifle, do you really suppose that means you're converted to the shopkeeper's religious faith? If this ceremony is forced on us by the law of the land you should not attach greater importance to it than it deserves. Only a weak faith would fear such a test."

"My lady, before I came to Toulouse I had never been inside a church at all; till today my body has had no truck with the Devil's sacraments. The priest will speak to me as though I were baptized in his Faith. He will raise his hands over me and bless me. He will even give me the crucifix to kiss!"

"My dear child, you know perfectly well it is impossible for us, here in Toulouse, to live according to the pious customs by which your family brought you up. We have learned outward submission as a means of keeping the Faith pure in our innermost hearts. The Bishop has never forbidden such a practice. Our bodies alone are obedient to the laws of this world: and if you can eat, drink, and sleep, why can you not also endure this outward humiliation, since it touches no part of your heart?"

Gentian was led to the altar by an elderly uncle of the Lady Alfaïs, and was joined in matrimony to Bérenger d'Aspremont, knight, to be his lawful wedded wife. The Lady de Miraval herself, who was sitting immediately behind the newly married couple, was afraid, from her appearance, that her ward might at any moment pass into a state of prophetic possession. The girl was deathly pale and shivering; she held herself absolutely stiff the whole time, as though she were afraid of falling. Bérenger glanced uneasily at his bride, wondering whether her condition might not be due to her aversion to him: he was deeply in love, and the girl's obvious terror merely served to increase his desire. Such chaste shyness showed great nobility of character. He had known too many women who beamed invitingly the moment they saw him in the distance.

Gentian thought: How cleverly Satan spreads his snares of the senses to entrap our hearts—the chanting and the candles, the ornate altar and painted walls, all this purple and gold, the too sweet smell of that blue incense smoke! How well he knows how to arouse concupiscence in our eyes and flesh! I hate this chanting, yet my ear tells me it is beautiful. The light that filters through these stained-glass windows touches my eyes like a caress. What my soul rejects my body receives with joyful acceptance. O Lord, have mercy on me: it is my father's butchers who now sing in this choir, the gold and enamel are all crimson with his blood. We are crucified by Rome and the Cross of Rome. Our land has been sold by Rome's priests. For the sake of tonsured monks and unleavened bread and Church treasures the sanctity of our soil has been violated; and our bodies remain imprisoned here, as though in a dream, enduring these devilish sorcerers' spells.

As though in a dream she saw the hand of the priest join her hand to Bérenger's; as though in a dream she took the ring and bowed low before the Cross. It seemed to her as though someone else were performing these gestures in her stead, an icy, lifeless body, a strange girl with nothing in her head but the clash and hammering of bells, and a gaping hole where her heart should be. She drew down the flame-colored bridal veil over her face: the whole church turned red, and the candles trembled, and under the light silken material she could feel her face flushing with heat. Yet now she was calmer: veiled, and therefore withdrawn; free to close her eyes and pray. No one was surprised by her gesture: rather they admired her nerve. The priest, who knew exactly what her behavior meant, affected not to notice anything.

The bride entered the Aspremont mansion on her husband's arm. The floor of the great hall was all spread with flowers, while garlands and freshly cut branches adorned the walls. The young bridesmaids sang in chorus to the music of flute and cittern; the table was set for fifty guests, and the gleaming white napery all embroidered in silver. Such a mass of candles had been lit in every sconce and chandelier that even by daylight their brightness hurt the eyes. It was indeed a gay wedding. Let them not suppose they have beaten and impoverished us, Bérenger thought. Let them not boast of having taken our happiness away. Let them envy in us what they cannot have themselves—the freedom to laugh and sing in our own homes, with our friends and womenfolk around us. They can, if they will, take all this from us; but they will not gain happiness thereby.

Gentian sat there in her high gilded chair, a little gray now, weary of smiling, and watched the candles guttering down in their sockets. It is evening, she thought: the church bells are ringing for Vespers, the town is fading from sunset-red to gray. The torches are being lit out in the streets, and the streets are crowded with foreign soldiers. And I am dressed all in red: red dress, red veil. Farewell to my black habit, that I so desperately longed to wear; I shall never sing the New Song now.

What was it you told me that day, Master Deacon? "You are nothing. A weak woman who raves and believes herself visited by the Holy Spirit simply because she is tormented by the devils of the flesh." Was it true, what you told me then? Doubtless you knew more of these things than I did. I have heard much, indeed, of the flesh and its diabolical delights; yet they might as well have been talking about the lands of the Indies where people have dogs' heads.

Suppose I got up and went now, away out of this house, still wearing the red dress and necklaces and earrings that are offerings from the man who has bought me. Suppose I went to the palace of the Devil's Bishop, and said: "My Lord, I have lived hitherto in the shadows of abominable heresy. I want to make my confession to you alone, and tell you everything I know about the heretics in this town." Once I was close to him, I know what I should do. He wears no coat of mail; I would stab him straight through the heart, a little to the left of his cross. How I died afterward would not matter: I should not have lived in vain. If I must lose my soul, let the loss at least be profitable.

Foolish creature! You are being asked to destroy yourself *for nothing,* to kill your pride and the vain urge to glory that is in you. *If you can eat, drink, and sleep, why can you not also endure this outward humiliation, since it touches no part of your heart?* After a Catholic marriage ceremony comes the ceremony of the bridal bed: back to the flock with you! Did you take yourself for the Mystic Lamb—*you,* the lowliest among the Shepherd's ewes? Later, after twenty or thirty years, you will begin to understand what God demands of your soul. You will come to Him an old, ugly woman, defiled by the habits of animal love and a dozen or more childbirths, who looks back on her younger virgin self as though on some extravagant child. Humble, O Lord? Yes, I shall be humble then, and with good reason. They all envy me my virginity: even you, Master Deacon, you were jealous of it as well.

In the eyes of the world you never broke the Rule. You remained pure—or so, at least, I believe and hope. Had you no idea, Monseigneur, how great a power you and your like possess? Did you not realize that one glance from you would weigh more heavily than a thousand kisses from anyone else, that it had the power of lightning falling from Heaven? You had no right to fall to earth from such a height.

Yet in truth I must forgive you: you have gone where I have not, and after nearly a year my heart still bleeds for you. It is useless for people to say: "He has been glorified, God has judged him worthy to bear witness," or again: "He has done his duty as a Christian." Why could you not keep out of the clutches of these accursed devils, who take living men and roast them like capons? For your soul I need have no pity; but your smile, your slender hands, your eagle eye, your flesh so cruelly destroyed, all these stir me to such deep compassion that I shall never be able to begrudge you them. You never raised your voice, but *they* made **you** shriek aloud. You were always as straight as a taper, and bore yourself with royal nobility; but *they* reduced you to a mere beast, howling and writhing in your bonds.

Every word you spoke to me was coldly dignified; you knew only too well how to avoid looking at me. Perhaps I dreamed— No, may I be condemned to the prison-cycle of a thousand lives if I know the least thing about such matters! I was virgin of heart as I am still in body, and your glance burned me like the red-hot iron with which criminals are branded. You possessed the power to turn shadow into substance, illusion into truth; and you looked at me as any shameless man would look at a beautiful girl!

I am not beautiful; yet even so my meager charms are still, I doubt not, more than is proper. Oh, I should have cut off my nose and lips—this very night a man will come in to me and say: "Be my lover"; he too will find me beautiful, and look at me as though he were dying of thirst. You were not forced into doing this by threats or blows, Gentian. It is your own pride that is your un-doing: you want to stop people from looking at you in pity, and talking about you behind your back. O my lady Alfaïs, I am no Dove, no torch of Truth; I am not among the elect.

The maidens attendant on the bride unhooked and unlaced her wedding dress, combed out her hair, and rubbed perfume into her arms. So tall and slender and solemn was Gentian that she had the air of a bishop being robed for the Paschal Mass. The Lady Alfaïs came and kissed her on the forehead. She said: "My child, I know very well that these customs are both pagan and impious, and that we should be weeping rather than laughing because of them. But if we needs must bow to secular rule, let us hide our sadness in our hearts. Remember that even the holiest of women have passed through this ordeal without so much as a murmur."

How should one receive a husband who, despite the most com-mendable efforts, has not in the end been able decently to refuse to drain two or three goblets of good wine? Now he was, not exactly drunk, but somewhat more excited than usual as he came to court his bride. He was wearing a long pink nightshirt: with his curly hair and clean, close-shaven face he looked a mere youth. He sat at Gentian's feet with his cittern, but his fingers were trembling so violently that he could not play it properly.

Finally he said: "I have no voice for singing this evening; my mind is too preoccupied with thoughts of you."

"I too," Gentian said, "am cruelly preoccupied."

"You feel nothing of what I feel," he retorted bitterly. "You have accepted me as one might accept some punishment. I have given my heart to the hardest woman on earth, who still torments me even after accepting my suit."

"It is you who torment yourself. I married you out of esteem and courtesy."

"I do not wish to boast, but I have known other girls who would have given me their hand with greater pleasure."

"My friend, I am glad to think that my father would have been proud to welcome you as his son-in-law. My parents always wanted to see me married. Master Jacques d'Ambialet gave me to understand that it is fitting a young girl should marry out of obedience rather than love."

He said: "I am neither old, nor ugly, nor gross in my ways. Will you become my lover tonight?"

Gentian had not expected so brutally direct a question: she felt her courage failing her.

"If I said yes," she replied, "would I not be wanting in the modesty becoming to my sex? Our nature urges us to flee such intimacy. Bérenger, if all you wanted was another concubine, would you have chosen a woman like me?"

Bérenger said: "You should know that I have put away all my concubines. I love you so much that I wish for no other woman."

"How can you call this love?" she asked. "True love spurns the gifts of the body."

"My lady, it is hard to tell what 'true love' is. When Love takes possession of us, we serve him as best we can, and speak of him according to our knowledge. He is a torment and a joy for body no less than soul, and even among the most famous lovers of history the two are inseparable. Such is the power of love that when

I see you there, so pure and chaste, my desire for you increases ten-fold. How miserable I would be if you spurned me I cannot even tell you."

Gentian turned her head so that she no longer need see that beseeching, humiliated face bent over her; she wished she could have stopped her ears as well. He seemed even more unhappy than he claimed to be: his voice was breaking, and tears stood in his eyes. He was saying now that she should take pity on him and not drive him out of his mind with grief; that she was too hard, that a woman should not put off a lover once she has opened the door of her chamber to him— So I am hardhearted, am I? she thought. Shall I show him pity, then? And why should I feel pity when the land is in such evil plight, when my father has been tortured, and my brother is dead, and my mother hunted through the woods like a wild animal, and Christians are burned in the public square? Am I to feel pity for a strong, well-favored man who breaks into most undignified lamentations simply because a woman is severe with him? In truth, any knight who grovelled thus to save his life would be scorned by his comrades! Is the agony of love so powerful? Can it be that he loves me as much as *that*?

Till this moment she had supposed Bérenger to be a sensible, levelheaded person.

"If you are a true lover," she said, "at least do not clasp me so close in your arms, or kiss me like that; it frightens me."

He said she ought not to be afraid, that he was her lover.

"Ugh!" she said, "this room is so tiny, I'm stifling—and all these perfumes, and the smell of the candles— At least open the window and let in some fresh air."

He snuffed the candles and threw open the small window. Through the lozenge pattern of the grille Gentian could see the house opposite, with its crenellated street wall. A prison? she wondered. Have I not always known that life was a prison?

"Are you not my enemy, then?" she said aloud.

In the darkness, dazed by a hail of tender words and kisses, she thought: So this is what they mean by the corruption of soul and body. She felt neither repugnance nor hatred; indeed, she was scarcely surprised. Yet neither her mother nor any of her companions had ever come so close to her. Was she then to permit a man, a stranger, to do what she had not tolerated at the hands of any woman—and not die of shame? My God, she thought, when I yield my body must I also yield my soul? They told me that if the soul remained vigilant it could avoid defilement; and now it is as though I had neither soul nor the power of thought.

Next morning the young bride shut herself in her room for a period of prayer and meditation: she refused to see anybody. Leaning on her lectern, she searched through Holy Writ for an answer to questions that she felt incapable of solving: Where is the boundary set between soul and body? What is the relationship between the will and the sinful act? *Whosoever looketh on a woman to lust after her hath committed adultery with her already in his heart:* if thought has such power, what matter if the whole body is given over to corruption? And if my body is now corrupt and rotten, what can I do to keep my soul unspotted? The holy women who taught me were preparing me for a virgin life; they never explained how one could detach soul from body at so formidable a moment of temptation. Yet we must suppose that they themselves remained pure of heart, even when married. And what of me? The very first time I all but experienced joy in my very shame—or if not joy, at least no great distress.

This man I have married is no true lover, but an ignorant creature, more skilled in the artifices of vulgar love-making than in true courtesy and affections of the mind. But how could I have known the way he was? It seems it is as foolish to judge a husband before you have slept in his bed as it would be to judge the sword by its scabbard.

Shortly before noon Bérenger came in search of her, with a request that she should come down and receive his friends and family: he was sorry, he added, but this was something she could not refuse to do.

"Tell them," Gentian said, "that you have married a provincial girl unacquainted with the finer points of etiquette, who prefers the company of books to theirs."

"Indeed I would," he said, half smiling, half annoyed, "if the finer points of etiquette did not forbid a man to discuss his wife. If you refuse to come down, my relations will regard it as a deliberate affront to me."

"It is possible that is what I want. *You* wanted to be happy; are you?"

He looked at her with a curious expression, in which a kind of desire mingled with something that might have been either impatience or regret.

"I must needs assume that I am," he said. "Less than I had hoped, since I can see you have very little affection for me."

"You once said you would be the happiest man in the world if you could possess me wholly."

"And you know very well that I have *not* possessed you wholly. Do you take me for a mere churl? I would have no more possessed you if I had taken you by rape. For a year now I have been trying to make you realize that I care for you more than anything else in the world. You should know me better by now."

"I am hardheaded," Gentian said.

"Hardhearted, rather. I wonder what I must do to win that heart of yours?"

Why does he look at me with those suffering eyes when it is he who has made *me* suffer? Gentian thought. And what is his complaint? Only a few hours ago he thought himself dying of bliss, and now look at him: like a gambler who has just staked his shirt and lost it. Surely he is old enough to realize that this devil's game of his is only for dupes?

She said: "Are *you* asking how a woman's heart should be won —and asking it of me, who know nothing of such matters?"

"Now is your chance to make mock of me, then. With you, truly, I have no notion how to proceed: you lack both the tenderness and the gentle disposition natural to your sex."

This criticism touched Gentian on the raw. "My friend," she

said, "that is not my fault. I will be frank with you: you think about love as people used to do before the war. Today there is only one way of winning a lady's heart—any lady worthy of the name, that is. You know very well what it is, and I would not wish you to win my heart in such a way. It is the dead who have the right to our love, from the noble King of Aragon to the lowliest foot soldier who has fallen spear in hand: it is for them our hearts bleed and mourn. To love those who have made the ultimate self-sacrifice is a natural instinct. The living cannot be blamed for this; but my heart has bled so much that I find the torments of love a futile thing."

Bérenger flushed and drew himself up as though he had been struck.

"Very well, my lady. I understand. I shall endeavor to act in the way that will win your love. When you are a widow, you will have my example to dangle in front of your next prospective husband."

He went out.

Ah, God, Gentian said to herself, did he think I was accusing him of cowardice? Why, had I not all the regard for him that is due to a fine and honorable man? Why does he demand tenderness of me at the precise moment when I am least capable of giving it— when by force of circumstance he has become my enemy? Yet I do not know where I am any longer myself—is it possible for us *not* to hate a person who violates our soul and reduces it to mere flesh? And can the soul be made flesh? I desired the highest Love of all, and was rejected. In twenty or thirty years, you told me, Master Deacon. Certainly I shall not begin to understand this new life in a day.

Bérenger was not proud of his behavior: only the lowest sort of churl could speak harshly to a woman after giving her proof of his affections. But this woman was so high-minded that she did not even think of feeling grateful to him: her marriage had merely brought her riches and security, to both of which advantages she was totally indifferent. She ignored them; she thought of nothing but her immortal soul. There are certain people who do not object to being beaten, especially when they are aware of their own strength; and so Bérenger found himself admiring this young girl, and reflecting that you could not expect the daughter of a man such as Ricord de Montgeil to coo like any dove. Despite all the services he had rendered his country, Ricord had a somewhat sinister reputation: patriotism, it was thought, did not perforce demand that extra hardihood necessary for slitting the throats of wounded men or monks.

Bérenger was the more satisfied with his marriage in that his uncle (who had himself married a Consul's daughter) criticized him for it severely.

"It's hard enough already for us to live peacefully," the old man said, "and now you have to squander a quarter of your inheritance on a match like that! People will think you've done it to honor the father rather than to please the daughter."

"How should I not honor a man who wreaked such havoc on our enemies?"

"I would have been very glad if I'd been able to do what he did; but courage is one thing, and madness another. Men like him put us in a compromising position. It is because of them that our knights are put on the same footing as brigands and bandits. He got a legal trial, anyhow."

"Yes: at Carcassonne."

"If we do not behave prudently, a year hence Toulouse will be another Carcassonne."

"Prudence, Uncle, is a seductive lady, but not always on intimate terms with Honor. I have been reproached enough already for being overprudent."

Before the wedding Bérenger had pledged the whole of his property apart from that which would revert to Gentian, and in this way had succeeded in raising a hundred silver marks. With such a sum he reckoned on being able to recruit about thirty good soldiers in Spain. He intended to leave town on some excuse or other, taking with him his squires and those of his servants who were fit to bear arms. Gentian had to sign a large number of documents: she now became the sole and only owner of all goods re-

ceived by her as dowry, and declared that her fortune could not
be used in any way for her husband's benefit, either to pay his debts
or in any other manner that made it liable to confiscation.

"So long as Toulouse preserves its charter and privileges,"
Bérenger said, "this legal contract will hold good, and whatever I
may do, no one will lay hands on your property." He seemed to
believe that the world would collapse sooner than Toulouse would
lose its rights.

"Why are you so determined to protect your worldly wealth?
You could put it all to good use. The day your goods are confiscated your creditors will accuse you of fraud. But if you lose
everything, people will see that you acted from patriotic motives."

"Do you want our children, one day, to hold it against us that
we left them no patrimony with which to make their friends gifts?
This war will not exactly have enriched us. Still, once the country
is liberated, we shall be able to get our property back from the
French—which is more than we shall be able to do from our own
bankers."

"Our children, Bérenger, if ever we have any, may rather reproach us for having brought them into the world at all; for this
war is nowhere near its end yet. There will be no peace for us
while any Christians remain in the country. We shall have to bring
our children up in poverty, fortitude, and the hatred of evil, not in
the luxuries and vanities of this world."

"God grant that you be mistaken!" Bérenger said. "We cannot
endure this sort of existence much longer."

How dismal it is to be a woman, Gentian thought. For him it is
all quite clear-cut: *he* is going to fight. Even though he may spend
six months trailing around from castle to castle, frittering all his
money away, simply because he cannot find a fighting force to join!
How many of our men have lost their time thus, and all for nothing? But we women cannot wage war; so what are we to do now?
We are of less use than bread and wine in a burning house.

Before he left Bérenger asked his wife if she still desired to see
him dead. A month had passed since the wedding, and the two of
them had spent more time talking of war than love—thanks to

which they got on well enough together. After that first night Bérenger promised himself not to exercise his marital rights again till he came home from the wars; so Gentian had perforce to admit that he was behaving with true lover's devotion. Besides, she believed herself to be with child, and she knew that men have a weakness for wanting to hand on both name and heritage to a son. If I tell him, she thought, he will doubtless experience worldly and inappropriate feelings of pleasure. And *how* am I to tell him?

"Did you not tell me," Bérenger said, "that only those who get themselves killed have the right to a lady's love? I dearly hope to give you the lie over this, since I want to kill rather than be killed. What more defeated a thing is there than a dead man?"

"There are those who are not defeated in death, but attain the highest glory. Bérenger, I know that you are a faithful member of our Church, but I feel you remain, despite everything, one of those who are neither hot nor cold. I cannot blame you for having Catholic friends; but the false sacraments to which you pay lip service will end by poisoning your soul."

"You will never change," he said, almost cheerfully. "I speak to you of love, and you reply with sermons. I only wanted to know whether you will think of me a little when I am gone."

She said: "Even though I might not wish it, in all likelihood I shall be forced to despite myself. You see, Bérenger, I believe myself to be with child by you. You can understand, then, how I may be forced to think of you."

He bit his lip, not knowing whether the news pleased or distressed him.

"I think," said he, "that I care too much for you, dear heart, to attach overmuch importance to what you have just told me. If you regard it as a misfortune, why then, so do I."

Gentian thought: I do not hate him after all. She came close to her husband and took his head in her hands.

"If such is our fate," she said, "let us submit to it with dignity. I shall not be sorry to have sons who may one day avenge my father. May this child live, then, and may I instill into its body through my blood and my milk everlasting hatred of our enemies!

Today I live according to the flesh, and henceforth hatred is a thing permitted me. May this child live to love our country and our Faith and, one day, to attain salvation. And for my sake no less than his, I long to see you come marching back into Toulouse with our Count's army—though it be in a year, or even five years from now!"

CHAPTER IX

Renaud of Limoux

TOWARD the end of September an armed troop, with a cleric
from the See of Narbonne at its head, appeared at the Ventajou sawmill. The owner was asked to produce "one Renaud, a
burgher of Limoux, wanted by the Bishop's Court as a heretic and
apostate." Renaud only just had time to escape into the forest,
taking his books with him. Both the owner and his workers swore
they had never known the said Renaud; despite this they were taken
off to Narbonne for further interrogation. Two days later, the inhabitants of Ventajou saw a grisly sight as they trudged out to their
vineyards: the corpse of a man, its hands and feet lopped off, its
arms and legs covered with brand marks in the shape of a cross,
lashed to a stone tethering post beside the horse trough. Its face
had been spared, so that everyone would be able to recognize it.
The man had worked at the sawmill for a fortnight, and then left
to go and visit his sick father in Narbonne. Whether he was an informer or not no one ever knew.

Arsen and Fabrisse left the sawmill and retreated as far as
Laurac, where they were given shelter by the lord of that fortress.
The whole place was in the hands of the Crusaders, and the Seigneur de Laurac passed for a staunch Catholic. The two women
were put to work in the kitchen; here they found several of the
brethren concealed, disguised for the nonce as cellarmen or masons.
At night they would hold meetings in the bedchamber of the Seigneur's wife. To these meetings only very close friends and completely trustworthy servants were admitted. It was a small room,
and very often some of the worshippers fainted from lack of air.
Fabrisse, who had chest trouble, said she wished they were still
living out in the woods.

In October the Seigneur de Laurac entertained Count Simon de Montfort himself in his castle; the Count was travelling across country on his way to Agenais. There was a great feast that day: hogsheads of wine were carried down to the soldiers encamped outside the walls, while the Count's knights received presents of mantles, rings, and embroidered fabrics for their wives. The ramparts were all ablaze with flaring torches, and every chamber was decorated. At the banquet itself, which lasted till nightfall, the minstrels of France and Languedoc vied with one another in a courtly contest: the lady of the castle strained good manners to the extent of awarding the Frenchmen the prize. Simon de Montfort, it was known, had little time for junketings; but he enjoyed listening to the songs of his country.

That evening Fabrisse lay stretched out on the flagstones in the kitchen, softly singing hymns to herself, and wondering if she would ever get her voice back.

"My sister," Arsen said to her, "would you have the courage to pray for this man?"

"For all men, my friend: else prayer would be nothing but vanity and mere mortal contrivance. The sun must shine alike upon the just and the wicked."

Arsen thought: My eyes have looked upon the Beast, my country's butcher. He has a man's face; he eats and drinks like other men. Can any human body have the power to do such great evil? He is one man; yet he weighs more heavily upon us than ten thousand of his fellows.

"Listen, Fabrisse," she said. "Our brother Aicart, who was taken at Carcassonne, was still a young man. If he had lived he might have saved hundreds of souls. He would never have gone into a town where everyone knew him unless he had been summoned to a dying person's bedside. So he gave his life for *one man*."

"If we had the right to pick and choose among the dying when they called upon us, what would our ministry be worth?"

"Fabrisse, my heart grieves when I think how early he was cut down: he might have grown greater yet in the Spirit and in grace."

"The wage is the same for all," Fabrisse said.

"True. But how much more joyful is the man who has labored from morning till evening, and slaved long hours in the service of Love! How sad it is to see the departure of those who still had so much left to love on this earth!"

"Up there, they love still better."

Arsen said, thoughtfully: "I have no desire to quit this vale of tears. Suffering only serves to prove our love the better."

"What does our love matter? Only God's love exists—in us, through us, or without us."

"I know that well. But the human heart yearns so powerfully for the joys of love that it would gladly endure torments for a thousand years for the greater glory of the Loved One."

Fabrisse sighed, and said nothing. She knew what martyrdoms her companion had been suffering since the news of her husband's death had reached her. "It is little profit to me knowing that one of our Brethren managed to see him the night before his death," Arsen had said. "How am I to be sure he did not succumb under torture? They say he called my name to the very end. And I was not there."

She had wept and moaned, tearing at her cheeks with clawed hands like any ordinary widow. The sorrow that racked her, this most un-Christian grief, was so overpowering that she could not even begin to control it. The flesh may be nothing, Arsen thought, but the sufferings of the flesh are not: they tear the soul apart as well. My loyal partner was tortured to death: ax, knife, and saw entered his soul through the thousand pangs he suffered. His fine and noble soul was cut to pieces; in what condition, then, did God receive it?

Why was I not there? The wood merchant's clerk, who saw it all, still wept when he thought of the scene. The whole town heard him crying out for me; yet I, his partner, was not there. "You could hear him far beyond the market place," the clerk said. "No man who had lost so much blood ever shouted so loud. And when he cried out, *Arsen!* the very soldiers hung their heads. Till that night we all had that name ringing in our ears, every one of us; we could think of nothing else. And when the executioner brandished the head aloft by its white hair, so many folk yelled out: *Down with the bloody butcher!* that the soldiers dared not bid them be quiet. Everyone knew he was a brave man who had never taken so much as a sou for himself."

Ricord, have you forgiven me my harsh words? Yours was a pure soul, and sinned greatly only through excess of love. How has God received your soul now? In what strange habit, all torn and bloody, have you presented yourself at the wedding feast?

For days on end Arsen's prayers were nothing but tears and lamentations. Never had she found herself so close to God. Never had she burned with so fierce a love for God's own image, so cruelly tortured and harried here on earth. O Lord, she prayed, how terrible is the earthly destiny of all that belongs to Thee in this world, all that seeks Thee and longs to love Thee in this world, this flame of love that is Thy sole possession in this world! Who can withstand love's madness? God is the love of lost souls. Here on this earth God is consuming pity and unwearying tenderness. And just as I will never weary of cherishing my dear comrade's mutilated soul, so likewise will the Father never weary of His infinite compassion.

He was, indeed, a great sinner; yet I know what love it was on which his soul spent itself, and can I not now forgive him for it? Lo, my eyes have seen the Butcher, the Beast with human face, and yet I cannot bring myself to pray for him. But, O Lord, perhaps in him too the flame of love still burns, however defaced and profaned by Satan's myriad lies. O Lord, Thy pity is folly, and Thy Image, mocked here by us, weeps on high among the angelic choirs!

In the silence of the night Arsen heard the wailing and sobbing of lost souls, defiled souls that cried and cried in vain: *Lord, Lord, let us see Thy face! We are sunk in a sea of filth, our eyelids are glued together, our ears filled with silt!*

She would see dozens of pure and gleaming souls fall, struggling, like birds with a broken wing, into the black pit of the womb, the warm and clinging prison of the flesh. For the whole earth was nothing more than shapeless flesh, peopled with lost souls struggling and writhing, about and about, in a vain urge to break out into the light. Have pity, she thought, on all tiny babies, opening their unfocussed eyes for the first time; on little children, prattling like birds, because they do not yet know they are in prison! Small desolate points of light, condemned to long burial in the night of the flesh—and then, scarcely have they torn themselves free, with tears and anguish, scarcely have they made one leap heavenward, when their broken wing plunges them back into darkness again. How long, O Lord? How long?

Of all those reunited with their lost Spirit through the grace of the Sacrament, how many held fast to it in their death agony? How many passed over the barrier without breaking their newly regained wings against it? Once we said not even death could part us; yet in four years I saw his face once only, and when death came to him I was far away. O Lord, I know nothing of his soul's great struggle; I am in the blackness myself.

Love is like the pangs of childbirth, and pity resembles our anguish when we hear the weeping of the child who has come forth from our belly. O Lord, behold this country, behold this earth, behold the souls, thousands upon thousands of them, who inhabit our world: in Your sight they are no more than a child, howling because he has bruised himself. Ah, Lord, the agony of it! Save us from this world, and the pangs of love that pierce us to the quick!

Aloud she said: "Fabrisse, my sister, what are we doing here? We have a refuge, true; but a refuge can also be a prison. No one will dare bring sick folk or the dying to us in this place. Unless we want to become mere barren fig trees, we must move on again."

"I agree, my sister; but we must do it in such a way that we avoid becoming, not fig trees—whether barren or no—but living torches. Our Bishop has exhorted us to be cautious."

"Fabrisse, who would have the folly to be *cautious* if he saw his father or his son tumble down a well? It was well said, Verily I say unto you, there is no man that hath left house, or brethren, or sisters, or father, or mother, or wife, or children, or lands, for my sake, and the gospel's, but he shall receive an hundredfold now in this time. Is it not for our brothers and children that we are risking our lives thus? If we must come to their aid, how can we now start thinking about caution?"

The two women asked the Lady de Laurac for warm clothes and money for their journey, and set out. A messenger had informed them that Renaud was hiding in the woods near Saissac: he was very much in need of a woman's help, since the town had for long been in the Crusaders' hands, and it was impossible for him to gain admission to the bedsides of dying women. And during that winter, because of famine and water pollution, many folk died in the area, especially among the old people.

So Arsen and Fabrisse were able to rejoin Renaud. In anticipation of their arrival he had built them a fine log cabin, about thirty paces away from his own, in the lee of a rocky hillside dotted with fir trees.

"I turn my hand to every craft, you see," he told them. "Previously I was a blacksmith; now I am woodman, joiner, and ditch-digger. Your hut is a better one than mine; I have dug it in so deep that you will never be in danger of freezing."

Renaud judged other people by his own standards: despite his age he was still so hot-blooded that he worked in shirt-sleeves in the depth of winter. At the moment he was very cheerful; it is always pleasant to be reunited with old friends and fellow workers. And besides, without in any way prejudicing the seriousness of his calling, he was a cheerful man by nature. The two women were wakened at dawn by his full-throated hymn-singing: he had a deep, powerful voice, unspoiled as yet by age, which resembled the bass notes of a horn. Coming from his lips, each supplication and act of contrition sounded like a song of victory.

He took Arsen with him on his tours of pastoral duty; Fabrisse was too weak to walk long distances. He knew "safe" houses in the nearby villages and towns where they could take turns preaching, and where Renaud would bless bread and break it. The two of them looked so exactly like a couple of poor townsfolk, husband and wife, that they could move among monks and clerics without any fear: no one ever thought of scrutinizing their faces more closely. In order to attract less attention, Renaud had allowed his beard to grow.

Then one day, in the market place at Saissac, two monks in white habits gripped him by the arm.

"Come now, friend," one of them said, "you must *fast* a lot to get so thin, eh?"

"Ah, let him be, brother," the other monk said. "You can see for yourself he's with a woman."

They stared after the couple, frowning.

Renaud said: "That was a lucky escape. We can't come here any more as long as these men are still in the town."

The two friars, itinerant preachers from a new order which received much encouragement from the Bishop of Toulouse, were charged with the special mission of tracking down heretics. In the sermon which he was due to deliver that day in the Bailiff of Saissac's house, Renaud exhorted the faithful to show their charity, and expressly forbade them to lay hands on the two monks.

"In what respect would we be superior to them if we fought them with their own weapons?" he asked. "Let none among you surrender to the spirit of Jehovah, and say that evil should be stamped out by the sword, and God's enemies by the edge of the sword! Is not the man who acts thus like a lunatic who tries to put out a fire with live coals? It is true that these two men are the minions of Satan; but when they walk the roads alone, from village to village, they are two poor men merely, naked and unarmed: you should see in them only their fleshly weakness, which is infinitely worthy of your compassion.

"My brethren, if God had revealed some infallible sign to us by which we might recognize the sons of perdition, we would have to esteem ourselves higher than the angels. Saul, who persecuted the Church so fiercely before his transformation into the greatest of the Apostles, should serve as a perennial warning to us. Do not risk putting out a heavenly flame when you suppose yourself to be smiting a son of Satan! Mark my words well: if I ever learn that these two men have come to any harm in the neighborhood of your town, I shall inform our Bishop that you are sheltering traitors and murderers among you."

"Monseigneur," the bailiff said, "it makes me nearly choke with rage to think that these men you speak of are determined to find you and put you to death. The more you preach charity to us, the more our hearts swell with fury. How could we allow such men as you to come to harm?"

"You must realize, my son, that no one can harm us. Do not regard us as men, for in truth we are much less than other men— dried husks, empty shells merely. If the Spirit is willing to make use of us, do not commit the blasphemy of supposing It to be a prisoner in our bodies. The day we cease to be of use, It will find new tools, better fitted to accomplish Its work."

When they had both retired to their chamber Arsen said: "Do you suppose, my brother Renaud, that the Church would have lost nothing if—by some inconceivable misfortune—the Blessed Apostle Paul had died at the very outset of his ministry?"

"Is not this too subtle a question, my sister? You might as well ask what would happen if one day the sun failed to rise. Besides, the sun is a mere lump of inanimate matter, while the works of the Blessed Paul were written in God's thought from all eternity. We think we are free to move right or left; but in reality all that is to befall us has been accomplished in God since the beginning of time. We are reading a book whose pages we cannot turn till the hour strikes."

Arsen said: "That is a hard thought, and one difficult to conceive. When you seek to turn souls aside from sin, do you suppose them free to do evil or not, as they choose?"

"No; any more than I am free not to speak to them as I do. I have no option, I cannot frame my words otherwise. If they hearken to what I say, that means they were not free to do evil."

After this they both bowed their heads, and then turned their backs on one another to devote themselves to prayer. Renaud prayed aloud, reciting the *Pater Noster* and the prescribed Commentaries on it: his delivery was solemn and monotonous, as

though he were chanting a psalm or litany. Arsen often wondered
if, beneath these familiar and oft-repeated words, another tongue
did not lie concealed, that which the Apostles spoke on the day of
Pentecost; for when she prayed with Renaud, she felt a new energy
and peace descend upon her. She did not think about him, any more
than he thought of her. But the two of them were like flint and
tinder: when they came together, the flame of prayer was kindled
between them.

It was the period of the great Christmas fast. At daybreak the
two companions ate a little bread and drank some cold water, and
then took leave of their hosts.

"If only my sister Fabrisse would at least think of warming her
water before she drank it!" Arsen said. "She suffers from such
terrible pains in her chest."

"The nourishment prescribed by the Rule could not possibly
harm anyone," Renaud said. "Your charity makes you torment
yourself unduly for the body's sake."

"Alas, how can I not love my dear friend's body? A man in
prison clings to the wall through which he can speak with his
comrade."

Not far from the path that led to their huts, Renaud and Arsen
stumbled upon a wounded man: he was fair-haired and looked like
a foreigner. His attackers had stripped him and left him there
naked.

"It's a miracle he didn't die during the night," Renaud said,
putting an ear to the young man's white chest. "He looks to me
as though he's lost a lot of blood." And with that he hefted him
up by the arms and onto his own broad back.

So this fair-haired youth was bedded down on Renaud's palliasse,
wrapped up in bearskins and woollen cloaks. The women placed
heated stones under his feet and prepared infusions of sedative
herbs for him, since he seemed to be in great pain. The next day
he had a burning fever, so much so, indeed, that Renaud was constrained to bleed him and apply damp cloths to his forehead. For
three days the invalid merely groaned and babbled a few discon-

nected words; on the fourth he came to himself again and asked for something to eat.

"What are we going to do with him?" Arsen said. "He's a Frenchman. We cannot conceal our identity from him for long."

"If he asks us no questions we are not obliged to tell him anything. What is important is to set him on his legs again as soon as possible."

The young man was so enfeebled that he scarcely opened his mouth, and never thought of asking the names of the people tending him. Renaud merely had to say his prayers outside—a sufficiently severe penance when it was pouring with rain.

The sick man had a nasty wound in his left side. Though not too deep, it was suppurating, and thus responsible for his feverish condition. He bore the pain bravely, without complaint, but Arsen's heart was wrung to see him bite his lip in agony. He was so young, younger than her own sons.

She said to him: "This must be a sore trial of your mother's love for you! How she must be counting the days and hours you are away!"

The boy smiled cheerfully and said, in a confident voice: "You certainly spoke the truth there! She promised to offer up a candle to St. Michael on my behalf, every day."

In the end he told her his name, which was Gautier de Maleterre, and that he was a knight's son, from the Île-de-France. He served in the company of Sire Manassé de Bury, the local commander, and had been in the district for only six months. He had been ambushed by brigands in the wood, and left for dead. The countryside wasn't safe, he admitted, and he would never have ventured out alone along a forest track, ordinarily. But he had wanted to keep a rendezvous with a certain girl, who was too scared of her family to let him come to her home.

Arsen sighed; she had often heard of such girls. They thought they were doing their country good service by luring soldiers into such traps.

"When am I going to be fit again?" Gautier asked. "For God's sake let my captain know that I'm still alive; he'll reward you well for your pains."

"No point in doing that," Renaud said. "You'll soon be on your feet again."

One day five young noblemen from the surrounding district called upon Renaud when he was sitting at the door of his hut; they told him they wanted his blessing, for they were about to leave the country secretly, to join the forces of the Count of Toulouse. Renaud could not tell them there was a Frenchman in the hut, and found some excuse to take them off in the direction of the women's hut. But Gautier had heard a little too much nevertheless. That evening, when Renaud brought him his supper—bread soaked in hot wine—he pushed the bowl away and said: "Why did you never tell me the truth: that you were a heretic?"

"Not a heretic," Renaud said, "a Christian."

"Why did those people ask a blessing of you? If you are not a priest, then *what are you?*"

"I cannot tell you a lie: in the eyes of your people we pass for heretics."

"Why have you lied to me all this time?" the young man asked harshly.

"I have not lied. I was more concerned with caring for you than talking to you."

Gautier gazed at him with an odd expression, in which fear, disgust, and astonishment mingled.

"You did *that,* for me?" he said, slowly. Then he fell back on the palliasse, hiding his face in his hands. "I would rather have died than been touched by you."

"I am not a leper, and I have not got the plague; so there is no way in which my touch can harm you."

"How can I ever be sure you didn't take advantage of my condition to inflict your Devil's baptism on me?" the young man cried.

Renaud said: "Baptism can never be administered except to those who understand what it means, and are willing to accept it. We have only tried to nurse you back to health."

"What is recovery by such means worth to me? How can I believe what you say? I was unconscious for days, at your mercy!"

It was useless for Renaud to try to show this boy that he was blinded by vain superstitions: he refused both nourishment and any other attention, and toward nightfall he became delirious once more. Renaud reflected that in certain instances the inability to lie was a harsh necessity, but that nevertheless the Rule was imposed by God, not men. For two days and nights he kept vigil by the young invalid's bedside, even going so far as to neglect his prayers: for it seemed to him that the boy's life was in great danger. His feet had to be kept warm constantly, the wet cloths around his head changed, and he himself made to drink. He was freezing cold; Arsen and Fabrisse took turns surrounding the sickbed with heated stones, which cooled almost immediately.

On the day that Gautier opened his eyes, Renaud was no longer there; he had had to go off with Arsen. A man lay dying near Montoulieu, and they must needs administer the Consolamentum to him. Fabrisse, who was shivering with fever herself, sat warming her hands over a jug of hot water. Gautier raised himself on one elbow, and then groaned and sank back again.

"Ah, God be praised," Fabrisse cried, "he is regaining consciousness! We thought we were going to lose you, Master Gautier."

"*Where is that man?*" the invalid demanded.

"He had things to do in the town. Don't get upset; I'm going to give you something to drink."

"Oh, that's all right. Give it to me anyway. I understand now: *you* belong to their sect as well. Yet you look like a lady of birth and breeding."

"I have no idea what *I* look like; but *you* seem a rather stupid boy to me. People take you in and look after you as best they can —and you do not even deign to speak to them with reasonable politeness!"

"Why have you looked after me, unless it is to induce me to accept your Faith?"

"Are you so eager, then, Master Gautier," Fabrisse said, a

flicker of gentle malice showing in her small, demure smile, "are you so eager to embrace our Faith?"

"Why do you mock me thus? I am too stupid to answer you, surely."

"Master Gautier: conversion to our Faith is a most profitable business. Look at the fine life we lead; consider our gorgeous palaces, our sumptuous feasts, our servants and bodyguards. If this is all we can offer in the way of temptation, how would we set about converting you? It was essential for us to save your body, so that your soul may one day have the chance of being saved in its turn."

Mistrustfully, but without anger, Gautier said: "You see? You are already speaking to me of my soul's salvation. You must be trying to seduce me into heresy."

"I sincerely hope," Fabrisse said, "that three days hence you will be in a fit state to leave us. And I have no intention of spending those three days instructing you in our doctrines."

"Do you really think I would be capable of abandoning my Faith for your abominations in three days?"

"To tell the truth, I don't know what you're capable of," Fabrisse said, and gave a little shrug of her shoulders, which made the young man reflect that she must once have been both pretty and flirtatious. "But," she went on, "I already cough quite enough when I keep quiet; and I would rather talk to the trees than to people who have made up their minds in advance not to listen to me."

Gautier said: "Do you mean your people mistrust us so much that they will not even take the trouble to talk to us?"

"Just now," Fabrisse retorted, "you were afraid I might be trying to seduce you into heresy."

"*Afraid?* You are very much mistaken. I was not afraid. I took a vow to defend my Faith and never to renounce it, either under torture or the threat of death. Even though you were, by your magic, to make me see stars and angels falling from Heaven, I yet should not believe a single word of what you say."

The sick man had his drink, and then fell asleep again. He suffered no further relapses. For two days Fabrisse kept him company, discussing problems of belief and salvation with him. It was, indeed, true that on occasion she would break off, shaken by so cruel a spasm of coughing that it made Gautier's own chest hurt and brought tears to his eyes. She would spit blood onto the ground, saying that it did her good, it was as beneficial as being bled. Gautier promised himself to speak of all this to his confessor. He felt weak and isolated, and this woman was a pleasant creature; sometimes he told himself that if she had been twenty or thirty years younger it would have been wonderful to make love to her.

He left before Renaud and Arsen got back. The uneasiness he had felt on this heretical woman's account had left him with certain feelings of remorse: he asked himself whether he had been right to leave her alone, ill and defenseless. Better not go back, though.

He was tricked out in breeches and a shirt of Renaud's, which was far too large for him; he felt both ridiculous and humiliated, the more so since he was still weak, and could only totter along; besides which, these garments, having been worn by a heretic, might render him more vulnerable still to the poison of heresy. A fine rig in which to turn up at the castle gates, he thought; but his comrades were so overjoyed to find him still alive that they did not think of laughing at his clothes.

Gautier de Maleterre was a sincere Catholic, and could not prevent himself from being concerned for his soul's salvation. But when he unfolded his position to the castle chaplain, he understood, in no uncertain terms, the dangers run by any man who is unlucky enough to be rescued by a heretic. The chaplain refused him Absolution, and treated him as an abettor of heresy and a traitor to his Faith: if the man had not been in Holy Orders Gautier would never have brooked such an insult.

"Father," he said, "it is impossible for me to do what you ask of me. If I did, I should be dishonored forever."

"You do yourself greater dishonor by trying to shield these

stinking foxes that defile and destroy the True Vine of our Lord. Do you not know what sort of people these are, with their crimes and blasphemies?"

"Yes, Father, I know; after all, I have taken up the Cross against them. I know equally well that I have contracted this debt against my own will, and that I would rather have been saved by good Christians. But if I tell you their hiding place, that is tantamount to condemning them to death; and afterward they would have some reason for saying that the people in our country are a worthless lot."

"I can see very clearly," the chaplain declared, "that these accursed devils have contaminated you already. Your faith and your Church are in peril; and yet you are worried about what *they* will think of you, when they are lower than the very dogs! You must have a very high opinion of them to fear their judgment so."

The young man was deeply distressed at this, for the priest had given his words a meaning he did not intend, and in the end Gautier began to believe in his own guilt.

"Have pity on me, Father! It is true that I spent too much time in converse with this woman: I was deceived by the friendliness of her manner. But never shall it be said that a Frenchman was responsible for the death of those who saved his life, were they a hundred times over the Church's enemies!"

"And do you realize," the priest asked him, "that a man who abuses the secrecy of the confessional in so unworthy a fashion as you is no longer a Christian, and that his confession is valueless? Do you even know, poor ignoramus that you are, who this man is you are so eager to defend? From what you have told me I have no doubt he is the heretic Renaud of Limoux, who has already corrupted hundreds of souls, and who has settled in this district like a crow, watching out for dying folk so that he can deliver them over to Satan. Why, the perversity of these devils is such that as soon as they hear of any grave illness, they pounce on the patient to try to make him renounce his Catholic Faith and commit every sort of abominable sacrilege, so that his soul may be damned beyond all doubt. Do you imagine I can keep the secret of your confession

when it is at the risk of letting God knows how many other souls
suffer all the torments of Hell? This man is a clever fox, you must
know: he has avoided us so skillfully hitherto that if it had not
been for your information we should have been quite unaware of
his presence in the area."

"Truly, Father, I had no notion that he was so evil a person; but
for me that makes no difference. I should not be here discussing
him with you if he had not picked me up half dead in the woods,
and spent night after night at my bedside. My own father could not
have cared for me better than this man did."

"You only think in this way through excessive simplicity. Could
we not also say that we are doing pigs 'good' when we fatten them
up for killing? This man was not acting for your benefit, but for
the profit of his master, who is Beelzebub. Would he otherwise
have left you alone with an artful female who took advantage of
your weakness to the point of inspiring you with such damnable
sentiments?"

"Father, she was an old woman!"

"Age is no bar to Satan's wiles; it is plain that the creature
seduced you by magical practices. Do you realize that despite all
their pretense of chaste behavior and austerity of life, these devils
perform the most abominable acts upon one another in private?
This man of whom you speak formerly lived with a handsome
young heretic whom they had made a 'deacon' in their sect, and
who was taken and burned at Carcassonne last year. At the moment he lives a life of debauchery with these two old women, who
are themselves Satan's minions, and who seduce the souls of
credulous women. Is it for this kind of person that you would risk
your chance of salvation?"

"In truth," the young man said, burying his face in his hands,
"I do not know what kind of persons these may be." (He could not
understand why he found it so distressing to picture that big,
tough, good-natured man living in sin with those two gentle-voiced
women.) "I do not know what kind of persons these may be, nor
—please forgive me—whether what you say of them is true,

Father; you might have got your information from their enemies. But I honestly believe that if the Devil himself had rendered me such a service, I should still hesitate to denounce him."

"In that case," said the priest contemptuously, "you must set a very high value on your life in the body, and a correspondingly small one on the salvation of your soul. Now listen to me. As to your own sins I must keep silence, even though I refuse you Absolution. But a priest is not bound to secrecy in respect of grave crimes which his penitent has only witnessed. We shall have no difficulty in finding these people without your aid: a thorough search through the woods in the area will take care of that. But you have hampered the execution of justice, and I pronounce you from this day forth to be under suspicion of culpable complicity, an abettor of heretics, one unworthy to bear the Cross of Jesus Christ."

Gautier left the confessional in such a state of misery and distress that he wished he were dead. He had come to this country to fight, not to get mixed up in sordid affairs such as this. He was in the mood to hate the priest, the man in the forest, and his two companions equally: they all knew so much more about good and evil than he did, they disposed of his soul as though it were a child's toy. He felt himself suddenly stripped naked, an object of suspicion in his own eyes, irremediably defiled. If faith in God demands such sacrifices, he thought, if the avoidance of one mortal sin leads us straight into another, to which voice ought we to hearken?

Unable to stand it any longer, he told the story of his misadventures to Jean d'Andilly, his fellow countryman and childhood friend, who had joined the Crusade on the same day as himself. In the guardroom, standing near the huge chimney piece, with laughing, singing comrades all about him, he no longer felt out of his element: he was ready to believe himself an ordinary man again, like the rest of them. Jean at first seemed shocked by his story, and then began to ask him innumerable questions about these famous heretics: he had never yet actually seen one.

"Well," he said, not without a certain admiration, "they're certainly wily, no doubt about that. They've got the better of you, all right: they saved your life, and that means you can't do a thing against them."

"There's a search party going out to find them now. If it hadn't been for me, no one would have known they were hiding in these woods."

"Devil take it! And supposing—supposing you were to warn them?"

"How? Who would take the message? Do you suppose we know just which citizens are on their side? To go myself would be the surest way of getting them caught."

Jean scratched his head in some embarrassment. "Well, anyhow," he said at last, "you're out of it all now; you've done what you could. And does it occur to you how many people you may have saved, despite yourself? They say that one of these fellows damns at least a thousand souls to perdition."

And perhaps he has damned me, too, Gautier thought. Shall I ever know? I have been so defiled by contact with them that I no longer know what I am myself. What profane abominations may they not have committed upon me when I was unconscious? He tried to recapture in his imagination the calm, austere features of the man who had so often bent over him to wipe his brow and induce him to drink. Can the Devil give a man's face such powers of lying deception? he wondered. Shall I be able to look at anyone henceforth without saying to myself: *Perhaps he is a devil?* The heretic's every gesture and glance now seemed in retrospect heavy with cunning malice; and this pierced Gautier's heart with an agony akin to nausea. He had no very high opinion of the castle chaplain, Dom Fulcrand, who was a Provençal, a harsh, quick-tempered man, always prone to accuse the Crusaders of lukewarm enthusiasm and worldly dissipations. But in six months Gautier had had time to realize that these invisible heretics were a good deal more dangerous than people in the North ever supposed.

Jean d'Andilly was a talkative fellow; by that same evening the whole garrison knew that Gautier de Maleterre had had the ex-

traordinary luck to see some real heretics at close quarters. Dom
Fulcrand realized that there was no time to be lost. He acquainted
the commandant, de Bury, with the facts; and at dawn the next day
every soldier and varlet in the fortress was out on the trail, while
the burghers and peasants were forbidden to leave their houses.
The men-at-arms spread out in small detachments along the woodland paths.

It was the chaplain himself, escorted by two mounted squires,
who was lucky enough to stumble on the path that led to Renaud's
hut. They found him there alone; both the women had gone to
gather firewood.

When he saw the horsemen approaching, Renaud's first thought
was for flight; but what cover was there behind bare trees? I
should have built my hut on the edge of a ravine, he thought. Here,
they're bound to catch me the moment I start up that slope. Quickly
he wrapped his Gospels in a piece of sheepskin and flung them
away into the bushes, as far as he could.

"You are the heretic Renaud, of Limoux?"

"Yes."

"Where are the women who live with you?"

"They have gone."

"They can't be far away," one of the soldiers said. "There's a
loaf in their hut with hardly anything cut off it."

The party hung about for a good half-hour. As it was freezing
cold, they decided that the chaplain and one of the men-at-arms
should take the heretic to the fortress at Saissac, while the other
soldier remained behind till the women returned.

But Arsen and Fabrisse managed to escape capture: when they
heard men's voices and the clatter of boots they dropped their firewood and concealed themselves behind a large rocky outcrop that
overhung the track. They were thus able to watch the chaplain and
soldier pass in front of them, dragging Renaud behind them by a
cord attached to his neck. The horses were moving at a smart trot,
and Renaud had to run to keep up with them. His arms were
bound behind his back, and he was making a vast effort to adapt
the natural movement of his long legs to the horses' alien rhythm.

Terrified, the two women buried their faces in the decayed leaves that lay thick on the icy ground. They remained a long while thus, numb with cold, not daring to move.

"Where can we go?" Arsen said at length. "It is out of the question to return to our hut now."

"Ah, let us stay where we are, and die here of hunger and cold!" Fabrisse cried, bursting into tears. "What good are we? We no longer even have our Books. How many times will God impose this ordeal on us?"

"My sister, do you suppose that child we nursed betrayed us?"

"Who else?" Fabrisse said bitterly. "What can one expect of such weak souls? Yet what does it matter? Has God sent us here only to help the strong and virtuous?"

The garrison commander and Father de Souillac, the Bishop's representative, were considerably embarrassed at landing so large a catch. Heretics were like burning resin, as dangerous to guard as to transport, and the Crusaders had only about fifty men at Saissac.

"I cannot part with all my men just to escort this limb of Satan to Carcassonne," de Bury said. "And if I send a small party, we shall lose both men and prisoner."

"Then notify my lord Bishop; ask him to let us have reinforcements."

De Bury said: "You don't suppose my men would agree to spend whole days and weeks here when there is such a plague-carrier within the walls, do you? And are they going to let the men of Carcassonne reap the benefits of their good action? Half of them have been on garrison duty for two years now without seeing a single burning. We must not let them forget that they are here to defend their Faith. At the moment they forget it only too readily."

"I will not allow them to take the law into their own hands," the priest said.

"You are the Bishop's lieutenant," de Bury said. "You have the power to condemn this man to death."

"God forfend, my lord: no man of the Church has that power."

"What I meant was that you have the power to pronounce the

sentence that will deliver him into our hands. The men in the small garrisons are complaining enough already that we treat them as mere watchdogs and not as fighters for the Faith."

The priest, though with an ill grace, was constrained to bow to the facts: it was not the best moment to create embarrassing procedural problems. He summoned for the morrow both the garrison chaplain and the parish priest of Saissac. In the guardroom and the courtyard of the castle soldiers bustled to and fro, as restless as on the night before a move. The presence of the heretic stirred their blood; a thunderbolt hung over the fortress, ready to fall. It is not every day that one can take part in an act of divine justice; nor does the opportunity fall to every man. More than one fist was clenched in a trembling desire to touch the very timber from which the faggots would be cut. The priests had such a passion for doing things according to the book: might they not give this emissary of the Devil a chance to escape? Heretics, it was said, were strong enough to strike off thirty-pound chains with one tap of the thumb, or turn themselves into crows and fly away the moment they were brought out into the open air.

So these men-at-arms stared somewhat suspiciously at the Saissac parish priest as he crossed the courtyard on his way to the keep. He was an elderly man, a bent, shabbily dressed figure, his expression one of melancholy preoccupation. With one vague hand he bestowed a blessing on the men as he passed, but did not raise his eyes from the ground.

Manassé de Bury wanted to be present at the trial; he had had a chair placed ready for himself, a few feet away from that of the Bishop's deputy. The clerk responsible for transcribing the proceedings was sharpening his pens; the three clerical judges, having said their prayers, gave the order for the prisoner to be brought in, and for his chains to be struck off.

Renaud had eaten nothing since the previous evening for fear of being unwittingly defiled by impure foodstuffs, and he now felt somewhat exhausted. He had not passed a bad night in his cell; safe within four walls one at least avoided suffering from cold. After having allowed himself several hours' sleep he had prayed, with more fervor than was his wont: *It is finished then, O Lord; Thou hast delivered me, my struggle is nearing its end; Thou hast no longer any need of Thy useless servant.*

All glory to Thy bounty, O Lord, he thought. At last Thou deignest to destroy this defiled and rotting body, which has given Thee so much offense for fifty long years. Glory be for all eternity to Thy infinitely tender love, which has not scorned to stoop so low that a flame of joy may be lit in our hearts! What is all mankind? Wisps of straw in an ocean of light. Open their eyes, O Lord, as Thou didst to Bartimaeus; give them the strength to walk toward Thee, as Thou didst to those who were paralyzed—for there is no end to Thy miracles!

The jailer broke into his prayers at this point, shaking him by the shoulder and saying: "What's the matter with you, sitting there like a lump—are you deaf, or paralyzed?"

Renaud had not heard him come in. Now he recalled the comrades who had travelled this road before him, so many that he could not count them: his first companion, Guiraud de Montpellier; Aicart, his second; and now it was his turn to pass through the crimson door.

He wondered why he felt no fear, thinking of Aicart—Aicart, who had had to struggle so fiercely to quell his rebellious flesh; Aicart, whose urge to live was so great. *I do not hate life,* he reflected, astonished. *Life is everywhere.*

Now he stared at the three men in their long robes: all were tonsured, and two of them had a silver cross on their breast over the white habit. For them he felt only that pity which is due to wild animals and all living flesh, since he could not but believe them to be infinitely far removed from the prospect of salvation. But the third, the parish priest of Saissac, was a man whom Renaud had known for many years. Before the war he would often come to hear Renaud's sermons, and invite Renaud to attend his own; they regarded one another as colleagues rather than as enemies. Now he sat among the judges, a mute hostage, the accomplice of a foreign power.

Ah, brother, Renaud thought now, can you still say I was wrong when I besought you to quit this den of perdition? You said to me: "Our Church is like a spotless soul in a suffering body; our Church takes on itself the sins of the world, just as Christ Jesus took on Himself the likeness of man—"

The prisoner was questioned in the Languedoc tongue, since neither he nor de Bury knew any Latin.

"You are indeed Renaud, are you not, son of one Jacques, formerly a master-blacksmith in Limoux?"

"I am."

"What is your age?"

"A little over fifty, I believe."

"Were you baptized and brought up in the Catholic Faith?"

"I was baptized."

"How long is it since you abjured the Catholic Faith?"

"Twenty years ago, after my wife's death."

"What persons incited you to abandon the Catholic Faith and embrace the abominable doctrines of the sect known as Cathars, or Albigensians?"

"No person, but God alone: He opened my eyes and gave me knowledge, so that I could choose good rather than evil. The day on which my eyes were opened I went to see those who dealt in good works."

"What are the names of the heretics who initiated you?"

"Monseigneur Bernard, Bishop of Carcassonne, and Monseigneur Peter, his elder son."

"Do you honestly dare to give the heresiarchs of your sect the title of *Bishop?*" the chaplain demanded.

"Why, yes; that is the name we use to designate our superiors, since we know no other. In this we conform to the testimony of Holy Writ and of the Blessed Apostle Paul."

"You are not among your fellow heretics now," the Bishop's deputy said. "While you are here you will moderate your language."

"I speak no other language."

"And yet, before your conversion to this damnable heresy, you practiced the Catholic religion, did you not?"

"I did not practice the Catholic religion; I was like the beasts of the field, lacking all religion, either good or bad."

At this, de Bury could not prevent himself from starting with anger. "It's outrageous!" he exclaimed. "How dare this fellow utter such filthy depravities?"

"Will you dare to assert," the Bishop's deputy continued, "that you did not believe in God before you surrendered your heart to the heretical faith?"

"I did not care for the God of drunken priests and bishops who fleeced the poor," Renaud said, and then regretted having spoken so harshly when he thought of the Saissac parish priest. Hastily he added: "I was a simple man; I am still. I did not mean to offend you."

"Do not suppose you can deceive us with false meekness," the Bishop's deputy said. "What are the insults you hurl at priests and bishops compared with those with which you load our Holy Mother Church? You received the grace and sacrament of baptism, and now you spurn it as swine trample pearls! Because you are an uneducated simpleton, you have allowed yourself to be taken unawares by the wiles of false teachers."

"You are right," Renaud said, smiling calmly. "Your priests were not in the habit of talking to us of God and Jesus Christ. They spoke of Hell and saints' days and the payment of dues. We found others who were ready and willing to tell us of God."

"This man," the chaplain said, "is trying to excuse his own crimes by making the Church responsible for that shameful and culpable ignorance in which his life has been spent! If you were a sincere person, should you not be ready to listen to the teachings of the learned doctors of the Church? After all, you yourself admit having rejected them without knowing them."

"I do not know them, it is true. But I judge the tree by its fruits."

The chaplain said, harshly: "A fool picks up a rotten windfall apple, with a worm at its core, and then protests that the apple is a detestable fruit. We know all this. If you had not, in your stupid pride, arrogated to yourself the title and prerogatives of a pastor of souls, we would not bother talking to such a bumpkin at all."

The Saissac parish priest was visibly embarrassed: he sat there telling his beads, and so far had not looked up at the accused man. Renaud, watching his hands slide over the rosary, saw that they were trembling slightly. Could he be afraid I might betray him? Renaud asked himself, sensing at least as much fear as pity in the priest's behavior. He can rest assured on that score; the gulf that separates us now is wider than the space between Toulouse and Barcelona. I know only too well that now I can no longer show friendship to anyone, not so much as by a single glance. The priest, Renaud reflected, was serving his country as best he could—hiding outlaws, interceding on behalf of those whose goods had been confiscated unjustly, and making so staunch a pretense of being wholly ignorant of his parishioners' goings-on that he incurred some suspicion himself.

"It seems to me, Reverend Father," de Bury said, "it seems to me—if I may say so without giving offense to your cloth—that we are now merely marking time. The fellow admits his crime, and doesn't look as though he intends repenting of it. What more do you want?"

Someone talking common sense at last, Renaud thought. At least men like him know what they want.

Aloud he said: "Master Frenchman, there is no harm in your being anxious to get this business settled, since it will turn out to my advantage rather than otherwise. Nevertheless, in your place I should try to realize that what is under discussion is no less than a man's death."

De Bury frowned and turned his head away.

"Churl, who gave you permission to speak to me, or address me as 'Master Frenchman'? I am not one of your judges."

"You are not yet accustomed to their insolence," Father de Souillac told him. And then to Renaud: "Listen to me: we know who you are, and we have very little hope of seeing you recant your errors—though we are always ready to show you mercy if you ever manifest the desire for repentance. But we still have some questions to put to you. How long have you been in the Saissac district?"

"For four months."

"To how many dying persons in this parish have you administered what you term baptism, or the Consolamentum?"

"I would prefer not to tell you that."

"You know very well that your religion forbids you to tell a lie."

Renaud said: "Does yours permit it, then?"

"We are not, like you, Pharisees who attach more importance to the letter than the spirit," de Souillac exclaimed angrily. "We do not crush a man's head just to kill a fly. If it is a matter of saving another's life, or some equally obvious good, yes, we are permitted to lie."

"I would not lie to save another man's life; but silence is not a lie. I will tell you nothing further."

"Tell us this: did the bailiff know you were in hiding nearby with those two women heretics?"

"I repeat: I will tell you nothing further."

"If the bailiff didn't know, you would have answered 'No.' "

"If you asked me if my name was Renaud, and if I had two eyes and a mouth, my answer would still be the same."

The Bishop's deputy shrugged his shoulders and asked the clerk who had been taking down the evidence to read his transcription over to the accused. Since this transcription was in Latin, Renaud demanded a translation; and even then he examined the manuscript with meticulous care to see if this clerk had happened, through excess of zeal, to insert any proper names in the evidence. Having found nothing suspicious, he signed his name.

Then Father de Souillac, speaking in the name of the Bishop whose local representative he was, read out the sentence: this declared Renaud, son of Jacques, a burgher of Limoux, to be an excommunicate heretic, whom, since she despaired of his salvation, the Church now cast forth, condemning him to the flames of Hell, and handing him over to the judgment of the secular arm.

"And where are my secular judges?" Renaud inquired.

Manassé de Bury rose, flung the long folds of his cloak across his shoulder with an impatient gesture, and made for the door.

"From now on," he snapped, "every good Christian is both your judge and your executioner. Before this night you will have settled your account with him to whom you have sold your soul."

"*Amen,*" Renaud said, his impassive eyes staring straight at the discomposed face of the Saissac parish priest. "May none of you feel remorse or regret over your decision. And do not feel pleasure, either; for this is no Christian act."

De Bury returned now, with an escort of soldiers. And then the parish priest sprang up and cried: "Reverend Fathers, you are not delivering this man to justice, but to a foreign soldiery, swollen with luxurious vice, thirsting for blood! You will bring down shame on our ministry if you act thus!"

The commandant glared at him so fiercely that Father de Souillac, even the chaplain himself, recoiled and turned pale. The wretched priest shrank back a full pace, as though he saw the point of a spear presented at his breast.

"That's enough," de Bury said. "Take this fellow along, too. They'll teach him to sing a different sort of song in prison. By Christ's blood, reverend sirs, it seems that your Southern stock is so rotten and degenerate that neither soutane nor tonsure can work any change in it! It was high time that we came to set your country to rights!"

The priest was thrown into the cell and the heretic led out into the courtyard, where the soldiers put on his head a miterlike bonnet, coated with tar. He underwent no other ordeals, since the men were scared of his maleficent powers, and, above all, were anxious to see him finally committed to the imprisoning flames. The pyre was prepared some two hundred paces from the town gates, in a fallow vineyard.

Alone now, the two priests and the clerk remained silent for a long time, furious at the affront de Bury had inflicted upon them. For a moment the heretic became one of them, and it was the Crusader who was their enemy; they were willing to condone even the rash words uttered by the parish priest of Saissac.

"What use will it be for us to lodge a complaint with the Bishop?" the chaplain said at length. "Father Aymeric is a whited sepulcher, and our Bishop, being a Frenchman himself, will hardly excommunicate a Crusader captain for the sake of a village priest with sympathetic leanings toward heretics."

"This is a most irregular procedure," Father de Souillac exclaimed, his face quivering with indignation. "The laity are already only too prone to meddle in our affairs. Father Aymeric was *our* responsibility: it was up to us to bring him before the Bishop's court. How long must we still endure the overweening pride of these Northerners? Where the sword rules there is no more justice."

Manassé de Bury swept back into the low chamber like a gust of wind, almost overturning a candlestick with his great blue cloak as he came. His face was still red, and his nostrils twitched; but his expression seemed somewhat milder than it had been.

"By all the saints in Paradise, reverend sirs," he exclaimed, "do not leave me to face such temptations a moment longer! It cost me a great effort not to hang the fellow out of hand for the infamous remarks he made about our Christian soldiers! We have a hard enough time of it in this country as it is, and my soldiers are not going to risk a knife in their backs at every street corner only to be insulted by the people they are here to defend! Our patience has its limits too, you know."

"The parish priest spoke foolishly," Father de Souillac said. "If you hand him back to us, we will conduct an inquiry into his behavior, and send a report to the Bishop. It is not fitting to wrangle over personal insults when God's justice is being fulfilled."

"I would not describe the vilification of God's army as a 'personal insult.' But we don't want to put the cart before the horse, I agree. Let's finish with this condemned heretic first. It seems to me," he added, with sudden distrust, "that you have shown him quite remarkable lenience. If you really wanted to make the fellow talk, I fancy the means are available."

"Why don't you accuse us of being on his side, and have done with it?" the chaplain said, tartly. "If you were better acquainted with these people, you would know they cannot be made to talk. Sometimes one can derive a certain advantage from their exaggerated hatred of lying; but when they decide to keep quiet, you might as well try beating a block of wood. The sooner the fire does its work, the better it will be for all concerned."

"I must be there in person," de Bury said. "But I am unfamiliar with this sort of—ceremony. Will you appear with me?"

"Such is our bounden duty. If ever God's grace were to touch his heart, even at the eleventh hour, he would have to be received back into the Church."

"In such a case," said de Bury, "I could not hold myself responsible for my troops."

The chaplain said: "If that man is converted, I will cheerfully go to the stake instead of him. Give the order to ring the bells and beat the drums."

Renaud stood outside in the courtyard, his back against the wall of the keep. He felt his strength deserting him; he was suffering cruelly from thirst. The tarred bonnet burned his scalp. He could see men all about him—how many? Several dozens, perhaps. Glances, faces, voices. For the first time in his life he was seized with horror at the sight of fellow human beings. It was as though no spark of humanity remained in all this swarming mass of flesh, as though the souls had suddenly fled from their bodies, and through their eyes the Beast looked out. And for a moment this incomprehensible and violent manifestation of sheer evil turned him giddy.

They were preparing to kill a man—what man, mattered little. He forgot that it was he himself who was to die. Human souls were defiling themselves by an act contrary to nature, and made ready for it as though for a feast. That faint glimmer of pity which can be seen even in the eyes of beasts, that last reflection of the soul, had vanished from these noisy, healthy, youthful bodies. Ah, God, Renaud thought, what have I ever done to them? Yet I cannot hate them.

He was cut off forever from mankind now, a loathsome encumbrance that was left in a corner till people found time to take it elsewhere and destroy it. They came and went, arming themselves for parade, laughing, complaining of the cold and the wind.

"Still, we'll get a bit of warmth soon, eh?"

"That's right; there'll be something to warm ourselves at. Have to hold your nose, though."

"Is it true that these chaps' bodies stink worse than anyone else's when they burn?"

"Sure it is; they smell of sulfur and rotten eggs."

"You seen them burned before?"

"Yes, at Lavaur. You think I only just got here? Four hundred of them roasted that day. God, how they howled! You couldn't have heard it thunder, there was such a row."

"Cocky, aren't you, you and your four hundred? Seems likely that lot weren't all real heretics anyway, from what I hear."

"Do you think this one is?"

"Well, of course! The priests have proved it, that's why he's here."

Could I ask *them* for something to drink? Renaud wondered. But then, whom else could I ask? He took one step forward, and saw them stiffen into watchfulness, like a pack of hounds about a badly wounded boar that unexpectedly staggers to its feet.

"Hey there, what d'you want, eh?" one of the men said.

"Give me a drink, for pity's sake," Renaud gasped. "I haven't had a drop since yesterday."

Several soldiers nudged each other at this, and exchanged surprised glances. It astonished them to see that their prisoner was a very ordinary-looking fellow, like any one of a dozen master-farriers or carpenters they had seen. Only his eyes were different—too serious, too penetrating, as though he were looking at you from the bottom of a well.

"You think we could?" someone asked.

"That'd come under the head of doing him a service."

"It's the jailer's business."

But despite everything, they were embarrassed.

"We haven't had orders about it," they told Renaud. "Don't talk to us any more."

Ah, Renaud thought, so close to death, and can I still yearn thus after a mouthful of water? What is to come will be crueler by far.

For God's sake, let them be quick about it, though! I can't hold out much longer. Destructible matter is not worth the trouble of thinking about—but I *am* suffering! O Lord, this body which so often has played You traitor is betraying You still. Old horse, old beast of burden, serve me a few moments longer: don't jib, don't torture me—let me speak to my Saviour!

He prayed, no longer knowing how many times he completed his prayer. Men came and ordered him to remove his shoes, and put a long white shirt upon him, and fastened a cord about his neck. It is done, he thought, they are taking me away now. O Lord, grant me a quick deliverance—do not reject me, O Lord! He raised his head and threw back his shoulders, filling his powerful lungs with great draughts of ice-cold air. Then he began to sing his last hymn on earth. I *will* sing, he thought, what does it matter if these men laugh at me? I have nothing more to do with them. I am alone with Thee now.

So he sang as he walked, but his cracked voice could not be heard above the tramp of feet and clanking armor. The procession moved slowly forward, with a town crier at its head, banging away on a copper gong; behind him marched a detachment of men-at-arms, with the garrison commander and the Bishop's deputy following them on horseback, their mounts caparisoned in white trappings on which scarlet crosses had been embroidered. Next came the clerics and the cantors. The chaplain marched on foot, brandishing a large copper cross, at the head of the soldiers who were leading the heretic himself. Behind the condemned man rode three cavalrymen, lances at the ready, while a crowd of archers and common foot soldiers brought up the rear.

It had been decided to perform this warlike ceremony in as orderly and dignified a manner as possible, so as to show the townsfolk (now gathered in the market place or crowding their doorways) that the old days were over for good, and that the Cross of Christ was no longer to be flouted with impunity in this country. The bailiff, the sacristan, the notary, and the wealthiest burghers were forced to join the procession.

Renaud was no longer conscious of the cold numbing his feet;

he was no longer even thirsty. He could not hear the sound—a sort
of strangled growl—that still issued from his throat; nor the tramp
of booted feet, nor the powerful voices of the cantors celebrating,
as he was, the glory of God. He heard other voices, upraised in a
chant more terrible than thunder, more solemn than the church
bell's burden at Eastertide, and achieving a harmony such as no
human voice could ever compass: for the peace of God is of so
annihilating a splendor that man's heart cannot bear it—his head
bursts, his whole body is crushed into nothingness. Can the sun
fall from heaven upon an earthworm? Everything flies to pieces,
and the last rags of flesh vanish like sparks up the chimney.

He was wrenched away from his vision by a man's voice, asking
him if he still persisted in his errors, whether he did not wish for
reconciliation with Holy Church. He saw that he was standing at
the foot of a vast pile of faggots, around which straw had been
heaped. Above them a wooden stake reared up. He shook his head,
unwilling to speak. Thoughtfully he surveyed the faggots, wondering what would be the most convenient way of clambering up
without toppling them over. Then a man dressed in red made the
ascent with him, and set about lashing him to the stake.

He glanced at the fortress opposite him, and the houses of the
town, oppressed now by a gray and lowering sky; at the black
woodland and reddish fields; at the hedge of lances and gleaming
helmets that ringed the scaffold—and at the few score men who
stood there, necks craning, eyes upturned toward him. Some of my
flock must be here among the crowd, he thought, and I can no
longer recognize them, they are so far away. Even this great tower
looks nearly as small as a gambler's dice.

He looked down by his feet and saw small yellow and blue
flames spreading through the straw, flickering, growing, till they
began to lick gently around the faggots. A pleasant warmth began
to steal through his frozen feet. With wide-eyed fascination he
watched the flames climb higher. O Lord, he prayed, now it comes.
Now it comes. Mercy on me! O Lord, may the flesh alone be defeated in this its final struggle!

A sudden gust of wind made straw and faggots crackle, and the fire sprang up at its human victim like a wild beast. Renaud felt his body arch and stiffen in a hopeless effort to shrink away from it.

Now the pain was there, gnawing his flesh with such sudden violence that he felt as though his whole body had burst apart, as though he were dead already. But this death was slow—how slow, no one will ever know. Every second is like an hour, with a thousand bees swarming simultaneously in a thousand raw wounds. His eyes were blinded by the smoke; by dint of violent shaking he managed to throw his head back. O Lord, he prayed, have no mercy on this flesh of mine! O Lord, now at last lettest Thou Thy servant depart in peace, according to Thy word!

The priests continued to chant, but the troops, and those citizens who either by compulsion or of their own free will had joined the procession, remained silent. All eyes were raised toward the victim, towering over them on his pyre. Too much wood had been piled up around it, so that the fire blazed with unlooked-for fierceness: the soldiers felt their helmets getting overhot, while their faces turned scarlet, and their horses snorted and pawed the ground. The man up on the scaffold moaned softly, but did not cry out aloud. Then, suddenly, with one fearful heave of his shoulders, he tore loose the cords that bound his arms. As he reached skyward with both hands a stupefied gasp burst from every mouth: all those present thought that the very next instant he would either fling himself down on them or else rise into the air above the pyre.

He tore off the pitch-smeared miter, and for a few seconds thrashed his arms about as though trying to ward off the flames that rose toward him. For one instant it looked as if he had put a spell on the fire: a gust of wind blew the tall yellowish tongues of flame back and down, toward the ground, so that they practically touched the hoofs of two horses, which reared up and shied away to one side.

"Get a pitchfork!" a voice called. "Pile those faggots up again, you clumsy idiots!"

The man stood aloft there in his shirt of fire, arms outstretched heavenward, straining to the last inch of his great height, as though trying to grasp some invisible cord that would have drawn him up into the sky. Then he thrust both arms back behind his head and gripped the top of the stake: he did not move again. But his head still showed signs of life: the wind would momentarily reveal it through the smoke, all blistered and bloody, while his mouth opened to howl the words "Our Father Which art in Heaven, Our Father Which art in Heaven— Our Father—"

And then a pitiable, childish voice, broken with sobs, cried out: "*It wasn't my fault!* I swear to you it wasn't my fault!" Gautier de Maleterre's horse plunged toward the pyre; he had spurred it cruelly, and Gautier's companions were hard put to it to get the beast under control. The young man himself had to be carried off struggling. Manassé de Bury regretted having imposed this penance on him; it was really too much of an ordeal for a convalescent.

The executioner poked the victim's body with a long iron bar to make sure he was really dead, and then raked the still unburned faggots in toward the stake. The show was over, and the burning mass a carcass only; besides which the stench given off by that thick black smoke was becoming well-nigh unbearable. De Bury turned his horse's head and rode off back to the town, in a thoughtful mood, with Father de Souillac beside him.

The priest stared grimly at the gray and red roofs that were visible through broken gaps in the ramparts. His mind was running on reprisals: it was, he reflected, a hard business carrying out God's justice in half-conquered territory. The soldier was like a sword, which protected you only when you had the time and skill to make use of it; and here there were something like fifty men to police a population of two thousand souls.

"The Devil must needs be very powerful, Father," de Bury said. "Otherwise we should be forced to suppose that this man held his deluded beliefs in all good faith. If it were not an offense against God, I could all but swear that the fellow died a brave death—and I've seen many enough die in my time. Yet he was an ordinary burgher, nothing more."

Father de Souillac frowned. "That should not surprise you, my lord," he said. "If you want my opinion, I honestly think these folk do not know the meaning of fear. That is how they win a lot of their converts. But you shouldn't turn this quality into a virtue. They have such a loathing of life, and are so enamored of death, that they actually claim suicide to be permissible, even desirable; in their blindness they rejoice when we condemn them to death. But this is less the result of courage than of morbid exaltation, a kind of mad delirium which they attain by repeatedly performing certain demoniacal rites known to them alone. God forfend we should ever envy them this courage: it is as contrary to Christian resignation as madness is to common sense."

"A good point," de Bury said. "It seems to me you should explain such matters in greater detail to my troops. They are simple souls, and might well be taken in otherwise. One of them has already been corrupted. He's a boy from my own district, and I don't want him to get into any trouble of that sort."

"If you value the lad's life," said the priest, "make sure he doesn't show himself for the next month or two, either here in the town or out in the countryside."

When the troops had marched back to their fortress, it was the poor folk's turn to take part in the feast. Many of them had followed the Crusaders, and stood there in little groups, well away from the scaffold, among the vines or at the roadside. From the top of the keep the sentry could see these groups swelling even while he watched. They all seemed to be wandering aimlessly, round about, coming and going as though it were pure accident that they found themselves where they did. They resembled a large flock of sheep, scattered over a meadow which has been cropped bare. Yet, insensibly, the ring of men continued to close in around the still flaming pyre.

With a loud crash the calcined stake collapsed into the furnace below, scattering fiery sparks for twenty paces around. The fire still crackled as it ate up the last few morsels of flesh, but already the pyre was turning black at its heart, with only isolated pockets of red-hot embers remaining. The last of the faggots alone still flared up, their gray, red-tinged smoke mingling with the thick black fumes given off by the body. Evening was falling. And as it was bitterly cold, one might have supposed from a distance that all these people were crowding around the dying fire to get themselves warm.

Some knelt, some stood, others sat on the ground: they looked like travellers preparing to make a halt for the night, or unlucky villagers watching with mournful resignation while the rest of their houses burned down. Some women wept. Some of the men passed around hunks of bread, a knife, a jug of wine. Little was said. No one so much as glanced up in the direction of the fortress: there are moments when hatred becomes as solemn and formal as a prayer, moments when grief is wordless.

The flames had consumed too great a body of love that day; what these men had seen burning had been for them their true bread, their sure refuge, the very warmth of God's own glance. When would their Bishop send them another such? Would he send any sort of replacement after so great a disaster? Here, they reflected, is all that remains to us of him whose compassion for us was so great: a few scraps of flesh and bone—blackened, bloody, smoking. It would have been better for us to lose our fathers and mothers than this man, who was more than the bread of life to us. When the sun goes down all becomes dark; when the righteous man goes hence, the world becomes an evil place.

There are so many of us keeping vigil over him that they have not arms enough to hang us all—more shame on our town! Will God still show us His mercy when we have allowed such a thing to happen? Through fear of ax and lance we have let them take our pastor away from us.

Among the women keeping watch in the fields were Arsen and Fabrisse; a charcoal burner had given them shelter in his hut, and they had promised not to stay long at the place of execution—just long enough to say goodbye to their old friend and companion. They had to move on once more that same night.

"Why are you weeping?" Fabrisse asked. "To cling to the body of a loved one is mere superstition. Our dear friend has lost nothing of his essence."

"But our country has lost a bright flaming torch. The Devil labors so mightily to extinguish every remaining light that many men will be forced to walk in darkness. How long, my sister, how long?"

"Long enough for us not to see the end of it in the flesh. Why trouble your mind with such thoughts?"

The Saissac village priest was brought out of his cell the morning after the execution; he had been severely manhandled and his face was bruised in several places. De Bury apologized for this to Father de Souillac, saying it was all the fault of his troops; and with that excuse the Bishop's deputy had perforce to be content. He gave the priest a severe and lengthy reprimand, threatening him with both suspension and imprisonment. Father Aymeric listened gloomily, blinking puffy-eyed at his superior the while.

"You will not find a replacement for me," he said.

"That will be no great loss," de Souillac replied tartly. "It appears that for the last thirty years you have performed your duties so well that your whole flock worships these heretics."

"No," the priest said, teeth clenched. "There are Catholics too. Even now. You cannot say as much for every village in the area."

"I would be extremely interested to meet these Catholics," Father de Souillac remarked skeptically.

"I prefer not to tell you their names. Your friends from the North are not making their lives very easy."

Outside his presbytery door Father Aymeric found a group of weeping women, and some men who eyed him in a hesitant way. Among the latter were one or two who never went to church. He felt afraid.

"What do you want of me?" he asked.

"You can count on us, Father. We shan't forget what you did yesterday."

"I did nothing, and I hope I never have to count on you."

"We just wanted to tell you. You're one of us now, whether you like it or not. They'll have their eye on you."

"What stupid blockheads you are," the priest said sadly. "I can no longer help anyone, nor can anyone help me. A little while, and I shall be gone from here. All I ask of you is that you leave my successor alone—if I ever have one."

De Bury went off to visit Gautier de Maleterre in the turret room where, because of his scandalous behavior, he had been obliged to confine the young man. He found Gautier stretched out on the ground, shedding hot tears, and saying over and over again that he was damned, that he didn't want to stay another moment in this country.

"Gautier," de Bury said, "you are no longer a child. You are a member of my company, and we are short of men as it is. It was a *man* who swore the oath of allegiance to me; and now I find myself in the presence of a weak womanish creature who cannot stand the sight of an execution."

The young man raised himself on his elbows and cried: "But don't you know that it was *I* who betrayed this man?"

"Not so. You were the only person who knew the way to his hut—and you refused to reveal it."

"But he might have thought it was I—he *must* have believed it! And it's true, it *was* my confession that gave him away! When you made me go and watch him die, my feelings had been so worked upon that I no longer cared about him. But they had deceived me. He was a saint! If it was through my doing that he died, then I am damned!"

De Bury knelt down and placed one hand on the young man's shoulder.

"Gautier," he said, "I have no intention of losing you. Be a man. If these fellows were not so skilled at the seduction of souls there would be nothing dangerous about them. You have a tender heart because you are young. You ought to realize that the Devil is more than a match for you in cunning, that he arms himself with soft phrases and winning ways in order to catch Christians off their guard. God grant that your father never learn the words you have uttered! Betraying one's Faith is even worse than betraying one's country."

"I have not betrayed my Faith," Gautier said, grimly. "I have betrayed the man who saved my life."

"Such are the hazards of war, my boy. What is the service he did you in comparison with the evil he has done us all? Who was it set about you, ten men against one, and left you for dead? Why, his friends. You know what the folk in this country are like, how they treat our people. You know their greatest pleasure is to catch a Crusader alive and then torture him to death. You know, too, that these minions of Satan are their masters and leaders, and that in this country they are stronger than we are. I have been campaigning here for four years now. I have had time to see how despised our Christian Faith is in this accursed place, how rotten and decadent the inhabitants: they are so fond of treachery that they will swear an oath to you simply for the pleasure of perjuring themselves the next minute. We cannot rely on *anyone* here. Even their priests are not always reliable. Here you are getting worked up about this fellow, without stopping to think that he and his like are the cause of all our troubles. It is because they have renounced their Faith that these people are now such a bad lot."

The young man hardly listened to all this. With gloomy obstinacy he said: "If the service he did me is nothing, that means that my life is worth nothing, and that I am to all intents and purposes dead. Why do you bother talking to a corpse?"

"You see how far they have already corrupted your spirit?" de Bury said gently. "It is they, not we, who scorn life. The truth is, this fellow *wanted* to die, so we have not done him a bad turn. They are so blinded by their false beliefs that they go to the stake as though to some high festivity. It is not right that you should suffer for such people."

Gautier said: "I too would be glad to die, now. I have committed so villainous a deed that I shall never obtain forgiveness for it."

"Come now, pull yourself together. You are a soldier, not some cleric, or a woman, to sit bewailing your sins in this fashion. It is by fighting, rather than lamentation, that you will obtain the pardon promised us for doing God's work."

"Who will grant me such a pardon? They say this man's death was a praiseworthy deed. Who then has the right to pardon me? Even though I went to our Holy Father the Pope, do you think *he* would give me absolution? The priests and clerics from these parts have deceived him, and now he believes that killing these people is an act of virtue."

No doubt about it, de Bury decided, this boy is becoming a menace. He took his leave of Gautier at this point, promising to send him back home in the spring on grounds of ill-health. Gautier's comrades were most distressed to see him shut away in this fashion, the more so since a strange rumor was circulating among the garrison troops. It was being whispered that the heretic who had been burned was only a brave simpleton who had sacrificed himself at the bidding of his superiors in order to deflect suspicion from the real heretic, now safely in hiding.

Three days later, with the help of his friends, Gautier managed to escape. He said he wanted to go to Carcassonne and put his case before the Bishop, and obtain permission to make a pilgrimage to Rome. He distrusted Father de Souillac, and could not stand the sight of the chaplain who had betrayed the secrets he had uttered in the confessional. He had managed to procure a horse and a small spear, suitable for travelling. Thus equipped, he reckoned, he ran little risk of attracting attention, so long as he stuck to cross-country tracks.

When the salvation of one's soul is in jeopardy, it is permissible to disobey one's superiors; and never had soul stood in greater peril than Gautier's. His heart was torn with a longing to see his forest rescuer once more. Truly, he thought, a defaulting debtor may be stripped of his goods and flung into prison; but the debt *I* owe is this living body, the sky above me and the air I breathe, none of which any longer belongs to me, but to this man who is dead through my fault. To whom can my debt be paid? He alone could honorably discharge it, and he died with contempt for me in his heart.

O Lord, if this man was an emissary of the Devil, who, pray, are God's emissaries? How can we live in a world where evil wears the appearance of good? If this man has blasphemed against the Cross and profaned the Sacraments, what is life worth? If he did such things he deserved his death a thousand times over—and yet my heart breaks with pity for him. Is this only one of their tricks? Did they only save my life the better to torment and damn my soul?

About a league outside Saissac Gautier observed four horsemen riding toward him. He did not even think of taking to his heels; two of them were the sons of a local landowner, reputedly a staunch Catholic, and he had drained more than one cup of wine in their company. Unsuspectingly he allowed them to approach. One of them greeted him, and then, with a quick, nonchalant movement, presented his spear-point at Gautier's throat. An instant later, Gautier was hemmed in by all four lances, one at his throat, one on each side, and the last in the small of his back. His spear, sword, and dagger were taken from him. Then one of the young men said: "Tell us, soldier: weren't you the one who betrayed the minister?"

"I did not want to betray him."

"It is you, then. Get down from your horse and come into this little pine wood with us. We'll be able to talk at our ease there."

Gautier thrust his head forward sharply, trying to spit himself on the spear-point; but the man in front of him was too quick, and whipped his lance away.

"Easy, friend, easy," he said. "Don't spoil the goods for us. Do you think you're the only people who have the right to a little fun?"

The four men had fresh young faces, and their every gesture was shot through with that distinction of manner—slightly formal, yet easy and unforced—which characterized the sons of the gentry, and could be instantly identified a dozen paces off. Gautier stared at them in bewilderment. They were young men of the same sort as himself. What shone from the depths of their dark eyes was not hatred or cruelty, though; they seemed above all to be filled with *joy*—and at the same time quite inhumanly calm. Gautier would have been less scared by the sight of wolves' heads on human shoulders.

Then they pulled him off his horse. He struggled a long time with his bare hands, trying in vain to grab hold of one of the lances; he was quick and skillful, and his attackers did their best not to wound him seriously. Finally, when they had him trussed up, he ceased to struggle, and said: "This is not a fight you will boast of before your ladies—unless your ladies, like yourselves, have lost all sense of honor. Now will you kindly give me time to say my prayers?"

"You'll have plenty of time for that; we won't be through with you for three or four hours."

Contemptuously he said: "A fine trade you practice."

"No less honorable than yours. Here, Gaucelm, you take the horses. Don't be afraid—*Frenchman;* your friends will sing splendid Masses for your soul."

That day Gautier paid his debt in full and with interest. Toward evening his horse returned to the fortress at Saissac, bearing his trussed-up body on its back. Gautier's head, hands, and feet were burned black through and through, carbonized, like vegetables roasted slowly over a brazier. His features, though calcined, remained intact: they were stamped into so awful a rictus of agony that one of the soldiers who led the horse, with its horrid burden, into the castle courtyard fell down in a fit, and was only with difficulty brought around again.

De Bury put the bailiff and other suspect citizens to the torture, but failed to discover who was responsible. So he picked out fifteen young men at random, and hanged them instead.

CHAPTER X

Love Defeated

ARSEN and Fabrisse now had no alternative but to flee the country. Their huts had been solemnly burned by Father de Souillac and his clergy, and they would not have dared to return to them in any case. They knew that the hunt was on for them. Doubtless they exaggerated the immediate danger, since the garrison commander had no inclination to begin hunting down heretics again so soon. He was heard to remark that Father de Souillac's zeal caused him, de Bury, nothing but trouble, and that all these priestly spells were none of his concern anyway. But Arsen and Fabrisse, knowing nothing of this, no longer dared either to show themselves in the town or to venture along any main road. They had walked some five leagues by forest paths in the hope of reaching Cammazes, where troops seldom appeared except to forage for food and supplies.

It was raining, an icy downpour that blew fitfully into the travellers' faces, plastering sodden garments to their skin. Neither woman had eaten anything worth mentioning for two days: their stock of bread was so small that they made do with a morsel the size of two walnuts, at dawn and at dusk. However accustomed one becomes to eating very little, the human body nevertheless cannot adjust itself to a diet of nothing at all—especially in winter, and when it is called upon to march long distances over rough tracks.

"We shall get there tomorrow, my sister," Arsen said. "Please take what is left of the bread. There is not enough for two people, anyway."

Fabrisse said: "No, my sister, it is you who must have it. I know beyond doubt that I shall never need bread again. Tomorrow I shall not be in this village of yours, but in another place altogether, where you will not be able to come and find me—not of your own will, at least."

Night was falling. Under these bare trees there was no chance of shelter.

"I suppose," Fabrisse continued, stretching herself out on the soaking-wet ground, "that cold water is far less agonizing a torture than death by fire; so I ought to consider myself lucky. But I am so frozen that I can scarcely bring myself to believe it."

Arsen made her a tent with her own cloak, which, though soaked, did not let too much rain through. Fabrisse was no longer coughing; instead an occasional tiny hoarse rattling sound escaped her lips.

"Take your cloak back," she gasped. "It will make no difference to me, and it would be a great pity if you fell ill for nothing."

But Arsen's heart was so consumed with sorrow at the thought of her companion's leaving her that she felt neither cold nor hunger.

"No, dear friend," she cried, "this is not our first ordeal together, and it will not be our last! How can you leave me here in this frozen forest, exposed to the wind and the rain, alone with the night? I will keep you warm with my own body—I will *not* let you go!"

"What can your poor cold shivering body do for me, my dove? The cold that is freezing me rises from within. I can scarcely feel how cold the ground is—even my feet no longer hurt me. If you love me, I beg you, eat this bread, for I am no longer able to take any nourishment, and you still need all your strength."

"I feel neither cold nor hunger. Misery provides its own strength, and love's suffering is our true bread. If only I could keep you with me by love alone, my friend, so that we might never be parted in this life!"

"It is becoming dark," Fabrisse said. "Our ways will separate during the night, and I shall never see your face again in the flesh. Tell me your plans, my sister: I would like to continue our journey together a moment longer."

"I shall try to get through by way of Toulouse, and get in touch with our brethren in that area. Afterward I shall take to the mountains and try to find our Bishop. He will give me a new companion, and, perhaps, send me on a fresh mission."

"Give our friends in Toulouse my greetings. Your daughter is thereabouts too, is she not?"

"I have heard that she married a Toulouse nobleman last year. Now she is to me much as a rich man's feast is to a beggar: something fine and desirable, but to be viewed only from a distance."

"I never had a daughter," Fabrisse said, "and all my sons died in childhood. Tell your daughter that to bear children is no great affliction; that road too leads to true Love."

The rain had stopped now, but Arsen was still quite unable to make a fire. The water had seeped into her leather pouch, and all its contents—tinder, candle ends, flint—were fatally damp. The sky was so black that it could barely be distinguished from the blackness of the tree trunks. Ah, my friend, Arsen thought, there is not even a candle to light you on your way when you go!

Fabrisse said: "Help me to die, Arsen. While the least breath still flutters on my lips we remain together. Say the words, and I will make the responses as long as I can."

"*In the beginning was the Word,*" Arsen said, "*and the Word was with God, and the Word was God.*"

"*The same was in the beginning with God,*" Fabrisse murmured, with a great effort. "*All things were made by Him, and without Him was not anything made that was made.*"

"*In Him was life; and the life was the light of men. And the light shineth in darkness; and the darkness comprehended it not.*"

"*. . . He came unto His own, and His own received Him not.*"

"It is too much of an effort for you to speak," Arsen said. "I will say the words for you."

"Ah, what are you worrying about, my well-beloved? You need think of me no longer. Farewell, Arsen, my companion: let us concern ourselves no more with one another."

"*But as many as received Him, to them gave He power to become the sons of God . . .*"

"*Which were born, not of blood, nor of the will of the flesh, nor of the will of man, but of God.*"

Fabrisse lasted till the thirteenth verse. Then she gave a short, dry, rattling cough, and her whole body shuddered. She did not move again. Arsen continued to recite the Word, alone, knowing that she would receive no further response.

A pale dawn broke, shrouding the trees in white mist. Neither sky nor earth was visible; all that showed through were a few bare tree trunks and one or two bushes. It was like being at the world's end, standing on the last patch of solid ground above the bottomless abyss.

Arsen bent over the frail body, its arms folded across its chest, and took a last farewell of her former companion. Fabrisse had died several hours before, and her stiff, icy features had acquired a new youthfulness. The tiny wrinkles had vanished, while those hollow cheeks had lifted the corners of her mouth in a calm, unastonished smile. Her complexion was no longer feverish, but waxy white, while there was a bluish tinge about her lips and eyelids. Long locks of fair hair, darkened by the rain, clung to her cheeks. Arsen stroked them with one hand, and briefly caressed that small, convex forehead, with the sort of tender gesture one would make over a wounded bird. Poor deserted flesh, she thought, how lovely you still are! You look like a betrothed girl asleep, and it is thus that the vultures will find you. Poor muddied snowdrift, poor mire-betrampled flower, ephemeral relic of God's own temple! My companion has found her haven of peace, her bright-lit Heaven.

Arsen took the cloak that was draped over the dead woman's body, leaving her clad in nothing but one thin linen shift, so that the vultures and wild beasts could the more easily devour her. Then she ate the last small fragment of bread, sticky and sodden though it was, and set off in search of the path to the village.

She no longer felt any grief. Death by death, step by step, one climbed the great stairway that led upward to Love. The dead, she thought, are like a country from which one is departing; and my heart has known so many homelands in this world that it must learn to take such upheavals for granted, and to be a stranger, an alien everywhere.

A woman on her own is not an object of suspicion. Arsen reached Toulouse without experiencing any annoyances apart from an unpleasant cough and a touch of fever and stiffness. She stayed in the house of a certain cloth-merchant, a rich and charitable member of the Faith who gave shelter to heretics passing through the town. She was cared for there by a sister born and bred in the district, who was renowned for her gifts as a healer.

"You need at least two or three months' rest," this woman told Arsen, "otherwise you will not be able to continue in your ministry much longer. In our times God has no use for flawed tools."

Through this woman Arsen learned that her daughter was now known as Madame d'Aspremont, owned a house, and was reckoned one of the most beautiful women in the Daurade district. She sighed at this, telling herself that city life had changed Gentian. To marry was just tolerable, but to deck oneself out and attract attention in this way less than two years after her father's death— It's true, though, she thought, that nowadays months are reckoned like years: too many missing, too many dead. The girl's husband had long since left the country.

When Gentian's companion, a cousin of Bérenger's, told her that there was a woman called Arsen, from her own part of the country, asking to see her, Gentian nearly fainted. She had not forgotten her mother; it was only that she seemed to be living a wholly different life now. She was weary of endless death and rebirth, and ghosts from the past frightened her.

Arsen crossed the courtyard behind Gentian's companion, and climbed the narrow spiral staircase which led to her daughter's private apartments. The house looked rich to her, but seemed lacking in comfort. So stuffy, she thought. I wonder the poor child doesn't stifle. The men and women sitting about in the small rooms which composed the suite were certainly not servants: the men were playing at dice or chess, the women reading or sewing. A young fair-haired girl was sitting on the floor playing a cittern and singing a plangent, oversweet air which made Arsen want to weep.

As she walked through, the men looked up, as though quite un-
interested in their gaming, while the women stopped their chatter
and lowered their eyes in mute but conspiratorial greeting. She
knew very well what it was; her six years in the ministry had already given her the kind of face that every believer recognized on
sight. Sometimes she did not even need to throw back her hood,
since her carriage betrayed her. In the streets men would press
against the wall for fear of brushing her with their cloaks, while
women stooped to touch—as though by accident—the hem of her
robe. With her plain brown mantle and gray woollen coif she felt
like a queen, rather badly disguised as a servant girl. The thought
embarrassed her. The Catholics are always talking about our pride,
she thought. Might they not be right? Wouldn't anyone think that
I had a message written out in full across my forehead—*Show me
respect: I am a saintly woman*? The lady companion beside her,
meanwhile, was talking away, half in a whisper, as though she
were afraid of interrupting Arsen's meditations.

"Madame d'Aspremont sends her apologies for not coming out
to meet you. She says she wants to meet you alone, without anyone
else present. Please don't take offense; she has been through a great
deal for a young woman."

"Why should I take offense, my friend?"

"She was not forewarned of your coming, my lady. Our house is
like all the rest, I fear; we live here under Pharaoh's laws."

Arsen frowned at this. She disliked anyone's making it too plain
that they knew who she was.

Gentian was awaiting her in a small room so thickly hung with
tapestries that it was impossible to see what color the walls were,
and all cluttered up with chests and cabinets on which branched
candlesticks stood among piles of copper and silver plate. A book
lay open on the tall carved lectern, and on the floor, with cloth-of-
gold cushions to support it, a cittern had been thrown down. The
young girl was sitting on a day bed, which was set half in, half out
of a low red-curtained alcove. Arsen closed the door behind her
and remained motionless for a few moments, not daring to look up.

"Here I am," she said at length. It was silly, but she could find nothing else to say; she felt her lips trembling. This tall lady with the hawklike expression, her tresses all plaited with gold thread—could *she*, Arsen wondered, be my daughter? Gentian rose slowly, went over to her mother, knelt before her, and asked a blessing. Her calm, crisp voice seemed to be saying: That *is* how I should greet you, isn't it?

"Let me at least see your eyes," Arsen said.

They were as lovely as ever, gray and almond-shaped, but quite expressionless: two closed windows.

"Thank you for your kindness, Mother. You do my house a great honor."

"It is you I have come to see, not your house. I find you a lovely and much-honored lady. Your father would have been happy had he lived to see you so well established."

"That was why I married," Gentian said. "Both you and Father always wanted to see me married."

"Why do you say that in so reproachful a fashion? Are you not happy?"

Arsen at once regretted this unthinking remark: the girl was obviously pregnant, and her husband was far away.

"Who *is* happy today?" Gentian asked. She seemed less frozen now, almost friendly. "You, maybe. The rest of us are like the grass of the field; the wind passes over us, and no trace of us is to be found."

Arsen smiled. "But the mercy of the Lord abides from generation to generation upon them that fear Him. I take it your husband is of our Faith?"

"I have not yet taken to the society of Catholics," the girl retorted, piqued. "What do you take me for?"

"For my daughter. Why does each word I utter wound you so? I only wanted to know if your husband was a man who knew how to win your regard."

"He is the best of men. It is not his fault if the great lords are always waiting to see whether the wind will blow one way or the other. We have such vast armies in Spain that there is no one left here to fight the French."

"My child, our Count is not a soldier of fortune, who fights where and when he pleases. It is right that so mighty a prince should have sought to plead his cause before other kings, before the Pope, in order to make good his claims. You should not blame the knights who have left home and family through loyalty to their liege lord."

"I do not blame my husband; but it is more than five months since he left me, and I have heard not a word of news concerning him, either for good or ill, apart from his own letters. Would it not be a little wanton of me to love a man who has done nothing as yet to free his native city?"

"Ah, why allow yourself to succumb to such worldly thoughts?" Arsen exclaimed, in a burst of wistful tenderness. "Have I come here merely to see you parade your pride before me?"

"I no longer know how to talk to you," Gentian said, taking her mother by the hand and drawing her down upon the bed. "You see, I always thought you were the most precious thing I had in all the world—yet now I'm not even pleased to see you! It's as though my heart had been removed and another one put in its place. *You're* the same as always, even though your face has altered a lot. But I'm different; I've lived at least three or four different lives since I left home."

"I see you are soon to become a mother," Arsen said, gently.

"Why do you remind me of the body's miseries? I know only too well that I shall become attached to this child stirring in my womb, just as a bitch becomes fond of her litter. What other affection did you ever have for me? Neither my heart nor my head nor my soul has anything to do with the matter. Why bring it up, then?"

"Because there is no greater compassion in the world than that which binds us to tiny babies; it is more tender than any other sort of love."

"I do not possess a tender heart. If it is a boy, I shall bring him up in such a way that he will be able to avenge my father, and all those others who died for our country. But is it not shameful to spend night after night watching anxiously over a cradle, at a time when the blood of our best men is held so cheap that it is spilled in any gutter like water from a jug? And how can I love this man, so handsome and strong and happy to be alive, when I tell myself constantly that the best are those who abandon everything, even life itself, in the service of true Love?"

"Gentian, when I married your father he too was a young man, strong, happy to be alive; and I was right to love him as I did. Should I have waited till he was dead before granting him my love?"

"You lived in different times. Oh, Mother, if only those days could come back—days when we could dispose of our lives as we pleased, and spring was a season of beauty! But each spring now brings us fresh anguish, and each summer another bloody harvesting, till the hanged and the mutilated and the burned and the drowned become more real to us than the living—for these people have come to kill our country, and those who survive will own nothing but their lives! All that remains to us is the honor of fighting on to the end."

"Do not be like those who say the whole town is burning when their own house is on fire. Simon de Montfort is an old man, yet he is never off his horse or out of his armor except on feast-days. He certainly cannot live much longer."

"God grant they do not send us a worse one than he! You will say that such a thing could not be; but I say that there is no limit set to evil, and that a day may come when we shall say that in de Montfort's time we were happier and enjoyed more freedom."

"It is no good spirit that inspires such terrible words," her mother said, in some alarm. "How do you find the courage to utter them? To declare yourself defeated in advance is a sin."

The girl hid her face in her hands.

"My sin is to have a heart that is oversensitive to evil," she said. "I can scent misfortune as a carrion crow scents a corpse. They thought I was mad, or inspired, and hustled me into marriage as though it were a prison cell. My years in the convent, you see, brought me lucidity and detachment but did not take me the whole way to Love; I am like a bird whose wings are clipped just as its pinions have grown.

"Would to God I may be wrong! But night after night I have prayed and meditated, and God has made me see the world as a battlefield where Satan holds the mastery, and evil is ever triumphant. I have had visions in which I saw men killed, tortured, and burned at the stake; but they were never the wicked. And though with all my heart I long for our country to win, I cannot believe in such a victory; for I know that we are better than our enemies, and that in order to win one must love evil.

"How could it be otherwise, Mother? Do we not know that this world has been created by the Devil for his own ends? By what magic can we change blades of steel into the spiritual swords wielded by God's archangels? Only those who love the power of the sword above all else can vanquish by the sword; only those who wish all men to be slaves can make themselves obeyed; only those in love with gold are rich, and only those without conscience have confidence in themselves.

"We have right on our side, yet Kings, Emperor, and Pope alike proclaim that our enemies are just and virtuous; the only monarch who drew sword on our behalf is dead. If we had conquered by the power of the sword, *then* we should have had right on our side; the day that we invade Northern territory, kill three hundred thousand Frenchmen, burn their lands and plunder their towns, *then* perhaps we shall be called 'good Christians.' But we are not mighty enough to be 'good Christians' in *their* fashion; we are only concerned with honor and freedom."

"Are we forbidden to believe that even in this world God can illuminate our hearts and minds?" Arsen cried. "Do our Bishops preach in vain? Dough rises slowly, and a tree does not grow in a day. You are wailing like a child because your faith in God is not greater!"

"No; a tree does not grow in a day, true; but it can be cut down in a day. In other words, evil will always have the dominance on earth. Our house boasted treasures beyond all price, luminaries of pure gold set about with diamonds and pearls and every sort of wonderful precious stone—treasures such as were never yet seen on earth, for the least of which one would have sold the entire house. But thieves came, and cast them upon the fire, and crushed them to powder, and threw them down the latrines; and now they seek to get those which yet remain to us, and to destroy them in like fashion for the hate they bear us.

"It is indeed true that in God's Heaven these luminaries shine eternally, bright as a thousand beacons; but our house has been stripped of them, here on earth they who were worth more than the earth itself have been destroyed. Why do you talk of dough rising, or the growth of trees? The dough is thrown into the embers now, the earth has been scorched into barrenness. As for ourselves, we are like those madmen who till the soil in the belief that gold will sprout from it: we actually expect charity and justice of this world."

"Certainly, since we are not yet in the next. How could this world change our hearts' desire?"

Gentian said, harshly: "*You* no longer belong here; you have found your peace. You are one of those torches I spoke of; you are numbered among our treasures and our glories; but for you the battle is over. The standard against which you measure all things is not an ell but a league, and he who lends you a penny receives a thousand crowns in return. People such as you have bodies that seem like ours; yet you resemble those golden lamps that shine only in kings' palaces, and are never used in the kitchen or carried down to the cellar."

Peace? Arsen wondered. What peace? It is not three weeks since I lost my companion; yet I have not so much as dared to mention it. On the subject of our personal sorrows we must preserve absolute silence. My whole body aches with the longing to find my companion again; here I am in this stuffy, tapestried chamber when I would far sooner be out in the chill forest where I left her body. Have pity on the servant who returns hungry and tired from the fields, for to him the Master says, not "Be seated and eat," but, "Wait upon Me at table."

She said, gently: "If you had had to swab out wounds and wash filthy linen, like us, you would not say that. We are appointed to perform those tasks which even the lowliest think beneath them."

"That is your vocation," the young woman said. "You chose it yourself. And so noble a vocation, indeed, that the rest of us lack the right so much as even to dream of it; so we have to make do with pretty dresses and curtained four-posters instead."

She took her cittern, sat down on the cushions, and began to pluck the strings; she seemed calm enough, but there was a golden, catlike glint in her eyes. Her mother thought: How lovely she is; how seductive men must find her beauty. Gentian was strumming a monotonous, gently melancholy air, which sounded to Arsen like a song of parting. She reproached herself for remembering her own distress when perhaps her daughter, too, was suffering, because of her separation from the man she loved. There are many girls, she reflected, who, either through pride or shame, make a show of denying their love. Surely I came here to comfort Gentian, not to argue with her?

She sat down beside her daughter and began to stroke the girl's hair and shoulders.

"My dove," she said, "pain cannot be told in words; the heart throbs and bleeds and remains dumb. You are quite right: I am an old woman, and can no longer understand a young girl's anguish. I wish I could go back to the days when I used to dandle you on my knees."

"Mother," Gentian said, suddenly, looking Arsen straight in the eye, "Mother, tell me this: have you known the longings and joys of carnal desire?"

Arsen blinked at this, but from surprise rather than embarrassment.

"I loved your father as any woman living in the world loves her husband—with all the longing and joy and sorrow of which our sex is capable."

Gentian shook her head impatiently. "How can I tell whether we are speaking of the same thing? When you speak to me of my father, it is as though you were speaking of the love of God. My heart burns with thoughts as cruel as they are impure; I know neither the Spirit nor the flesh. Spilled blood turns our heads like overstrong wine; and the flame in our hearts flickers so faintly when set beside all these bonfires and conflagrations that we must constantly burn our breast with live coals in order to keep it alight."

"I know this," Arsen said. "Many young girls have told me a similar story. We live in a time of temptation. Do not distress yourself because of this, my child: you are no more to blame than the wounded or the sick. Even those young women who fall short of the honorable standards proper to their sex are not really to blame. War is a sickness of the soul; it is not men alone who are infected by it."

Gentian gave a harsh smile, with the faintest hint of gaiety in it.

"Since Bérenger went away," she said, "plenty of men have come a-wooing me. The people in these parts are very different from those back home; they make a firm distinction between honor and chastity, love and pleasure. I am forced to believe that what I feel for my husband is love, since I do not think I will ever wrong him, as long as I live."

Gentian sought out all the very best things she could find among the kinds of nourishment her mother was allowed, and herself washed the plates and the cup in Arsen's presence. But Arsen would touch nothing except bread and water: since her friend's death she had been observing a strict fast, through fear lest she fall into the weaknesses of sorrow according to the flesh.

"You eat, though," she told Gentian. "There is no call for you to weaken your unborn child's body out of respect for me. Even in its present condition it already possesses a soul, which is being made ready for a harsh Calvary. The woman who is lacking in regard toward the child she carries sins gravely against charity."

Gentian drank her wine and nibbled at the dried figs and hazelnuts. All the time she kept her eyes fixed on her mother.

"I am greedy," she said. "I am keeping you all to myself tonight. Is that a sin?"

"No, I have time and to spare; I shall not resume my journey until the fine weather comes, unless I am forced to. Do the Bishop's men keep a watch on your house?"

Gentian shrugged.

"They do," she said. "But I should be very much surprised if they tried to force their way into it; you see, Bérenger's uncle is the son-in-law of one of our Consuls. I will give you a change of clothes and have a man keep you company in public."

Arsen said: "Have you any news of your brothers?"

"Yes; Bérenger says in a letter that he saw Sicart at Saragossa. All three of them are in good health, and must go to Roussillon with their liege lord. They have seen a good deal of the world since we parted."

"Ah, when shall I see them again?" Arsen said. "We are all like seeds sown in the wind." She turned to her prayers, and Gentian lit the lamps: night had fallen, and little remained visible but the grille over the little square window, and the reflections of the silver ewers on their cabinets.

Gentian, lying on her bed with her mother beside her, could almost believe herself back in the days of her childhood.

"What has happened to our house at Montgeil, Mother?" she asked. "Who lives there now?"

"Maybe folk in need of shelter, maybe brigands—the Crusaders wouldn't bother with it, the country around there is too poor and out of the way."

"Or perhaps it's been burned down. A fine harvest of nettles and brambles my brothers will find on their land if they ever get it back! Mother—do you remember William de Frémiac, who was so desperately in love with me and wanted my hand in marriage? He's gone too, now."

"To lose all in a good cause remains a great honor. Even though it be a sin, courage is worth more than cowardice."

Gentian, chin resting on clasped hands, stared at the flame of the little oil lamp that hung above her bed.

"Mother," she said, "why am I a woman? Courage is a man's concern: then what remains for us? Even our enemies scorn us; our hatred causes them no fear. All that we can do is to love those who show themselves brave. Mother—there is something I must tell you. My heart has been trapped in the snare of earthly things, because of the great agony our country is enduring. Instead of longing for the Spirit, I think only of fleshly things."

"Every part of us, even the purest of our thoughts, is according to the flesh," Arsen said. "Only two things are not: the Word of God, and the Spirit of which our flesh knows nothing."

"Ah, the things you speak of are too high for me, Mother. How can I ever attain to them? I want to tell you something I have told to no other living soul: how my heart came to be seduced by the world. Oh, it was a day of great rejoicing for our country, a great honor for this town, the day that good King Peter entered Toulouse, with our Counts and the flower of his knighthood riding behind him, to deliver us from our enemies! All the trumpets sounded that day, and the drums and the fifes, and never a girl so modest but she ran out into the streets shouting for joy, carrying her sash or olive branch to fling under the horses' hoofs as they passed.

"I was in Capitol Square with my friend Beatrix de Miraval and her mother, and a crowd of other women all got up in their best clothes. I can't tell you how we all shouted for joy, how madly our hearts beat in our breasts! It was a beautiful day, and the knights' helms shone in the sunlight like crystal. And I saw the King come riding past in his gilded armor, bareheaded, so that we could all see his nobility and the great good will he had for our people. And oh, Mother, his face was as beautiful as a fine warm summer's day, and his smile a wide, joyous smile—you could see his teeth gleaming, so white and splendid! At the sight of him our hearts were full to overflowing, and tears sprang from our eyes. At that moment I felt such heat spread throughout my body that I felt as though I were enveloped in a great sheet of flame.

"I took such delight in watching this noble King, this flower of knighthood—so tall and strong he was, so perfect in every point of his person—that I would not have looked up even though the heavens had opened at that very moment to reveal a thousand arch-angels. That day I told myself: Now Heaven has come down on earth, for goodness and justice are reckoned at their true price. And beyond doubt my friends thought as I did, for we all said the same thing: *Here is the Saviour we have awaited so long!*

"You yourself know how brief was our joy, and how Satan duped us all. What I want to tell you is how I spent the day of that great battle, and the way my heart went where my body never did. We did not even know if battle had been joined or not; but while I sat at Dame Alfaïs's feet with my cittern, I began to hear shouts, and a mighty clash of spears, and I saw King Peter with a throng of men-at-arms about him. He was not wearing the same armor now, but his visor was up and I saw his face, and I knew he was in sore straits, for he was wounded, and fighting alone against four foemen. They bore him down off his horse and hacked at him with their swords, and all the time I watched and watched, unable to look away, thinking that help would come to him soon; but so thick was the press of battle, with wounded horses careering past on all sides, that his friends could not get to him in time. So sav-agely had he been mauled that he no longer struggled now; blood poured from his mouth in a great flood, till his helmet was full of it. I went into a sort of frenzy, shrieking out: *The King is dead! The King is dead! They have killed the King!*

"I have little recollection of what happened then, except that I saw a group of our knights defending themselves against a vast body of Crusaders; they were hard put to it to prevent their horses from shying away, for the onslaught was very fierce, and I saw more than one of them borne down and slain. They took me away to my room, and I struggled and cried, thinking that *my* mouth, too, was full of blood.

"I have no idea now how long I continued to weep. I lay on my bed, feeling as though I were bruised all over, and the blood was there, pouring from my nose and mouth. I had all the sensations of someone dizzy-drunk with bloodshed and hard knocks—which is not surprising, for on the day of that battle more than twenty thou-sand souls were torn violently from their bodies, weeping and shrieking in distress; and among the first was that of the King.

"They did not get news of all this in the town till evening; but then they saw very clearly that I had not been raving, and that God had chosen me to be a harbinger of evil tidings. You can have no idea of the weeping and mourning and tears that filled Toulouse in the days that followed; of the city burghers who had obeyed the call to arms, more than half had perished. Such was our mood that the accursed Simon did not dare to show his face among us; disarmed and desolate though we were, we burned with such fierce hatred of the King's murderer that the very stones of the houses would of their own accord have fallen and crushed him.

"For months on end I remained, as it were, the victim of my ailment—or rather of that gift of weeping with every soul wrenched from its body in blood and ghastliness. Through mourning this King, so cruelly slain, I had lost all desire for prayer. It was no good my spending time in meditation, or reading Holy Scripture; I could not check my burning love for all those who unstintingly risk their lives in the defense of our country. And those whom I begged to take pity on my soul, to let me be united with my Spirit, told me that I was unworthy, and that God would purify only those souls that were already pure."

"How can you blame them?" Arsen said. "You yourself have admitted to no longer possessing a true longing for God."

"I don't know now. I just don't know. Who can desire the sun before he has seen it? I was weary of my wretched condition, sick and tired of being a soulless body, a bodiless soul. Then, one fine day, a man I shall not name came to me armed with the authority of the Spirit, and told me I had neither faith nor charity, that even now it would be better for me to prostitute myself to Satan according to the way of the world: that would at least teach me humility. What would you say of a man who spoke thus?"

"What can I say? It is possible he was inspired by the Spirit."

"Mother, how can one speak to you? *You* see the Spirit everywhere. Tell me, do you know how a man looks at a woman when he lusts after her in love—and I do not speak of God's Love now, make no mistake about that! Even the stupidest girl knows that

look, just as a wild beast recognizes its hunter. If a man looks at
you like *that,* can he be inspired by the Spirit?"

"How should I know? We feel hunger and pain like other people; even the best of us can know humiliation in the flesh through
the Devil's wiles. The Spirit makes use of us despite our weaknesses."

Arsen's voice was sad and weary. What will she ask me next?
she wondered. Was ever child so inquisitive?

"Mother," Gentian said, "you are beginning to talk like the
Catholics."

"Heaven forfend! I know life rather better than you do, that is
all. If one of our brethren has been a cause of scandal to you, he
is greatly to be pitied."

"Mother, I swear to you it wasn't my fault—I would never have
thought of him as a man, for all his handsome face! He told me to
take a husband and live according to the secular law—it was like a
slap in the face, don't you see that? But worse than that, I accepted
the verdict. I told myself that no one would any longer treat me as
a lunatic visionary, or upbraid me for trying to seduce a man of
God—"

"Could anyone have dared make such an accusation, against
you?" Arsen cried, cut to the quick.

"Mother, you still don't understand at all, do you? No one actually uttered such a reproach—except perhaps in thought; but I am
always tortured by people's thoughts, that's something stronger
than I, I can't help it. If I told you the tenth part of my own
thoughts you'd have a headache for three days. Now listen: I chose
to become engaged to a man who was no worse than the common
run and perhaps rather better. I did this not through mere vulgar
desire, but out of respect for my father, and you, and my brothers.
I accepted him in all friendship, though my heart was forever for-
feit to a higher Love. Did I do wrong to marry?"

"No, my dove. All our actions are written beforehand in God's
book. You must believe that this is the way in which it has pleased
God to seek you out. There are countless Christian women who

come to Him after passing through the ordeal of maternal love."

Gentian sighed. "It may be so," she said. "But, Mother—if it pleases me to surrender my heart to too high a Love, who can forbid me?"

"I have never forbidden you anything," Arsen said.

Arsen stayed in her daughter's house for nearly a fortnight, and was able to see Jacques d'Ambialet and two of the brethren from the Carcassès area, who were in Toulouse on a special mission. They talked much of Renaud and Fabrisse, and did their best to comfort the grieving Arsen.

"It is proper," they said, "that you should languish after our late sister, now translated into the heavenly sphere, even as the dove languishes after its mate: such is the law of nature. There was never a better, gentler, more gracious lady in the land. It is a loss for us all—but not for her; she has attained once more to the fullness of joy, and at last can share in the glory of that one true Love, which is God's."

"Ah, do I not know this?" Arsen said. "She was more pure than the clearest crystal. My friends, what breaks my heart is not so much to be separated from her as the thought that two such fine workers have been taken from us in the very midst of their labors. The harvest is rich, the year well advanced, and full many a corn-stalk is losing its grain and rotting back to earth for want of harvesters! Take the district in which we have been working, the district where our brother Renaud lost his earthly life: there is such misery and hardship there because of the burning of the fields that the burghers themselves have scarcely any bread, and the common folk lack even bran soup. The men rob and murder on the highways when they get the chance, and their young daughters sell themselves to soldiers. In the town of Saissac six people died with their sins upon them this winter because their families did not dare to send for us. I can no longer return there myself, since I am too well known in the area; but the Bishop of Toulouse should send them two of the newly ordained brethren. I will let them have the names of those persons with whom they ought to establish contact. The faithful from those parts are so stricken by Renaud's death that they more or less feel this is God's punishment upon them, and that they are marked for eternal damnation."

"This town lies in the Carcassonne diocese," Jacques d'Ambialet said. "Our own Bishop is away on a pastoral tour of the Moissac area, and to tell the truth he spends more time on the road than he does in his house. Remember, though, that he is not as old as all that, and was only recently ordained. If he sent his own ordinands to Saissac, would he not be accused of encroaching on Monseigneur Bernard's rights? Your demand is a just one, but we must take care to avoid provoking scandals among the brethren."

"What scandal?" Arsen asked. "When a house is on fire, the first person on the spot has every right to carry the water buckets. Since this Deluge first broke upon our diocese, we have lost nearly seven hundred of our sisters and brethren. God forbid we should now harbor bitterness or jealousies against you! Your own venerable Bishop is the light of our land, who by the power of his discourse and the sanctity of his life has shown himself as it were a new St. Paul; how could *he* ever take offense at anyone? Let him but send God's Bread to the hungry. It is not I, the least of God's servants, who ask this; it is our dead brethren, who gave their lives for their flock."

"We shall speak of the matter to him," the old man said with a sigh. "In these troubled times many of the faithful lose contact with their Church, and some do not even know to which diocese they belong, since we are obliged to send them any preacher available. Through lack of pastors, many folk in the country districts have allowed themselves to be seduced by the Leonist heresy—a consequence of ignorance rather than evil intentions.

"Here in Toulouse we have to spend so much time avoiding the hooks and nets of our enemies that we are scarcely able to give our postulants the instruction they need. Certain of our younger members acquire such a taste for this undercover game that they spend more time inventing secret codes than assimilating intelligible lectures. I will repeat what I have said before: the real danger does not lie in the Bishop's Brotherhood,* with their noisy, hymn-bawling, Cross-waving assaults on private houses. It is the Bishop's spies whom we really have to fear. They worm their way in everywhere, humility written all over their faces, and falsely proclaiming their desire for instruction. We have lost seven men this way already, not counting those who have been forced to flee the town. We have to keep shifting our premises and looking for new houses. In such conditions it becomes about as easy to conduct a seminary as to write with a broken pen. Very often we have to ordain a candidate without possessing the means necessary to test his sense of vocation as we ought."

Arsen said: "Let us trust in God's bounty. He will know how to make good our weaknesses." It struck her that this venerable minister, probably because of his great age, was prone to misjudge both the knowledge and the zeal of his new recruits. Had there, she wondered, ever been so great a religious fervor among the young people in this area? How many girls had knelt weeping at her feet, begging her to let them accompany her, wanting to be taken into the mountains so that they might withdraw from the world and lead a hermit's life!

Gentian bade her mother farewell, and besought her to take good care of herself, and not to go back anywhere where her life was in danger.

"Always remember," she said, "that the death of any one of you is a cause of despair and denial among the faithful—and that each time the faggots are lit, our hearts conceive more hatred for the executioners than love for the martyrs thus butchered by them. *Never forget that we are not saints.*"

How hard love can become in times of great hatred, Arsen thought. Can untrammelled love cause actual harm? She trudged

---

* This refers to the so-called White Brotherhood, instituted by Bishop Foulques in Toulouse: a species of civil militia that attacked and ransacked the homes of known heretics.—Trs.

on beside the swollen Garonne, a lonely figure, with her staff and the new copy of the Gospels that the brethren in her diocese had given her, thinking of those comrades who had already rendered to God the trust they held from Him, increased and multiplied threefold, fivefold, or tenfold.

Many had been bowed by age and infirmities, and when the flames devoured them alive were already eagerly awaiting the day of their coming face to face with God. But many more, too many, had still had a long life ahead of them: the lamp had been snuffed out when it was still charged with oil. Take Renaud, who had still been strong enough to carry a man a good half-league on his back, and whose voice before sunrise was strong and melodious enough to wake the very birds: Renaud, who said that nothing which partook of the Spirit could be lost, and that a man's death could never hinder God's work! And yet, Arsen thought, never again, anywhere on this earth, will there be another Renaud—citizen of Limoux, God's minister in the districts round about Minerve and Carcassonne; and never will we be certain that those who so cruelly put him to death did no harm to God's cause.

Take Aicart, who could have become a mighty husbandman in the Father's vineyard, and who was cut down when his work was scarce begun: in one day he gave his all that he might honor the promise he had made. And in that one day God achieved his perfection. But here on earth a great flame of love was extinguished before it had time to shine out brightly.

O Lord, in what hearts and bodies will these extinguished flames be relit? We are not proud enough to suppose that Thou hast need of us—but what about those others, our well-beloved ones, the poor, the desolate, the distraught, those whom we served in our presumption, and who put their trust in us because they have no knowledge of Thee, O Lord? Where will *they* find again the faces they have loved so dearly, now that every day we are forced to abandon them further?

Have You sent us only to be an open wound in their hearts? Ah, pity the martyrs and the strong! When they have nothing left to

give but their lives they become like a fire that devours where it
should spread warmth. My poor child was right: when a righteous
man is executed, ten men will be found willing to follow his example, a thousand who long to avenge him, ten thousand who are
stricken by terror and robbed of their resolution—but only one or
two at the very most who feel themselves fired by a genuine love
of God.

Our enemies think we are mad, while our friends offer us the
veneration due only to saints; and thus a death that is true and
honorable before God becomes, in men's eyes, a mere lie.

O Lord, we are fragile instruments: to break us, a word—no,
less, a glass of milk only—will suffice. We are more subject than
others to mere matter, and our Rule leaves us defenseless in the
face of our enemies. When I go into a house heads are bent respectfully, and each face takes on an anxious expression: if ever I
am caught, will the person responsible ever be known, much less
made to answer for his deed? When I go through a town all eyes
stare after me, sometimes ashamedly, sometimes full of reproach,
as though to ask why I should come and lay such a burden upon
them. Yet in truth they do not think thus, for they never do reproach us; but their hearts are troubled. They all say, "Do not risk
your life for our sakes!" For whom else, then, my well-beloved
ones? Do you believe we play this game out of vainglory and a contempt for life?

A little while ago I visited a dying woman, who lay beside the
dead body of her newborn child. Her face was wrung with agony,
and she scarcely had the strength to repeat the Lord's Prayer after
me. When I laid my hands upon her she scarcely managed to keep
still; she turned her hunted, hope-crazy eyes on me and gasped:
"Am I saved, my lady?" "Trust in God's bounty, my sister," I told
her. These people do not believe in God; they believe in us. God
forbid we should ever become idols!

Arsen continued her journey on foot till she reached the safe
retreat of Montségur, where Bishop Bernard had taken temporary

refuge. It was a very quiet place; the Crusaders had passed through four years earlier, burning the village and devastating the fields, but that was all. Now the village was twice the size it had been before the war, and the road leading to it big enough for large carts to pass each other. The only armed men one was likely to meet in the area belonged to the Count of Foix.

Arsen felt as though she were ten years younger. Here was a district that had never abandoned its ancient customs, where sisters and brethren of the Faith still wore their habits and could be openly greeted in the streets, where people spoke of the seminary as casually as they would of the bailiff's house. She breathed freely again, feeling as though she had come into a warm house after a long journey through the wind and rain.

In the guesthouse kept specially for the use of itinerant sisters, Arsen was able to have a bath and obtain habit, veil, and new sandals. To her surprise this gave her a feeling of happy pride, as though she were a young girl again and getting a new feast-day dress. When, at long last, she put the habit on, over a clean shift (it was made of black wool, and gathered in at the waist with a silken cord) she felt for a moment that she had become, not more pure, but at least more truly herself. And yet, she thought, God knows this habit will never be dearer to me than my little girdle, blackened and sweat-sodden though it is. Since the great day when it was given me, no other eye has seen that girdle. It is my true raiment, my secret ring, the only object I possess which is truly mine. But how great is God's bounty in according us at times the simple happiness which the habit can bring, by proclaiming our servitude openly to mankind!

The heart is so made that it can compel the eyes to find beauty in the thing it loves. When she entered the guesthouse refectory, Arsen derived more pleasure from the sight of her sisters' austere black robes than she ever could have done by contemplating fine brocades or precious stones. Ah, she thought, if only Fabrisse had held out for another two months—if only she could have died here!

They were in the first weeks of the Paschal fast; so the cups and platters solemnly borne in by serving-maids contained, of course, only water, bread, and a little salt. Arsen, who had been weakened by ill-health and the rigors of her journey, felt somewhat hungry —hungry enough, at least, to recall that she was still subject to bodily afflictions, though otherwise she felt as though she were in Paradise.

There were several other women there who had been on missions in the regions around Toulouse and Carcassonne. The stories they had to tell were far from cheerful. The Church, they said, suffered as much at the hands of brigands and itinerant monks as from the Crusaders. The monks in particular were just like a pack of hunts-men's hounds, eager to sniff out any true Christians. Their master and leader, the renowned Dominic, was regarded as a visible in-carnation of the Devil, and it was he who put the audacity into them—"so much so, indeed," someone said, "that there is some doubt now whether they should be protected against overzealous champions of the Faith or, on the contrary, indicted as traitors to their country; some of them are persuasive talkers, and have suc-ceeded in converting a few credulous women."

Arsen found herself remembering the two white-clad friars whom she and Renaud had met in Saissac.

"My sisters," she said, "is it our task to condemn these men as traitors? The whole world is only too well aware of their treachery. God forbid we should cast oil on the flames; that is not our func-tion."

"Dear sister, our function is to protect our sheep against the wolf—and never before in this country have we known wolves so cruel and cunning. I have listened to one of their sermons: they paint the imaginary torments of Hell in such lurid colors that old women tremble and young girls shriek aloud. How can we stand by and see souls corrupted in such a fashion?"

Arsen covered her face with both hands. Ah, God, God, she thought, and here was I in my miserable selfishness hoping for peace and quiet! We sit here at peace ourselves, but leave our flock a prey to the tempters who rot their souls with tormenting fears. Every single word we hear reminds us of the awful plight in which

the occupied areas remain. It is not enough for them to kill the
body.

Her mind was on the faithful at Saissac, and around Minerve
and Lantarès. Alas, she thought, ten preachers would barely suffice
in such regions, and today there are one or two left at most. Because of our weakness the wolves grow stronger and multiply.
Who knows, they may well be saying: "Look, your pastors have
deserted you. They have run away. They are cowards." These
greedy wolves fear nothing. They say: "Kill us, and then we shall
be martyrs for God." Since the Devil, their master, makes them
insensitive both to pain and to fear, it is easy enough for them to
become martyrs.

The following day Arsen, together with several other women
from her diocese, climbed up to the fortress of Montségur. This
fortress was set so high that (since it was an early spring day with
mist in the air) it seemed to float among the clouds. The ascent was
both long and arduous, and twice the women stopped at little rest
huts built on the side of the mountain. These huts were for the
most part occupied either by postulants or by men still young
enough for a constantly active life: they were few in number, perhaps a dozen at most, and served as emergency shelters for the
sick in bad weather. It was not till they reached the very foot of the
walls that they saw the real convents. These were a series of tiny
huts piled one above the other; since space was exceedingly
cramped, they more or less hung suspended over the abyss. This
mountain was the biggest, highest, steepest rock formation in the
whole region: those old folk who preferred to live close to the
fortress rather than in the woods had at least to conserve strength
enough not to be afraid of giddiness.

The road that led up to the main gate was still of a fair width:
horses could pass on it easily enough, and so could small carts.
But at any time the courtyard was liable to be overcrowded; at
present a detachment of soldiers in transit were installed there. In
wartime the soldier has a right to be served first, and this lot had
made a six-league detour in order to hear the Bishop preach. The

women in black sat down at the foot of the staircase leading up to
the ramparts, and humbly awaited their turn.

Monseigneur Bernard had to remain in Montségur till Easter.
He was receiving all the visitors he could, and the women from the
Carcassès district were obliged to wait two days. Harried on all
sides by demands for money and hundreds of written complaints
from the brethren and lesser members of his flock, busy with the
composition and dictation of pastoral letters, constantly badgered
by visitors demanding his advice, the old Bishop could preach no
more than twice a week. Moreover his "minor son," Raymond
William, was obliged—without the Bishop's knowledge—to pick
and choose among the visitors who came begging an audience.
Monseigneur Bernard was capable of spending two hours listening
to the grievances of some utterly unimportant old crone: he would
never have shown any member of his flock that such conversations
might be either boring or a plain nuisance. When Raymond William pointed out to him that certain persons were abusing his generosity, the Bishop replied: "If I allowed myself to discriminate
in that fashion, I should no longer be the servant of all. Who am
I to decide that my neighbor is unworthy to address me?"

Arsen and her companions had no alternative but to be patient.
They passed the time by visiting the recluses who lived there on
the rock. It was wonderful to feel oneself relegated, at last, to the
ranks of the apprentices, the undistinguished beginners, those who
had all their discoveries before them still. Among the recluses of
Montségur there were several elderly ladies renowned for their
saintliness: simply to look at their faces was to feel firm ground
beneath one's feet again. They were as solid, massive, and un-
shakable as rocks themselves. Despite external differences, their
general resemblance to one another was quite terrifying: fired, not
once but again and again, in that same refining flame, each of them
revealed, glowing through thin, dry features, the light of ageless
youth—eternal spring, skies forever unclouded. What, Arsen
thought, are our miseries in comparison with peace such as this?
We are like tiny wayside lanterns, while these blessed ones are

already bathed in full sunlight. Such a one was my aunt, Dame Serrone; and many others besides, who, like her, have been burned at the stake—focal points of prayer, each one of them. Why must the earth be deprived of their presence? Our life is hard enough as it is.

The Bishop received them one evening after supper, in the room set aside for his use by the civil authorities. Monseigneur Bernard was seated in a high-backed chair, with a clutter of writing desks, lecterns, books, and papers all around him, dictating a letter to the postulant who acted as his secretary. He was very old now, and found it difficult to write, let alone to read—though his eyes were piercing enough still when he focussed them on any more distant object.

He made a habit of giving private interviews to each lay member of his flock, but never accorded the same privilege to those who had been ordained, saying, quite reasonably, that the corporate Church, being One, had a single soul. The five women knelt to receive his blessing, after which the Bishop pointed to a bench, indicating that they should sit down till he had finished his letter. He was dictating in Latin; the letter was to one of the brethren in Italy, a saintly and aged deacon who was in charge of one of the Rome seminaries. In the midst of terrible tribulations this most learned man kept up lengthy theological arguments by means of correspondence, since, as he put it, nothing threatened the Church's unity more than any falling off in the purity of her dogma.

God, Arsen thought, how he has changed in these three years! That large, bony countenance had acquired the brownish tinge normally to be seen on the faces of very old, very sick men. Deep pouches had formed below his quick, glinting eyes. The locks of white hair that hung down to his shoulders were sparser now, while his body, for all its natural stiffness of carriage, was so bowed that it seemed in imminent danger of collapse.

His voice, when he spoke, was hoarse and curt.

"My sisters," he said at length, "I am now at your disposal. I have been informed of your missions, and the work you have accomplished. If your acts have been wholly praiseworthy and in every respect worthy of the rank you hold, then it is not for me to thank you, nor, indeed, for you to expect thanks; for all that is good comes from God, and belongs to Him alone. But if there are any weaknesses you should reveal to me, any sins of omission or commission, then I will endeavor to examine the cause of each error with you, and help you henceforth to avoid such lapses from grace."

One by one the women came forward and knelt beside his chair, and said what they had to say. The Bishop heard them out, eyes lowered, chin in hand, as though his mind were on something quite different. Not a muscle moved in that lined, weary, impassive face.

When all was done he rose, wiped his hands on a white napkin that hung folded over the arm of his chair, and picked up the copy of the Gospels from his desk. He opened it, and began to read:

"He that entereth in by the door is the shepherd of the sheep. To him the porter openeth; and the sheep hear his voice: and he calleth his own sheep by name, and leadeth them out. And when he putteth forth his own sheep, he goeth before them, and the sheep follow him: for they know his voice. And a stranger will they not follow, but will flee from him: for they know not the voice of strangers."

At this point he stopped and said: "I will not read any further; you know the rest as well as I do. But according to the little understanding which has been granted me, I will endeavor to expound to you the way in which you should understand the twelfth and thirteenth verses; for many of our brethren have refused to abandon their posts through fear of being like the hireling who flees when he sees the wolf approach, and wish rather to resemble the good shepherd who gives his life for his flock.

"Such conduct, my sisters, while praiseworthy, is not always prudent. None of us is the Good Shepherd; there is only one Good Shepherd, and He has never fled away, but will remain with his flock forever, until the end of time.

"Hear once again that which is written in an earlier verse: *A stranger will they not follow.* God forfend you should ever doubt these words! Though the Enemy has absolute power over our bodies, he holds none over our souls—unless we count the power exercised by the suffering flesh over the soul which it holds imprisoned. Our enemies do well to fear us; for we let our flock hear the Shepherd's voice, and those sheep of which they thought to rob Him now follow Him instead. But we have no cause to fear *them;* none will follow them except the sons of perdition.

"And now, if I may, I will tell you a kind of parable. There was once a man who had, for no reason, incurred his neighbor's enmity. The neighbor, in a fit of insensate rage, started throwing stones and javelins at this man's sheep, and killed a large number of them. Seeing that he could do nothing to stop this fellow's mad fury, but rather that his efforts would only serve to augment it, and thus do the flock irreparable harm, the man took to the hills in search of his friends, and armed them all with sticks and staves. Together, he thought, we shall be strong enough to get this madman under control; and perhaps when I am out of his sight the wretched creature will stop slaughtering my sheep, for it is I, not they, against whom he bears a grudge."

"Ah, Monseigneur," cried one of the women, Guillelme by name, clasping her hands, "what advice is this you have given us? Men and women are dying in their sins for lack of Christians to give them solace!"

The Bishop said: "Do you believe, like the idolaters, that an ignorant soul can be judged and condemned merely because it has been unable to receive baptism? Those who die sincerely contrite, and earnestly desiring baptism, will not in any way have prejudiced their chance of salvation; they will obtain it again in a new life. But if the man in my story stays where he is, and fights the madman, there will be no one left to go for help, and the flock will lack a shepherd.

"My sisters, in time gone by, thanks to the authority with which, through the Church's decision, I have been invested, I used to preach in public and before princes, seeking openly to convince our enemies of their errors, face to face and man to man. Now I must

hide like a thief, and accept hospitality from our brethren of Toulouse. I cannot show myself in my own diocese unless I have a
strong bodyguard and am clad in garments unbecoming to my station. If tomorrow I went and preached in the main square of Carcassonne, I would be behaving like a madman, not as a servant of
Christ.

"Our Church has endured more ordeals than any other. My sisters, we cannot risk leaving the flock without its shepherds. Any
shepherd who gave his life for his sheep without shielding them
from danger would be out of his wits. We are responsible for our
lives to babes in the cradle and children yet unborn, for the times
are not yet fulfilled, and the Church must endure for centuries
rather than generations. Let us not sow our seed in a flooded field
with a hurricane blowing: every grain is numbered, and we ourselves are very few.

"It is not advice I am giving you, my sisters, but an order. You
are free to disregard it if you believe, before God and in all conscience, that you should act otherwise. But you must know that in
such a case you will have neither help nor support nor blessing
from me; I was not elected to serve you, but the faithful."

"Monseigneur," Arsen said, "the reason we stand before you
now is, precisely, to receive your orders. It is for you to decide into
which province you need to send us."

The Bishop said that, for the time being, he was not sending
them out at all, but imposing a year's retreat on them, to be spent
there, on the rock of Montségur. A sword, he told them, became
blunted with overuse, and needed the whetstone. The reverend
sisters had been exposed for too long to the impurities of this
world, and, by losing contact with the Church, risked falling into
the snares of willfulness and worldly fancy.

"I have already observed this disease in many of our brethren,"
he said, "and this is not the time for the salt to lose its savor. My
dear sister Arsen, I share your grief for your noble companion,
who was a Christian adorned with every most precious grace of the
Spirit. From this day forward you will have instead of her a newly

ordained young woman, a brave soul in a sorely tried body, who will stand in great need of your support. Your place of retreat will be told to you tomorrow."

"How long, Monseigneur," Guillelme asked, "must we stand by and watch the wolves decimate our flock?"

"Not so long as you suppose," the Bishop replied calmly. "Although for us there can be neither victory nor defeat, but only obedience to the Rule, I can assure you that the minions of Antichrist will be cast down in confusion sooner than they suppose. From the news I have been given by various members of the Faith —I will not name them to you, but they hold high office in the secular world—I can predict that very soon our land will spew up the foreign poison it now endures, that from the very excess of evil good will come. Your tears will be dried; you will return to the vintage with more fellow laborers than you ever had. And the harvest will be richer than in all previous years."

Reassured and greatly comforted by the Bishop's words, the women retired to the apartments of the Governor's lady, and found her already surrounded by a group of sisters from the nobility. Among them Arsen recognized her new companion, Esclarmonde de Ventenac, a girl of about thirty, and Bishop Bernard's greatniece. She suffered from acute shortsightedness, being unable to see anything more than a few inches in front of her nose. She was in the habit of saying how lucky she was in fact, since very soon she would be quite blind. And yet her eyes were very beautiful, like two huge black olives: only perhaps a little too fixed and brilliant. Arsen kissed her on both cheeks.

"God has sent me a companion as lovely as she is noble," she exclaimed. "May He grant that we remain long together!"

Esclarmonde inclined her head. "My lady," she replied, "may God grant that my imperfections do not make you miss too bitterly the companion you have lost."

"Ah," Arsen said, "I shall miss *her* till my dying day. I must needs love you the more dearly in memory of her; for you too are her sister."

The next day Arsen and Esclarmonde were taken to their new dwelling place, which lay in a patch of woodland on the east flank of the mountain, some three hundred yards from the castle itself. It was a hut of sorts, half excavated from the solid rock, half built out with large blocks of dressed stone. It was extremely pleasant. There was a hearth for a fire, and two stone beds had been cut from the rock face. Its doorway was so large that light penetrated inside for nearly the whole day. From the threshold one got a direct view of the fortress, its long, lofty bastions looking as though they hung in space above the boulders and brushwood. There, too, was the sheer fall of the huge cliff, bare rock plunging from the foot of the wall as though into infinity; even by bending over the edge it was impossible to see the bottom of the valley.

On both sides of the path the slope was dotted with sparse, twisted pines, growing almost above each other's heads. The path itself wound upward through the bushes like a snake, leading to other huts, and, above them, to a series of grottoes. Behind the tops of the nearest trees a superb panorama unfolded itself: a vast mountainous valley, gently undulating, covered with dark green woodland that faded to smoky blue in the distance. Against the horizon lay a range of blue peaks.

How will I face a year here? Arsen wondered. Only three months ago I would have dreamed of this as the most wonderful thing that could befall me. And no doubt if my friend had been here I would have said that we well deserved this period of respite. How she would have sung for joy, and decorated the hut with fresh greenery! *We have gone up a degree,* I can hear her saying, *we could almost be taken for old ladies now!* Old? She must have been very nearly fifty, like myself. *Since my lord Bishop regards us as blunted blades,* she would have said, *let us sharpen ourselves as best we may.* She would have said— Ah, in every tree, in each stone of this hut I can hear the voice of my beloved, my comrade in battle, the dove who was hunted to her death.

Fabrisse, my sister, your gentle hands still linger on my forehead, and your smile hovers about my lips; it is through your eyes that I look out at this beautiful landscape stretching away before me. You have never left me, beloved; night and day you are at my side. Only my body suffers from the void that your going has left in me; but the body is a restive steed, and hard to master.

Arsen stood with her back resting against the wall of the hut and gazed at the lofty walls of the fortress, dominating the mountaintop; it looked like a great stone ship, so gigantic in comparison with the minuscule houses piled up at its foot that it seemed as though human hands could not have built it. Ark and shield of the faithful, Arsen thought, impregnable sanctuary, tonight the shadow of your mighty wing will cover us, and we shall sleep in the shelter of your strength. Fabrisse, you must be happy to know that I have found safe haven for many months to come. And I have a new companion, Fabrisse: let me try to describe her for you. She is young and nobly born, but cruelly humiliated in the flesh. The Bishop in his wisdom has given me this girl, just as an overmettlesome horse is given a heavy, powerful rider. I shall not go striding across the countryside and hiding in barns with *her*.

Esclarmonde was singing as she broke bread and poured out water into the earthenware cups; being the younger, she had taken it upon herself to look after the domestic chores. She swept the floor and tidied the coverlets on their beds. Sometimes she bumped into the wall. "It's three months and more since I've been up here," she said by way of excuse. "I don't recognize anything now. I could still see a bit at the time."

Arsen said: "You'll soon get used to it."

The girl ran her fingers over a design carved in the wall of the hut: a series of circles enclosing square-cut crosses.

"This is a nice house, isn't it?" she said. "My grandmother—Monseigneur Bernard's eldest sister, that is—lived in it for twenty-five years. It is three months since she quit this vale of tears, and since then the house has remained empty. When I used to come up and visit her as a child she would say to me: 'If ever you choose the Way of Truth, I will leave you my house.' That was why Monseigneur gave it to no one else: he was waiting for my ordination."

Arsen said: "It is a great honor for me to be living in the venerable Lady Braïda's house. I had not expected so great a favor."

"The favor is not as great as that," Esclarmonde said. She spoke in a broken voice, its bitterness of tone outweighed only by her genuine humility. "It is your charity to which Monseigneur pays tribute when he saddles you with a blind companion. My mother was always telling me to get married—she said no Christian sister would want me as a companion, they needed a girl who was a help rather than a liability."

"You will be a help to me," Arsen said. "You know as well as I do that the flesh is nothing."

Since Esclarmonde saw nothing, she talked a great deal—more, certainly, than propriety, or the Rule, demanded. She was an educated girl, who knew Latin, and even a little Greek and Arabic; was tolerably well acquainted with music and astrology; and could discuss Plato or Aristotle in an intelligent fashion. Where on earth did I find such a little goose? Arsen thought, with a certain wry tenderness, when Esclarmonde blushed and trembled with emotion during a discussion of Plato and Socrates.

"Do you think I'll be good enough to teach others when I'm old?" the girl would ask. "When the war is over they'll open the schools again, and I mustn't forget all I learned in the days when I was able to read."

Esclarmonde used to pray aloud, with immense fervor. She did not content herself with reciting the Lord's Prayer, but improvised additions to it that were no more nor less than hymns in prose. It occurred to Arsen that, since all she could see in front of her eyes was a luminous mist, the girl in all likelihood must picture angels to herself, and other such glorious visions: very often she appeared to be speaking to someone actually visible to her.

Arsen loved her as she would have loved a niece or a young cousin. She tried to steer her toward a calmer and more restrained mode of prayer, but Esclarmonde was not easily steered. Once or twice a week they both went up to the castle to hear a sermon and attend the Blessing of Bread. But after a three months' stay Monseigneur Bernard left Montségur and resumed his wandering existence.

In the midst of solitude and prayer grief will reawaken like a ravening lion. Arsen's first months in retreat were months of tears. It seemed as though she had lost everything to no purpose. Her sons were far away, her husband martyred, her only daughter in a foreign town, her companions burned at the stake, Fabrisse lost to her. There were no more sick persons needing her care, no more little ones for her to comfort, no more dying women to be ordained. In this place there was no lack of preachers and doctors—and, in consequence, no need of her.

Peace, too, can annihilate, Arsen thought. O Lord, one day I will see Thee face to face. Dost Thou wish me to forget even the names of those I have loved? To be worthy of Thy service I must become smoother than a pebble, more transparent than glass. Grant that in the features of my humble brethren I may see Thy face, so that I, who have loved so dearly that which was not Thee, may henceforth love Thee only!

In the spring she received a visit from her sons. They were at present serving in the Count of Foix's army, and had come up to keep Easter at Montségur, together with a score of their comrades. They had no idea that they would find their mother there; they had long since lost trace of her. But a member of the garrison, on learning that they were Ricord de Montgeil's sons, said to them: "I know that some relative of yours is spending her period of retreat on the rock here. I'm sure she'd be pleased to see you."

When the three young men had climbed the rough stone steps that led up from the path to their mother's house, they stopped ten paces from the doorway, and sat down in the moss at the foot of the nearest tree, not daring to disturb these recluses in the midst of their meditation. All three stared at one another in silence, pensive and amazed, as though really *seeing* themselves for the first time in seven years. Sicart was now a man of thirty, hollow-cheeked, dark-complexioned, his hair and beard trimmed short; there was a long scar across his forehead, and all his front teeth were missing— this last the result of a heavy blow to the jaw from a cudgel. Renaud still had his teeth; but he lacked three fingers of his left hand, and still had internal injuries from being trampled on when he fell in a moat. His complexion was muddy, and he had blue rings under his eyes. Only Imbert had improved in appearance. He was now a lean, muscular, elegant figure of a man: his face was hard, and tanned a rich golden brown, like overbaked bread; it fairly glowed with health. All three still possessed the quick, eager expression that had characterized them as youths; they had not noticed themselves changing. But now they were thinking: So *that's* what we really look like! A pretty comic sight we are, and no mistake.

Outside the door of the hut, on a small stone platform, stood a large earthenware jug and a stone to grind corn. A young girl's voice could be heard singing a hymn: a strong, pure voice, which at times soared so high that the budding leaves on the bushes and the dew-spangled grass seemed to shiver and vibrate. For a few moments the three brothers felt like the man who spent a hundred years listening to the song of a bird, in the belief that he had only lent an ear to it for a minute or so. This mountain, from topmost peak to the very depths of the valley below, was so steeped in silence and peace; and the voice in the air was so tender; and it seemed so strange to them to know that their mother was nearby, yet not dare to approach her.

Suddenly another voice called out: "Sister, there are some men outside the house. Ask them what they want."

They could not be sure they had recognized this voice. Then a slim young woman clad all in black appeared on the threshold, and took a few steps in their direction, hands stretched out in front of her. The three men all knelt; and then Sicart asked whether they might speak with the Lady Arsen de Montgeil, seeing that they were her sons and had not seen her for seven years. The young woman blessed them, and bade them come into the house.

Arsen sat on her bed, hands clasped, and stared at the three kneeling men in silence. My children, she thought. My children. These are *my children*. She could not understand it. They were terribly changed; they were ordinary soldiers, the sort you could see anywhere in their scores and hundreds. This war has branded my children. They used to be like nobody but themselves, and now they have become the same as all the rest. But you, Olivier, I shall never see again; my "four Aymon boys" are only three now.

With unthinking pride she glanced down at their black, calloused hands.

"I see you still serve on horseback," she said.

This was so unexpected a remark that her sons burst out laughing, with cheerful heartiness.

"Oh, we will never put you to shame," Sicart said. "We have better horses than we used to."

Esclarmonde made them sit down near the door, and set out on the ground before them a jug of wine, some wheaten griddlecakes, and portions of dried fish. Seeing that their hostesses did not eat at all the three young men, somewhat intimidated, scarcely touched their own platefuls.

"Go on," Arsen said, in a near-beseeching voice, "please eat—you must be hungry. Would you refuse this favor to your mother? There is nothing else I can give you now. I cannot touch you or fold you in my arms; let me at least see you eat as you used to."

Renaud said: "My lady, for us this is the same as consecrated bread."

He felt shy, thinking how often they had been drunk, or had eaten spoiled meat.

Arsen said: "You used to be great talkers, but you say hardly anything now."

Imbert smiled.

"Oh, we still talk a lot," he assured her. "But usually it's a lot of words and not much sense."

"It hasn't been the same since Olivier got that arrow through his eye," Sicart added. "We're still close comrades, but it's rather like a cart with only three wheels."

Renaud raised his pallid face under its heavy thatch of brown hair and said: "All the same, the cart goes quite smoothly. Now we're out of winter quarters we'll be able to put in some useful work."

Imbert nudged him with his elbow: it was not fitting to speak thus of war and murder in the presence of such saintly ladies.

"You must forgive us, my lady," Sicart said. "We cannot help discussing these things; we know no other life."

Arsen could not take her eyes off her eldest son's face: that split lip imperfectly concealed by the mustache, that old man's mouth in a young man's face, that casual expression characteristic of one peacefully resigned to risking his life daily— She no longer felt pity for him: this man was following the occupation to which he had been born, and paying his debts in hard cash.

"What else is there to talk about?" she asked gently. "All our lives are bound up with war nowadays. When our country is free again you can discuss other things."

"That will be a long while yet," Imbert said. "Mother, after the things they did to Father, do you still maintain that fighting is a sin?"

"No," said his mother, eyes downcast. "It *is* a sin indeed, just as living is a sin; but we are no longer masters of this life that has been imposed upon us. When his country and Faith are attacked, no man is free to stand by, arms folded. But to kill or torture defenseless men, *that* is indeed a sin."

There was a short silence at this. Then Renaud said: "Mother, which is better, to cut off a man's feet and hands, or to kill him?"

"Renaud, Renaud, I am not your leader or your captain! But you know yourself that you only have the right to strike so long as your own life is in danger. A disarmed man is your brother."

"Not so," Sicart said. "You cannot make these people promise to fight no longer; they say a promise given to us is not binding. How can we take prisoners when they stand a good chance of regaining their liberty the next day? This is not an ordinary kind of war; even if you treat your prisoners well you do not win their friendship."

And for the tremor of unhappiness in his voice as he said this Arsen forgave him everything. How they would have loved the sort of war, he and his brothers, in which your adversary could be treated as a friend!

She thought: This question must have been tormenting them

sorely; they would not have dared to tell me of it otherwise. A question that all too many men have asked me—"Which is the lesser evil?" Is it a mother's place to answer it? She thought of Olivier, of his body that had been so like the three big sunburned bodies now confronting her, but for two years and more had rotted underground, and was now a mere skeleton. Then for one moment she glimpsed her dead son—not, in her vision, dead, but with his hands and feet chopped off, shuffling along on a pair of crutches and pushing bread into his mouth with his deformed stumps. A wave of horror and sheer animal pity swept over her, and she clapped both hands before her eyes. Not *that,* O God; praise be, Thou hast spared him that.

She said, in a low voice: "If you have no alternative, then kill. Whenever possible, kill painlessly. A quick death is better than twenty years' slow guttering out; for life comes and goes, but suffering endures, and gnaws at our very souls. And as you have treated your enemies, so will they in their turn treat you if you ever fall into their hands."

"Ah, Mother!" Imbert cried impulsively, "have we come here only to cause you such anguish? Here we are talking to you about sorrow and sin—you who should know nothing of such matters! Why have we been fighting all these seven long years if not to win toleration for our Faith, and undisturbed peace for those who bring us the gift of Life? Tell us—will that day ever come?"

"Surely it will," Arsen said. "But oh, my darlings, I beg you not to put your lives too much in jeopardy till it does—though indeed our lives no longer depend on our own efforts but on your courage."

PART FOUR

CHAPTER XI

Toulouse

IN the town of Toulouse, on that fresh and misty September night, the day began well before the dawn. The day had begun, and yet the townsfolk did not know it yet. They stood by their doors and listened to the sound of horsemen moving through the streets. The horses' hoofs squelched in the mud, and the metallic jingle of arms drowned the sound of voices—voices that spoke a tongue that was not French, voices quick with laughter and tears. Confused shouting could be heard at the crossroads; torches flared and vanished in the thick fog, horses whinnied, doors and windows everywhere were banging to and fro as though in a high wind.

Who is this coming among us? What soldiers are these, who enter the town like thieves? It is easy enough to enter here; the walls are razed to the ground, the drawbridge chains removed, our strong stone houses knocked down, our moats and ditches filled in and turned into ring roads. Anyone can come and go as he pleases, there is nothing to fear; they have stripped us so bare that a thief could rifle these houses and find nothing. The poor folk are living out in the open among the ruins and trying to keep themselves warm with wood fires. Their children cry with hunger all night.

The sky was gray, and the mist so thick that the town, the river, and the wharves were hidden beneath one huge blank pall, through which only the towers protruded. The fires flickered and went out; and from the direction of the Bazacle ford, across the fog-enshrouded water, there came an endless sound of splashing and trampling—heavy breathing, muffled shouts, horses pawing the ground. People hurried along the demolished ramparts, knocking at house doors. *What news, neighbors? What are they up to now? Are they going to set the town on fire?* Hurriedly citizens packed up bundles, while their wives slung wicker cradles from their shoulders. *Ought we to stay put or take refuge in the churches? Can anything worse happen than what we have seen already?*

For a long while yet, till dawn broke, in fact, they could hear horses moving through the fog into the town, though the riders' banners remained invisible. From time to time a high, strident cry would go up, and then swiftly be choked into silence. And then, abruptly, the whole town burst into a tremendous, clamorous hub-bub. People ran jostling through the streets, some to Saint-Sernin Square, others toward the Capitol, others again in the direction of the Garonne. Old folk standing on doorsteps used their fists to force a passage through the throng; women ran along with their children on their shoulders. Men could be heard sobbing aloud: *Where is he?* they cried. *Which way will he come? From what direction? God of mercy, that our eyes should once again behold him!* Houses emptied, doors were left wide open; cooking food was left to burn, and half-finished meals were abandoned.

Gentian joined the crowd together with the women of her own household and the Lady de Miraval's: the latter were lodging with her, since their own town house had been destroyed. A cry went up: *To the Capitol!* It was impossible to see a thing, so dense was the crowd. They just kept moving. Boys clambered up on turrets and rooftops to see the Count's banners fluttering in the square.

Gentian was hugging her son in her arms. The noise and the crowd terrified him, and he clung to her neck with his tiny hands: he was a heavy burden, being already eighteen months old; but on such a day his mother had not wanted to leave him in charge of a nurse. She felt as though she were drunk; and still inside her head echoed that great shout, *The Count is here!* Like the sun at midnight, like spring flowers in midwinter was this saviour who had come to reclaim his own and to get back his stolen heritage. *Now we can see him, and see that he has kept his promise. Despite the Church and the Kings, he has come to deliver us. Our own rightful lord is among us again. In the very teeth of the Frenchmen he has won back his town. Our menfolk have kept their promise.*

Old Count Raymond's horse took over an hour to get from the

Capitol to Saint-Sernin Square. So thick was the crowd that he was tossed about like a shallop in a rough sea. The knights and barons in his train dared not thrust the people aside: they advanced with arms raised and faces uncovered, themselves caught between laughter and tears. The uproar swelled from street to street. So jostled on all sides was the Count that he could do nothing but stop, and stretch out his hands. Men and women alike clung to his stirrups and feet and the trappings of his horse, hanging there; when they let go others at once took their place. Never were relics of the saints or the Blessed Virgin kissed with greater fervor. Children were held up to touch his hands in their gold-embroidered vair gloves. He had only to raise his eyes or turn his head for the shouting to redouble in volume, as though each of his movements were a divine act of grace.

Till evening they kept holiday in the streets—a bloody holiday to mark those few days when fear was forgotten. Soldiers sat indoors drinking to celebrate their return, while workers and burghers, women and youths armed themselves with hammers and pitchforks, and the Frenchmen's bodies were dragged through the streets, and little children stoned them. Banners blazed out in the public squares, and men went storming through house after house, ax in hand, faces radiant with joy.

The Capitol was all decked with flags and lit up with torches: outside, women of the lower orders were dancing about to the sound of bugles, waving here a Crusader's surcoat, there a spear or a halberd. Some citizens were rolling their last barrels of wine into the square. In the wealthier houses ladies were lighting candles as though for Christmas; and that day every soldier was a guest of honor, be he relative, friend, or stranger.

Of those Frenchmen who had not had time to shut themselves in the castle, not one remained alive. All along the torch-lit, beflagged streets the knights of Toulouse were returning once more to their own quarters, their horses stumbling over the mutilated bodies of their foes.

In her house near the Daurade, Gentian d'Aspremont had neither tapestries nor tableware left, neither chandeliers nor rugs. Walls and tables alike were bare; she had scarcely been able to muster up enough wooden platters and pewter mugs. Some skins of immature wine had been brought up from the cellar, together with some scrawny ham and the last of the smoked goose. It was a modest meal, but nobody present cared: in any case, no one was hungry. They talked by the light of tallow candles, set in earthenware pots.

The Lady de Miraval was celebrating the return of her son, who had brought two Catalan knights with him, his companions-in-arms. She no longer had a home, and she had lost her beauty as well—in two years she had become an old woman—yet both losses were forgotten now: her ravaged face, framed in its two blond braids, glowed with pride. Tonight everyone was at home, and there was no thought of sleep. The cup went around, laughter rose and mingled in the air. People peered through windows and went down into the streets to see what was going on. Here and there behind the roofs reddish smoke curled skyward; the fighting still continued around the Narbonnese Castle. Houses were all lit up, windows flung wide open, and from within came sounds of singing. Now and then a solitary knight would pass the crossroads beside the church; while citizens went roaming through the streets, knocking at doors, looking for their friends, in search of news.

Gentian sat beside the big chimney breast, her son in his cradle at her feet, listening to the tales of young Miraval and his Catalan friends, and trembling at every noise from the town outside. Her head was spinning; she had become unaccustomed to drinking wine, and she felt that she had been plunged, with brutal abruptness, into a new life where she no longer even recognized her own voice. She had seen blood and fire that day; and her head had been full of that great joyful shout which eclipsed laughter, singing, tears, and death throes alike: *The Count is here! The Count has come back!*

For hours on end she had wandered through the town, her arms aching from the weight of her child—her child with his curly black hair and silver-laced red dress: he seemed to get heavier and heavier as time went on. She had pushed him up to the Count's very hand; she had held him aloft while the banners of Foix and Comminges and Roussillon and Toulouse and Carcassonne went by; she had brandished him like a flag, so that his tiny hands might bestow a blessing on those who came to redeem the city's honor. She had lifted him over the corpses of men hacked to death with axes at street corners, and shown him the Capitol all twinkling in the light of a thousand torches. She had made him kiss the pillars of the church where the Count had gone to pray. You will not remember all this, my first-born child, she thought, but your eyes will have beheld it. When you are grown up I will remind you of it—and remind you that there is still a God in this world, and that our dead will be avenged; and that this day our town took an oath to hold out to the last man, woman, and child!

Now the tiny man-child was asleep in his cradle, so exhausted that neither bright lights nor shouting could disturb his slumbers. His face was flushed pink all over, with the luminous texture of some big flower on which the tiny crescents of eyebrows and eyelashes had been pencilled. He was still wearing his red dress; his mother had not dared to take it off him. He was very much like his father; Gentian often wondered how her body had ever contrived to form this alien flesh. One embrace had sufficed: there was the man himself, living again through her—the same expression, the same smile, even the same curl of the nostrils. Though the child might be named Ricord, she was endlessly tempted to call him Bérenger.

Bérenger d'Aspremont was in the town; but he had sent word to his wife by one of his squires that he would not be home before dawn, and that she should not wait up for him. Have I seen him? she wondered. Has he seen me? He must have passed through the streets along with the rest, shouting *Toulouse! Christ Jesus!* Other women had cheered as he passed by, and raised their infants in the air. On this day there were no husbands and wives, no lovers or mistresses; there was only one lover, the Count; only one lady—

Toulouse. The men who had slipped past the enemy's guard in the fog, when they crossed the Garonne, these men bore the name of Toulouse inscribed on their hearts, in letters of blood.

Gentian begged her guests and relatives to go upstairs and get some sleep. She herself waited in the great hall, alone except for two maidservants, and some varlets keeping guard at the door in case of prowling footpads. The candles guttered down, and Gentian replaced them. She had fresh water poured into the caldron that hung over the brazier; she saw that clean shirts, woollen doublets, and jugs of cold water were laid ready to hand. She had emptied her store chests, indeed, and was terribly afraid lest Bérenger bring too numerous a retinue of guests back with him; she had already shared the little property that remained with the Lady de Miraval. "We shall get it all back again," Lady Alfaïs had said. "Tenfold, a hundredfold—and even though we were to lose everything, it would still be worth it." She herself had lost so much that she had not a single horse or gold necklace left to her.

Do our men realize how utterly ruined we are? Gentian wondered. Everything had to be sold, and I was lucky to keep the house. She stood there, struggling against sleep, her face pressed to the grille of the open window. When she looked up she could see gables and weathercocks silhouetted against the sky. In the distance bugles sounded; and a detachment of horse came trotting from the direction of the church. She could hear the clack of their hoofs, and a faint jingle of metal: about half a dozen men, perhaps more. They pulled up in front of the house.

"For Toulouse and Christ Jesus!" a voice called. "This is Bérenger d'Aspremont and his men. Open, friends; do not be afraid."

The varlets hurriedly drew back the great iron bars and ran forward to take the horses. Bérenger strode into the hall, his cloak flung over a short coat of mail, his helmet under his arm. His face was haggard with fatigue, and his hair plastered down over his temples: but his eyes blazed with joy.

Gentian took a step forward, wrapping her green mantle about her in order to hide her worn, stained dress.

In a voice hoarse with emotion she said: "God has heard our prayers. Welcome to your home."

In two strides Bérenger was before her, kneeling, his helmet at his feet.

"At last your servant can do you homage, my lady. Will you now deign to accept me as your true and faithful lover?"

"Ah, Bérenger," Gentian said, "why do you speak of love when our hearts are so full? I am waiting here to serve you, not to accept your homage."

The squires and soldiers came forward now, greeted their master's lady, and after a brief prayer sat down to table. They were cheerful but utterly exhausted, too tired even to change their clothes.

"They tried to regain a foothold in the town," Bérenger was saying. "We had to drive them back and mount guard all around the castle. They won't risk another sortie unless they get reinforcements—but that won't be till tomorrow, whatever happens."

His eye travelled around the walls in some consternation.

"They've robbed you of everything!" he cried. "This is a poor man's house now."

"Not everything," Gentian said, and drew him toward the cradle. "Come and look. See—is not this better than gold or silver?"

He had turned very pale.

"Do you know," he said, hesitantly, "that I dared not speak of it to you for fear that—"

He was so overcome that he could not go on. Quickly he bent down to take the baby in his arms.

"He is tired," his mother said. "Let him sleep."

Bérenger stopped short and stepped back two paces; then he stood contemplating his child from a distance, with a solemn yet enraptured expression on his face.

"I never thought he could be so lovely," he half whispered. "You never told me in your letters how beautiful he was."

The soldiers were stretched out on the floor or the benches, suddenly tipsy, oblivious of the very presence of the lady of the house.

"These poor devils have had about all they can take for today,"
Bérenger observed. "The Countess de Montfort has taken it upon
herself to command the troops in the castle like a man, you see.
With the new ditches they've dug all around there's no hope of
taking the place by storm. And they're still likely to attempt another sortie."

"Nonsense. They'd be massacred."

Bérenger was pacing to and fro between the table and the chimney breast.

"The Beast is not beaten yet," he went on, "and this new Pope
is not a whit better than the old one. In the eyes of the Kings and
the Emperor we are all rebels, and our Count the archrebel. What
would become of you if the French ever recaptured the town?"

"They will never recapture it while we remain alive, Bérenger.
There are more than fifty thousand of us here to support you,
counting both men and women. We shall fight in the streets and
on the housetops. We have done it before; we know what it
means."

Bérenger said, bitterly: "We were like a madman who arms
himself with two halberds, takes a ten-foot shield with him, and yet
leaves his head exposed: we went out to fight and left our own city
open to attack. May God repay them in the next world for all the
suffering they caused you! But it is over now. Henceforth our son
will be able to sleep in his cradle, as he is sleeping now. How
courageous you were to call him Ricord! I should never have dared
to do it."

"Why? I want him to have my father's heart. As for our destiny,
we are not free to choose it."

Husband and wife eyed each other questioningly, in a solemn,
thoughtful fashion. There were so many things they dared not say.
Finally Bérenger took his wife's hand and said, somewhat hesitantly: "I see you are not wearing any other ring but mine."

"And what would you have said," she asked, "if I *had* been
wearing another ring?"

"For God's sake, my lady, do not torment me thus! It was not easy for me to leave my guard duties before the castle, and I must return there at dawn. In the two years and more that I have not seen you I have suffered agonies of jealousy. You know full well why I have come to you; you know, too, that a man cannot speak of love without knowing first whether the way is clear before him."

"It is no fault of yours," Gentian said, with a flash of bitterness, "that I was not forcibly taken by the Crusaders. The way is as clear as it could be; did I not promise to wait for you? God knows I have prepared your bed in our room after such a fashion that, once in it, you could forget how the French have stripped us of all our possessions. There is nothing I could rightfully refuse you on such a day as this."

He bent over her, suddenly (it seemed) fever-stricken, his cheeks aflame, his eyes overbright.

"I ached for you so desperately," he said, "that I was afraid to come here. Not once in two years has any woman made me forget your face. I would have given anything to know that you wanted to see me beside you in your bed—that you would receive me as a lover, not as a man returning from a day's hunting to find a good dinner waiting for him on the table! I have so little time to spend with you this night."

She said: "I will have a bath prepared for you, and new raiment laid out."

"Not so, my lady. I have taken a vow never to sleep with a woman other than in chain mail until the French are finally driven from our town."

How sweet it was, Gentian thought, to have her naked arms and breast crushed against a shirt of steel, to be bruised and pulverized and lacerated, to give back bite for bite and kiss for kiss! Stolen pleasures, wartime pleasures; we shall know no others till we are free again. In one short night Gentian had discovered the delights of love without even thinking of denying them. Henceforward, because of past sufferings and sufferings yet to come, all was permissible. It will be a long time yet, she told herself, that I must needs fear for the bodily safety of my husband and lover. *May I never see you again,* he had written, *may I never see my son at all, so long as our liege lord remains exiled from the town that is his.*

Was it day or night? The shadow of her husband's head wavered and faded against the bed curtains; the rosy dawn streamed in through their little window, highlighting the gray links of chain mail and Bérenger's heavy, sweat-soaked, leathery neck.

"What matter if the house be poor if I still have you, my beloved?" he said. "We shall win it back tenfold, no, a hundredfold."

"We have won everything back already, Bérenger: there is no longer any need for us to be humiliated."

"If we have conceived a child this night, I hope it is a girl: then she may have your eyes and face."

"We shall call her Toulousaine."

"We shall call her Joy."

"We shall call her Honor."

"We shall call her Raymonde."

"Bérenger," Gentian said, "I am your own true love now. Promise me that you will never think of another woman."

But he did not hear her; he had suddenly fallen asleep. Gentian lay there, weary, utterly astonished by the strange feeling of tenderness that enveloped her, and listened as though in a dream to the sounds of horses outside, the shouting and trumpet calls. The sun was burning her eyelids; she felt as though she were wrapped in a great robe of crimson fire. It was very unusual for her to wake up in broad daylight. But the madness was not over; it was only beginning. It would begin all over again every day. Every day they would rush to the Capitol, and welcome the troops, and await the approach of an enemy army, and build barricades, and dig earth for new ramparts. Every night they would make love between one armed vigil and the next. And they would see the Count's banners floating above the rooftops and church spires.

How deeply he sleeps, she thought. The house could fall, and still he would not wake. He is so terribly calm: like a dead man. Ah, all our dead have risen on this day; they are here, by our side. Shall I take pity on him for the sake of that handsome, marble-still face of his? Shall I leave him to sleep on in peace? But he is a soldier. He has to relieve the guard. It is no valid excuse to say that he overslept at his wife's side. No; we have not yet done with sleepless nights.

When a whole town is engaged in a life-or-death struggle, the battle can go on, not for weeks and months only, but for years. What can foreign troops do against a people who settle into war as though it were a peaceful house; people who, night and day, are busy digging ditches and manning the ramparts and knocking down houses to make towers or engines of war?

By every road, and down the Garonne, such quantities of troops, corn, cattle, and forage are flowing into Toulouse that this ruined town has never been more crowded or better fed—or, indeed, needed to be. The siege is so grimly fought that, on some days, corpses plunge into the moat by the dozen, like nuts from a thrashed hazel tree. Stones shatter the wooden barricades, towers go up in flames, and arrows fall thick as hail. No prisoners are ever taken: severed heads are used in lieu of cannon balls, and smash themselves to bits against the walls of houses.

This war has become each person's daily bread, his trade, his prayers, his sport, his only festivity. Urchins spend their time practicing with slings and making bows. Priests go about shovel in hand, and every man is now a mason and a carpenter. Women no longer have time to sew or to spin; they are too busy running soup kitchens, repairing chain mail, and burying the dead. Spring comes, and summer; a second winter and a second spring; and still our hearts do not weary of this life. So drunk are we with blood, and the spirit of hope, that we forget that any other kind of life has ever existed.

In spring the plain around Toulouse is a mass of white tents, and wagons, and horses. The Pope has promised salvation to all who destroy us—salvation for destroying people who believe in Christ and His Mother, and in God. But this time their lies and their treachery will avail them nothing. Nor will they obtain their salvation. For Christ Jesus never said that any bishop or Pope could turn theft into a deed of piety, or make a noble action out of rapine.

The day after Pentecost fires were lit all through the town, in the public squares, at every crossroads, and outside the churches. The ramparts were all aflare, and blazing torches were flung across the ditches in the direction of the enemy camp, itself brightly lit up: under that clear night sky the whole plain twinkled with points of fire. On the ramparts before the Narbonnese Castle they were singing; this served to drown the shrieks of the prisoners and the wounded, who were already being dragged off through the bonfires and the dancing when the alarm sounded. Both on the wall and in the ditch there was hand-to-hand fighting with axes; men rolled about the ground under a hail of stones and faggots, their clothing all ablaze.

That night three prisoners were burned alive in the square before the Capitol. That night, too, the noble Bérenger d'Aspremont was brought home with an ax wound in one shoulder, and his face and left arm badly burned. His wife was out on the ramparts, busy cooking meals for the soldiers manning the stone-guns. It was the Lady Alfaïs who gave the wounded man first aid—a task she was beginning to understand fairly well, since the house was now more or less converted into a hospital.

"Be of good cheer, cousin," she said. "I do not think you will lose your sight."

But Bérenger was in such agony from his burns that he could not even speak.

In the morning there was a new assault, and the heralds went through the streets shouting: "By the Count's orders! All knights of Toulouse to the Narbonnese Gate! All the men of Navarre to the Narbonnese Gate!" The women stood in file close behind the ramparts, passing forward buckets of boiling oil and water.

Gentian was standing beside one of the caldrons, busy stoking the fire beneath it with slivers of wood from beams and planks that children carried, by the armful, up to the ramparts. Her face was burning with heat, and also because of the sleepless night she had just passed. She had to lean back for support against one of the wooden posts on which the siege tower stood. It's awful, she thought, you can't see anything from here; you can only hear the din they're making. They've started in on the big stones now. And at that moment one of the men in the tower was hit in the head, and fell almost on top of her from a height of ten feet or more. She bent over him, but there was nothing to be done; his skull had been split wide open. He had not even had time to cry out.

"Hey," a voice called down, "send someone up here to pass the ammunition!"

Gentian knotted her skirt up around her knees and mounted the ladder.

"A *woman?*" the captain of the tower exclaimed. "Oh, very well—it's all right if you just pass the gun-stones, they're no great weight. But for God's sake hurry up—things are getting damned hot!"

And indeed, the framework of planks and beams was shaking under so heavy a fusillade of stones that there was scarcely time to load, and sighting became extremely difficult.

"Here, you, duck your head, my pretty! Over here—pass me one *here,* and get out of the way, damn you!"

Toward midday the attack was called off, and Gentian, dazed and feverish, staggered down from the wooden tower thinking: At last I can get some sleep. But close to the ramparts she ran into one of her maidservants, who was running along, a distracted expression on her face, apparently looking for someone.

"Ferrande!" Gentian exclaimed. "What's the matter? Bad news of your father?"

"No, my lady, thanks be to God! Not my father. It was you I was looking for, my lady."

"Tell me everything. I am not afraid to hear it."

"My lord Bérenger was wounded during the night. Don't worry, he's not going to die; but for all that he's in a bad way."

Gentian felt her head spinning; but out of pride she gently pushed the girl back as she sprang forward to support her mistress.

She said: "It is our common destiny, Ferrande. How many men have we not seen fall already who were like husbands and brothers to us?"

She began to run, clutching her kerchief to her head: obstinately it would keep slipping to one side, leaving her hair exposed. No path had ever seemed so long to her.

Eight days later Bérenger's burns were giving him less pain, and he began to become more aware of his surroundings. But he was still in a very poor way, feverish and scarcely able to eat. He begged Gentian not to stay by his side, saying that a wounded man was an ugly sight, and that she should take care of herself because of the child she was expecting—she had already lost one prematurely, three months earlier.

"Who would take care of himself nowadays except a madman?" Gentian snapped. "And have I not seen dozens of wounded men?"

"I dare to hope that at least you do not regard me as you might any other wounded man. You are torturing your own heart by staying here with me."

Nevertheless, she stayed on. Why, she did not know; it merely made him irritable. He hated her to see him suffering.

Never till this day had she known real exhaustion or fear. If he dies, she thought now, I shall be alone. The boy she had borne by him was there, close beside her, and looking at him she felt her heart freeze. It was as though this child were threatened with the loss of half his life.

"Bérenger," she said, "ah, Bérenger, if you do not recover there will be nothing for me but to kill myself on the very day of your death."

"So, so," he replied. "Does one man the more or less make any difference now? If only we could be sure of victory!"

On the tenth day after Pentecost he summoned to his bedside his sisters, his uncle, the Lady Alfaïs, and Gentian, and announced to them that he was resolved to ask for baptism. Not that he thought himself at death's door, but he did not want to risk the possibility. The fever was tormenting him so badly that at times he feared he might lose consciousness of what he was doing. Out of respect for traditional custom, and loyalty to his liege lord, he had, he said, often allowed himself to be led into practicing a false religion, and that with more fervor than was seemly. Weakened by wounds as he was, he could no longer endure this life without the knowledge that he was purified.

The women wept, saying he should not think of such things. But Gentian said: "We must do as he desires," and gave the order for the room to be made ready, and torches to be brought in.

"How can you do this?" one of Bérenger's sisters asked her. "You might as well prepare his shroud and have done with it."

"Not so, my lady," Gentian said. "This is to give him life. But the life of the body is not in our hands."

When his bandages were removed, Bérenger bore an even grimmer appearance; his skull was peeling, and his face all crisscrossed with black and red scabs. His eyes had escaped injury: their expression was clear, though perhaps a shade too brilliant and feverish. Tranquilly his wife busied herself with the preparation of the white napkins and the ewers required for the ceremony. She did not say a word.

Bérenger had asked to be left alone with her; and now, it seemed to him, her only motive in tidying up the room was fear of looking in his direction.

"Are you ashamed of my face, perhaps?" he asked her.

She turned around, cheeks aflame. "I have never found it more handsome!" she cried.

He smiled at that, a little sadly, but trustingly too. He said: "I know it is not hardness of heart that has made you accede to my request."

"No," she replied. "It is because I know what it feels like to long for God."

"That is why I have a higher regard for you than for any other living creature," Bérenger told her. "Now, take that casket which is standing by my bedside; it contains my will. Read it, and see whether you find its terms agreeable. If it contains anything that provokes your displeasure, I will have it changed. I made it two years ago, when I learned of Ricord's birth."

In his will, Bérenger d'Aspremont bequeathed all the worldly goods lately in his possession, which would be rendered up to him

again when the French were driven from the country, to his legitimate son, Ricord, born of the noble Lady Gentian de Montgeil, re-
serving only such fees as were the Count's by right and preroga-
tive; and the said Lady Gentian was to dispose of these goods as
she thought fit until the boy's majority, except in the case of her
remarriage: under such conditions the guardianship was to be
shared between the boy's mother and Imbert d'Aspremont, the
testator's uncle. Item, the said Lady Gentian was to give a solemn
assurance that she would recompense, whether in cash or kind, all
persons to whom the testator had caused substantial loss, and
whom, by reason of his absence from the country, he had neglected
to indemnify. (Here there followed a list of names.) Item, the said
Lady Gentian was to subsidize three poor persons in the "heretics'
hostel" in Toulouse; to provide for the support of the testator's
natural children, two sons and a daughter, and to set them up in a
fitting manner when they attained their majority; and to hold a
feast every year, at Eastertide, to which should be bidden every
high-born or free-born person from those lands over which the
d'Aspremont family held sway. And so on.

"Of course," Bérenger said, "it is understood that you will
pledge yourself to pay the Church the value of the fourth part of
my estate, in Toulouse coin; to do that you will need to sell my
property at Belvèse, with the same reservations on the Count's behalf. I know that this will be called dismembering the beast before
he is caught; you may have to wait two or three years for the restitu-
tion of my goods. But in any case, the people of Toulouse will be
the first to obtain redress."

Never, Gentian thought, had she loved him so deeply. He spoke
of victory now with such calm assurance that one might have
thought it was already at hand. She thought it a wonderful gesture
to dispose thus in detail of an estate which one did not possess.

"Is there anything else you wish to tell me?" she asked. "To
keep you alone to myself for so long will offend your family."

He gave her a keen, thoughtful glance.

"In your youth," he said, "you long cherished a desire for the
Love of God. For my part, I desire it now because of my bodily

sufferings rather than through the free choice of my will. But I wish you to know that it is, nevertheless, a sincere desire, and that I am not a man who promises to give his all only on the day when he finds himself with nothing left to lose."

"If you recover," she said, "will you renounce the profession of arms?"

"I do not feel I have the right to do that. But in all other respects I will do my utmost to lead a truly Christian life."

She said: "Bérenger, we will not have had enough time to love one another as we should."

"I have loved you as best I could. During these last few days I have thought much about my sins. I see now I was no better than the rat which is crushed by a wagon wheel."

Gentian said: "Tonight will be a great occasion for you—and a great honor for our house."

The ceremony was an extremely solemn one, for Bérenger d'Aspremont had numerous relatives and friends living in the town. The great hall at street level was crowded as though for a wedding, and the courtyard was so crammed with horses that it was impossible to walk across it.

In the wounded man's bedchamber, despite the windows' being thrown open, it was scarcely possible to breathe, because of the blazing candles and the throng of visitors: there must have been at least fifty persons present, children included. The two ministers had only just room in which to wash their hands. The invalid was arrayed in new clothes, with a scarlet jerkin laced up over his white shirt: his uncle was supporting him, since he insisted, at all costs, on kneeling for the ceremony. His flayed, shaking, outthrust countenance did not arouse pity: the seriousness of purpose that blazed from beneath those puffy eyelids, the eagerness with which he seemed to drink in every word which the black-clad minister uttered—these precluded such an emotion. He repeated the Lord's Prayer jerkily, but without hesitation. When the Book was placed on his head, he thrust away the arm that supported him, and rose to his feet.

He was to say later that at this moment he felt his scars close from within, and his fever drop; so sharp a spasm of pain shook him that he felt as though his whole skin were splitting apart. When he once more lay stretched out on his bed to reply to his relatives' congratulations, he remained a great while prostrate, unable to utter a single word, eyes wide open, lips frozen in a smile like a dead man's.

The two ministers bent their heads before the newly ordained Christian and begged leave to retire; they had other dying men to visit that night.

"Surely," said Lady Alfaïs, "you will not shame us by refusing to spend the night under our roof?"

"Do not take it as a slight, my daughter. There are not enough of us to deal with all those who have been mortally wounded during these last few days. So many of our brotherhood have been forced to leave the town that there are scarcely twenty of us left in all, to deal with the entire population; of these, three are so sick that they cannot stir from their beds."

The two men, who had only recently been ordained, were both young, but terribly thin and harassed-looking. They now wrapped themselves up in their big brown cloaks: these concealed their black robes. There were quite a number of Spanish soldiers in the besieged town, capable of taking offense at the sight of a heretic: these soldiers insisted on priest, Cross, and chalice. Besides this, there were many people in the area who still invoked the aid of Catholic priests, despite the Church's interdict on such a practice. Some of them summoned both priest and minister: life was becoming so hard that there were no longer saints enough in Heaven, nor enough relics, or prayers, or candles to burn. The bells would ring out at the Daurade, at St. Stephen's, and at Saint-Sernin, while the Count had the images of the Blessed Virgin and the holy martyrs carried in procession.

In the depths of the night bugles and drums sounded the alarm —a new attack near the Old Bridge and the outlying quarters of the town. The knights who had come to witness their comrade's ordination ran for their horses, shouting to their men. There was no need for them to arm themselves: they had come straight from the ramparts, just as they were, in chain mail and steel greaves. If these dogs managed to recapture the Saint-Cyprian district, there would be no peace thenceforward, day or night.

In the hall, all decked now for the feasting, the women kept an excited silence, doing their best not to let any unbecoming emotion be remarked. During this night God had visited the house, and one of their menfolk had given himself up to Christ. At this moment the peace of God was present in the midst of the tumult —the noise of gun-stones and night-riding forays, the wild battle cries. The Old Bridge was so close that when they went out into the street they could see the smoke of the burning siege engines, and hear voices yelling: "Montfort! Montfort! God with us!"

Gentian went up into her husband's bedchamber. He had been left alone, to avoid disturbing the great peace which now enfolded him. The candles were still lit, and the bed gleamed white. Ah, Gentian thought, will God grant him deliverance now, when his soul is as bright and fresh as the morning star?

"Bérenger," she called, "Bérenger—are you still there?"

Motionless, head thrown back, the sick man lay listening to the sounds that drifted in to him through the open window.

"They are fighting by the bridge," he said.

"Ah, my friend, is this the moment to think of such things? They are so unworthy in comparison with the thing that has been wrought in you!"

"No," he said. "God is giving me back my life that I may fight again."

"How has He revealed this to you?"

"I know it. Do not give my arms to anyone else. Very soon I will don them again myself."

Gentian stood at the foot of the bed and gazed at this body, sacrosanct henceforth, through which she had known the joys and agonies of sin. Ah, Gentian thought, the fleshly love with which he loved me is finished forever, his beauty destroyed, his body become so pure that I dare not even touch it. No more compassion, then, for earthly love: the love that burns in us all today is too deadly a flame.

Slowly she knelt before the bed; then went downstairs, took her cloak, and went out into the street.

Till dawn broke she stayed on the wall among the soldiers, carrying gun-stones, collecting fallen weapons, and shouting "Toulouse and Christ Jesus!" with the rest of them. A dozen times arrows passed so close to her face that she felt the cold wind of them on her cheek, and was amazed to find her head still in one piece. She stood leaning over the wooden parapet, half shot away by gun-stones, and looked down into Hell. Helmeted men, the scarlet cross blazoned on their breast, were clambering up ladders set against the walls; horses, their bellies ripped open, were writhing about in the ditch; flames were licking over the bridge, and not a dozen feet beneath her was a pile of shouting, struggling, bleeding bodies, all mixed up, friend and foe. Flaming firebrands shot past them; the ladders wavered and tilted backward, dragging a whole string of living bodies with them as they fell, and crashing down into yet more bodies below.

Glory be to God, Gentian thought, they will never get the upper hand of us; we are holding our own so well that they will not take one inch of our town. Our blood is mightier than theirs; they have forged us hearts of fire and brass.

"Come here, my fine lady," a voice called. "Help me lug these stones along; I'm wounded. It's by the gate that things are hottest."

The soldier collapsed, and Gentian began to drag his stone-laden sledge on for him, stumbling into the bodies of dead and wounded alike as she went. Up onto some shaky beams she clambered, and began to hurl stones down, brandishing them above her head as an executioner would his ax. No one said "The woman's mad"; they were all as mad themselves. Then the beam collapsed, and Gentian managed to leap back just in time. She felt that her own body no longer existed, that she was down there in the bodies of all those men below the wall, so busy thrusting their swords and spears into human flesh.

It's over! the cry went up. *God be thanked! They're beating the retreat!* A great paean of joy rose all along the wall, and spread into the town itself. Through the open gates men streamed back, bleeding and exhausted, leading horses that trembled with sheer fatigue. The bells rang, and the sun shone high in the heavens; but no one had noticed its ascent.

Gentian strode forward at the head of a group of women, arms upraised, singing as she went. As she passed by, people stopped and stared at her, the words dying on their lips as though they were observing a religious procession.

A thin, black-bearded man, his mail-clad jerkin ripped open from shoulder to waist, ran across the square in front of the church to her.

"My lady," he said, "are you—are you not my sister? You have her voice."

She shivered, as though suddenly awakened, and looked at him. Surely I know him, she thought, he's like someone I— The man grinned broadly; since he had no front teeth, this gave him a somewhat sinister appearance despite himself.

"Sicart?" she said. "Sicart—it can't be you, surely?"

He kept his mouth open in that poor hesitant smile: at the back of his eyes there was a kind of hunted, astonished agony.

"We have been here in Toulouse since Pentecost. Renaud was killed this morning, just before dawn, out on the Old Bridge."

She flung herself into his arms. "Come with me," she said, "both of you—come home with me. My husband received the Consolamentum yesterday evening."

She shed no tears; she simply thought: How much longer will our blood continue to be shed? What Paradise shall we not have merited in the end? So now his body lies there in the muddy riverbank, and horses trample over it.

Because a stone missile cracked a certain man's skull, so many bugles and drums and trumpets and bells and cymbals sounded throughout the town on the day after the Feast of St. John that God's own thunder would have gone unheard. The shouts of joy swelled into chanting, and the chanting rose up till it turned into clamor.

Ah, long live Toulouse, that has snatched this miracle from the hands of God and the Devil! The Beast is dead, the butcher, the man of the bloody cross. The whole town could see him from the top of the ramparts. His body was not made of brass, his head was less hard than stone: we saw it crack open like a nutshell, we saw his brains spurt out and his teeth scattered broadcast.

His friends have borne away his body to wrap it in white linen and fine embroidered cloth. Let them adorn and embalm the dead man how they will, they still will not give him back a new head. Let them mourn and honor his passing: they do well, for they will never recover from this loss. When once the vulture is slain, what need to fear a flight of crows? The wind has turned, and the fire they lit is blowing back on them now.

Death went by the name of Simon de Montfort. Now Death has been slain. Our shame has been killed in that death.

The flames of a thousand candles burn in the churches for St. John, St. Stephen, and St. Sernin. The Pope of Rome who betrayed us will not be able to say that his hired killer lacked well-lit chapels; not a woman so poor that she would not give her last mite to celebrate the death of the soldier of Antichrist.

They could not rob us of our true wealth: the old and the young Count, father and son, so stripped and betrayed by the Church and the Kings of Christendom! The very paving stones rose for them, and for them spades and plowshares were turned into swords.

Victory is not here yet; it is like the rosy flush that spreads across the horizon before dawn breaks. It is not here yet; but it is not far away. The sky is growing lighter; never before has the sun turned back in his path.

When the time of the wine harvest comes around, there will be no more French tents before Toulouse. It will be our turn to hunt them, and put their garrisons to the sword: neither the walls of Carcassonne nor those of Narbonne will be strong enough to protect them. In every fortress they have captured there will be ten free men for one traitor, a hundred citizens to each Crusader. And

of the property that they have stolen they will not take back enough
to their own country to buy themselves a pair of gloves.
Thanks be to God, for this joy comes to us from Him.

Bérenger d'Aspremont was buying new arms for himself and
his men. Of all the tradesmen in Toulouse the armorers were, beyond any doubt, the richest and the most in demand. During the
siege so much good tempered steel had come into their hands, from
Spain, Aquitaine, and the North, that counts and knights could
now take their pick among it. The forges and workshops were far
from idle, despite the tricks of the French—not a single weapon
left in the town except their own, *they* thought. Ladies now accompanied their husbands and lovers to help them choose their arms,
being unable to make a choice of furs and jewelry as they had
formerly done. (There were very few women whose lovers were
rich enough to offer them such luxuries still, and in any case the
market had little to offer.) They had become connoisseurs in coats
of mail, thigh-pieces, and steel gauntlets.

For himself, Bérenger picked out a black-painted helmet and
a shield polished as smooth as glass, with no decoration on it except for a ring of copper studs around the outer edge. Gentian
stood beside him, her eyes flickering eagerly from one piece to the
other. Little Ricord, whom she was holding by the hand, was so
determined to go and play with all the shiny objects he saw in the
shop that finally his father had to pick him up and carry him.

"For this one," Bérenger declared, "we will buy a gilded helmet
with enamel buckles, and a shirt of mail wrought in Toledo steel."

"A fine child," said the assistant, busy spreading out brand-new
gleaming coats of mail on the counter. "He will surely be more
beloved of women than ever Lancelot or Gawain was. See how he
is already enamored of knightly gear!"

Gentian reflected that Bérenger, on the other hand, would doubtless never be beloved of women again. His scarred face was, indeed, growing fresh skin; but it was so puckered and seamed that
at the very best he might, one day, look as though he had suffered
from smallpox. Well, she thought, I care very little about such

"ladies," and in any case they are not overfussy; but it is heart-breaking to see a fine, handsome face so disfigured. So many beautiful things have been wiped off the earth forever that our country will long resemble a garden laid waste by a hailstorm.

They will send fresh armies against us; our fields are not done with burning. Bishop Foulques, our city's sworn lord—may God's curse light on him—has gone to Paris to preach a Holy War against us once more.

"My love," Bérenger said, "I have promised God I will not lay down my arms till the day peace comes. I know that He has not purified me that I may withdraw my body from danger, but that I may be more worthy to defend my Faith. It is not by anger or hatred that we shall conquer, but by love of all creation. Today I no more hate our enemies than I would my adversary in a tournament. In truth, we are waging war much as a laborer works his field; and if we, too, must needs start over again every year, our toil will be great, yet we have no choice."

"Why can I not find peace?" Gentian cried. "The blood of our dead consumes my heart; I shall never be able to forgive. Do you wish me to withdraw to a convent, seeing that you no longer have need of a wife? I should be in no danger there; at present our enemies are more concerned to protect themselves than to hunt out Christians."

Bérenger stared at her thoughtfully across the table. A tall candle stood between them, its flame trembling.

"Let me say this, my love: I no longer feel desire for you after the flesh—but it would go very hard with me to be separated from you. Ricord and the child who is yet unborn will have need of you. If you are willing to remain in my house I shall be very happy: we still have a hard fight ahead of us, and we need to face it together."

Gentian looked up and said: "I realize I must now act as bailiff of your estates, and chatelaine of your house, besides caring for your children—I, who once dreamed of love so lofty that the whole earth seemed too little to contain it! While the battle lasted I

could go on living, for when one's nerves are strung tight as a bow-
string there is no time to think.

"But now my heart cries out with anguish. We stand before a
seven-headed dragon, and though we have slashed off a head or
two, the others still live—and even those that are gone may grow
again. No Emperor or King will ever dare to speak up on behalf of
our excommunicated country. Because we fought in our own defense, we are treated as traitors and rebels; and so long as the
Great Whore remains uncrushed we shall be like men fighting with
flawed weapons. We shall be choked in the filthy stench of her
whoredoms; while we fight against soldiers, the bishops and clergy
will stab us in the back."

Bérenger said: "Why speak ill of our Count's Faith? The present
Pope is bad, but his successor may show himself less harsh. And
not all the bishops are traitors."

Gentian rose, her face flushed: "How do you expect me to bring
up our children?" she said. "I was never baptized; my parents
never taught me to worship scraps of rotting bone and bits of unleavened bread! I was forced to let my son Ricord be carried to the
baptismal font, even though he bore my father's name, because we
have to live like everyone else; we have to treat the Devil's Church
as we would a tailor's shop—anyone who refuses to enter it at all
is like a man walking about stark naked.

"And if our Count, together with his great barons, must needs
bow to that Church, out of respect for old customs, and through
fear of the great liar that sits on the throne of Babylon—why, then
he makes liars of us all. I shall have to tell my children that they
should not hate the Cross, abominable object though it is. Yes, it
is red with our blood, I shall say, but you will bow before it nevertheless. The churches are haunts of Satan—yet you must prostrate
yourselves inside them. Honor the bishops, though they have sold
and betrayed our country.

"How can you wish me to live after this fashion? You have been
clothed in the fire of the Spirit, yet already you are condoning this
life of lies; you imagine that evil can change its nature, can cease
to be evil. I do not hold that against you; it is your duty as a sol-

dier. Yet even so my father preferred to live the life of a hunted vagabond, to be numbered among brigands and footpads, rather than defile himself by an oath of allegiance to a Catholic overlord! Through your love of our Count you will go into their churches, and bare your head before the relics, and tell yourself: It means nothing, it is bodily submission only, my soul remains undefiled by it. But men who have received the Spirit would rather be burned alive than soil themselves with the least impure contact!"

"What do you want of me?" Bérenger asked. "When will you leave me in peace? Was I made to be a preacher? Can I at one and the same time serve my overlord and wear the black habit? If you are so exacting as to make a crime out of my loyalty to the Count and my obedience to our country's laws, then how *do* you want me to live? I am not alone in this; all my friends think as I do—that once the war is over, the Count will grant us the freedom of living according to our Faith.

"And when the war *is* over, I will renew my vows and give myself up to God wholly and irrevocably. More than that I cannot promise you."

"I have told you before, Bérenger: God grant that our sons, at least, live to see the end of it! You are choosing the worse course when you say: Tomorrow will be soon enough to retrace my steps. You say you must serve your overlord—you, whose only Lord henceforward should be Christ Jesus! Since our Bishop allows you to do so, I am willing to believe that there is no evil in what you are doing; but for my own part, I am no soldier. I want to bring up our children in such a way that they know the Faith of their fathers has always been the true Faith: I don't want them to feel ashamed of it, or call themselves 'heretics.' I am going to take them away to my part of the country, since my brothers intend to reclaim their lands there. You can come and visit us whenever you please. For the time has come, my love, when we must be steadfast, and build our house on the solidest rock we can find; we are beginning to understand what rain and storms and winds can be like."

"Very well, my beloved," Bérenger said. "Since such is your desire, I will have you escorted thither as soon as your luggage is ready. If your unborn child is a boy, what name will you give him?"

"Renaud. But if it is a girl, I shall call her Raymonde, as you wanted me to."

Bérenger picked up the candlestick and accompanied his wife as far as the door of her chamber. He thought: Even if I had not promised to abstain from all further carnal knowledge of woman-kind, I could not desire her now. We have passed through such cruel ordeals that my desires have become as hateful to me as the burned scars on my face. I love her now with so great a love that I could no longer use her for my bodily pleasures. For our love is as hard as well-tempered steel; and I know now that she loves me with all the strength that is in her heart.

When he was back in the guardroom, where he slept with his men, he drew from his travelling case the New Testament, which he read now every night, and opened it at random—he was not yet free of the superstitious urge to ask God questions. He read:

And I saw thrones, and they sat upon them, and judgment was given unto them: and I saw the souls of them that were beheaded for the witness of Jesus, and for the word of God, and which had not worshipped the Beast, neither his image, neither had received his mark upon their foreheads, or in their hands; and they lived and reigned with Christ a thousand years. But the rest of the dead lived not again until the thousand years were finished. This is the first resurrection. Blessed and holy is he that hath part in the first resurrection: on such the second death hath no power, but they shall be priests of God and of Christ, and shall reign with Him a thousand years.

Bérenger closed the Book; the words he had just read seemed written on the wall in letters of fire. The mark of the Beast is mighty, he thought, and terrible the power of the flesh. The Great Whore decks herself with such wealth of gold and jewelry and dazzling lights, with music and singing, incense and myrrh; she wears kings' crowns as bracelets, and all about her are helmets, lances, swords, oriflammes. Through all the earth she goes, crying: No one can match me for splendor and sanctity!

So great is her power that I, who was marked by her at my baptism, am already well-nigh ready to receive that mark again, to say: I am a man, made of human flesh; it must needs be that I have commerce with whores.

For this Great Whore has been loved by kings and princes; and I too, all unwillingly, have also loved her, for the sound of church bells around my house, and for her painted and gilded altars, all blazing with candles.

What shall we say to them who have had part in the first resurrection?

We have fought for our country and our Faith, but in cowardly wise; instead of bearing witness we have merely followed our trade as killers of men. . . .

He snuffed the candle and stretched out on the straw-covered floor. For a long while there rose before his wakeful eyes a vision of the thrones where men and women who had been burned alive now sat gleaming in their fiery robes. Let me not betray them, he thought, let me not plunge into the abyss of endless shame that is the second death, and which awaits all imperfect souls! Today such a fire has been lit on earth that we cannot but watch it till our eyes are scorched.

CHAPTER XII

Montségur (April 1243)

A RSEN stayed on the great rock of Montségur for more than
twenty-five years.

She had learned that the heart does not grow weary of loving,
but is like a tree that blossoms and bears fruit each year. Today's
blossom is the same as that of twenty years ago: there is no weariness in God.

She had wandered through the countryside, on foot or muleback,
caring for the sick, giving women instruction in the Faith, and
always followed by her blind companion, who had the gift of
words and song, and could make even the most hardened sinner
weep. These were good years they had. From Niort to Fanjeaux,
from Minerve to Cabaret, there were new convents for them to
visit, and congregations more numerous—and far more fervent—
than the prewar ones. This ordeal was necessary, then, Arsen
thought, in order to fortify the Christian Faith. Our friends did not
die in vain.

She had the pleasure of meeting many of her former flock from
Minerve and Saissac; when they saw her again they wept as though
it were their mother they had found. The memory of those hard
times passed together, and the friends they had lost, brought joy
rather than pain. The child whose wooden horse Renaud had repaired long ago was now a grown man—yet he still remembered.
And the woman who had hidden Fabrisse under a pile of brushwood one day: what a laugh they had had about it afterward! *A
very light lady she was,* the woman said. *No smaller than the next
one, and weighed hardly more than a baby.* Ah, my companion,
you were light as the grass of the field, light as a flame! Now you

are gone I no longer feel the weight of my life; it is as though your blood flowed in my veins.

In her cell on the rock Arsen rediscovered the calm, eternal ardor of the dead. While she was at prayer with Esclarmonde, she felt so strong an impression of another's presence that she moved cautiously, for fear of brushing against Renaud's shoulder. Heaven knows Renaud occupied enough space when he was alive; but dead, he was bigger and taller still. His praying was like silent thunder, an avalanche of silence. Arsen never spoke of this to her companion.

Esclarmonde was an ardent creature, who spoke of death as though it were a longed-for meeting with the Beloved. She longed for it, indeed, with such fervor that on several occasions Bishop Peter, who had succeeded her great-uncle in the see, was forced to beg her to take some nourishment and to keep vigil, lamp in hand, rather than hasten so rashly into the presence of her Betrothed.

Arsen loved her companion as one loves flowers in springtime: she alone knew of the childish freshness hidden in this dried-up, sorrowful, and impassioned virgin. Despite all her learning and her gifts, Esclarmonde would go into ecstasies at the song of a thrush; and when she went into a believer's house, she was terribly afraid of being thought bad-mannered because, since she could not see people, she did not greet them in the proper manner.

Sometimes she asked Arsen: "Do you know what kind of death we shall die?"

"How should I know?"

"If it is at the stake, promise you will hold my hand—or if they tie us up, talk to me as long as you can."

"When that moment comes," Arsen said, "you will no longer have need of me."

"It's not that I'm afraid; but in my dreams I often see so huge a fire lit, and so many people thrown into it, that I feel a kind of agony because of my infirmity—the thought of never finding you again."

"You are like a child," Arsen said tenderly. "Which of us has not dreamed of such fires at some time or other?"

And indeed the fires were lit again, throughout the country. Monseigneur Peter, Bishop of Carcassonne, was among the first to be burned, by the special order of the King of France; and a most solemn occasion they made of it. The war had flared up so fiercely that it was becoming difficult to travel again. Arsen was like a white wolf, because of her blind companion: Esclarmonde was only too easy to recognize, and correspondingly difficult to protect. Wherever they went, her voice, and her rapt face, ensured that she was noticed. Besides, the great rock of Montségur was so crowded with the brethren and the sisterhood and novices, that very soon they would be forced to feed on berries and acorns. Provisions were running short in the village at the foot of the mountain, and people were forced to beg their food in the neighboring towns.

Once again the crops were burned, while corpses on gibbets and mutilated cripples were scattered by the hundreds along every roadside. Famine spread her great mantle of dearth over the countryside. Once again the soldier with the scarlet cross on his breast was there, spear in fist, outside the walls of every town and settlement.

Dear God, neither plague nor locusts return as quickly as these. Children born in the midst of war have not yet lost their milk teeth, and the newly planted vines have barely begun to bear fruit! The bishops and clergy have called upon them, and brought them hither, and thrown open the gates of the towns to them. The country has been sold for tithes and prebendaries and privilege.

What can we do against these accursed people? So many of them died of disease on the way that their corpses made the air stink for a league around; and their King, Louis—not the Lion but the Vulture rather—reaped so fair a recompense from his God that he returned to his own country feet first, sewn up in an ox-hide. And still they come, as though they were so miserable on their own soil that they must needs flee beyond their borders. One wants to avenge a father, another his brother, yet another a friend; another wants to win back his stolen booty from its lawful owners. Today it is the thieves who are robbed, and men are returning the land of their fathers to those same wandering soldiers who previously ruined it.

Such is justice today, and such the law: the true master of this country is treated as a thief, and condemned for having kept what is his. He must needs surrender his property to those with no claim on it; and besides this he is censured for acts that should rightly earn any man praise. He defends himself, and is branded as an aggressor; he protects his own, and is called traitor for it.

If they treat the Count himself in so outrageous a fashion, to what Gethsemane of suffering will they not condemn our country? The new peace brings new justice in its train: the innocent will be guilty, only liars will tell the truth, victims will be chastised, thieves compensated, and honors loaded upon dishonorable men. Loyalty and treachery will wear each other's titles. And all this comes through the archduplicity of Pope Gregory: not content with installing French garrisons inside Toulouse itself, he has handed the country over to the Dominicans, as one might surrender a flock of sheep to the wolves.

Woe to those who live in such times! Woe to the men who fought for twenty years only to come to such a pass!

In the small white hall of Montségur Castle, Bishop Bertrand was ordaining a number of the newly elect. So many were the men and women in black who had come to pray for these postulants that the hall could not hold them all: only the most aged were allowed inside, and the rest waited out in the courtyard, together with ordinary members of the Faith who had come to keep Easter at Montségur, and members of the garrison with their families.

There were about a score of postulants, of whom only half were old people. The need for new preachers was more pressing than ever. In the thirteen years that had elapsed since the Frenchmen and the clerics had signed their peace treaty,[*] the Church had been more sorely tested than ever in the days of the Crusaders. For the Devil's minions had succeeded in rousing brother against brother

---

[*] This was the Treaty of Meaux, ratified in 1229. For full details of this treaty see Oldenbourg, *Le Bûcher de Montségur* (1959; translation in preparation), pp. 246–54.—Trs.

through fear of prison and the stake. So many Christians had been burned and tortured that there were none left in the towns to comfort the dying; and even in the countryside no heretic could stay in the same place for a month on end.

"I am sending you forth among wolves," Bishop Bertrand told his congregation. "I am sending you forth into the fiery furnace, into the jaws of Hell. Let your hearts not be troubled, for so treated they the prophets that lived before you. If you live forever in the Love of Christ, and keep His commandments, neither fire nor any other torture will have power over you: you will pass through unharmed and without blemish, and come forth washed in the blood of the Lamb.

"His commandment is to love without stint or limit, sisters and brethren; and today that Love is the hardest road of all, the road which most surely leads to death in the body. The time has come when God's Love here on earth wears the face of Death. Every man who sees you will know that it is with your lives that you are paying for the right to speak of God. Those who are not born of the Devil will believe in your words; for words that can bring us to our deaths are not mere empty verbiage.

"Therefore beware against profaning your ministry with any vain utterance: hold fast to the One Word, as it is expounded by the ancients and the Fathers of our Church. In times such as these, my brethren, the seed you sow will plant itself in men's hearts like arrows of fire; and against it neither the thorns nor the birds of the fields will prevail.

"Let the wisdom of the serpent be your guide: do not break the tool before it has fulfilled its purpose. Yet let Christ find you ready to bear witness at the first summons, lest excessive caution be accounted cowardice in you. Never forget that our yet unenlightened brethren measure the truth of our words by the contempt we show for death. Contempt of death is not a good in itself; but for those souls that are rooted in the flesh it remains the sole proof of a sincere faith. The times in which we live are such that all who enter upon the Way of Truth risk their lives wherever they go, wherever they are, and at every hour of the day and night.

"Do not tempt the weak. Avoid entering houses or asking for hospitality and other such services, except from tried and trusty members of the Faith. Do not ask too much even of these: they may have to pay for their loyalty with their freedom—or their life. They also run the risk of weakening under threats, and damning themselves by betraying you.

"If you are ever put to torture, and are forced to speak by reason of weakness of the flesh, I hereby authorize you to reveal the names of those who are dead; for our enemies find the dead a delectable object of attack, and in their vain superstition believe they can do harm to souls by expending their wrath on decaying flesh or ashes. Nevertheless, do not even do this except under the pressure of necessity, lest you cause suffering to the relatives of the deceased, in their property or their affections. If you are made to suffer such agony that in all good faith you feel you cannot keep silent, I hereby authorize you to refuse all nourishment, and thus starve yourselves to death. Better to be reduced to this rather than denounce those who trust you.

"May the love of Christ be your sole guide; and may that love henceforward be mingled with no earthly considerations. The misfortunes and reverses that we have undergone during these last few months have shown us, only too well, that neither strength of arms, nor a just cause, nor love of an earthly country has prevailed against the might of the Evil One. Let Christ from now on be your Alpha and Omega, your beginning and your end, your only goal and Way and Saviour."

The new initiates were now taken to their cells out on the mountain, in order to prepare themselves for their mission. The congregation, warriors for the most part, discussed the Bishop's sermon respectfully, but with a touch of bitterness too: if you had to renounce fighting, how could you ever hope to live like a man?

It was thirteen years since Bérenger d'Aspremont had been once more deprived of his lands and goods, and five since he had been condemned to death *in absentia*. Now he led a vagabond existence with others like him, moving from Cerdagne to Catalonia, from

Corbières to Ariégeois, sometimes lodging with one of his wife's relatives, and sometimes under the open sky. Three years before he had received a wound in the leg before Carcassonne, which left him with a slight limp. Since then opportunities for fighting had somehow slipped through his fingers. He hoped and waited for them, and spent days on end discussing the possibilities with his friends. When you have a family trailing behind you, you needs must find food once a day at least. In a poor country not everyone is lucky enough to get work.

In the village of Montségur, under the shadow of the great rock, day-by-day miseries were partly forgotten. Hope was as tenacious as the scab. The Emperor will come and deliver us, they said. The King of England will bring an army of Gascons and besiege Carcassonne. The French can't stay here forever. People have never hung on to stolen territory for so long. . . .

Despite her clothes, which were so patched and mended that the original cloth was hardly visible, Gentian de Montgeil remained a great lady. In the hostel for women of the Faith, where she was lodging with her daughter over Eastertide, she had a right to the place of honor; and women in brocaded dresses, with belts of wrought gold, gladly gave way to her. She had been condemned to the stake in her absence at the same time as her husband and was regarded as one of those pious women who, without actually having received baptism, ranked only a little below an ordained Christian. She had a penetrating voice, and let no one forget that her mother had lived in a cell up on the great rock for the past twenty-five years, nor that her father had been hacked to bits in the great square of Carcassonne for the murder of more than three hundred Crusaders. She rightfully could claim a place among the highest nobility in the land. So respected was she that she frequently spoke in public, and spoke well.

Whence do body and heart draw the strength not to give up? Gentian wondered. I never would have believed I should live so long; and yet I feel scarcely any older than the day I left home for the very first time. Scarcely any older—and yet I am nearly fifty! We have gone on looking forward to life; all the time we have said, "Tomorrow." Tomorrow there will be victory, tomorrow we shall be happy, tomorrow we shall have rest. We have so got into the habit that we always say it. And for thirty years now the vise has been tightening around us. We used to say: God grant that our children see the end of this war. Now we must say: God grant our children are spared the end of it, and that our grandchildren still have the strength to hold out. Yet we cannot ask that of them. It is too cruel.

It is a cruel life that we have led—but a free one.

All that our children know of freedom is that it means hunger, misery, and exhaustion. Honored and respected though we are, even our best friends do not willingly receive us in their homes: a discontented servant, a scared girl—these are enough to betray them. So many people tell us nowadays: "I don't know whether I can rely on my servants." Alas: soon they will no longer know whether they can rely on themselves.

It was a hard climb up to the fortress. Bérenger had to lean on his stick, for his wounded leg tired quickly. Out of tact the young folk, too, schooled themselves to walk slowly. There was a great throng of pilgrims this year, as there was all the time from Easter to Ascension Day; but this year it was even larger than usual. It was known that very soon a Crusader army under the Seneschal of Carcassonne intended to occupy the area, doubtless for many a long month.

Gentian was walking beside her husband, eyes raised toward the fortress. Sitting there on its rock, it put her in mind of a great ship, sailing high in the heavens.

"Bérenger," she said, "will you ask leave to enter your period of probation this year?"

"I think not, my love. I am still an able-bodied man, and my leg will not prevent me from fighting if I need to. But I am not holding *you* back. If they are willing to accept you, you would be better off here than in the valley."

"We have been together too long to part now. If you are taken, I want to go with you."

He shrugged. "If they wanted to execute everyone condemned

in his absence they would not find faggots enough to burn them. They are well enough content to let us live this sort of life."

Gentian glanced back at her children, who were following close behind, pausing at each bend of the zigzag track to look out over the wide mountain valley and the heavy massif of Mount Tabor.

There were four of them: Ricord, Raymonde, Bernard de Frémiac, Raymonde's husband, and Izarn, the son that Bérenger had had in his fortieth year, when, driven by the Devil, he had taken a concubine. All four possessed the somewhat rough grace of young mountain animals—the supple limbs, the sure eye, always watchful, and the head carried high above straight shoulders. From the very cradle they had been taught to love good and hate evil—so thoroughly, indeed, that they sought only Good or Evil in everything they saw. They were eager and greedy for life; yet it never crossed their minds that they had a *right* to live. Life, the True Life, lay up aloft for them, up on the great rock where the fortress stood; Life was contained in the Bishops, the deacons, the ministers; it resided in the Count, in the King of Aragon or the Emperor of Germany; it lurked in the dungeons and the burning faggots. It was in their hymns and prayers, and in the blood of God's enemies.

Their life was so lofty and remote that they had developed the habit of gazing out to the far horizon, lost to the world, and of feeling great contempt for their own bodies. They too were all condemned *in absentia*—all, that is, except Izarn, who was not yet fourteen at the time of the trials. They regarded this as a kind of badge of honor. Many of their comrades were in the same position, and not a penny the worse for it: they merely had to avoid being seen too often in the towns.

Any one of those three young men, if they met a Dominican friar, would have cheerfully sprung on him and slit his throat; yet they showed neither malice nor pride, as is so often the case with boys who have been brought up to a hard life. Luckily, they had not yet found the occasion to commit a noble act of this nature. When we are gone, Gentian thought, they will be lost. It was because of this that she did not want to withdraw from the world.

With rapt emotions Gentian contemplated the unfamiliar old woman whom her mother had now become: dried-up, frail almost, her skin as tough as parchment, her eyes large still, but sunk between deep-scored eyelids, her teeth still unblemished, lips withered but firm. It was not a beautiful face: it was, rather, like the ruins of a face that had once been more beautiful than Arsen's ever was.

From beneath the folds of her black veil her eyes smiled at them, brimming over with simple cheerfulness: it was always a treat for her to see her children again. She received them as though it were they who were doing her an honor. The cell was very small, so the visitors had to squat as best they might on the stone platform outside the entrance, above a little gorge where hazels grew.

"This part of the rock has become quite a village," Arsen said. "Holy women sprout here like mushrooms. There's a long queue to draw water from the well."

It was true that, ever since they had reached the foot of the castle ramparts, the visitors had been conscious of the odor of sanctity that hung about the summit of the rock. This odor was stronger when they got near the little piled-up huts, and yet different from the normal smell of human habitation. The breath and sweat of these perpetually fasting hermits seemed to hold an aroma of old wax, or resin, or tart apples: one very soon got used to it. But the mere presence of so many persons who had been shaped and molded by prayer went to one's head like a rough wine. The most villainous of men could not long withstand its effects; so much so that the ignorant claimed the place was bewitched.

Bérenger and the young people were amazed to see this old lady smiling and discussing banal matters with them, after having given them her solemn blessing. Each of her words, too, had a hidden meaning for them, as though it came from a world in which they had no place. Because she was pleased to see them they felt as though it were God who had blessed them.

"I can't put you all up, we haven't the room," she was saying, "and it's getting too cold to sleep outside." She let her thoughtful gaze rest on each of the four young people in turn.

"What lovely little children!" she said, which must have annoyed them: they were far from little. Ricord, in fact, was more than twenty-six. But the old lady's eyes, so radiant with warm, tranquil tenderness, made them feel that beside her they were really little children, and even less.

"Ricord," she said again, and her lips trembled. "Ricord. Not yet married, at your age?"

The young man shrugged and half smiled, as though to say: How could I be?

"He took it into his head," Bérenger put in, "to marry the Chalabre wheelwright's daughter. It appears, however, that we are not good enough to aspire to a wheelwright's daughter. He should have been content with a daughter of the nobility, as Bernard was."

He flashed an affectionate and conspiratorial glance at his son-in-law. His devotion to these three boys and the girl was all the stronger since, despite himself, he felt himself at fault in his treatment of them.

Arsen lowered her eyes. She too felt not so much at fault as embarrassed by the presence of these people who, it seemed to her, were paying too high a price for their loyalty to the Faith. It is not just, she thought, to condemn to death those who have neither received baptism nor taken the habit; you might as well demand a thousand crowns from someone who owes you only ten. Could one treat as a heretic a man who had received the baptism for the dying, and then resumed his military career? In our day, she thought, only the Christians were condemned.

Sicart and Imbert, her two surviving sons, had been forced to enlist with a troop of Aragonese mercenaries, as common soldiers. Must these handsome boys, with their clean, golden-brown faces, also drink of the same cup? Men are far more often driven to a brigand's life by unhappiness than by natural cruelty.

Bérenger was talking. For once he was bitter, and depressed: he was thinking the same thoughts as Arsen.

He said: "All the time I lived sinfully, I was honored by my fellow men, wealthy, surrounded by friends and sure of my rights. In the Toulouse area I have a number of relatives and friends who belonged to our Faith, yet who took the oath each time it was required of them, and now go to Mass every Sunday and communicate thrice yearly. As a result they have kept their property, and have money to spend on the Church and the upkeep of our ministers. Quite apart from the fact that they live in houses and can marry their children to whom they please.

"I have done many things which are sins before God, but not in the sight of men. I have never violated any of my country's laws. I can tell you in all honesty, my lady, that I have never incurred any reproach save touching my Faith—of such crimes as rape and sedition and looting I am wholly innocent. Even at my trial, so far as I can ascertain, they found no case against me except those of having received baptism when I lay wounded, and giving lodging or shelter to Christians. This I never bothered to conceal; my wife and I were denounced by more than a hundred witnesses. I make no complaint as regards that; I would far prefer to lead the kind of life I do now than be forced to attend Mass every Sunday.

"But you see, we still thought that if the Count succeeded in regaining the castles stolen from him by the King of France, and ejecting the Dominican preaching friars, then part at least of our sentences might be quashed, and our children would be left to live as seemed best to them, and to enter the service of whatever overlord they chose. For even rough justice must needs be executed by sane men, not by lunatics; no one could leave all these young folk to rot away in woods and caves. But now that the Count has bowed the knee as he never did before, and the only justice left to us—if you can call it that—is provided by the Inquisition, I do not know where to turn. If we have held out so long only to flee into Lombardy at the last, we ought to have done it when the children were smaller and I still had some money left."

Arsen shook her head.

"I know too well how hard life can be for poor folk in a foreign country. But in Lombardy no one will stop you from living according to your Faith."

At that Ricord started back, and blushed; his dark, smoldering eyes flickered away to one side, as though he dared not look at his grandmother.

"As long as there remain any enemies of Christ in this country," he said, in a hoarse voice, "we shall stay here too."

His father frowned, and blushed in his turn at what he considered a tactless piece of braggadocio. But it was, in fact, a genuine *cri de coeur*.

"Ah, Bérenger," Arsen said, "let them speak freely in my presence! It's plain enough to me that they feel awed because I am so old; I can hardly hear a word they say. And God all too seldom grants me the joy of seeing my children."

The young people were not really awed or intimidated so much as held by a kind of rapt contemplation. The old lady was their most precious worldly possession, their heritage and pride, their share in God. She was old, so old: more than seventy-five, and they supposed her nearer a hundred. So old, indeed, that the power of the Spirit had accumulated within her, had multiplied and burgeoned, and had transformed her into this great spiritual lover who drew souls to herself as the magnet gathers iron filings. Kinship in the flesh is a thing of little worth; but it was no little thing for them to be able to say: She is of our kin. Our flesh and blood lives on the holy mountain, we too are of the family who have their dwelling in the high places. Bernard and Izarn, who were not related to the old lady by ties of blood, felt exactly as the others did: the bond which united them all was far stronger than any blood kinship.

There she sat, a living prayer, relic and sacrament, protector most humble and tender; and this protector they would have shielded at the price of their lives—since God's power is not of this world. Speak to her? But she knew everything before it was said. Raymonde would not even have dared to say, aloud: "I would like to stay here near you." Who deserved so great an honor? Not even their own mother; scarcely, perhaps, even this tall, thin, blind woman who moved about the cell with the abrupt yet graceful gait of a tame fawn.

Gentian and Raymonde spent the night in the cell, while their menfolk went off to find quarters somewhere on the mountain, along with other visitors. At Eastertide the whole rock was swarming with pilgrims, and there was only just room in the brethren's cells for the old and the sick. The other pilgrims camped on the rock, close to the track, lighting fires to warm up the wheaten cakes and smoked fish they had been given, or which they had brought up from the village. Hunger is not an easy thing to accustom oneself to; very many of them gabbled off their two, or perhaps eight, *Pater Nosters,* so as to begin their meal that much the sooner.

After saying her prayers Arsen came out and sat on her threshold: with advancing age she had almost lost the need for sleep altogether. Inside the cell Esclarmonde was praying aloud, while Raymonde lay stretched out asleep on the floor. Gentian spread a cloak over her, since it was a chilly night, and then went out and sat at her mother's feet.

Long thin clouds were scudding across the sky, in pursuit of a white, gleaming crescent moon. The night air was filled with the dull hum of voices, praying, singing, talking. The mountain itself seemed more urgently alive than it did during the daytime. A few steps below them, the two women could see the path plunge out of sight into a bottomless abyss; on their left the fortress reared up, a vast black gateway in the smoke-gray sky. The sentries on the ramparts and the guards in the main keep were signalling to each other with their lamps.

"Do they light all those torches every night?" Gentian asked.

"No. But you know how it is these days: the soldiers are uneasy. In a few weeks' time we shall be in a state of siege here. Already the bishops and the clergy are recruiting men throughout the countryside."

Gentian sighed.

"So you will be cut off from the outside world for the whole summer. It is a great misfortune for all of us."

"My daughter, they will not stay just for the summer but

throughout the winter too. Here, you see, we know more or less all that passes in the councils of the wicked. A month from now the only people left on the mountain will be those who have to stay there; there is nowhere else so safe as the fortress itself and the huts above it. My companion and I will have to leave this home of ours and take up lodgings with a sister who lives in the angle of the west wall. For me," she added, sadly, "it will be a little like changing my country. Though at least we shall be closer to the House of Prayer."

"Mother, they can never capture the fortress!"

"It would certainly be a difficult business. But they will wreak much evil on us, that I can feel in my heart. Christ has manifested Himself too powerfully in these parts; that is why we are fated to have no peace here. The Beast is arming himself, sharpening every fang and claw for the fray: all who speak of God on earth are intolerable to him. In truth he can do nothing to us; but my heart mourns for those to whom the Lord has entrusted us—for of them he will devour full many."

Gentian let her head rest on her mother's knees.

"I am weary," she said. "I am not ashamed to say it, since I would still keep walking even though I had twenty pounds' weight hung from my hands and feet. Every road is blocked for us now, even that of exile: we have reached such a degree of poverty that we remain better off in our own mountains—a condition, truly, nearer that of wolves than of men.

"Mother, my daughter has borne two children. The second lived three whole months. She wept bitterly for it: flesh will cleave powerfully to its own flesh. Suppose she has other children, what will become of them? Our sons have served honorably enough hitherto; but now the lords who were well disposed toward us have all changed sides. I would rather see my sons dead than turned into brigands—and you know very well I do not say *that* through any hardness of heart! Half the time we live by the charity of the Church, which is hardly fitting, seeing that we are neither aged nor sick.

"It is only now that I have come to see that the Christian's life on this earth can be none other than this: endless, hopeless misery, without goal or issue. So long as we nursed hope we were no true Christians, but pagans like the rest of them. Mother, since we stand condemned for our Faith alone, it follows that this condemnation is just according to the laws of the world. It is said: Men shall persecute you for My sake. At least this is certain: we are persecuted for no other reason.

"I wanted to make Christians of our children, and to teach them that nothing counts except Christ's Truth, and the Church. But they say, 'We shall arm ourselves with keen-edged swords and stout spears, and smite God's enemies.' That is all they think about. For them our life of hunger and humiliation is no life, and I lack the strength to tell them how right it is they should know none other. It *is* just, Mother—yet at the same time it offends all justice. I don't know how to explain this to you; I can't really understand it myself, though I've racked my brains over it.

"But, you see, they are as innocent as it is humanly possible for them to be, free of all defilement—even though Ricord was baptized, but that was my fault—and brought up in the Faith, ignorant of all evil save the common weaknesses of the flesh. Christ took pity on the little ones—they must not be offended, He said—and on the naked and hungry and imprisoned. He did not say: Make these little ones hungrier and colder yet, send them to the dungeon and the stake. If He did not say it, how should I?"

"They no longer have the choice," Arsen said.

Gentian sat a long time without answering, her eyes following the bright dance of signal flares on the roof of the keep. They were blazing more fiercely than ever now, and to judge by their size must be directed to the folk in the village below. Even in this haven of deep peace, she thought, war lurks like fire under the ashes. The only freedom left to us is that of spilling blood.

At last she replied: "I should have said, Blessed are those who have never been forced to choose. They have been forcibly thrust onto the path of righteousness, since the other road they might have taken was a mire of ugliness and treachery. But God have mercy on the children when they say to Him, as one day they will: 'Lord, we have not knocked or searched; we have not been able to sell all we possessed to gain the pearl of great price; all was sold long before.'

"Mother, this life drains one's heart, just as too hot a sun will wither plants. For a long while now our hearts have been parched and burned: what I feel for our enemies is not so much hatred as a sort of insatiable contempt, akin to hunger. I shall never be a Christian, and I know that we must remain faithful to God without any hope of salvation, for our enemies in this day and age are such that it will never be possible to love or forgive them."

"They know not what they do," the old woman said, slowly. "Forget the evil man, and see the wild beast he is in reality. We are delivered up to beasts, as the early Christians were: beasts more intelligent and crueler than lions, but not one whit more responsible for their acts. Only their Maker is responsible and guilty. The leader of these lost creatures, whom they call Dominic, was, it is said, like a dog—always arching his back and barking furiously and gobbling up Christians. Can you find it in your heart to feel contempt or loathing for a *dog*? A beast can frighten us; it can even make us turn cowards because of that fear; but in itself it is nothing. We must learn to feel love for it in its carnal misery, and pity the wretched soul that may be screaming in agony at the thought of being lodged in the body of a beast."

"I have not your insight; for me a man will never be a beast. Listen, Mother! They are going to bring an army in order to storm this castle and burn our Bishop and all our ministers, and every Christian sister here, and *you*, Mother, and your companion, and many of our friends' mothers and grandmothers. They want to gain possession of this castle so that they may defile and profane the place where we come to pray, and to mock our Faith according to their fashion! Before, they only consumed our bodies; now they devour body and soul together, a thing no beast could do."

"And supposing they were to capture this castle? How many

Christians have they not burned already—and among them the most steadfast both in word and in deed? We have no need to fear them; it is they rather who fear us."

"Mother, what will become of us if even this refuge is taken from us?"

"It is said: 'The gates of Hell shall not prevail against it.' The Rock on which the Church is built is neither the rock of Montségur nor any other rock fortress, however strong, you may be quite sure of that."

"Ah, that I know well," Gentian said. "But we are here on earth, and that Rock is in Heaven."

In the morning the whole valley was shrouded in a mist of quite dazzling whiteness, from which the mountain rose, clear and sun-gilded as though on the first day of Creation. The castle, thus freshly painted, and with its frail girdle of gray, stony huts strung about it, brought to mind the image of some huge white bird that had made its nest on the rocky summit. Huge windows glittered against the rising sun as though they were eyes.

Gentian and her daughter had climbed down in the direction of the track, so as not to disturb the reverend sisters' prayers. Raymonde supported herself against a pine tree that practically hung over the sheer rock face, and looked down. All around her was the same vertiginous drop, ramparts of close-growing pines and oaks split by stony spurs, and that blanket of mist at the bottom. Sleep had wiped every trace of weariness and distress from the young girl's face; pale and slender though she was, with hollow eyes and chapped lips, she still radiated freshness. Her astonished eyes seemed to see magic symbols or dancing fairies in the wisps of mist that drifted through the blue-shaded trees.

Raymonde was as slim as a boy and had all the agility of a young goat. Her bare feet were black and hardened, and the two tresses in which her hair was plaited resembled a couple of sodden dogs' tails. She laughed at her state, with the delightful indifference of a healthy young girl who is in love and spends every night in her lover's arms. A lucky child, Gentian thought. This hard life is a wind that fans the flames of love. Though Bernard had married her seven years before, he was still as mad for her as on his wedding night; he had never known another woman.

Scattered among the heavy boulders, around a dead fire, was a group of young men. Having now said their prayers in a seemly manner, they were preparing to strike camp. They buckled on their belts, laced up the black gartering around their thighs, and shook out their dew-dampened jerkins. There was a good score of them, all either related by blood or—what was better—made brothers by the same love and the same hatred. Some of them wore fine leather shoes and new doublets, bright red or purple or green in hue. This earned them neither envy nor contempt: chance had turned them into "temporary Catholics" ere now, and chance tomorrow might send them to prison or the Holy Land—or simply into the wide kingdom of the forests and rocks, where their new clothes would have ample time to fade. These young men were not like their fathers: they did not spend their time looking into the future in hope or desperation. Life is not over at twenty; someone was bound to work a miracle for them. In the last three years the country had twice risen in revolt, and twice all but gained the victory: the third time—or the fourth—all would go well.

The enemy was unreal, far away, in Rome or Paris, in the monasteries and palaces, everywhere *they* were not. They alone were true and real: they, and their friends. They thought themselves as strong as the whole world.

They strolled up to the castle in little groups, exchanging greetings with the troops in the watchtower that stood in the midst of the rocks; this tower was encircled by a huge, brand-new palisade, its timber so freshly cut that it still exuded a smell of resin. Here on this mountain freedom was something you breathed in the air, something you met in everyone's eye, something you ate with the bread blessed by the ministers. Who could ever suppose that this high place would ever be taken? Let those dogs bark as they would; once they came they would get a hot reception.

From far off Bérenger observed his three sons as they were swallowed up among a crowd of their fellows. That morning he felt neither compassion nor distress on their behalf; he was wholly conquered by the atmosphere of austere peacefulness that rose from the hermits' cells and seemed to throb like some slow, deep heartbeat in the very rock itself. My sons, he thought: my sons. They have been sacrificed, rejected by this world, proscribed and excommunicated, condemned by every court in our country. Condemned for nothing, condemned for their parents' acts. We never asked them what *they* felt.

Consider this, O Lord: how could I say to my son: Ricord, go and present yourself at the Dominican friary in Toulouse. Wait your turn in the crowd you will find outside the door. Tell them that you have always abominated our Faith, and that you wish to submit yourself to their so-called Holy Church. Names, they will ask you. My parents. Your parents? they will say, mockingly. Your parents are far away. Tell us the names of those you know in the town. Dead men? We know all about them. Name someone still alive. Not one or two names, either, but ten, twenty, thirty—if you don't give us enough names you might as well not have come. Don't forget that you did not come here entirely of your own free will. You were under summons. You have been denounced as a Cathar. Now, you're no fool: you have the choice. Life imprisonment, or all the names we care to ask for. Your repentance is not sincere. You are the dog that returns to its vomit.

O Lord, should I have exposed my children to that? Many other fathers have done so. Suppose I had: they would have been packed off to the Holy Land for two or three years—which means they would have been back again by now, and on a regular engagement in the Count's army. Just a nasty moment to get through, the shame of it quickly forgotten—after all, they are young. I never thought of doing it; I always believed our Count would be able to protect us and drive out those accursed devils. But they have proved stronger than he: see how he sides with them now to destroy our Church! Yet we served him, through thick and thin. Hunted, betrayed, stripped of our lands, we still served him. God knows it was not only our lands that we fought for, but respect for our Faith.

Now our lawful lord has betrayed us. He says: It is for the sake of their accursed Faith that my country has been destroyed. God forgive him, his father would never have said that: you could search till the Day of Judgment and not find more loyal vassals than we have proved ourselves. Now, O Lord, we are no longer his vassals: our allegiance is to Thy spotless Church, which has never failed us.

It is better, Lord, that they should be in Thy service than in the Count's. It is true that Thou givest us neither horses, nor coats of mail, nor money; Thy service is in pride and poverty. There they go now, clad in that rich armor which Christ Jesus has promised to those who serve Him: no shirt and one coat only—and even that one split at every seam!

The young men were chatting with one another, seriously as befitted their age, but with a kind of borrowed gravity that seemed to be cracking under their sheer high-blooded *joie de vivre*. Blood coursed proudly through their veins: nothing was forbidden them, all was signed and sealed in advance. Their life was hard enough to give them the right to do anything they chose. Their faces were burned black by the sun, their hair rain-washed and wind-knotted, their cheeks nicked and scarred by blunt razors; but when they looked at you their eyes shone so hard and certain that no one could outface them.

They stood talking to the soldiers in the watchtower, soldiers who were boys like themselves, the forest nobility, prison bait, brethren in Christ. They spoke of the siege. Everyone was well informed concerning the latest events at Carcassonne. They knew the exact day by which the village down below would have to be evacuated; they knew which roads would be the best to travel, and which of the city militiamen could be relied upon. Not all these Crusaders, it was certain, were genuine enemies.

The thing nobody knew was the most important of all—whether the noble Emperor Frederick would raise a great army and come down the Rhone, to further his aim of occupying Provence and thence taking the Frenchmen in the rear. When that day came the Count would recall every banished exile, and not a Dominican would be left in the land: every one of them would be massacred, and each soldier would be able to make a mantle for his mistress out of their white robes. The Pope in his gilded palace trembled before the Emperor; for such deep insults had passed between them that they would never be able to make peace again.

The prisons would be thrown open, and the exiles allowed to return home, and every traitor duly punished.

"No, not all of them. Only the biggest."

"You know which they are, eh?"

"No, my friends, we will punish none of them. Their shame will be sufficient punishment. When that day comes, we will all ride up to the gates of Montségur Castle on Crusaders' horses, and offer up the booty we have taken as a tribute to our Bishop."

They don't really believe it, Bérenger thought. Who *could* believe it? They've got heads on their shoulders. No, they don't believe it; but at their age people want there to be some sort of justice in this world. Blessed are they who hunger after justice. These boys may hunger after it for their own sakes—but not for that alone.

Arsen blessed her children before their departure.

"I have a feeling we shall never see each other again," she told them. "I am old, and there are dark days ahead for us. You, my daughter, my only reminder of the companion I once loved so dearly, do not forget us, either your father or myself. It is years since he died; yet I feel that he still is calling me as he called me on that dreadful day. If, despite my age, I am still fated to die in torment, I do not know what name I shall couple with God's in my own cries. My flesh is too weak, and has loved greatly. The faces and voices of all those I have loved still live within me, like seeds in a clod of earth. You too, my daughter, will live in me, so long as I have a drop of blood left in my veins—like your dead brothers, and those other brothers lost on the paths of misfortune. On the day of my death I will call out to you, and you will hear me.

"I cannot tell what I shall say to you when that day comes. But I know what your father told me when he was in the executioner's hands: that there is no hatred, only love, unreasoning love, love without a beginning or an end. Love is never destroyed, never dies, never exists in vain. If I have lived so long it is to be better able to tell you that. We shall never be defeated, either on earth or in Heaven, if we have loved to the very end."

"Pray God," Gentian said, kneeling, "that He grant us the grace to love in this fashion."

She embraced Arsen and her blind companion, and then went up to the castle. It seemed to her that her mother would never die, or else that she was dead already: it seemed the same thing. She was living timelessly, world without end, with her restless, quivering, immutable, stubborn love; love unwavering, like fire and water; love too patient, too enduring. No one could do anything against her. Then why, Gentian wondered, does my heart ache so at the thought of her old and withered flesh being delivered to the flames? So much, indeed, that I would give my life to prevent it. What is this power of the flesh?

"Bérenger," she said. "Bérenger, our Lord said, did He not, in St. Luke: 'He that hath no sword, let him sell his garment, and buy one'?"

Her husband shrugged his shoulders.

"We have nothing left to sell," he said.

What was left of their arms lay hidden in a cave some four leagues distant, in a wood near Chalabre. And that in truth was little enough.

"Bérenger, when the disciples showed Him two swords he said: 'It is enough.' But it was not enough; and He told Peter to put his sword up in its sheath again. Then what did He want them to do with these swords?"

"Monseigneur Raymond said that He was speaking here of the

two spiritual swords, Faith and Charity, that it was a kind of parable."

"Yet they were real swords, Bérenger. There were all too few of them—but He did not say, Cast them aside."

"Then we will not cast ours aside either. But we have so few ourselves that they, too, will in the end become a kind of parable, not real weapons."

"This castle will never surrender, Bérenger. Even in this world God permits the existence of visible signs that testify to Him. Otherwise there would no longer be any salvation for men's souls."

Bérenger slowly shook his grizzled head.

"Do not speak thus," he said. "Our children can say that; we cannot. Even though such a calamity befell us, God would be neither richer nor poorer by reason of it."

"But *we* would, Bérenger! Ah, *we* would become poorer than Job! God will never allow this thing to be taken from us!"

The fortress of Montségur was stormed a year later. Nearly two hundred ordained heretics were burned, and more than a score of believers converted at the eleventh hour. Among the heretics were Bishop Bertrand Marty, the deacons Raymond Aguilher, Raymond de Saint-Martin, William Clamens, and Peter Bonnet; and a vast number of other Christians, known and unknown.

CHAPTER XIII

The Faithful (1246)

IT was two years after the fall of Montségur that Bérenger and Gentian d'Aspremont came to the end of their life of wandering. Their children were with them no longer; the boys were serving in a company formed of outlaws like themselves, which roamed from Corbières to Roussillon and from Roussillon to Cerdagne, living off the land. The line which divides an outlaw from a mercenary is very easily crossed: real hunger, and a weapon at your side—these are enough to push a man over. These broken-down soldiers still cherished a faith that would have sent them ten leagues over the mountains in midwinter to catch a minister passing through the district; but such travelling pastors were becoming rarer and rarer. A soldier's sins lie heavy on him—especially when that soldier has no one to pay his wages.

Bérenger was too old and exhausted for this kind of life; he went from village to village, getting his bread as best he could. He could read and write, and he understood Latin; he also taught his hosts songs that he knew, or made up himself, which resulted in his being known as "the Troubadour." Gentian still had her fine voice, too, but would sing only when other women were present. Obviously they could never stay more than a fortnight in the same town: it was quite clear to everyone that they were condemned outlaws.

And yet it was in a wood that they were finally caught, during a search organized by the Seigneur de Mirepoix's bailiff. (His men were looking for a heretical sister who, in point of fact, had already left the country.) Gentian, who had climbed up onto a big rock overlooking the road, was spotted by the commander of the small armed detachment; Bérenger, sitting behind the same rock, had not noticed their approach.

Gentian pretended to feel ill, and begged her husband to go and find some water for her. The nearest spring was about a mile away.

"How can I leave you here in this state?" he said.

"For God's sake, my love, don't delay—go quickly, unless you want me to die! Run, run—I'll be all right till you get back."

He picked up the water bottle.

"I *can't* leave you! You're shivering with fever."

"No, it's thirst. Go, now! Do you want me to die?"

As he hurried away she murmured: "Bérenger—" He looked back, and she waved him on. Then she walked out onto the road, thinking: If they are looking for a woman heretic, they won't stray far from here now they've caught sight of me. And very soon the bailiff's men came up with her.

"Are you the woman known as Braïda de Bélesta?" they asked. She said that she was.

But her trick was of no use to her. Like the wolf that lets itself be caught when following the trail of his captured mate, Bérenger voluntarily surrendered to the bailiff, knowing very well that his wife could not have vanished into thin air while he was away. Both of them were sent under escort to Toulouse.

During the journey they had time to discuss their position: while they were bivouacked for the night they were left shut up in a cellar, with only a single sentry mounting guard over them. In such cases the Church recommended its unordained members to bow to secular law, and not to bear witness unless they felt an uncontrollable desire to do so. Even in these circumstances it was better to abstain, unless they were sure of finding a Christian in prison, who could administer baptism to them *in extremis*.

Bérenger said: "At the age of sixty, I have no intention of bringing dishonor on myself by abjuring my Faith, just to gain a few extra years of life in prison. What sort of life would it be, tell me that? The best I could hope for would be one of those common dungeons where they live twenty or thirty to a cell. Such places are full of spies and informers; we would undoubtedly be burned as relapsed heretics a month or so after our trial."

"Bérenger, when I was young I wanted to become a martyr for God. You know about that. But martyrdom is not the prize at a tournament; it cannot be plucked up on the point of a spear. It is the God of our enemies, not the true God, who delights in torments, and in the shrieks and smoke of the executioner's bonfire. We must beware of committing a grave sin by going to His feast in foul linen."

"Would it be any the less foul if we were to recant?"

"Neither more nor less. We are heavy with years and the weight of our sins. You see—already you are speaking as though it were a question of your 'honor.' You reckon nothing of *my* agony. Do you think I want to watch the flames devour you alive before my very eyes? Do you want to see me, yes, *me,* burned at the stake, and have the whole town listening to my shrieks of pain? Such a death is not beautiful, it is ugly—the ugliest thing conceivable in the world."

"Whatever you do, that shall I do also," Bérenger said. "God forbid that *I* should drive you to your death—and to such a death as this! But I must needs believe that God has granted you a new vision, for you would not have spoken in such a way once."

"Ah, it may be that I am wrong to fear such torments. My courage is not broken, though; perhaps it is merely that my love for you has become greater. So many human beings that I loved have endured this death now that my heart feels as though it were flayed alive. It is all very well knowing that my mother is blessed and glorified—when I think of what they did to her body, I have to bite my lips to stop myself from crying out. Age has not hardened me, my beloved: I have become a sort of pincushion, so pierced and transfixed at every point that there is not space for another wound in me. I want to live a few more years beside you, though it be in prison; our parting will come all too soon as it is."

"You do not really know what you want, my poor darling; you were quite prepared to leave me alone and take this road without me."

"Yes. In that instant my only thought was to prevent your being captured. Why did you have to surrender yourself? Did you think you would give me great joy by such an act?"

"You must believe me—I too only thought of—no, truly, I do not know what I was thinking of."

Bérenger and Gentian spent two months in prison in Toulouse before they were questioned—a harsh imposition, since there was very little room available for them. There was not a single cell empty; the newcomers were flung pell-mell into a kind of refectory, where sixty or more were forced to sleep practically on top of one another. Since it was summer, they were so tormented by flies, mosquitoes, lice, and fleas that many said it was better to get the whole thing over and done with, for good. They might talk of building new prisons; but that wouldn't happen overnight.

The day that Bérenger and Gentian were at last taken before the Tribunal of the Holy Office, they all but fainted on coming out into the fresh air: they felt as though they were choking. To be haled through the streets in rags, with shackles on their legs, did not disturb them at all. Dear God, they prayed, let it go on a long time. Let us not be taken back to prison too quickly.

When they were outside the gate of the Dominican friary Gentian realized she was trembling. She had never seen any of these folk close to, and she had got so exaggerated a notion of their diabolical powers that she feared their least glance might cast a spell on her.

Bérenger had to go in first. "Whatever you do," she told him, "do not think of me. Answer as you think best."

In that neat, whitewashed room, confronted with clean-shaven men who wore fine white robes and black cloaks and bore the scarlet cross on their breast, Bérenger found some difficulty in remembering that he was a high-born gentleman, a knight of Toulouse. His judgment and condemnation were read to him in Latin. He said: "I understand: there is no need for a translation."

The clerk reading the Instrument of Accusation then proceeded as follows: "Though Holy Mother Church has recognized you,

Bérenger, being of noble birth and formerly Lord of Aspremont, as a man notoriously and publicly known for your invincible attachment to that depraved heretical sect commonly called Cathars, concerning whom we possess the formal testimony of more than one hundred and fifteen separate witnesses;

"And though, in consideration of your obstinate and persistent refusal to submit to the Church and appear before this present Tribunal to justify those crimes which are laid to your charge, you have been declared an infamous person, excommunicate and unworthy of all mercy, cast forth from the bosom of the Church, and delivered to the secular arm;

"And though you have thereby been lawfully and constitutionally condemned in a secular court to be burned alive as a heretic and a rebel; and though you have for many years past willfully withdrawn yourself from Holy Church's maternal authority, and have thereby fully merited this condemnation;

"Nevertheless: judging that Holy Church should not close her arms against any repentant sinner, and being unwilling to cast forth any man finally and irrevocably before hearing him, we, Brother Peter, Friar of the Order of Blessed Dominic, do adjure you, in the name of Holy Mother Church, to renounce those errors into which you have been led by wicked shepherds, to abjure this pestilential heresy and return to the bosom of the Catholic Church, that your body may be preserved from the fire on this earth, and your soul from the flames of Hell."

What am I to say to them? Bérenger pondered. If only I could tell them that I repented! He stood there without opening his mouth, trying to make himself realize that he was playing with his life, that by keeping silent he was condemning himself to death, that day or the next. He felt neither hatred nor bitterness; he did not think of his wife, or even of God. Everything he had loved, hated, or venerated till that moment now seemed suddenly meaningless to him.

Words, he thought. I am letting myself be killed for the sake of a few words. For a long time now the words "depraved, pestilential heresy," "infamous errors and crimes" had ceased to be insults, and had become mere ecclesiastical jargon. For a long time, indeed, words had had no meaning at all: these accursed men had killed falsehood as well as the truth. A man robbed of the right to speak has nothing to deny. Too many honorable persons had recanted as they would have handed their purse to a bandit when his knife was at their throat—with a clear conscience.

He stared before him into space, with a slight, embarrassed smile on his face that seemed to say: Please do not take it amiss if I can find nothing to say to you. His wretched appearance and ravaged countenance—his hair as bleached and faded as his clothes—must have stirred a spark of compassion in one of the judge's assessors, who asked leave of his superior to address the accused.

"Is it not," he said, "a most unhappy thing to see you, formerly a knight and citizen of high repute, who were once among the handsomest, richest, and most courteous men in your district—to see you, I say, reduced to such a state that even those who knew you can scarce believe their eyes? Would you be mad enough to attempt to persevere in a Faith that has brought you to so lamentable a pass?"

Confronted with a man who treated him as an equal, Bérenger recovered something of his self-assurance.

"It is not *my* Faith that has brought me where I now stand," he observed, "but *yours*. It was not we who began the war."

"Is that all you have to say in your own defense?" the judge asked, icily.

Bérenger looked at him, and felt afraid. He was old, so old that, for all his sixty years, Bérenger felt almost a young man beside him. His bloodless, clean-shaven face, with its deep network of wrinkles, already had the chill of the tomb upon it. His calm, weary eyes, heavy with hundreds of unregretted capital sentences, held a power seldom seen in any human being. Death dwelt in them, more surely than in the ax of the executioner.

Bérenger said, hesitantly: "I am very willing to submit myself to the Church. I have never been a heretic. But I cannot do penance unless I am guaranteed my life, and a communal prison where I can have my wife with me. I am legally married."

The Inquisitor reminded him that the said woman was herself condemned and excommunicate, and had not yet done penance; still, the Church's indulgence did not temper the punishment to the gravity of the fault, but to the sincerity of the repentance. If the accused gave sure proof of his attachment to the Church, his sentence would be quashed and the penalty of death commuted to one of life imprisonment—always granted that the accused did not relapse into his former errors.

"I am not a heretic," Bérenger repeated. "It is years now since I have been in the company of any heretic. Those whom I knew have all been tried and executed."

The clerk looked up and said: "Shall I put down 'Refuses to talk'?"

"We shall wait until the next interrogation. That is enough for today. Let him simply sign his declaration. If his repentance is sincere, he will speak."

Bérenger went over to the desk to read the previously prepared document, in which the clerk had just inserted his name. Never had anything seemed so hard of decipherment to him: the letters danced in a jumbled mass before his eyes, and his eyes themselves were swimming with tears, which he was ashamed to wipe away. He took the pen that was held out to him, and abruptly, without thinking what he was doing, scratched a great cross over the paper, and flung the pen away.

"There are enough sins on my conscience already," he exclaimed, in a hoarse voice. "I will not add this one to them."

He was informed that he could henceforth regard himself as a relapsed heretic, and that he would not be empowered to make any further appeal. He shrugged his shoulders and glanced indifferently at the old man, enthroned there on his dais. There was nothing more the Inquisitor could do to him now, and he no longer felt afraid of him.

Gentian, who was waiting out in the corridor with about fifteen other prisoners (most of them also condemned *in absentia*), saw the guards lead her husband out. He tried to smile at her, hoping she would guess nothing of what had passed. Women are so silly, he thought. If she knows I did not yield she will be quite capable of doing the same thing herself, simply out of love for me. She stirred him to pity, so thin and feverish she was, her eyes haggard, her hair plastered down on her temples with sweat and scarcely covered by a small, almost threadbare gray kerchief. What, then, is life, he wondered, that I should so want her to stay alive, even though it be in misery, fear, and humiliation?

The clerk read: "Gentian, daughter of the noble-born Ricord, joint Lord of Montgeil in the Sault district, a rebel and bandit leader drawn and quartered at Carcassonne in the time of Count Simon de Montfort, and of Arsen de Cadéjac, an ordained heretic, burned at the taking of Montségur; wife of the noble-born Bérenger of Toulouse, formerly Lord of Aspremont, knight;

"Accused of having spent three years in a convent for heretical women in Foix; of having further, at the time of her sojourn in Toulouse, on many occasions done adoration to heretics and heresiarchs; of having, after the ceremony of a Catholic marriage, relapsed into her former aberrations; of having taken part, with great fervor, in the heretical baptism of divers persons, and notably that of her husband, the latter being grievously wounded at the siege of Toulouse (on this last occasion, five witnesses attest that the heretics Arnaud and Guiraud were summoned at the express desire and insistence of the accused);

"Item, numerous witnesses agree in their statements that the said Lady Gentian did, both before and after her marriage, on divers occasions utter abominable curses and blasphemies against the Holy Roman Church, our Holy Father the Pope, and my lord Bishop of Toulouse; that she pressed her malignity and evil spite so far as to drag her husband into her perverse beliefs, and to refuse Holy Baptism both to her legitimate daughter, Raymonde, and to the bastard that her husband had had by the girl Saurine Mercier, the which Saurine was likewise perverted by the accused and contaminated with the poison of heresy, so much so that she persisted in her false beliefs even unto death;

"Item, the said Gentian, not content with performing most humble, reverent, and devoted salutations to such heretics or heresiarchs as, in her perversity, she might seek out in all such places as she could find them, did also hold it for an honor to receive them in her house, to carry their messages, and to bring numerous persons to hear their sermons;

"Also by innumerable arguments and pleas she did persuade persons of the Catholic Faith, or heretics reconciled with the Church, to abandon the true Faith and turn again to heretical abominations: so much so that more than ten witnesses have testified to being led into error by the persuasions of the said Gentian;

"Item, the accused did press her devilish malice so far as to forbid a Catholic priest access to the chamber of the Lady de Miraval, her cousin, when the latter was in her death agony; and, further, did spit in the face of this minister of God, calling him idolater and traitor;

"Item, the accused did on many occasions declare that the Friars of the Order of St. Dominic were minions of the Devil and visible incarnations of Satan, and that it was not unlawful to slay them; item . . ."

Gentian listened carefully, sometimes trying to guess which person had supplied her judges with some particular piece of information. These revelations stirred her to a compassion that was barely tinged with bitterness. But she was no longer afraid. The Instrument of Accusation, as solemn and interminable as a Litany, was slowly forging her a steely barricade against all fear. It is you they are talking about, she told herself. Here is the truth concerning your life, set forth in judgment. How fortunate they are who are judged only for acts of which they have every right to be proud!

To the judge's adjuration, asking her whether she would not repent that she might be spared from the flames both on earth and in Hell, she replied, her face a mingled study of contempt and astonishment: "Have you not been listening to the accusation? I am over fifty years old. Can a person of my age start learning to tell falsehoods? And what is there for me to repent of? You accuse me of nothing but virtuous and praiseworthy acts."

The Inquisitor said, slowly: "Your husband has not proved as obstinate as you."

She gave him a startled glance, herself momentarily fascinated, like Bérenger, by the deathly chill that emanated from him. One could not look unmoved at a man who wielded such vast authority.

"I would rather have it that way," she said, half to herself. "I would rather he lived. For my own part, I could tell you no more, even if I so desired."

"You realize, do you not," the judge said, "that a condemnation *in absentia* does not release you from the obligation to answer for any crimes you may have committed since the date of that condemnation?"

At that Gentian turned red, and then very pale, and flung her head back.

"I have committed less than I might have done, but more than enough for your purposes!" she cried. "If you put me to the torture, be warned that I shall not tell you a word of truth. I have already learned by heart the names of a hundred persons who never really existed."

The friars exchanged disappointed glances: they were familiar with this sort of woman. The judge gave an order for the condemned woman to be removed and the next prisoner brought in. Gentian d'Aspremont belonged now as of right to the secular arm: what was yet to be done lay between provost and executioner.

There were four of them to make the trip out to the Pré du Comte that day: three men and a woman. The others returned to their cells, with the exception of two who were kept for further questioning.

In the prison courtyard Gentian was astonished to find her husband. She had been so dumfounded by what had just happened to her that she had well-nigh forgotten him, believing that he had saved his life. Then she saw him, leaning against the wall, talking to two other men who were, like him, in chains. There was a squad of soldiers in the courtyard, armed with spears and axes.

Ah, my God, she thought, that is for us; they will have time to take us out there before Vespers.

Lord, Lord, I shall never receive Thy Baptism in this life now. Is it just, O Lord? Behold, I am dying because of Thee.

She was now led over to join the three men, still not daring to believe that Bérenger was there for the same reason as herself. They looked at one another for a moment, with the same dumb reproach in their eyes, and the same gratitude. In that one brief glance they told each other more than they had ever done in thirty years' fighting and suffering side by side.

The three men's faces were dripping with sweat; their eyes were strangely hollow and enlarged, and seemed to have some difficulty in discerning their surroundings; their jaws dropped. They held themselves stiffly in order to still their trembling hands: each spasmodic shudder made their chains rattle audibly.

"Did they—torture you?" Gentian asked. She could not know that her own face was just as ghastly.

"Best get it over quickly," Bérenger said, in a jerky voice that his wife did not recognize as his. He seemed to be fumbling for his words.

One of the men said: "There are people who pay the executioner to strangle them when the smoke's beginning to rise. You have to be rich even for that."

He was a relapsed heretic, a shoemaker from the Saint-Remésy district. The other man, who had been condemned *in absentia,* was a forty-year-old banker's son; he had been captured two days before, and still seemed stunned by the brutal abruptness of his passing from life to death.

"If I could only know who gave me away," he kept saying. "It's certainly not my brother. My sister-in-law, perhaps—"

"Bérenger," Gentian said, "my head is a blank. There were so many things I meant to tell you when this day came, and now it's too late: I shall never recall them."

"We're both mad. I was going to sign their paper. I don't know what stopped me."

"This is the way it had to be. Many others have trodden this road before us."

"Our Father, Which art in Heaven, hallowed be Thy name; Thy kingdom come, Thy will be done . . ." The four condemned prisoners began to recite the Lord's Prayer in turns, and went on for a good ten minutes, each of them carefully keeping his voice under control, and never missing his cue. Then they were taken away and clothed in the shifts and paper miters that condemned heretics wore to the stake. Thus they found themselves entitled to the name of heretic; and despite themselves they still felt they had been the victims of some ridiculous mistake. For more than ten years now this crazy kind of justice had ruled the country, and they were not used to it yet. Every man likes to see his local customs respected; it was both cruel and contrary to the law to burn those who had never received the Consolamentum.

Sadly Gentian watched her long tresses fall to the ground at her feet: lice-ridden, alas, but still fine and black, despite a few scattered white hairs.

Did they cut off yours too, Mother? she wondered. No; they would not have had the time. You were all taken just as you were, wearing your proper garb, your faces revealed in their truth. All together. Mother, do you remember the night I came and lay down on the ground that was still black with the ashes of the great burning? In that supremely sacred place I besought God to let my earthly body die; for during that night the souls of God's saints spoke to me with mighty voices, and I was encompassed by the flames of the Spirit as a coffin in a well-lit chapel is ringed all around with candles. On that night Christ spoke to me in your voice, saying: "My daughter, another shall gird thee, and carry thee whither thou wouldest not." Ah, if the blessed Apostle Peter did not go willingly to his death, how then should such a one as I?

Thy kingdom come. Thy will be done, on earth as it is in Heaven. Give us this day our supersubstantial bread, and forgive us our trespasses, as we forgive them that trespass against us—ah, I do *not* forgive them, nor shall my own be forgiven. Like the foolish virgins I shall go and knock at the door and find it closed

—O Lord, Lord, I have only known how to keep faith according to the laws of this world!

Through the streets the procession wound its way, with soldiers and drums and town-criers, and white-clad men who bore the scarlet cross on their breast, and lifted up their voices in solemn chant to the glory of God. Before them went a great gilded cross, held high and gleaming in the sunlight.

The four condemned prisoners sang too, to keep their courage up; their chains had been knocked off, and each of them carried a great wax candle. They had been arrayed in their penitential dress like those straw puppets that are burned or hanged on fair-days; for in truth these were men no longer, but mere lumps of flesh for the burning, objects destined to provide an edifying spectacle for the faithful.

In front of the houses and at every window the townsfolk crowded: scared and curious, and a little disappointed too, since it was known that none of the four was a proper heretic. They thought to themselves: These are poor folk they caught because they had nothing better to hand. A heretic was always expected to produce some miracle or other—God knows what.

The four prisoners went on singing, with the desperate defiance of men trying to drug themselves with sheer noise in order to drive away fear. They were not a pretty sight: their faces were gray and drawn, worn hollow with age and misery. Someone said: "The one in front is a woman." You could tell that by the extraordinary slenderness of her body, and the stiff grace of her carriage. A high-born lady, one who almost had the face of a heretic. But the noble Bérenger d'Aspremont (whom some people in the Daurade quarter still remembered) had no trace left of his knightly status save his stiff, lofty bearing and his half-shaven chin. Ah, the pity of it! A man we saw disable three Crusaders in succession on the Old Bridge, during the siege—how can the Count let such things happen? A man who used to wear fine clothes all sewn with strips of gold brocade, and the strips as wide as your hand—

How was I to know I would die in my own town? The bells are ringing for me now, as they did on my wedding day. Ah, my poor companion, Bérenger thought: if it had not been for her I should not be here today. Poor, proud woman: too proud. Memories caught him by the throat, memories of joys wrongly belittled: fine clothes at the feast, dancing in rooms all painted and flower-bedecked, the gilded armor of the chase, the music of viols and the long note of a hunting horn, the white breasts of beautiful mistresses. My life has been a good life, he thought, and embellished with every pleasure that a man could desire. It was not of my own free will that I renounced these pleasures, but through obedience to honor's law.

They have robbed me of my life. Come, all you good people of Toulouse who did not act as I did, look upon this mad fellow who spent his time hurling himself on the spear-points dressed against him, saying: I can do no other. But it is true, O Lord: I could do no other. I would have done it if I could; but I could not.

O my God, Gentian was thinking, by all the martyrs and just ones, by all those of our country burned at the stake; by Master Peter, Bishop of Carcassonne, by Master William, Bishop of Albi; by Master Bertrand, Bishop of Toulouse, our own reverend father, by Master Raymond and Master John, deacons—and by the Lady Agnes, and the Lady Beatrix and the Lady Guillelme, and by the noble Lady Serrone, who was my great-aunt, and by my beloved friend Beatrix de Miraval—by Master Aicart the deacon who was so handsome of countenance, and Master Raymond de Ribeyre who was as pure and brilliant as an angel from Heaven; by that noble and beautiful Lady Hélis, who smiled and sang amid the flames; by my much-honored mother, Thy servant Arsen who loved me so dearly, and by all those others, O Lord, who have passed through this stern ordeal, all those who now know what it is, and hold it in their memories, and for all eternity will never forget it—

By them and in their name I, who know not how to pray, now conjure Thee: by those hands of theirs that were charged with Thy Holy Spirit, and after reduced to ashes; by all those pure hands that will never be laid upon us again to purify us—have mercy on us, O Lord, for we know not whither we are going, nor what Satan will wreak on our souls; we only know that at least we have not denied Thee before men.

At the foot of the pyre the clerk of the Holy Office read the sentences out loud. Gentian and Peter Boursier, the banker's son, were asked if they persisted in their errors; the other two, as relapsed heretics, no longer had any right to this final chance.

"We are not mountebanks or jugglers," Peter Boursier said, "who say one thing today and another tomorrow for people's amusement. If I had wanted to recant I should have done it this morning."

Gentian was praying, and merely shook her head.

Hallowed be Thy name. Thy kingdom come. Thy will be done, on earth as it is in Heaven. Give us this day our supersubstantial bread. Today and no other day. On this day whose end we shall not see in this world. And lead us not into temptation, but deliver us from evil. Deliver us . . .

Bérenger was the first to mount the scaffold of piled-up faggots.

"Good people of Toulouse," he cried, "have pity on us, for we are suffering, not for theft or murder or treason, but merely for those ordinary sins that each man commits, and for the Faith of Jesus Christ! Know, all of you, that our Faith is so good that we would die rather than abandon it!"

The executioner dragged him violently toward the stake.

"Come on, you old rogue, it's no use your bawling. You'll be able to shout your head off soon enough, and for as long as you like."

Bérenger turned toward him, a strange smile on his face: thoughtful, surprised, almost tender.

"Thank you, brother," he said. "Good luck."

The executioner shuddered and shrank back, as though a red-hot iron had been laid across him.

He takes me for a madman, Bérenger thought. It is true that I spoke like a madman. If only he knew! A man is a beautiful creature—a living man, a man who will see tomorrow's sun rise; he himself cannot tell how beautiful he is. A man, whatever kind of man he be— And to think I made a profession of *killing* men!

Gentian watched as the fire crackled and caught, very gently, in the small twigs protruding from the faggots. She strained so violently at the cords that she drew blood from her wrists and elbows. It's pure madness, she thought—how could they tie me up like this, how can they stand there looking on so calmly, and do nothing to get us out of it, how can they stand there and not understand what's happening? *O Lord, when a soul is destroyed by such great fear, what can it do?*

When a house catches fire you hurry to save even your animals, if you can. What are you doing, why are you doing this to us, you who know nothing of fire, none of you, except to cook your food on it? No one will raise a finger, they're all at a fairground peep-show. She gazed beyond the soldiers to where the men in white were chanting to the glory of God, their glittering crosses brandished aloft. Their fairground God, she thought, their masquerading God, their bloodthirsty God who has ground us up in His maw!

Lord, Lord, if one of these men said, now, "Bring them down from there and take them back to prison," I would go over to their Faith. I would sell my soul for one cry of pity. Nobody knows, no one can understand that in our present plight nothing signifies except pity, the voice crying, "Bring them down!"

She pressed herself back against the stake, drawing in her shoulders and legs as though to make herself smaller, to hide herself. Her shift was in flames now, and it felt as though every part of her skin was peeling off and cracking. *My hands, my hands! Why did they tie up my hands?* That was too much.

"Bérenger!" she screamed.

He was so close to her that by bending her head down she could touch his shoulder. She threw him one panic-stricken, pain-maddened glance, through a surging smoke-eddy. His eyes were starting from his head, and every muscle in his face was so tense that she did not recognize him. Then she saw that he was trying to smile.

For one instant she forgot where she was: she knew only that something terrible, yet utterly impossible to avoid, was happening to both of them. As though it surprised her, she said: "We are burning."

Hoarsely he muttered: "And yet it is not so bad as I thought."

Beside them a raucous, heart-rending voice cried: "If there is a Christian among you, good people, let him pray for us! Let him pray for us! We are dying for the Church!"

Ah, why does he shout like that? Gentian wondered. What is the use of it? The pride of men—

We are dying.

Remember us, O Lord, in Your kingdom.

The faithful who did not adore the Beast, and whom the Beast has slain.

The faithful who served You because they could do no other, who lived in an age when the right to be a man must needs be bought with a man's life.

Remember those who gave more than they could, more indeed than they possessed; more than they ever should have given. They could do no other.

This pain is too great to be borne; they are men no longer now, mere howling beasts.

Of the four who were burned, Gentian was the first to die. Bérenger had managed to get his right hand free in order to protect his face: with his half-blinded eyes he saw his companion's head, raw, bloody, smoking, drop forward over the calcined cords that held her. The fire still licked about her, crackling and sputtering, but she no longer writhed in its embrace. Thank God, he thought, she is out of Hell.

Pain was no longer there: it had destroyed itself. He did not know now whether it was heat or cold that devoured him, whether the smoke that surged before his eyes was red or black, whether he could still hear those cries. *My God,* he thought, *I am still alive. How hard a thing it is to die.*

Mercy, Lord, on all the burned ones of this world. Mercy on

all who have loved beyond this world. On all who have loved. On all who had some true thing to love.

For they were one against a thousand, and throughout the land there were no more than ten thousand of them, in a hundred years.

And among those who watched them burn, there was not one who dared to say: They were wrongly condemned.

Paris, May 1959